SELF-MADE
SCOUNDREL

The Valley of Ten Crescents Book Two

TRISTAN J. TARWATER

Cover Artist: Sam Wood
Editor: Annetta Ribkin
Design: Chrisanthropic Studios

ISBN: 0-9840089-1-8
ISBN-13: 978-0-9840089-1-9

Dedicated to Sopi.

ACKNOWLEDGMENTS

Thank you to all of our high tier Kickstarter Backers:

Jeron Richardson
Ellen
Mitch Davis, Rockstar
Fran Stewart

Admiral Ackbar & Mandrew Murderbow
Andreas V. Heitmann
Chris Harris
Donovan & Angel
JEDII
Justin
Rob Stockdale
Sarah Stewart

Thank you so much for backing this elf up.
We really appreciate it.

Chapter 1
The Sword and the Seat

When Dershik Cartaskin was twelve years of age he saw his father Baron Darix Cartaskin beat down a farmer with the hilt of his sword in full daylight. The apologies made by the man's wife and son, cowering a few paces away did nothing to stay the Baron's hand. The sound of finely crafted metal and wood smacked against bone and flesh reverberated in Dershik's ears; the glint of metal shone not with light but with blood. Mother and son stood there, holding each other, frozen although their faces were pulled in horror. They didn't shout "no," or "stop." They only sobbed "Please, mercy!" The wife called out the name of her husband, trying to pull away from her son as one last smack sent the man plummeting to the ground. He fell with a low thud, dust kicking up around him. The woman cried out again, but still the man didn't move.

Dershik could only swallow and try to ignore the roll passing through his stomach, turning his face from the scene. He saw his father pull out a handkerchief, wiping the stained hilt of his sword with it before he let the square of fabric fall to the ground. He fastened his sword to his belt quickly and quietly; the sobs of the family were quieter. The Baron then turned and mounted his horse in one fluid movement and dug his heels into the beast's side, spurring it on to continue their survey of the village. Dershik's hands felt dead on the reins but still his horse managed to follow after the Baron, pulling up along the other horse with a smooth, steady pace.

"Don't look back," his father commanded, low and deep. Dershik managed to keep his eyes forward though he desperately wanted to disobey. He wanted to see if the man lived, to see if the family went to the man's aid. The boy couldn't even remember why his father had done it. First, the Baron and the farmer had exchanged words and then without a shout, without warning the sword had been pulled out. The landscape blurred before him and Dershik looked down at his hands. He and his father continued down the dusty road and turned at the bend. Out of the corner of his eye the boy thought he saw some movement, but his fear of the man riding beside him kept his eyes on the road, his view marred by the tears he tried to keep from falling.

"The sword and the seat," his father said when they were back in their home, the large stone keep. The magistrates and scribes had all left in a bustle of activity. Dershik meant to leave with them but his father called his name loudly, freezing him in his seat. The boy squirmed in spite of the cushion. He placed his arms on the arm-rests, thinking it would feel more natural, but it didn't so Dershik put his hands in his lap and waited. His father's steps echoed in the large room. The boy heard his brother and other children playing in the yard, ignoring the priestess calling them indoors. He tried to keep his eyes focused on some detail of the room, the room he had been forced to sit in so many times. He felt his father's cold blue eyes on him, drawing his own up to meet his.

"This is our lot in life," his father continued, walking in front of the tapestries. Gold and azure, the Cartaskin colors. His father stood there, like a monument to the Cartaskin lineage. His blond hair shone in the lamplight and his face just barely showed the golden stubble of his beard. "It is my calling and yours. In order to hold both well, you must have a firm hand. I know it's hard to keep interest. You're young and wish to play in the yard with your brother and the other children, climb trees. But the time will come when you'll have to take up the sword and the seat and you will be grateful for the training and in-struction I have given you." His father smiled and Dershik felt like he should smile back so he tried. His father placed his hands on the back of the Seat, the chair a symbol of his authority, ornately carved with the Cartaskin symbols and the moon.

Dershik leaned forward in his chair, momentarily not caring his posture was so relaxed. "But I don't understand why you beat that...man earlier today. Why? How does that help us hold the Seat? Doesn't that make people afraid?" His father smiled again though Dershik saw his grip on the chair tighten, his knuckles white against the deep brown.

"The farmer questioned the Seat. So he received the sword. He was reminded where there is one, there is the other. He won't die," his father said in a voice not meant to reassure Dershik. "You should remember the two go together." He placed his hand on the pommel of his sword, his other hand still on the seat. Darix Cartaskin looked so natural there Dershik couldn't help but wonder if he himself could ever stand there as his father did now. Would the magistrates all quiet when he entered a room? Or would they have to be asked and shouted at, like his friends?

Dershik heard his father take in a breath and then sigh quietly. "Dershik, when you are the Baron and not the Baron-to-be you will learn fear works better than love. If you are wise and take my lessons to heart now, it would make your life and your training much easier." His father finally looked toward the window, hearing the sounds of the children as if for the first time and he let go of the chair, nodding his head to his son. "Go. Play. You have sparring at first watch and you won't be late. Your proficiency is not an excuse for delinquency." His father smiled wryly at him as the boy vaulted out of his seat, rushing from the room and into the hallways of the keep.

As he approached the yard the boy slowed his steps, placing one foot in front of the other, bending low so he wouldn't be seen by the other children. He gazed over the scene and unfastened his cape, letting it fall to the ground. Dershik spied his brother, strawberry blond hair and blue eyes, his longer face from their mother's side of the family. He watched his brother catch the leather ball and heard his triumphant whoop. His brother threw it in the direction of another child before he darted off again, like a longfly in summer. Dershik watched and waited till he was certain no one was looking his way before slinking behind the bales of hay piled in the yard for visiting horses.

The ball passed back and forth, the children all running about and shouting, too engrossed in their game to notice him. His brother, red cheeked from running, laughed and took a step away from where Dershik lay in hiding. He sucked in his breath thinking his little brother ran away but the little boy bolted toward him, unaware. Dershik felt his heart beat faster. As his brother rushed toward him Dershik scrambled up from the bale of hay. He shrieked as he leaped down upon his brother. The younger boy's eyes went white and wide with fear. He screamed in response, throwing his hands in front of his face. They both tumbled to the ground in a mess of gangly limbs and high pitched curses, the other children rushing toward them.

"Derry, get off of me! Get off!" His brother struggled under him. Dershik felt his brother's fist smack across his mouth, salt and metal flowing over his tongue. It made Dershik angry and he grabbed his brother's wrists as he sat on top of him.

"What was that?" Dershik asked. He was a lot bigger than Ceric and hadn't played all day, being confined to his saddle and then the meeting with his father. He was angry and jealous. Ceric had played all day. He remembered Ceric chatting happily to the priestess about the games he had planned, his happiness that the metal merchant was bringing his daughter. Dershik pulled back his fist for another punch.

"Get up off of him, Master Dershik, please!" said one of the other children. All the heat in Dershik's body drained away and he felt cold. He saw Ceric's face, afraid. His brother's face was already starting to swell. He looked up and saw the faces of the other children. Some of them had their hands over their mouths. Shame yanked him off of his brother and he scrambled up, tripping over himself as he sped away from the other children, pushing past the servants who had come out to see what all the commotion was about.

The autumn evening air felt good against his skin as he ran, his boots clunking against the earth. The crisp air and the aroma from the kitchen mixed in his nostrils and he ducked into the kitchen through the back door. A quick glance showed all the servants were probably in the yard tending to Ceric. Alone, he pulled part of a cold roasted animal off of a plate and shoved it into a small loaf of bread. Two servants emerged from the pantry with braids of garlic and a bucket of whiteroots, nodding in greeting. Dershik nodded back and ducked out of the kitchen, ignoring the shouts from the yard as he continued on his path.

The temple was cold and quiet. Vespers were over for the day and most people were busy getting chores done before the last watch. The temple was smaller than most keep temples Dershik was told, but it was familiar so he loved it. The boy took a bite of his meal and chewed as quietly as he could, not wanting to disturb the sanctity of the holy place. It was only here people never yelled. Everyone sat as equals before the Goddess for one purpose. It was where every child born into the area was named, every child acknowledged as a man or a woman,

every pair of lovers bound, every prayer for the dead recited. He gazed up at the life-sized statue of the Goddess,
dressed in actual cloth garments which moved in the
slight breeze from the window

Footsteps came from behind him but he didn't bother
to turn and look. He knew by the cadence and quietness
to whom they belonged. The priestess walked toward him
and sat beside him. She was of an age with his father with
long, brown hair, eyes grey like mirrorstone, and a square
face. Her robes were various shades of grey that both hid
and revealed the female form beneath them. The boy and
the priestess sat there for a moment regarding one another quietly in the temple. Dershik ripped his food in two
pieces, and when he offered her half she took it. He heard
her chew quietly and the low swallow of her mouthful before she drew in her breath and spoke.

"Fighting again?" she asked simply. Dershik wasn't
surprised she knew. Sister Kiyla had probably passed the
commotion in the yard or at least heard it. His mouth was
still bloody. He could taste it in his food. It wasn't the first
time he had shown up to temple bleeding. "I'm not surprised it came to blows. However, I did think you would
want to play for a little while before you excused yourself
by making yourself unwelcome." She took another bite of
her food, giving the boy some time to collect his thoughts
before he finally spoke.

"I'm not welcome, anyway," he said, his voice cracking. It was true. Dershik was older than most of the children of the keep, children of servants or visiting
merchants or magistrates. The older children who visited
all knew who he was. They wouldn't spar or sneak with

their future Baron, regardless of how much he asked and insisted. His own brother was four years younger and annoying. Ceric wasn't quiet or brave, which meant he couldn't participate in many of the activities Dershik was interested in. Dershik had tried to get him to explore the abandoned cellars one time, knowing Ceric's bizarrely keen knowledge of Cartaskin history would reveal more, but he started crying actual tears when Dershik pushed him through the door and slammed it shut. Ceric was a baby. The friendships Dershik fostered with some of the servant's children all dissolved once his father started 'advising' him to join in on his meetings, accompany him on his surveys. He had tried to get a game of kick-the-ball going just last phase, but Gerik the baker's boy and Arn the lamp minder had all quieted, saying they had too many things to do to play. He saw them playing later out by the old well. He had showed them where the well was in the first place.

Dershik gulped down his anger with the children and took another bite of his food, talking through it noisily. "Nobody wants to play with the Baron's son. It's the Sword and the Seat, not kick-the-ball for me." He took another bite, cramming his mouth full.

Sister Kiyla brushed some crumbs off of her lap with a pale hand, a large moonstone ring on her finger flashing in the light. She nodded in agreement with him and Dershik's face fell, wishing for a way out of his problem, not resignation. "It is true, your position in life means people will treat you a certain way. You have responsibilities many do not know or understand. People fear this, though the Goddess tries to offer comfort and wisdom. And there is an estrangement between those who rule and the ruled. Even in the clergy, this happens."

Her words were meant to comfort him but they didn't. He fidgeted in his seat and he felt his face grow somber as he remembered that morning and the farmer. "Why? Why does this happen?" Dershik shrugged and winced before he could hear the answer, hoping she wouldn't have an explanation. "Why are things this way? Why can my father...do what he does?" He didn't want to say what he had seen. But the look on the priestess' face told him she knew. Dershik looked away.

"Why did you strike your brother?" It wasn't an accusation. It sounded like one of her lessons but he couldn't figure out what she was trying to teach him.

"I was angry!" he said. "But...but not with him. I was just...it's hard, learning from my father all day. And Ceric gets to play all day. It's not fair."

"He had to come to lessons after morning meal. And he still had riding lessons after midday."

"I know, it's just...." Dershik looked down. His hasty meal felt heavy in his stomach. "I stopped myself from hitting him. Too much. He just...he looked scared." He remembered the faces of the peasants and those of the children. "Why the sword? Why does there have to be a division? Such a sharp one? Why does my father want people to fear him?"

For a few breaths the priestess said nothing, her grey eyes focused on him. It made him feel comfortable. Finally she spoke. "Do you fear the Goddess? Do you resent Her for being over you?"

Dershik blinked. "No, of course not." He shook his head and looked toward the statue of the Goddess set behind the altar, alabaster white. The expression on Her face was serene, but strong. At Her feet were representations of those she subdued to make the Valley fit for Her people. A black-palmed hand painted with a silver spiral held Her staff; the other hand lay on the head of the maned bear, the sign of his household. How could he feel anything bad toward the Goddess, the Lady of the Night, who watched over them when they slept, who protected them from harm?

"Why?" Sister Kiyla asked.

Dershik tried to figure out what she was getting at, wondering if what either of them was saying or was about to say would be blasphemy. He licked his lips and tried to think of what he should say. "She's full of goodness and grace." That was from his lessons. "And she made this place for us."

"The Valley was already here before our people came here."

"But it was barren and full of Freemen," Dershik insisted, knowing the stories well. "She prepared the way and set the Crescents in the land, as a sign of Her favor." He felt his face get hot, wondering why he was arguing in favor of the Goddess to the priestess but couldn't stop himself. "She keeps us safe."

Sister Kiyla shrugged, looking at her food. "Some would say your father does that. He fortified the walls just two springs ago and beat back the Freemen in his youth. I doubt your brother would remember an attack, it's been that long."

"But my father is just a man," Dershik said and his words echoed through the temple. He looked to the statue of the Goddess and thought about what he said while the priestess finished the food he brought her. He thought of the stone representation of the Holy Mother and his flesh and blood father. He thought of the blood of the farmer and the strength in his father's arm, wrapped in leather and metal.

"I do believe that is what makes all the difference," Sister Kiyla said. "In our hearts we know we are all flesh and blood. The same. The seat is given, passed down from father to son and it is easily sat upon but it must be held somehow. And sometimes it means seeming more than flesh and blood. Accruing some sort of quality to make oneself...."

"Stand apart." Dershik looked down at the floor. It wouldn't be enough to be the Baron's son. The seat felt hard under him and he drew his knees up to his chest, biting his bottom lip as he thought over her words. When he fixed his eyes on her, she smiled.

"I fear I've drawn you even deeper into a somber mood, Dershik," Sister Kiyla mused. "Forgive me. I do have some good news though, something which might brighten your face." Dershik sat up and raised his eyebrows waiting for the news. "While your lack of friends these days is troubling to me, hopefully you can find the time to make one out of a young person new to the Home Cartaskin?" The priestess stood up from her seat and Dershik rose as well, not sure why. "I'm to receive a student within the phase, an apprentice priestess if you will. It would be good if you grew to know her since she will most likely be your counselor when you are the Baron proper."

"What about you?" he asked, following her as she walked into the main aisle, following her toward the head of the church. The priestess smiled and took his hand. Her fingers felt cold in his, and dry. The moonstone ring she wore was even colder than her skin.

"I am your father's priestess and counselor, you know that." For a moment he thought she would ruffle his hair but she didn't, just led him toward the front of the temple. "I've been here a long time and when you marry and he steps down, you will need your own counselor. One who knows you best."

Dershik leaned against the altar as the priestess lifted the altar cloth and pulled out a bowl and incense. "You know my father best of anyone."

"Probably," she said. When she said it she sounded tired. "It is difficult to be a Baron and it is difficult to be his priestess. One must know when to give comfort and when to give council. I hope my student can learn from some of my shortcomings and serve you well." Sister Kiyla smiled at Dershik and he smiled back, thinking she looked sad. She sighed and this time she did ruffle his curls which made him blush and she looked toward the door of the temple. "I must say, I hope to see you more often, Dershik. I miss you at my lessons."

"I miss them too, but I know most of it by now anyway," he said, laughing. He had outgrown the little bench where he and Ceric sat with other children for lessons. He knew all of the Goddess' Triumphs by heart and could read and write, though his penmanship was a bit too sloppy for his father's tastes. "But I miss it, too. I know all the stories but I still like hearing them." Even after he had heard them fifty times, they were still more interesting than the bale counts for the last ten harvests, the surveys of the fish in the ponds, the taxes collected from each household.

"Ceric's attention has improved since your absence, though, and that I cannot complain about." She laughed and bowed to him in departure, Dershik bowing back. Ceric was probably already asleep, he thought as he headed toward the temple door.

It was a quick trip from the temple to the tower door but he still checked to make sure no one was watching before he ran across the shadow of the keep. The guardsman on duty inside the tower only sighed and smiled at the boy, not bothering to watch him as he ran up the stairs, taking the steps two at a time. Silence filled the hall, lamplight spilling across the carpeted floor. The room he shared with his brother was on this floor, as well as a room for servants and several extra rooms seldom used nowadays. His father's room was upstairs but at this time of night he was probably still in his study, maybe entertaining the metal merchant before fourth watch.

The door to their bedroom creaked, so Dershik put his head against it and listened for voices before he opened it slowly, cringing as the hinges grated against themselves. Movement within told Dershik his brother was still awake. He crept into the room anyway, sitting on the bench to pull off his boots as Ceric sat up in his bed. The lamp was still lit, its light showing Ceric's face was still red. He would probably have a black eye in the morning. Dershik felt his own lip swelling. He pulled one boot off and then the other, setting them by the bench beside one another. Ceric's clothes were strewn all about. Dershik pulled his clothes off, folding them before setting them on the bench. The fireplace hadn't warmed the room up enough and he felt cold air creeping in under the door, shivering in his bare skin. Clutching himself with one arm he yanked down the quilt and then the blankets, leaping into the bed, but when he pulled the sheets up they felt almost as cold as the air. He heard Ceric laugh as he grunted in discomfort, kicking around under the blankets to try and warm them up.

"My sheets are already warm," Ceric said brightly. He was smiling. His hair looked redder in the firelight. Dershik wiggled up to a sitting position in the bed, holding the blankets around his neck. Ceric's smile faded. "Aren't you going to say sorry?" he asked.

"What for?" the older boy asked. He saw Ceric's face grow dark and sad. Dershik tried not to roll his eyes. "I just had a bit of fun with you, Ceric. If you hadn't tried to fight back, I would've played kick-the-ball with you."

"You know I don't like being scared, Derry." For a few moments they just sat in the low light, not speaking to one another. Finally Ceric sniffled. "All the other kids think I'm a baby."

Dershik fought the urge to tell him he was a baby, knowing it would be an easy jab. Instead he thought about a way to make Ceric feel better. He was still his brother. "Well, you know you're not a baby. Besides, if I had jumped out at anyone else, they would have screamed just as loud." Dershik lay back down in his bed, trying to find a warm spot and failing. "As a matter of fact, I scared Hilik the blacksmith last waning. He was headed to the latrine and I jumped out of from behind where the old wall used to be and he screamed louder than you did."

"Really?"

"Yeah. I think he might have pissed himself too." Dershik was pretty sure the man had. The man went to the latrine because he had been drinking too much the night before and was still drunk at the forge. Had he been sober he would have spared his breeches and probably caught Dershik as well. The boy had been lucky to escape with just a curse placed on his head. Dershik moved so he could see his brother. "If you want, I'll scare someone for you just to show them it's not so easy to keep calm. How about it?"

Ceric was grinning now. "Maybe the metal merchant's daughter?"

"Didn't she help you?" Dershik asked. He was a bit confused by Ceric's request. The man and his daughter had visited several times this season and she and Ceric seemed to get on well. Ceric sat up in bed and shrugged.

"Well, if you scared her...she might get upset. And then I can help her! Return the favor, you know?"

"That doesn't make any sense Ceric," Dershik huffed. "How about someone else? What about Piles, the chicken boy? He was there, he-"

"You said anyone I want, Derry," Ceric insisted. His eyes reflected the fireplace light. Footsteps in the hallway made them both turn their heads toward the door. Before it creaked open, they both managed to fake their states of slumber. Dershik kept his breath low and even, knowing not to scrunch his eyes shut but to relax, opening his mouth slightly. He had tried to share this knowledge with his brother. He hoped the younger boy was following suit.

The servant cursed in his direction, seeing him already abed and then sighed in Ceric's. Dershik listened as she scooped up the clothing, placing the pile of garments on Ceric's bench. She then placed another log or two on the fire, stabbing at it with the poker. Dershik saw the fire glow behind closed eyes, red and black dancing. Eventually the servant retreated, muttering as she left, the door thumping closed behind her. He waited a few breaths and heard the door creak open again and he risked smiling, knowing his face was turned away from the door. Finally it closed for good and the footsteps walked away down the hall.

"When are you going to play with us again, Derry?" Dershik heard the question but didn't know the answer. He spent his days doing what his father ordered. This included sparring practice, sitting in on meetings, looking over old records of crop yields, almanacs and weather records, histories of the houses and more. He was 'allowed' to go for a ride on his horse, Ripple, on the grounds if his duties didn't take him and his father away from the keep. Every day was eaten up more and more by responsibility. "Everybody asks for you. You were the best at coming up with games." He heard Ceric move within his sheets, his small voice muffled by his cushion. "They ask me to come up with something, but I can't. And when I come up with something, they think it's silly."

Dershik slid over to one side of his bed, feeling the coolness of the sheets creep over and into his skin and he shivered. "I wouldn't worry too much about it, Ceric," he assured him, hoping it was true. "You'll find the people who want to play with you. Not everyone likes to play the same way." He couldn't come up with a truthful answer to Ceric's question so he just avoided it, changing the subject altogether. He didn't want to lie about it, not about this. It was one thing to lie and say his younger brother was stolen from a wet nurse who was now dead and would come one night to claim her blood son as her own. Scaring him with lies was one thing. Scaring him with the truth was another.

Dershik felt old as he lay there in bed. He imagined himself as an adult standing before the banners of the Cartaskin household, his brother playing at his feet. "I bet my bed's warmer than yours," he said finally, trying to sound cheerful.

"I don't think it is," Ceric said back, sounding suspiciously sleepy. Dershik thrashed around under the covers, feeling cold air creep in.

"I'm certain it is. I'm bigger than you, I heat things up better. There's more of me to warm the bed." He heard Ceric squirm. "Also, my bed is closer to the fireplace."

"It isn't, I measured it. They're exactly the same distance."

"Okay," Dershik sighed. One last attempt. "Try not to think about the wet nurse." Dershik rolled over and started to count. This always worked. He liked to see how long it would take for Ceric to break. So far he had never made it past twenty breaths. Dershik counted in his head and was surprised to make it to twenty, but at twenty five he heard Ceric stir in his bed and then his bare feet run across the stone floor, squeaks of fear as he crawled into bed beside his brother. "What're you doing here?" Dershik demanded, tucking him in as he asked. "Don't be a baby, Ceric."

"Please, Dershik, I'm scared." Ceric had his fists pressed into his chin and he curled up in a ball, trying to warm up after skipping across the room.

"Fine. And switch sides with me, this one's warmer." Quickly the boys climbed over and under each other, switching positions in the bed so the younger one had the warmer side. Ceric cuddled up to him and Dershik pushed him away a bit but rolled over and threw his arm around his brother. He couldn't help but wonder when even this would be denied to him.

When he woke up in the morning the room was warm but he was alone in his bed. Someone had moved Ceric in the night while the both slept, the lump in the bed across from him rising slowly and steadily. Dershik considered throwing a pillow at him or dragging him out of bed but there was no point. It wasn't Ceric's fault.

Quietly and soberly the boy dressed, noticing his trousers needed to be lengthened if not replaced. He washed his face quickly in the bowl of water left out and looked at his reflection. Dershik knew he had his father's blond, wavy hair and bright blue eyes and their jaws were the same, which made them look very similar. But certainly something about him was different? Something his own? Dershik pushed and pulled on his cheeks, distorting his features as he looked for something he couldn't place.

Off in the distance the bells rang, signaling fourth watch had ended and first was about to begin. Splashing water on his hair he grabbed his wooden sword, and as he wrapped his fingers around the hilt he remembered the day before, his father's hilt stained with the blood of the farmer. Dershik gulped hard and slipped out of the room, tying the sword about his waist. He knew he was different in some way, he told himself. He would just have to find out how.

Chapter 2
The Point of a Dagger

Dershik knocked on the door as loud as he dared, unable to keep the grin from pulling at his mouth. He looked over his shoulder to see if anyone had followed him, but the yard was dark. The sounds of the Coming of Spring party carried through the air, music and the occasional laugh making its way to his ears. He was supposed to be at the party but he didn't care. Parties were boring and full of people who knew who he was and constantly reminded him, bowing, introducing themselves and saying where they were from even though he already knew. Even his step-mother looked bored during the greetings, excusing herself to make sure the new tapestries were hung correctly.

Dershik wished he could make an equally ridiculous excuse. He hated the feel of everyone's hand in his. Some were so dry they felt like autumn leaves, others so wet it took effort to not make a horrid face in response. Dershik knocked on the door again, louder, looking back before he called through it. "Cira!" he whispered as loud as he dared. "It's me, Derry. Open up!"

The door swung open. He thought his heart had beat quickly during the dance, but when his eyes fell upon the young priestess his heart thumped in his chest as he entered her room. She hadn't been sleeping, he knew that. Her light grey eyes were bright though weary, a book open on her bed. Her dark, wavy hair was still plaited and fell over her shoulder. She must have been reading; the tail of her braid was wet from chewing on it, one of her habits. Getting to know one another was part of the acclimating process, although Dershik had been surprised when his father approved it. Still, he rarely entered the young priestess' small room. He gazed about the simple trappings, the carved chest at the foot of her bed, the quilt her mother had made. "You left early," he said.

"I did. It wasn't my party," she accused, laughing. "And I've already changed. You look as if you should still be there." Both Cira and Sister Kiyla had come to the celebration, dressed in their second finest robes. Dershik wore his best, brand new clothes decked in azure and gold. His father had even gifted him a new brooch carved with the maned bear. What was supposed to be an imperfection in the rich blue stone turned into a silver fish in the bear's jaws. Ceric had whooped when they received their new clothes, yammering about the Spring Party held at the keep after Baron's Day. Dershik tried not to stand up straighter and show off but he felt his spine tighten, his toes wiggle in his boots as he took a wide stance. He couldn't help it. The way Cira smiled at him made him want to be taller, broader. Dershik reached into his cloak to bring out what he wanted to show her. "Maybe I'll go back after but first, look at this!" He held out the dagger, his hands trembling as he held it, careful not to cut himself on its naked edge. The hilt was delicately carved, several stones glittering among the crescent pattern. When he turned, it caught the light of the lamp and the feel of the cold metal sent shivers down Dershik's spine. Even Cira drew in her breath.

"It's beautiful, Dershik," Cira said. She looked to him and her eyes met his. "Did your father give this to you?"

His heart thumped again as he weighed the dagger in his hands. "No," he said. "I...I took it." He raised his eyebrows at her and smiled, not able to keep from being excited. "Do you remember the boy in the dark blue tunic, with the green trim?"

Cira's frown disappeared and she nodded. "I do. He didn't seem very...."

"He's an ass," Dershik assured her. "He thinks he's important because his father runs the eastern silver mine. Anyway," Dershik continued, waving the formalities away with his hand. "All us sons had to sit together and he was going on and on about this dagger, how his father had given it to him after he had his Moon dream." Dershik laughed, thinking about how ridiculous the boy's story had been, how big he had pantomimed the Goddess' bosom when she visited him in the night and made a man of him. Dershik's father promised him a sword if he would just admit the Goddess had visited him already. The Goddess had already visited him in the night but Dershik wouldn't admit it, not yet.

The youth tossed the dagger in his hand, catching it by the hilt effortlessly. "But then he goes on about what he's going to do with it. He said he threatened his little sister with the blade before he and his father left for the festivities, and said he'd use it on one of their servants if they didn't watch themselves." Dershik tossed it again and caught it, loving how it felt, the weight of the metal, the texture of the hilt. "What was that all about?"

"So you stole it from him?" Cira asked. She asked him in her priestess way, not her friend way.

"I took it from him," he answered. He couldn't keep a smile from creeping onto his face as he remembered. "You should have seen his face when he realized it was missing." Karic was the boy's name. His expression when he realized it was gone, only noticing when someone asked to see it. Plates were overturned and a pitcher of beer broken when he ransacked everything on the table looking for it. Dershik's father laughed at the boy's reaction but Karic's own father's face was red. He grabbed the boy by the arm and escorted him out of the hall. Dershik took the opportunity to slip out to the priestess' chambers.

"Are you going to give it back?" she asked. Cira took the blade from him and held it, seeming interested in the dagger. Dershik wondered if she'd ever held anything this nice before, something which wasn't a tool used in the temple. His guess was she hadn't.

Dershik looked back and forth from the dagger to the young priestess quickly. "Don't you want to know how I got it?" he asked, dodging her question. When he said it he knew he had no intention of returning the dagger to its previous owner. What Karic had been given Dershik had won. Seeing Cira hold it only made his victory sweeter. When he had dreams of the Goddess visiting him, she usually looked like Cira. Of course he never told her this.

"Are you offering to show off for me?" she asked, a taunting smile on her mouth. She held the dagger behind her back. Cira often accused him of being a show-off; for some reason it didn't bother him. At least he had something to show off. He reached to grab it from her, reaching behind her but she turned and stepped back. Dershik smirked and lunged for it, still missing but meaning to do so. Cira let him stand very close to her, his arm brushing against hers as he reached for the dagger. "I'm starting to think maybe he just left it on the table and you took it," she laughed.

"Please, have some faith in me," he said, backing off. "Besides, he wasn't holding it like you are. Do you know 'Ten Petals On Spring's First Bloom'? The dance?" Cira shook her head and Dershik pressed his lips together, try-ing to think of the best way to explain the dance with only two people and in such tiny quarters. "Well, there's a circle of people in the middle and then there are the petals, which are pairs of people, so there are actually three rings of people."

"You know, it is possible to dance with only two people involved," she joked.

"I didn't make up the dance! I'm just telling you how it's done!" Dershik couldn't help but chuckle along. "Look, just come here. You pretend to be Karic, I'll be myself, of course. You stand here," he said, putting his hands on her shoulders and moving her slightly to the right. He took a step back and to the right. "Now, you would have a girl in front of you and I had a girl in front of me so we bow," he said, bowing at the knees with his hand out toward his imaginary partner, Cira mimicking him a breath later. "Put your hand out and do a half turn, right?"

By now they were both smiling, knowing they looked ridiculous, performing the dance to no music and no one else around. Dershik watched as she turned toward him, wisps of dark hair framing her pretty face. He wished she had stayed at the party. He wished he could have danced with Cira the way people did in the barns and in the dance halls, hands on waists and hand in hand. There was the Lovers Dance done at weddings but he wouldn't be doing this for some years he hoped. When he would, it wouldn't be with Cira.

"I don't think I need to know all the steps of the dance to know how you got it from him," she said, tilting her head at him. "Just do the part where you relieved him of it."

"But you have to understand how well I planned it out, how I counted-"

"I'm glad you can count, Dershik but I don't have all night." Cira folded her arms across her chest, holding the dagger in one hand.

"Fine," he huffed. "Hold the dagger behind your back but not too tightly. The hilt wasn't tight. I know because I checked when Karic showed me earlier." Dershik waited for her to comply then nodded again. "Now, turn toward me, an eighth turn. Reach your hand forward." He reached forward and grabbed her by the forearm, pulling her toward him and around so they traded places. When they were back to back, he reached behind him with his free hand and took the dagger from her, the same place Karic had kept the knife.

Dershik wore his cape to the dance so he had tucked the dagger into the back of his trousers quickly while facing Karic, hands behind his back as the song indicated. He tried not to grin as they looked at each other, knowing the boy had no idea what just happened. At the next count Dershik had traded spots with someone else and when the song was over, he retreated to await the commotion that ensued. "See?" he said, holding the dagger up, a grin on his face. "Easy as that. For me."

Cira looked like she was trying to frown but her mouth twisted into a smile. "Yes, you are clever, aren't you?"

"I'd say so," he answered, looking the dagger over again. He could see his blue eyes in its shine and he grinned again. He didn't have a sheath for it but he didn't need one, not right now. Dershik knew where he could keep the blade hidden. The wooden box with a key his father had given him last spring would be the perfect spot.

"How're you going to get it back without him noticing?" Cira asked. There was a hint of judgment in her voice. Dershik furrowed his brow at her in response

"I'm not giving it back," he said simply. "I took it, it's mine. Besides," he said, walking past her and sitting down on her bed, "He's just going to do something stupid with it. I told you what he said." Dershik gazed at her, then looked to the book opened on her bed. "I'm doing everyone a favor."

"Except for Karic." Her arms were crossed over her chest. Dershik stood up from her bed and put his hands on her shoulders, putting his forehead on hers.

"Look, Cira," he said. "Please, don't tell. I just...I wanted to take it from him. I wanted to see if I could, and I did!" He was beseeching her now. "You have to understand, I did something I wanted to do, not something my father told me or something they expected from me. Please? I know you can keep a secret."

Cira broke away from him, leaving an empty space where she had stood. She sat on the edge of her bed, eyes on the book she had been reading. "Of course I can keep a secret," she answered. It was part of her calling, to keep the matters of the hearts of others to herself. It was why Dershik could talk to her about this, about his unease at becoming the next Baron, about how much he hated reading the ledgers and records of past harvests and past censuses, the commissioning of mines to be further explored. It wasn't just boredom. It was something else, a disjoint between what he wanted to be and what his father said he had to be. It didn't excite him, the promise of being the Baron. Holding the stolen dagger in his hand did.

"Then you have to keep this one," he said, tucking the dagger away. "Please." He walked over to her bed and felt bold, sitting beside her. Dershik reached out slowly and took her hands in his, his arm touching hers. Cira was the prettiest girl he knew and he wondered how she felt about him. She didn't pull her hands away or shift away from him. "Please."

Cira held his hands in hers. She rubbed the palm of his hand with her thumb. "I will. Of course I will keep your secret. But please remember, sometimes you have to look for the joy in the things you do. Happiness rarely comes easily. For everyone, not just you." Cira wasn't moving away from him. Derk bit the inside of his lip, his mouth wanting to meet hers. Should he? What would she say? What would she do? Would she just become a priestess to him, no longer a friend? She could tell Kiyla or worse, his father. Dershik had no idea what his father would do if he knew of his feelings for the priestess. Cira was the only friend he had. He didn't think he could risk losing her. Dershik let go of her hands, standing up from the bed before he did something stupid.

"I know," he said. This was her constant advice to him. But the reading and the surveying never yielded anything but disdain. Disdain for his father and the way the Barony was run. For telling people what to do and having them blindly obey. Cira tried to tell him he could earn their respect, govern differently from his father. He could make the seat what he wanted it to be. But Dershik would always feel like it had been handed to him. "I'm trying, Cira, I am."

He pulled the door open slightly, making sure there was no one on the grounds before he looked to her one last time. Cira sat on the bed, hands in her lap. As beautiful as always, her round face framed by her dark hair, light eyes sparkling above a freckled nose. Dershik sighed. "See you in the morning." He checked one more time before he slipped through the door.

Dershik still heard the clamor of the party. The windows to the hall were open and he saw the lights within, people dancing and talking. He crept up to the window, crouching down so he wouldn't be seen by the revelers in the large hall. His step-mother was back and leading a dance, graceful as always. His father watched her dance with something like pleasure on his face, flanked by two men Dershik knew to be important magistrates.

It took him a while to find Ceric but eventually he did. He sat in a corner of the room with a girl, Jerila. They both looked flushed. Right when Dershik was about to duck and leave he saw Ceric lean in and kiss Jerila on the mouth, quickly. Dershik stood up and ran, ran away from the party. He passed the first tower and came to the second, flinging open the door and ignoring the guard yet again, racing up the stairs. Everyone was at the party so he didn't bother trying to sneak to his room. The door creaked open and closed as he slipped in. In a few short moments he pulled both the box and key from their respective hiding places, opening the lid and pulling the dagger out of his belt.

Dershik stared at the dagger. The full moon shone through the window, lighting the room like lamplight. The blade glinted in the white glow and he caught his reflection in its shine once more. Maybe he could run away. Take the dagger, his grubbier clothes, steal a horse from the stable. It wouldn't be too hard. He could try to sell some of his nicer clothes since all his jewelry was stamped with the Cartaskin seal. But he'd take his good boots. The party would last till well into the evening. No one would notice he was gone. All the guard shifts were running light as the extra help was needed in the kitchen and the hall itself, as well as allowing the guards a chance to join in the festivities.

Footsteps approached and Dershik slammed the dagger into the box and locked it, sliding it under his bed. The key he dropped in his pocket. He'd put it on a chain later and keep it close from now on. He gulped as the door was pushed open and the shape of his father filled the frame.

"What're you doing in here?" his father asked. He sounded tired and Dershik wondered if he'd been looking for him.

"I...I was tired and thought I'd go to bed," Dershik lied.

His father stepped into the room, his boots loud against the floor. "A boy of fourteen years, too tired to attend a party." His father walked up to his bed and sat on the edge of his bed, his back toward him. "Very curious."

"I don't like the parties," Dershik said. "They're boring and everyone is just pretending to like us. They just want things from us."

"Good," his father said, turning to him. "If they want things, we can provide them. Keep them in our service. Make them support our house in our endeavors." His father sighed and turned to him. "Dershik, I know you're too young to remember, but it was our house who organized and provided for the people when we were dealing with Freemen attacks. Your grandfather trained his soldiers himself, and trained me."

"But the Freeman haven't attacked since I was a baby," Dershik interrupted. "So there's no need for an army anymore." Dershik knew the number of soldiers had been reduced drastically in the last ten years, most of the trained soldiers relegated to guards in the cities and towns. The magistrates hadn't requested more than their quotas, content with the numbers his father provided.

"Peace is the time for progress, not passivity," his father said, quoting one of the journals of Dershik's great-grandfather, who had built the keep as it stood today. "I have spent time trying to make you into the leader the people will need and leave you with a legacy people will talk about for generations to come. I know you don't see it in yourself, but I see a young man who can stay calm under trying circumstances. Who is well-liked by those around him, even if they don't know him. Who thinks about things differently. A natural leader. You will make a great Baron, Dershik."

"I don't want to be the Baron," Dershik blurted out. As soon as he said the words he wished he could shove them back into his mouth. His father turned his head slowly toward him, his lack of reaction filling Dershik with dread.

"What did you say?" his father asked. His voice was too quiet. Dershik took a step back and when he did his father rose from the bed, facing him. Dershik noticed his father wasn't much taller than him now, but he was definitely bigger, stronger. His father's eyes shone as they looked over his face, waiting for the answer Dershik didn't want to give.

"I...I don't." He had to give some answer. "I don't want to do it." Dershik tried to sound brave but it didn't matter. The next thing he knew he was on the floor, his head spinning as pain shot through his skull. The sound of footsteps barely registered in his brain as his father approached him, standing over him. Dershik looked up woozily, not able to keep his eyes focused.

"It's not about what you want," his father growled, sounding more animal than man. "You are too young to make decisions like this. You are being stupid and selfish. You are going to do as I say. You are going to study and train, and in two year's time, you will marry Jerila." Now he had Dershik's attention, the boy's eyes wide as he stared at his father. "I've talked to her father. She's moving into the keep so you can get to know her."

"No," Dershik said, pushing himself up. He brought a hand to his head, still disoriented from the blow but unable to keep quiet. "Not her. Please." He remembered how Ceric talked about Jerila after her visits and how they looked at each other. He remembered the kiss he had seen them exchange in the hall. "Ceric-"

"Ceric's going to become a priest," his father spat. "He's leaving in the summer for Whitfield. He's already chosen."

"So Ceric gets a choice as to what he wants but I don't?" Dershik shouted, too upset to care what happened. It wasn't fair. "How does that work out?"

"Ceric made the right decision." His father started to walk away, heading for the door. "He knows you'll get the seat. He could go into the clergy or try to find an industry in which to excel. We both know where his strengths lie. He's an excellent student and having a brother in the Church would be beneficial to you, as you get older." His father headed to the door and opened it, the light from the hall spilling into the room but leaving Dershik in the dark. "And," his father added.

"It's about time you had your own room. Tomorrow I expect you to be upstairs."

"There's a room on this floor," Dershik suggested feebly, feeling he was being punished.

"I know that. Upstairs." His father turned to leave but looked at him once more, his eyes moving over the boy. " Looks like you got something you wanted. Don't bother coming back to the party." His father left and let the door close with a thud, leaving Dershik alone in his room.

He balled his fists and waited before he screamed in frustration, pushing the mattress off of his bed. It flopped to the floor noiselessly and he kicked his wooden box across the room, sending it skittering, splintering across the floor. The dagger fell out and slid across the stones, dull. Dershik stood up and scooped it, feeling the hilt in his hand. Without thinking he drove it into his mattress and stabbed, over and over again, feathers and wool bursting from the lashes. He stopped after a few breaths, seeing what he had done, and felt stupid. What had he done? Nothing. Just taken out his anger on something which wasn't even alive. He punched the mattress and stood up, wiping the tears which had fallen from his eyes during his outburst.

His head still ached but he ignored the pain as he went to his trunk and pulled out some clothes. Derk stripped and changed into his riding gear, fastening his cloak about his shoulders and leaving his new brooch on the tattered bed. He shoved some clothes into his pack and looked around for something without the house seal on them, something he could sell. He had already torn up the sheets, and those would be too large to travel with anyway.

Dershik knew the clothes he wore would have the seal of his house on it, embroidered in yellow and blue somewhere. Even his boots would have the mark, under the fold where it wouldn't be seen during normal wear. What about the books and scrolls? Dershik went to Ceric's side of the room and flipped them open, unrolling them. All of them were marked, some with the seals of several houses as they had been passed from Barony to Barony.

To Her Hems with this, he thought, throwing a few more clothes items into his bag and grabbing a pair of gloves, wrapping them around the newly obtained dagger. He was already sweating both from wearing too many clothes and his nervousness as the reality of what he was going to do sunk in. His hand against the door, he took a deep breath.

The door pushed open from the other side and Dershik stepped back, fear clawing his throat. He thought it was his father about to find him in his current state. Instead a strawberry blond head popped in, dark blue eyes and a lantern lighting up the room. "Derry?" Ceric said, walking into the room. "Are you okay? Papa looked cross after he went to look for you."

"I'm leaving," Dershik said, slinging his pack over one shoulder. He tried to make it sound as convincing as possible but his resolve was already faltering. The look Ceric gave him shattered it. Dershik shook his head. "There's no use arguing. I can't be the Baron."

Ceric burst into tears and rushed Dershik, hugging him tightly. He was fairly certain his brother was talking but he couldn't understand what he was saying. His determination dissolved into shame as he felt his brother's tears soak through his tunic to his skin. Dershik pried Ceric off of him, his head still hurting as he looked him over, trying to keep his remorse off his face. "Please, stop crying, Ceric. Ceric. Ceric!"

"You can't go!" Ceric managed. His face was all red now from crying and his eyelashes stuck to each other. "You can't! If you go, I'll have no one here. And you have to be the Baron. It's your birthright!"

"You're not even going to be here after the spring, Ceric! Father's sending you away to Whitfield!" The look on Ceric's face told Dershik his brother already knew this. "You know about Whitfield already?"

"Of course," Ceric said, picking up the lantern. He wiped his face with his free hand, taking a deep breath. "I talked it over with the Sisters and Father. Whitfield would be the best place for me to study and be taken seriously. Not many men don grey robes."

So Cira knew and hadn't told him. Dershik cocked his head to the side. "Did you, now? Did Father also tell you Jerila is moving to the keep?" Now Ceric's eyes went wide and then he colored, biting his lip. "Did he tell you that? And I'm to take vows with her?" Now he got a reaction out of his brother he wanted. Surprise followed by disbelief.

"It isn't true," Ceric said. It sounded like he was trying to convince himself more than anything else. "You don't even like Jerila."

"I know I don't but she's...her father owns the largest mines in the Barony."

"So that's why?" Ceric shouted, looking angrier than Dershik had ever seen him. "You want something from her family, so you're going to marry her?"

"I don't want to marry her, Ceric!" he shouted over him, resisting the urge to grab him by the shoulders and shake him. "I told Father! I know you like her! I saw you kissing at the party." His face still hurt and shouting had made the pain worse. He walked over to Ceric's bed and sat on the edge, setting his pack on the floor. His head was spinning and he felt like he might throw up. Even though it was dark in the room he still saw sparks out of the corner of his eyes. "I saw you."

"Are you okay?" Ceric finally asked, walking toward him with the lantern. Dershik blinked and shielded his eyes, turning away from its light as well as from his brother's face. He didn't want to see Ceric worried about him, or angry with him. It would make leaving harder.

"I'm fine," Dershik said. "Ceric, if I go then maybe you can be the Baron. And marry Jerila. What do you think?"

"Father would look for you," Ceric insisted. "You would never get away. And I can't be the Baron. Father says I'm too timid. He says people won't take me seriously as a leader and says I could never hold the seat. I want to be a priest."

"But what about Jerila?" Dershik asked, hoping the mention of the girl might steel his younger brother against his fears. Ceric looked down at the ground and shook his head.

"I like Jerila but...I'm only a boy. We're both young. She might just like me now. Sister Kiyla says young hearts often change." His brother looked sad. "She might grow to like you better. And well, there will be girls in Whitfield." At this Ceric's face brightened. Dershik was a little surprised to see his brother's fondness for girls, given his age. His brother shrugged. "But please don't go. Please."

Dershik sighed. He didn't know what he should do now. He knew his brother was right. His father would try to find him. How long could he last out in the Valley by himself? How far would he get? And what would happen upon his return? His head throbbed.

"If you go, I'll tell on you right now." Dershik looked up. His brother was trying to seem formidable but it just made Dershik tilt his head to the side and laugh.

"I could just tie you up and gag you. It could be a whole watch before they come looking for you." He offered the information to his brother and saw him gulp down his fear. Still, the boy stood there, steadfast in his resolve.

"Well, they would come find me and I would tell them. So they'd know to go out and look for you straight-away instead of searching the grounds first." Ceric nodded as he spoke, as if trying to reassure himself this was a good enough deterrent for his brother.

"Look, why are we setting ourselves against each other?" Dershik mused, taking the lantern from his brother. "I'm not going." Sighing he surveyed the bed and kicked the butchered remains of the mattress. "We've got enough problems without taking things out on each other."

"Why did you do that to your bed?" Ceric squawked, seeing it for the first time. "Where're you going to sleep?"

"Upstairs," Dershik revealed, looking to his brother. Ceric's head fell to his chest and Dershik indicated the lantern. "You mind if I take this?" Ceric shook his head and waited as Dershik gathered up his sheets and blankets, leaving the torn ones behind. He balled them up and slung his pack over his shoulders.

"What about Jerila?" Ceric asked, following him to the door. Dershik shrugged and waited while Ceric pulled the door open, holding it for him.

"I don't know, Ceric. We'll figure it out as it happens. I'll see what I can do." It was all he could say, in all honesty. Jerila hadn't even moved in yet. They both walked up the stairs to the third floor, the guard looking at them strangely when they approached. "I'm moving my room, Garic," Dershik answered his look.

"In the middle of a party, sir?" The guard laughed, shaking his head. "Couldn't wait till morning?"

"No," Dershik said, not wanting to continue the conversation. He walked past him, hearing Ceric mouth an apology to the guard and walked to one of the rooms he knew was empty. Dershik held the door open, shining the lantern in so Ceric could enter unafraid.

It was a simple room, right above his old one. The difference was it had one bed and a library within it, as well as a writing desk. The room was dusty and he was sure not to note the cobwebs lest his brother run from the room. Double doors opened out onto a balcony and the full moon's light shone through the colored glass.

Dershik couldn't remember the last time he had slept in a room by himself. He had been sharing a room with Ceric ever since his brother had been weaned, and before Ceric, a servant had slept across from him, his mother and father in the next room. Now he had a room to himself. By himself. Even though Ceric was there, Dershik couldn't help but feel lonely.

"Are you all right?" Ceric asked. Dershik nodded quickly, trying to push his emotions from his face before he set the lantern down and busied himself with getting his bed ready.

"I'm fine. Just tired and a bit dizzy. I think I danced too much." He pulled his shirt off and folded it quickly, going to set it where his chest would normally be. It was still downstairs. He set it on the edge of the bed instead, knowing he would probably kick it off during the night. Dershik waved Ceric away. "I just need to sleep."

"Okay then," Ceric said quietly, turning to leave but turning back. "Do you want me to leave the lantern?"

"I'll be fine. The moon's full." Dershik wasn't afraid of the dark. "You go back and enjoy the party."

Before Dershik knew what was happening, Ceric set down the lantern and rushed him, embracing him again. Dershik held his brother to him, feeling tears come to his eyes. His brother finally let go and drew away from him and Dershik wiped his eyes quickly, not wanting his brother to see his tears. The door closed with a thud and he was alone in the room.

A quiet scuffle in the corner made Dershik jump, but he realized it was probably only a mouse, his brain telling his heart to slow its pace. The light in the room was enough to see some of the details of the tapestries hanging on the wall, older in style but well maintained. The fireplace was clean and cold, but one night in a chilly room wouldn't kill him. With a few quick movements the extra blankets were put on the bed and he slipped out of his clothes, setting them on top of his pack before he hopped into the bed.

The sheets were icier than he had imagined they would be and so clean they scratched at his skin. The boy shivered beneath the sheets, trying to warm up and managing to do so after a few breaths. On the third floor he couldn't tell a party was taking place in the keep. All he could see was the full moon shining through the window, the Goddess' beautiful face glowing down with pride upon her children. Dershik crawled out of bed and found the dagger, feeling the coolness of the object as he wrapped his hand around it and looked at it once more.

It was his. He would never give it up. His father had his ways of getting what he wanted, Dershik would make his own methods, his own way. His father had the sword, strapped to his waist. Even at the dance the Baron wore it, the hilt and scabbard done in their colors. Dershik had this dagger. He would have to keep it hidden, tucked away. He eased it under his pillow, feeling its shape under his head. What kind of path could a dagger cut? Could Dershik carve out something for himself and Ceric as well? He couldn't keep from pulling out the dagger once more and look at his face reflected there. It wasn't his father's gaze looking back at him. It was his own.

Chapter 3
Born and Bred

The servant screamed and stepped back, her eyes wide with fright as her shout echoed through the hall. It was followed by raucous laughter as Dershik stepped out from his hiding place to reveal himself to the other servants. The woman's face grew red as the laughter of other servants soon followed. Dershik gave her a boyish grin, a grin which had endeared him to many of the servants of the household over the last four years. For all his tricks and sneaking, he proved he was harmless. Dershik had taken it upon himself to work alongside the smith, the baker, the field hand and many more, trying to gain an understanding of their crafts and callings. He listened to their suggestions and valued their input in interpreting the patterns and trends he saw in the carefully kept records. Dershik had kneaded bread and pumped bellows and planted seeds in the ground. It meant the servants forgave his obnoxious hobby of lurking about the house, hiding himself in spaces long forgotten and revealing himself in the most surprising manner possible.

Dershik was still laughing when the servant woman grabbed him by the arm. "You ass-eared boy, hiding about, and Jerila's been having labor pains since the start of the watch. We've been looking for you!" Dershik's smile melted from his face and he pulled his arm from the servant's grasp, running ahead of her.

"My brother?" he asked, calling over his shoulder. He heard the servant shout Ceric was already there. Quickly Dershik ran through the keep, barely avoiding colliding with a pair of servants filling up the lamps. He shouted an apology behind him before he clipped up the stairs, throwing open the door and rushing into the room where other men were waiting. Dark blue eyes met his and Dershik ignored the other men in the room, grabbing his brother by the shoulders. "Is she all right?" He wanted to ask Ceric if he was all right but he couldn't, not here in front of everyone.

"As far as we can tell," Ceric managed, looking paler than usual. He had reason to worry. It was his child Jerila was birthing in the women's room. Dershik was legally married to Jerila, as his father had commanded. He and Ceric's hope his brother and Jerila's love for each other would wane was for nothing. Jerila and Ceric had written to each other in letters while Ceric was at Whitfield. Dershik would never have Jerila's heart and he was fine with it; he didn't want it. When Ceric came back to the keep for Dershik's wedding, he had been the one in the marriage bed. Dershik waited out on the balcony while the pair consummated their love.

"She'll be fine," Dershik said. Jerila was strong. She had handled her pregnancy extremely well. Just yesterday they had gone horseback riding through the estate and she was frequently seen walking about the keep, helping her mother-in-law with her portion of the household duties. Ceric nodded, tears in his dark blue eyes as he went to sit down on one of the benches.

The seal had already been placed over the door. The rope and a special knot tied in the rope to keep malevolent wishes or spirits from entering the room also hung there to keep the energy of the women within to aid the laboring mother. Sister Kiyla would be with her and Cira...Dershik tried not to think about her. She would be inside, her dark hair slipping out of its plait, her round, beautiful face encouraging Jerila as she did whatever it was mothers did. She and Dershik kept up their friendship, but after his brother told him Cira knew about Whitfield...there were enough secrets kept between them. They were close but not 'skin to skin,' not the best friends he had hoped.

Everyone in the room stood and Dershik looked up, startled out of his own thoughts. Ceric pulled him up in time for them to rise as his father entered, dismissing the people's formal stances with a nod of his head. "Any word?" his father asked. He was still wearing his riding clothes, gold and silver hair swept by the wind, his cloak fastened about his shoulders.

"No," Dershik said. He had only gotten out of the meeting with the owner of the new silver mine because of Jerila's impending labor, but had spent the day sneaking around the house and hiding in the weeds. He had scared Big Hilik the smith when the bulk of a man had come across his hiding spot in the outhouse and then shared the story of the Bleeding Tree with some of the servant children, keeping his voice low and shaky so their eyes went big and their mouths dropped open.

He had lingered at the temple and prayed before the statue of the Goddess as he always did. Dershik prayed for revelation. He prayed for guidance. He prayed for a feeling of contentment deep within his soul, something he hadn't felt since the night he stole the dagger from that boy. The statue of the Goddess held a sword, two of her fingers on the snout of the maned bear, keeping its jaws shut. It was a symbol of strength, like the Cartaskin words: Strength from Within. Dershik needed strength. He felt powerless. Powerless and alone.

"Well, have food brought up. Dershik will have to keep up his strength as he keeps vigil. And cushions." His father gave the orders and servants ducked their heads and scurried down the stairs. Dershik sat down, not waiting for his father to say anything else.

"Ceric, can we have a prayer?" he asked, feeling nervous, He didn't know why he was nervous. It wasn't his child, or his love. He considered Jerila a friend though, and the child would be his son by law and his nephew by blood. It was a woman he was close with giving birth. The threat of death lingered on the outskirt of his thoughts, and he worried for the mother and child in the room and the lives outside connected to them. His own mother had been affected by Ceric's birth, never regaining her strength and dying because of it.

Dershik looked at his father and then to Ceric, wondering at how time had caused them to trade places, and how they were unaware of their common bond. Ceric finally realized what Dershik had asked and nodded, motioning for Dershik to stand up. Those in the room surrounded Dershik for the prayer and it made him anxious and self-conscious, trying to ignore them as they all placed their hands over their hearts to pray.

"Holy Mother, Blessed Woman, Ever-Changing and-Ever Loving, hear the words of your grateful children," Ceric began the prayer. "Extend your gracious hand toward Jerila and the other women in the room. Grant them wisdom and give Jerila the strength she will need to give us this child. What is hidden shall be brought forth into your gentle light.

"Comfort the husband and the father in his time of need. Grant him patience and put strength in his arm so he might protect the family you have given him. Help him in this next stage of his life and give him discernment, that he would make righteous decisions for his life and the lives of those he loves. May your Black Hand guide us all."

Dershik lifted his head and his eyes met Ceric's. There was a hardness there he couldn't mistake and he couldn't tell what it meant. The men around them repeated the end of the prayer and broke away just as several servants brought in cushions and pitchers. Dershik sat back down, arms over his chest. A servant offered him a glass of something and he took it, draining it when he found it was alcohol. His father ordered someone to bring his house clothes to a nearby room so he could change without straying too far from the birthing room and more people trickled in and out. Some of them said something to Dershik as they left but he didn't hear them, though he nodded in reply.

"You should have seen your father at your birth, Dershik," Kera the baker said. Dershik raised his eyes to her and smirked. Her apron was still covered with flour. He remembered when her son was born several years ago. Now he was four and played under the large table where Kera kneaded and mixed and rolled. He was a happy little boy with curly brown hair who always had flour or dough in his hair or on his clothes.. "We thought he would break the door down when your mother started screaming. He gave Big Hilik a black eye and broke Garn's nose."

Dershik looked over at Ceric. He remembered Ceric's birth. He remembered his father holding Dershik too tight, almost crushing him and Dershik finally breaking away and hiding in the bramble bushes. By the time the servants found him Ceric had already been born and Dershik was covered in scratches and berry juice. His brother had been a pink, scrunch faced little beast, a hint of strawberry blond hair barely covering the spot on his head pulsing like a heartbeat. His mother had looked pale and his father gripped his shoulder tight, too tight.

Ceric's eyes stared straight forward, visibly trying to control himself. Dershik was about to take his hand when a cry came through the door.

Both Dershik and Ceric stood up, the whole room coming to life as another cry came. It was the cry of a woman, of Jerila. After a few breaths another cry came, louder, with moaning following the cry. The voices of the other women could be heard faintly through the door and some of the servants ran out of the room, probably to tell others something was happening. Dershik began trembling as another moan, louder and more painful came to his ears. He sat down on the bench, ignoring the words other people spoke to him, wishing he could comfort his brother but unable to do so, not with everyone here.

The air seemed heavy and hot and he was having trouble breathing. He wondered how Jerila felt, how great her pain must be and if she was thinking about the lies she was bringing her child into and if it made it hurt more. He wondered if she wanted Ceric or if she hated him now, wishing he was birthing instead of her. Dershik remembered the nights he had slept alongside her, the discomfort she felt, the feel of something moving beneath her stretched skin, all alien joints with a mind of its own. Most of the time he had slept in a chair and let her have the bed. He would probably let her and the baby have the bed once she was able to leave the birthing room. Another scream came from the room and the hair on his neck stood up as his imagination filled in what was happening.

The watch went by in a blur. His father came back, dressed in house clothes which made the setting even more tense. Dershik asked one of the lampers if he had his cards on him and if they could play. Every time another moan came from the room they would look up but they were helpless to do anything else but stare and wonder and pray. Ceric looked as if he might throw up so Dershik had him dealt in. It took the priest three games to finally understand the rules and he lost fifteen blueies in the process before refusing to play again.

"How about you? Would you like to play?" Dershik asked his father. The Baron had been watching them whole time and everyone but Dershik was too busy counting and timing the sounds coming from the room to notice the Baron's disdain. His father just narrowed his eyes at him and turned away. Someone brought up filled buns and he managed to eat one savory and one sweet roll while he waited. The moans died down and people expected the door to open and the seal to be broken, but no priestess came to the door. Dershik eventually laid on an empty bench, most of those who had been waiting around leaving to sleep or tend to their duties. Ceric sat at his head, hands in his lap and as Dershik nodded off he could hear him praying quietly under his breath.

A hand on his shoulder roused him from a dreamless sleep, the sounds from the room making him bolt upright on the bench. People ran to get others as the cries and encouragements of women came through the door. Dershik pushed past those there and put his ear against the door, careful not to touch the rope making up the seal. He could hear the voice of the midwife and Jerila grunting, groaning and Sister Kiyla praying loudly, all of the noise finally punctuated by the small, lusty cry of a baby. Dershik stepped back from the door as if a shock went through him, turning to the crowd with a grin on his face. A cheer went through the room and more people poured in, all hoping to get a glimpse of the newborn who would be Baron one day. Ceric came up alongside Dershik, some of the color having returned to his face. There was the sound of a lock being undone and then a creak as the door was opened, the midwife appearing at the door with a knife in her hand.

She cut the rope sealing the door and put an arm around Dershik's shoulders, ushering him into the birthing room while everyone else hung back, waiting. Dershik gulped as he looked inside, curious as to what he would see within.

The room was dim and it smelled of sweat and blood. A servant filled a lamp with scented oil to clear the air and the heady aroma of the flowers and resins mixing with the human odors was strange. Piles of cloth were being put into a bundle, stained pink and red and brown. A strange chair with no true seat to it sat in the middle of the room. Dershik saw Jerila laying in bed, her face sweaty and peppered with red dots but smiling. Her light eyes looked weary but she smiled at Dershik as he approached, all the women in the room watching.

"Here he is," Jerila said. Dershik saw the baby, its smushed face pressed up against Jerila's breast, its mouth sleepily trying to nurse. A hint of strawberry blond hair sprouted from his small head. He could only stare at him, hands at his sides, not sure what to do. Sister Kiyla laughed, pouring a glass of beer.

"Take him from her so she can have a drink," Sister Kiyla said. Dershik looked to her and noticed how old she appeared. Silver strands ran through dark brown hair and wrinkles framed her eyes. Dershik pressed his lips together, wondering how to take the baby. Jerila smiled as she unlatched the baby from her breast and wrapped him in the yellow and blue blanket specially made for the child. Dershik reached out and she placed the babe in his hands.

He was so little, so loose-jointed. His skin was a mottled pink and white and pale eyelashes and brows barely showed on his face. One tiny fist sneaked out from the various blankets, jerking clumsily as the baby tried to control its limbs. Dershik cradled the boy in his arms and sucked in his breath as the infant opened its eyes, deep blue and watching. Ceric's eyes. The baby's real father was outside the door, waiting to see him. Dershik made sure the blankets were wrapped around the baby tightly so it wouldn't catch a chill and he walked to the door.

As was the custom, he placed a hand to support the baby's head and neck and lifted the child slowly over his head, for all the people into the room. "A boy," he announced, trying to shout it but holding back, feeling suddenly awkward. The people cheered loudly, which promptly startled the baby. The baby cried out, over the shouts which made everyone cheer even more, slapping each other on the back. Dershik saw his brother and smiled nervously, holding his nephew close to him as his brother lowered his eyes and nodded. The ritual done, he took the crying baby back into the room.

The baby's crying sounded louder in the smallness of the room and Jerila sat up and reached out her arms, taking the baby from him. As soon he was with his mother he quieted down, nuzzling against her and soon suckling once more.

"He's got a lusty cry," the midwife said, beaming happily. Her blood-stained apron had been removed, her homespun brown dress and red belt setting her apart from the others in the room. "It's a good sign, means he's strong. He'll make the family proud, that's for sure."

"He'll need a strong name," Dershik said. "I've got a few ideas." He nodded at Jerila. "I should go and see to the household. Arrange for the naming ceremony. Do you...need anything?" He looked to Jerila hopefully, feeling awkward yet again.

"Be sure to answer anyone's questions about the baby," Jerila said, giving him a look saying much more.

"And have bone broth and bloodroot salad brought up, rare meat as well." The midwife put her hands on Dershik's shoulders and directed him out of the room gently. "Go on, you can come back later." Dershik stumbled into the throng of people still hanging around, some of them exchanging money for bets they had made regarding the baby's sex. Dershik laughed as Little Hilik came up to him and handed him five blueies. He had told Dershik it would be a girl.

"Aren't we supposed to carry the new father to the feasting hall?" Dershik tried to hide his true feelings, wishing to forego the tradition. But everyone started shouting and before he knew it, people were grabbing his legs and lifting him up. The midwife shouted for them to leave, and soon Dershik found himself being carried awkwardly through the hallway, down two flights of stairs and through another hall, everyone singing and trying to touch him in hopes his virility would rub off onto them. Dershik wished for a quick death. Maybe they would drop him and he would hit his head on the floor. But he made it to the feasting hall safely and was finally set down before the seat of honor, plates of steamed and roasted grains already set on the table. Long strings of sausages were piled up in bowls and everyone shouted and sang. Dershik mouthed a 'thank you' as his brother poured him a glass of sweet barley wine.

People placed bets on the name of the baby, trying to guess what letter it would start with and Dershik drained his glass. He tapped it and someone filled it again, which he promptly drained. Someone set a plate of food in front of him, slapping him on the shoulders and ruffling his hair. When someone asked if he needed anything he simply relayed the request for meat and bloodroot to be sent to the birthing room on his behalf. When Dershik looked over at his father, the man only looked amused, allowing his oldest son his time in the light.

Dershik ate and answered questions about the baby, which weren't many. Who did he look like more, what color hair did he have, what color were his eyes, was he heavy? Soon the musicians started to play and dishes of salads with colored eggs were put out. He drank another glass of wine and picked at his grains and sausage, the grease from the meat starting to congeal on the plate. Ceric didn't seem to have much of an appetite either, drinking only herbal tea. When someone asked Dershik to join in a dance he politely refused, nursing a glass of spirits mixed with heartberry juice as the people spun round and round.

Whether to spite him or encourage him, his father got up and actually sang. His father was well known for his singing voice, so when he climbed on the platform and asked the band to play "Three Are the Aspects of Love," a shout went up and the people banged their fists on the table, making the plates jump and a pitcher overturn. "Don't mind Dershik," his father called over the crowd. "He's just saving his energy so he can give his son a sibling once Jerila comes out of the birthing room." His father raised his glass to Dershik, who slowly sank in his chair, his face burning with embarrassment. Ceric sat there, still as a stone.

The celebration was for the birth of the child, not for Dershik himself so eventually he was able to excuse himself. The music was raucous and when it seemed it couldn't get any louder, he pushed himself out of his chair, ready to make his exit. The room spun as if it was joining in the dance itself and he took a few breaths before he pushed the chair back, grabbing a half full pitcher and hitting Ceric on the shoulder with his hand. "I can't take this anymore," he said, carefully making his way out of the hall and toward the staircase. If Ceric responded, he hadn't heard it. Anything his brother would have said could only make him feel worse.

Dershik clutched his stomach and leaned over, vomiting on the first landing. The sound of digested food hitting stones and the smell made him heave again, emptying his stomach of its contents. "I'm all right," he said, in the off chance anyone was around and watching, waving imaginary onlookers away before he walked up the steps. He took them carefully, knowing a great uncle had died on these steps, too heavy with drink. He was an uncle, wasn't he? Not a father. Not that anyone knew it, anyone besides himself and Ceric and Jerila. Maybe he should have tried harder, harder to get Jerila to like him, harder to dissuade Ceric from her. But he didn't. He hadn't wanted to. It seemed wrong.

Dershik found the second landing and almost exited but remembered his room was on the third floor. As he took the first step he heard the familiar sound of kissing, squinting in the low light to see who was up ahead. A young man came down the stairs from around the corner, averting his gaze from Dershik and another young man followed, tying his trousers. Dershik just shrugged and called after them. "Don't slip. I got sick on the stairs."

The third floor was found, all the windows open to let in fresh air and moonlight, a half moon already making its way west. Dershik stared at the moon and put a hand over his heart, drinking from the wine jug in honor of the Goddess. Where was his sign? Where was the answer he needed? Where was his room? The hallway seemed impossibly long all of a sudden. His door had a maned bear in a cave on it, he reminded himself, feeling stupid. It had been affixed to the door after he and Jerila had taken their vows. Another lie. He found the door and pushed it open.

The room was as tidy, the way he preferred it now Jerila's items were all put away or moved to the birthing room. His items were all in their drawers or chests, the sheepskin rug freshly washed. He pulled his boots off and set them neatly at the foot of the bed, pulling off his socks. The floor was cold so he just crawled up onto the bed and sat there, pulling his dagger out and flipping it over and over in his hand as he held the jug, sipping from it occasionally.

He didn't know how long he sat there on the bed, playing with the blade and sipping wine. Eventually he finished the jug and he managed to set it on the floor without falling off the bed. He began nursing a pitcher of water, knowing he would regret it later if he didn't. Even drunk he handled the dagger skillfully, the metal warming in his hand. It warmed to him. It cut true. It kept his secrets and didn't foist any more secrets on him.

A knock came at the door and Dershik hid the dagger at his side, eyes wide. "What is it?" he called, trying not to slur his words. He expected it to be Ceric or if the Goddess hated him, his father, bidding him to return to the festivities below. Instead a female voice came through the door. It was Cira.

"It's me," she said. It was obvious she wanted him to hear but didn't want to shout. Dershik blinked in the dark and wondered if he should put his shoes back on before he remembered she wanted him to answer her.

"Oh," he started. He found a quilt and covered his feet, not sure why he did it but finding it necessary all the same. "Uh, come in." Dershik managed to make it a statement and not a question. It was a breath before the door opened and Cira's form filled the doorway, the priestess opening the door only enough to enter the room. The door closed with a thud behind her.

"You're sitting here alone in the dark." Cira held her hands together in front of her, clasped. Her hair was loose, the way she'd been wearing it lately. Dershik swore he smelled her sweet perfume already, moonflower incense and spices. It made him bite his lip.

"You know me. Not one for parties. Especially if I'm the guest of honor." He smirked and shrugged, taking a sip of water from the jug. Cira walked across the room slowly, her eyes wandering over the furniture and decorations. She'd never been in here before. Not since Jerila moved in.

Cira sat on the edge of the bed and Dershik found himself shifting away from her, wondering what she was doing here. She took the pitcher from him and sipped from it, her brows furrowing as she swallowed. "This is water," she laughed, looking at him. Even in the dark, her grey eyes looked so pale.

"Only the best for the heir to the seat," he laughed, taking it from her. He took another sip and then sat back in his bed, leaning against the headboard as he wrapped his hands around the vessel. "To be honest, I had too much to drink. I'm doing my best to not be totally useless tomorrow." He managed a pathetic grin and looked into the pitcher again.

"Well, it's already tomorrow," she said. "First watch has already come."

"Has it, now?" Dershik shrugged. "Well, here I am. Useless." He took another sip of water, wishing his head would clear up faster. At least his mouth didn't taste like vomit anymore.

"I wouldn't say that," Cira offered. She put her hand on his and moved closer to him. Dershik forced himself to move away from her, just a bit. "I mean, right now, yes. I don't think you'd be any good to anyone now, drunk as you are."

"You're right," he agreed, laughing and finding it nice he still could. He gave her the pitcher and laid on his side, his head propped up in one hand. "But besides this. I can't be a good husband to Jerila. I can't be a good father to the baby. And I can't be a good Baron." He wanted to add he couldn't be a good son, but it went without saying. It was tied with holding the Seat, his unwillingness to do it his Father's way.

"Dershik, what can you do?" Cira asked. There was exasperation in her voice and it surprised him. "You're always talking about how you can't do this or that. What can you do? What do you want to do?"

"I want my brother to be happy," Dershik started, anger beginning to simmer within. "I want Jerila to be happy. I want this child to know his father and for the people of the Barony to have peace, within and without. I want to be happy."

"Can all these things exist at the same time?"

"I don't know!" Dershik shouted. "I don't know! It doesn't matter what I want, nobody seems to care what I want. I don't want people to be afraid of me, or to take money from them."

"But Dershik, people are afraid of you," Cira said gently. "It's well known you lurk about the keep and scare the servants and visitors alike. And you take their money. You gamble with them in the stable."

"That's different," he insisted, sitting up on the bed. "It's not the same. Riding down a road on a horse and having people bow is different from making Big Hilik piss himself in the privy. Making a law so money comes in from eight towns over is different from beating someone at cards. It's not the same!" Dershik felt his heart thump in his chest, panting with insistence. Is this why Cira had come, to make him angry? "I am tired of secrets," he said at last, not able to keep his tone from being accusatory. "I am tired of hiding things away. Of hiding myself away, to make other people happy." He took a deep breath and wished he hadn't finished his wine. "I know you say my place in life is a gift from the Goddess, and I should be grateful for it. But haven't you ever been given a gift you didn't like? Or didn't use and gave to someone else? What if blindly accepting the gift is the mistake?"

He was ready for her to admonish him, to encourage him toward the Seat. It's what she had always done in the end. Instead she put a hand on the side of his face. Her hand felt cool and soft and he wanted to kiss her. But she looked as if she was going to say something so he didn't, his eyes set on her lips. "If you feel this is what the Goddess is telling you, Dershik," she finally said. "...do what you can."

What was this? Dershik looked into her eyes. Was this permission? Permission for what? Something like relief spread over him, as well as fear. If he was free to do what he wanted, what would he do?

"Cira," he said. He leaned over and kissed her. She dropped her hand from his face but didn't pull away from him. She returned the kiss and when Dershik pulled away she didn't look surprised. "I wish I was married to you," he blurted. He realized how stupid it sounded after he said it. He laughed nervously and she joined him, the two of them giggling in the dark room. "I don't want to be married to Jerila," he admitted. "I'm not the one who loves her. It's not fair to her or to me." He wondered how much Cira knew. Jerila went to Cira for council but Jerila never told Dershik what secrets she divulged. Ceric answered to Kiyla while he was here. He considered the fact he might have just admitted to the entire mess. Still, the priestesses had no obligation to reveal their secrets to his father. They answered to their Order and the Goddess so their secrets were safe with them. All the same Dershik wondered if it had been wise to share what he had with Cira. He shouldn't have kissed her, though the recent memory would stay etched in his mind for a long time.

"But you are still kind to Jerila," Cira said, smiling. "I know if nothing else you are friends. I see how you trust her. I know you admire her. You're not the first son to be forced into a marriage like this, but you are dealing with it with grace and humility. You could just ignore her and take mistresses more to your liking. It happens in other Baronies." Dershik raised his eyebrows, surprised to hear this. He didn't see the point of treating someone who was in the same bad situation terribly. Maybe it helped the feeling of misery, to share it with others. He remembered how he had often attacked and fought with Ceric and thought it was similar.

"Are things very different? In other Baronies? Other Baron families?" He knew the Barons were free to run their lands in the way they saw fit. His father went to the Valley Colloquium every year in the summer but had never brought him along. Dershik had met the Ayilkin and the Darakin barons. Ceric had gotten on with the Ayil boy, as they talked about books and letters and the Daras had been...rough. The 'Wicks were always fighting with one another.

"Every family is different, but every family is also the same," she responded.

"That's a terrible answer," he said. "Though I guess it doesn't matter how Baron Darakin treats his son. I'm not his son." Dershik shrugged and laid back on his bed, hands behind his head. "If I said, 'Father, the Darakin heir was allowed to wait to get married. And when he does, he'll marry who he chooses,' my father wouldn't care. He thinks he's above the other Barons." Dershik sighed and looked at Cira.

"Your father thinks he's above many things." There was something in her voice sharp, striking Dershik as bitter. Cira smiled though, and put her hand on his arm. "But you're right. You're you. It wouldn't be the first time a Baron would be better served by following his heart and not the advice of his priestess."

"Are you trying to confuse me?" Dershik asked, sitting up again. He was still drunk and thought maybe he heard her incorrectly. "What?"

"We're not infallible, you know this. We have faults. We sometimes put the needs of others before those we're supposed to care for. Or we follow the law of the land more closely than the law of the heart." Cira sighed and put her hand on his, sitting close to him. The scent of her perfume mingled with the alcohol in his brain. "It's hard to find a balance," she continued, her voice low and steady.

"You should go," Dershik said suddenly. Cira turned her face toward him abruptly, surprise in her eyes. He wanted to kiss her, touch her as he had imagined, dreamed so many times but he knew it was one of the worst ideas he ever had. Not now. Not like this. Depressed and drunk in the bed he shared with his lawful wife. He would have laughed if he didn't feel so ashamed. She rose from the bed slowly, taking her fragrance and her warmth with her.

"I wish we could have been better friends," she said, laying her hand on the door. She sounded sad and Dershik couldn't help but feeling somber as well.

"Me too," he replied. Cira's mouth pulled to the side in a melancholy smile and she left the room, the sound of the door closing sounding ominous.

Dershik cursed himself, rolling over in the bed. He didn't bother getting undressed. He yanked the bed sheets down and climbed in, pulling the blankets over his head. He was either the Valley's stupidest man or unluckiest. That couldn't be true, he thought. He had once seen a man born with no legs in a circus show, doing handstands and walking about, shaking hands with anyone who was willing. A man born with no legs was less lucky than him, right? However, the man with no legs smiled and laughed. He even had a wife in the circus, a woman with flaming red hair who could do tricks with fires and a baby who had legs. Even the people in the circus were happier than him.

It was too much. Dershik remembered what Cira said. To do what he could. What could he do? What did he want? Drunk and woozy as he was, he couldn't sleep. A wish turned into an idea and he sat up in bed, realizing what he needed to to do. Swinging his legs over the side of the bed, he put on his socks and boots, trudging slowly out of the room and back toward the party. He heard the music and the boisterous talking from the staircase, his hand on the wall as he guided himself down, avoiding the puddle of vomit he had left earlier. People were still dancing at this hour and the band had changed musicians but still played on.

Feeling emboldened by his secret, Dershik stepped up on the stage, all the dancers and musicians winding down as they realized he was there. He cleared his throat and turned back to the musicians.

"Do you know 'Long Are Her Skirts'?" he asked with a grin. A laugh went through the room, the bawdy song more popular in bars and inns than the Barony hall. If his father was in the room, he would be frowning at him with disapproval. As far as Dershik was concerned, he wasn't there nor did he care if he was. Ceric was absent as well. The band began playing the melody and Dershik tapped his foot in time, counting time before he began the song. He needed a bit of fun. It was a good way to start off his plan.

Chapter 4
The Crown and the Coin

It turned out his father had a plan as well.

Dershik almost dropped the baby on his naming day. He was so nervous he shook the whole time, so much his father smacked him across the back of the head before they entered the temple in an effort to calm him. Kiyla performed the ritual, Cira assisted her and Ceric stood beside her, all of them dressed in grey. Ceric looked as if he had been crying. Dershik kept fiddling with his belt, the air in the temple seeming too hot although the weather outside was pleasant with a slight breeze. Jerila and Dershik walked up to the altar with the baby, all three of them dressed in the household colors. Kiyla filled the bowl with water from a silver pitcher, sanctifying it. When Jerila handed Dershik the baby, he tripped on the way to the alter, almost spilling with the baby. But he caught himself, his heart in his throat as he turned to Kiyla, nervously laughing. Ceric looked as if he wanted to kill him. Dershik could only give him an apologetic nod as Kiyla sprinkled holy water on the baby's head and breast.

Dershik realized everyone was staring at him, waiting, and the whole of the congregation gathered was silent. Kiyla raised her dark eyebrows at him, expectant. Dershik froze.

"The name of the baby," Cira whispered under her breath, just loud enough for Dershik to hear. Someone in the congregation coughed, the sound echoing through the building.

"Sorry, I was just trying to keep up the suspense," he said to the people gathered in the temple, drawing a chuckle from those seated. "Deril."

Kiyla was trying not to laugh, Dershik could see it. She sighed quietly and blessed the baby again, the baby wincing as he felt more water sprinkled onto his forehead. "Deril Cartaskin, we welcome you to the Valley and into the grace of the Holy Mother. May you find love and peace in your life. May Her Black Hand guide us all." The congregation applauded and Dershik held the baby up once more for the people to see, careful with Deril.

Once the child had been presented, Dershik handed the baby back to Jerila before they all left to rejoin the temple attenders for the liturgy. As was the custom they sang "We Are Your Children," with his father leading the hymn for once. Dershik tried to ignore the intense look his father gave him from the altar. When he looked to

Ceric, his brother looked as if he might leap from the front of the temple and strangle him. Dershik gulped and looked to Deril, strawberry blond hair starting to curl gently around his small, pink head. Skinny, long feet kicked out of the blue and yellow blanket. Ceric's features, both of them. But Deril had his mother's nose. What had Dershik given him? What would he leave him? For the Cartaskins? Dershik felt like he didn't have anything to give. And it didn't bother him one bit.

Dershik didn't like the feeling in the room. He sat in the first seat, on the right side of his father. Jerila's father sat across from him, grey bearded, older than his own father, eyes a steely, intense grey. Beside Dershik sat one of the magistrates, Gedrix of Clefthill, one of the biggest towns in the barony. Across from him was the magistrate of the next biggest town, Kersen of Pines-Below-Water. Opposite his father, Ceric sat, still in his grey and brown robes. A book and ink and pen sat in front of him. As soon as the door was closed his father looked to Ceric.

"No need to record any of this yet, son," Darix Cartaskin said. Ceric blushed and closed the book, putting his hands in his lap as the men all looked up at their Baron. "Deril has survived the phase. For that we are thankful." Dershik waited for his father to thank the Goddess but the Baron just looked down to the table, as if collecting his thoughts before he looked up again. "Dershik and Jerila are a good match both in attitude and body. Perhaps they will be as lucky as I was and have another child."

Dershik's face grew hot and he concentrated on the grain of the table and not the words his father said. He could feel Ceric staring at him. His father started talking about allegiance and transformation and legacy. He gestured to Dershik when he said it. Dershik was sitting where he was because as the next Baron it was his place. He had been put there. Fine. He listened lazily, sitting without attention in his chair.

"The time to mint our own coins and remove the Baronies from the grip of the Church has come."

What? Dershik sat up in his chair, suddenly interested in what his father had to say. What? He looked to Ceric. His brother looked like a ghost.

"With our households joined, we now have enough metal. Both of your towns have priestesses we can trust to be on our side. With Ceric as the spiritual adviser of Dershik we will have the discretion needed to undertake this project." His father looked to him, his eyes bright and keen, stifling all of the questions Dershik wanted to ask. What about Kiyla? And Cira? Coinage? The Church controlled the coin as a way to relieve the Barons of the burden and keep balance within the region. The Church didn't pay taxes. They were an objective third party when it came to the economy of the Valley. And now his father wanted to remove them.

Dershik felt sick. He listened as his father gave figures, named locations and listed the order in which the other Barons would be approached. "Ceric is our man on the inside, able to ascertain who among the clergy will work with us. They keep it under their beds but there are factions within the clergy. We can use this to our gain." Dershik glanced to Ceric. His brother looked ashamed.

"If all goes according to plan, we can go from the Sword and the Seat to the Crown and the Coin," his father said, looking to Dershik. Hope shone in his eyes. "A sword is a cruel thing with which to rule. With your help and our careful planning, the Cartaskin household will establish a throne and a legacy in the Ten Crescents, ruled not with the wisdom of religion like Haran or the whims of its Barons. It will be a proper country with all of us helping to establish it as a small but great nation, something to pass on to our children and our children's children." Now the old men all looked to each other. They all had ambition on their faces. Dershik tried to keep the terror off his own face.

"Do I have your oaths and your hand, as well as your secrecy?" his father asked.

"You have all three of these from me, my lord and future king," Jerila's father said very quickly, putting his hand to his forehead in salute.

"And from me, my lord and future king," said Gedrix.

"I as well." Now all the older men looked to Dershik, seeming to ignore Ceric for the moment.

Dershik didn't know what to do or say. It sounded like blasphemy, but was it? A king? There had been a king in Haran but he was a King and the High Priest, head of the Holy Family. There was no Family here, only the Goddess and she needed no consort, no husband. She took on as she desired. If Dershik agreed, he was agreeing to be the future king of the Valley and he wanted that even less than he wanted to be the Baron. But if there was no legacy...there was no use standing up to him now. Dershik would find another way.

"Yes," Dershik said, trying to sound as confident as he knew his father wanted him to be. Darix Cartaskin actually looked surprised for a breath, then pleased. Dershik was relieved to have his father turn his attention to his brother.

"Of course, my lord," Ceric said. His voice squeaked when he spoke. Dershik turned to Ceric as well, glaring at his brother. Once again his brother seemed to know more than he did. Keeping an eye on other members of the clergy as well as agreeing to take the place of Cira. What would Dershik have left?

"You all know what is at stake. We must all do our parts. Strength from Within," his father concluded. He smiled broadly and except for the silver in his hair and the wrinkles at his eyes, Darix Cartaskin seemed the same young man Dershik remembered from his boyhood. He himself felt like a little boy, playing underfoot while the adults carried on their business. How long would he be forced under the table? As the old men came together to talk about less serious matters, Dershik slipped out of the room, needing fresh air.

"Derry!" His brother called after him, chasing him down the hall. There were servants in the halls, swapping the tapestries on the walls for the newer ones. They featured the maned bear of the house with the silver fish in its mouth. Dershik wanted to rip them all down, but he concentrated on ignoring Ceric and made for the stairs.

"Derry!" Ceric called again, louder. Dershik ducked into the staircase and took a step down before finally Ceric caught up, panting and tired.

"Don't call me that any more!" Dershik snapped. He felt the tension in his jaw, the anger in him grow. "We're not children anymore. And I'm through with you."

"What? Why?!" Ceric called, following him down the steps. Dershik growled and spun around, grabbing his brother by his robes. He slammed him against the wall and pinned him there.

"You hem chewer, you knew father meant to get Cira out of here and put you at the head of the temple. Like you could ever lead anyone. Like I need you."

"Der-ick" Ceric croaked. It almost sounded funny, except his face was terrified and his skin was changing colors. He tried to speak but couldn't, Dershik crushing his throat with his arm. He just flailed his arms at his sides. Dershik held him there a breath longer than he would have liked to before he released him, watching as he gasped for air.

Faster than thought, Ceric punched Dershik so hard he almost fell down the stairs. "You stupid fapper, you don't get it. I have to stay here. To be by them. I need them." It sounded like a plea, like it was begging. But it just made Dershik more angry.

"I hate you. You're just as bad as our father, keeping secrets from me, sneaking about and taking everything people give to you, just piling it up for yourself! Chew Her Hems, you greedy slave!"

"If the world wasn't run by asses like you and father, I could take for myself!" Ceric shouted, his face red, his eyes shining with anger and tears.

"Well, take this," Dershik spat, making an obscene gesture at him. "I hope you die as miserable as I am now, and as lonely. To Her Hems with you." Dershik tried to ignore the look of anguish on Ceric's face, but even when he turned and walked away from him he saw it, the pain, how lonely he felt. He tried to push it out of his mind and he remembered words he had said as a younger man, a less angry man. "We have enough to deal with as it is, we don't need to fight each other." And what had he just done? He considered going back to Ceric and begging for his forgiveness, but if Ceric said the wrong thing he might blow up at him again. Worse, Dershik could run into their father and he didn't want to see him, not now.

Dershik walked through the keep, ignoring the greetings of anyone he came across. Through the kitchen, under the overhang, past the clucking chickens and the herb gardens. The stable was open of course. Ripple had been put out to pasture now, retired, and Eddy waited to be saddled and ridden, the blue roan stallion already pawing at the ground. Dershik shooed the servants away and saddled the horse himself, leading the snuffling beast out toward the gardens that lay to the north of the keep.

Servants shouted as he galloped the horse through the field, trampling the ornamental flowers. Dershik just laughed and whooped, standing in his stirrups and shouting encouragement to the beast. He rode the horse till they reached the woods, still in eyesight of the keep but far enough away they couldn't see him. There was a small stream here he knew of and so he tied the horse up close to drink, pulling out the food he had taken from the kitchen and shoved in the saddlebag. There were a few carrots there for the horse and Dershik handed them over, scratching the horse on the cheeks as it snorted with happiness.

Dershik was about to sit down and enjoy his stolen food when something caught his eye. He blinked, wondering if the failing light was playing a trick on him, but he scrambled up from the ground and walked over.

A large tree about as wide as his torso, off the path but close enough to the stream he could find it. It was unremarkable except for the fact that close to its base, it was hollow. Big enough to hide a few things. Dershik put his hand inside. A pack would easily fit in here. A set of boots. And the stream could be followed. The recent memory of the accusations he made to his brother still stung. And he knew their father was serious about going through with his fashioning of a Throne instead of a Seat. The tree was here, as well as a way out. Dershik could give one more thing to his brother, especially if it meant taking away from the Baron who would take from them all.

"You seem to be in a better mood," Jerila said one evening. They ate supper in their room and Dershik held Deril in the crook of his arm. Dershik brought a spoon of stew to his mouth, the baby waving his arms at the food in acknowledgment.

"Maybe because the weather's getting better. I like the summer," Dershik said. A chubby hand smacked him on the cheek, scratching his beard. Dershik looked down into the dark blue eyes, sticking his tongue out at Deril, who cooed. "You'll like the summer too," he said to the babe. "Maybe you can go swimming. Or just play in the garden and eat all of Gia's herbs, you'd like that."

"He shouldn't be eating herbs," Jerila laughed, reaching over the table. Dershik set down his spoon and held the baby under his armpits, handing him over. "Only milk for little Deril, right?" Jerila cradled the baby in one arm, quickly bringing the baby to her breast so they could both eat at the same time. "Is Ceric back from Whitfield yet?"

"He should be back at the end of the phase," Dershik said, managing to keep the annoyance out of his voice. She asked him every day the last two phases. That and the constant reminder his brother had someone to love him wore at him. Ceric had been called back for testing and his father was paranoid they might assign his brother to another church. Dershik was worried as well, but he managed to put on a nonchalant face, which seemed to make his father more worried. Dershik thought about the clothes hidden under the tree, the cards lying on the nightstand. "Jerila," he said, taking a sip of his wine. "Do you love my brother?"

Jerila looked up with a start, a slight blush coloring her cheeks. She nodded, a small gesture barely moving her head, her eyes set on his. "Of course I do. You know this." Jerila stared down at the baby after she said it.

"Would you do anything for him?" Dershik asked. He sat back in his chair and waited for her reaction and response. She must have started thinking about what that might entail exactly, because she looked down to the table, her eyes moving back and forth as she searched over scenarios in her mind. Jerila sat up straight in her chair, shifting the baby in her arms.

"Yes, I would. And I am." She wasn't accusing Dershik of anything, nor did he fault her for anything. Her father had decided an alliance with the Baron would be best cemented by willing his mines to his grandson and not his daughter. If she was complicit, so was he.

"You are good for him, you know that," Dershik mused. He pushed his grains around his plate with his spoon, wondering what was being cooked in the kitchen right now. "You remember what he was like, as a boy. So nervous. Now he's more sure of himself, more ambitious."

"More melancholy," she said. Jerila moved the baby to her lap and patted him on the back. She looked at Dershik, tilting her head to the side. "And what about you? I remember you when you were young. You've changed as well."

"Taller, stronger," he offered. "And I eat bloodroot now, I couldn't stand it when I was little."

"That's not what I meant," she laughed. The baby burped loudly. Dershik watched as she held the baby to her, the little boy moving his head around to look about the room. Jerila put a diaper on her shoulder to soak anything the baby might spit up and looked to Dershik again. "You used to be so...you loved everything, you were so enthusiastic. You used to love playing, 'Lead the Party.' I remember you used to say, 'When I'm Baron, we'll have honeybread for breakfast, not porridge,' or other things."

"I was a child," he huffed. "These are the kinds of things children do."

"Everyone looked up to you," she said. "Ceric most of all."

"Even after I locked him in the tunnel on the second floor," Dershik sighed, remembering. "I told him if he would just come with me, he would be safe. There were books in there, old ones I wanted him to see." Dershik shook his head, the memory old but still clear. He remembered grabbing Ceric by the shoulders and throwing him into the small space, holding the door closed with his back while Ceric pounded and screamed, his voice muffled by the wood between them.

"He was scared of the dark for a long time after that," Jerila said. Now she sounded as if she was chastising him.

"Jerila," he said, standing up from his seat. "Would you believe me if I said...I do love my brother? And I do care for you. And Deril." He gripped the back of his chair, his knuckles turning white as he thought of what to say. "And anything I do? It's not just for selfish reasons. I am not a selfish person." They stared at each other for a breath. He thought Jerila would say something but she didn't. He wasn't sure if she agreed with him or not but he knew what was true. Dershik grabbed his cloak from the peg beside the door and left. He had lamp oil to store in the abandoned stable.

It was difficult to pick the person who would be his stand in, to realize his options. This part of the plan was the hardest. If he was to fake his own death, there would have to be a body, and obviously not his own. Bodies took hours to burn down to bones, so a pile of bones would look suspicious. He would need flesh. Dershik listened and asked questions of the servants he gambled with. Most had families, loved ones also working in the keep, people he had grown up with. But rumors were going around about one of the newer servants. A lamp keeper everyone called Fil had been jailed in the Tyeskin territory for violent behavior. He was quiet and kept to himself though he did frequent the card and dice games wherever they were held around the keep. Fil did like to drink and gamble. And he was of a height and build with Dershik, which sealed his fate.

The day Dershik decided to enact his plan he finally went to see Cira. His mind went back and forth, regarding the wisdom of his decision, but if he followed through he would never see her again. His feet seemed heavy as he walked to the temple, memories he had made with her playing through his mind, conversations they'd shared. Dershik remembered all the disappointment he had revealed to her, all the secrets of his heart and how he held back these last few years. He wondered if she would miss him once she thought he was dead. Would she cry? But then he began thinking about the real man who would die and it turned his thoughts away from phantom pity. He took a deep breath before he put his hand on the door and pushed it open.

Cira was praying in the pew, her hands over her heart, head bowed. Dershik walked as quietly as he could, running his hand over the smooth wood of the benches. He sat down beside her on the bench, the pew creaking in a familiar way. Her eyes fluttered open and she let her hands drop as she looked toward him.

"I'd say I'm sorry to disturb you, but I'm not," he said. Dershik smiled wolfishly at her and she rolled her eyes eyes, rising from her seat. "What were you praying for?" he asked. His hand draped across the back of the bench, one leg crossed over a knee.

"I was praying for myself, actually," she said, folding her hands in front of her. Her long robes dragged along the floor but never seemed to get dirty. Maybe because they were grey. He thought about what it implied, the larger connotations of the grey garb and the priestesses. His own brother wore family colors under his priestly robes. He wondered what Cira wore.

"I thought I might do the same," he said. He reached into his pocket and pulled out a small blue coin. "Would you please get out the devotional incense?" He stood and placed the coin on the altar, the sound muffled against the fabric covering the sacred space.

Cira turned to go but she stopped. "Which incense would be appropriate for your devotion?" she asked. She stepped behind the altar and lifted up the altar cloth hiding the tools they used for services. The chalice still sat on the altar, alabaster white with the whirls and designs accented with gold paint. How many times had he dipped his fingers into this chalice?

"I think I could use some encouragement right now." He left it at that. Cira just eyed him before she pulled out a box and opened it with a key she wore tied to her wrist, pulling out the lamp and the small vial of the appropriate oil. She poured a few drops before she put the lamp on a stand, lighting it with a match. The oil in the lamp burned and the scent of rich woods and night blooming flowers wafted through the temple.

Dershik thought of the dagger in his boot, the lamp oil in the stable, the hollow under the tree. The hole he would leave when he was gone, that he hoped Ceric would be able to fill. Even if his brother wasn't the Baron, he could still be with Jerila. And with Dershik gone, would his father's plan to usurp the Church and become a king hold? It was an act of defiance against his father, leaving, the only one that would stick. Dershik's protests were worthless to his father. The idea of killing a man rose in his mind and the scent of the devotional incense seemed too heavy in his nose, almost suffocating. Would Fil be missed? They would assume Fil killed him, wouldn't they? In a drunken rage, if it made any difference. They'd bury Fil's body in Derk's grave, beside his mother. He wondered if his father would cry at his wake or if he would immediately start making new plans.

"Do you need prayer, Dershik?" Cira asked finally, interrupting his dark thoughts. Dershik jerked his head toward her before staring back at the floor, shaking his head.

"No," he sighed. He put his hands on his thighs and stood up, walking over to her. Dershik took both her hands in his, their eyes meeting. His heart thumped in his chest but when he leaned over, he kissed her on the cheek. It was a kiss full of restraint. His mouth lingered on the side of her face and when he pulled his lips off of her skin, he rested his forehead on her temple, smelling the unique scent of her skin and hair, feeling her hands gripping his.

Then she kissed him on the mouth. Dershik pulled away from her but still held her hands in his, not sure if he should let go. He looked toward the door and then back to her, biting his bottom lip in anticipation. The look on her face told him she wanted more than a kiss. Dershik remembered the night in his room when he had chased her away, too drunk to make good decisions. He was sober now and tomorrow, he would be gone. Would sleeping with Cira make leaving more difficult or easier?

They both looked to the door, not surprised to find they were still alone. Dershik took her in his arms and kissed her, letting her pull him out of the temple through the side door. They walked through the shadow of the keep, the sun already setting. Cira led him into her room and locked the door behind him, throwing him down onto the bed.

When they were done, Dershik watched as she dressed quickly, pulling on her skirts and robes over her pale skin. She had a birthmark on her stomach he had never seen before, and he sat up in her bed, realizing he'd probably never see it again. Not unless he came back to her room before tomorrow night. Cira smiled at him as she plaited her thick, dark hair with long, slender fingers. Before he got too comfortable in the bed he was up, looking for his clothes.

As he walked back to the keep he thought not about Cira but tomorrow night and what he would have to do. A part of him wondered if having Cira would make life more bearable at the keep, and what it would mean for Jerila. Priestesses were allowed to take as lovers whomever they wished and did occasionally marry but he and Cira could obviously never be. And when his father found out, he would send Cira away sooner rather than later.

Dershik knew what he wanted. He had to put all this behind him and move forward. But first, there would have to be blood. Blood and fire.

Dershik sat in the abandoned stable, holding his breath. Fil sat across from him, eyes barely open. The cards were strewn on straw-littered ground and the pitcher of spirits he had brought was empty. The lamp gave off a feeble light, low and hidden behind a barrel. Fil had come easily enough, already in his cups when Dershik had put the question to him and offering something he didn't think Fil would refuse. He'd brought up a bottle of ten year old barley wine from the stores, an excellent vintage noted for being subtle with its fruit and smooth in the mouth. It probably helped Dershik drugged it with a sleeping aid given to him by the midwife to help him through the night and through Deril's evening wakings. Dershik preferred to walk off his anxiety and so he mixed the herbs into the wine. It was a waste of the wine. Fil had drank all of it.

The man leaned in his chair, his eyes rolling back in his head before he keeled over, too drunk and drugged to stay upright. He landed on the floor with a thump that seemed too loud and Dershik waited to see if he had roused him. Instead a low snore emitted from the man's nose, his mouth open.

Dershik had to kill him. This was the body which would be buried in his grave, the body his family would mourn and watch over till the next new moon. But he couldn't burn him alive. Dershik took up a rock in his hand and stood over the man, as if waiting for him to wake up and fight back or at least scream. But his eyes were closed. Maybe he had broken his neck falling off the stool. Dershik shook his head and brought his hand to his hair, pulling at it. He snored. Fil was alive.

The rock was large and bulky but he wrapped his hand around it and knelt at Fil's side. His mouth was dry as parchment, and sweat popped on his forehead, despite the coolness of the night. Fil just lay there, unmoving except for his chest. Dershik couldn't help but reach out with his free hand and poke him, to see if he could get a reaction. The man just breathed. Dershik licked his lips and moved Fil's head so it lay against the ground, giving him a clear shot at his temple.

Dershik grit his teeth and held in a scream as he brought the rock down on the man's head, feeling the bones give way under the force. He lifted the rock again. Blood and something else dripped from it and he bashed the man's head in again. The bones of Fil's face buckled and folded into something unrecognizable. Dershik let the stone drop from his hand and he fell back. His stomach heaved and he vomited on the floor, adrenaline and disgust emptying his stomach. He couldn't believe he had done it. But he had. His father had struck down a peasant for speaking out against him and what had Fil done?

Dershik wiped his mouth with the back of his hand. He hated himself. What he had done? He was worse than his father. His father had at least had a reason for striking the farmer down years ago and the man probably survived. Fil...he couldn't look at him but he forced himself. His plan was unfolding and he had to follow it through.

First he exchanged their boots and belts. The fabric would probably burn but he wasn't sure if the metal would and Dershik's boots always had buckles, his belt pressed with the house standard. He cringed as he put on Fil's boots, old things which didn't fit and were wet and warm inside. Dershik pulled his rings off and put them on Fil's fingers, removing the chain Jerila had given him on their wedding day and fastened it around Fil's neck. As he did, the misshapen eyes of the man seemed to stare at him and blood pooled on the floor, crawling toward him. Dershik took a step back and forced himself to look at the man who was taking his place, who would take the seeds out of his father's soil. Who would help Ceric and Jerila be together. He retrieved the lamp oil.

He poured the lamp oil all over the body, putting a few handfuls of straw on the face so something would burn there. Hay was stacked on one side of the body so anyone at the keep wouldn't see the light and come inspect too soon, before the body had properly burned. How long did it take a body to burn? He had heard about barns burning and homes burning. Animals escaping but screaming in pain as chunks of their flesh sloughed off, gnarled, blackened bodies unidentifiable. At least Fil was dead. He had killed him. Dershik poured the last of the lamp oil on hay stacked against a wall and picked up the lamp, catching a handful of hay on fire. It licked at his hand and he threw it on the body, smacking his hand against his leg to make sure his own skin wasn't on fire.

The small tongues of fire took to the lamp oil and became hungry mouths, catching the clothes and floor on fire. Fil's face burned, the hair catching first and Dershik watched, partially to make sure the body was burning and partially out of a morbid fascination. Dershik took apart another bale of hay, tipping it into the flames to fuel its burn. Smoke started to fill the barn, black and thick. Dershik coughed, looking around to find the door. He panicked as he spun around, trying to orient himself in the smoke but then remembered the barrel hiding the lamp light had been across from the door and he ran toward it.

Dershik fled from the barn toward the riding trail, the stream, and then the tree. The moon was a sliver tonight, like a bowl in the sky and the smoke from the barn barely showed against the dark night. The walls of the barn hid most of the light, giving him time to escape. Dershik ran, the boots ill fitting and his heart racing but still he found his way.

The hollow of the tree held his now meager belongings. He changed his boots and wondered what he to do with the dead man's, deciding to carry them for a spell and leave them in the forest somewhere. He changed his shirt and rolled it up, throwing it in his pack before he slung it over his shoulder, making sure his lucky dagger was in its hilt before he looked back at the keep and the barn.

The barn was aflame now and he heard bells in the keep. The fire had been seen. Everyone was awake now, he was sure, required to safely abandon whatever they were doing in order to combat the fire. They would wet the grass around the barn, remove debris and try to keep the fire contained to the stables. The fire would just have to consume itself and they would try to mitigate the damage. It was far enough away from the keep to not put the main building in jeopardy.

Dershik took one last look, wondering where the people he loved were during all this. Ceric was in Whitfield. Cira was probably leading a prayer with Kiyla, for mercy. His father was probably trying to run the count, trying to account for everyone in the household. Dershik would be missing. Fil would be as well. He had to get gone. Taking one last look at the flames, he turned and ran down the path, not able to keep a triumphant grin from breaking across his smoke stained face. He had done it. He was free from the life of Dershik, son of Darix Cartaskin. He was Derk now. Despite the dark, he ran, the light from the Goddess enough for him to safely maneuver away from this life and into the next.

Chapter 5
A Contract of Devotion

"Then, she turns to me and says I owe her five blueies!" Derk set his tankard down on the bar top with a thump, the foam leaping out of cup and spilling onto the wooden surface. "If I'd known she was still filling her purse, I'da left her on the street corner, I would've." He shook his head and took in a deep breath, trying to ignore the laughter coming from the woman sitting beside him. Its volume and intensity hinted she wouldn't be done laughing soon and Derk felt a hand come down on his shoulder as she steadied herself on her stool.

If it wasn't such a pleasant sound, he could have stayed angrier longer, but Celeel had an annoying way of putting people in good spirits just by being in their presence. He took a gulp of his beer, waiting for her to finish laughing, running a hand over his stubbled cheek. He needed a shave sooner than later. Did he still have his razor?

"I say, for someone who swims with fish, you come up for air quite often," she said, wrapping her fingers around her cup, still giggling at his story. She drank the same thing as Derk, just a smaller serving. Celeel wasn't a bad looking woman. She was more pretty than beautiful. Her long, brown curly hair framed her heart shaped face and hung down to her waist. Her hazel eyes glittered merrily when she was in good spirits, which was most of the time. The terrible scar on her leg didn't put him off either.

What made Derk stick by Old Gam wasn't her looks, which were fair, but her wits. She was smart and funny and conversed with him, even argued. They met at a dance where she had stolen his purse. He stole it back and threatened to call the the brown cloaks after pretending to find it missing. She primly replied it was in his possession and therefore there was nothing he could accuse her of as he had no proof. He introduced himself to her as Derk and she had hesitated before introducing herself as Celeel, but more often called Old Gam. She added with a smirk, if he was lucky, he'd find out why. She could turn a phrase and knew a hundred sayings he never heard before, most of which he didn't understand. He caught the meaning of this one though. Derk glared at her, eyes glinting with annoyance. She was unfazed and took a drink before speaking to him again.

"You're telling me you can't recognize a girl at work still? All women are gilded in your eyes, aren't they?" The woman laughed again, the pleasant sound almost drowned out by some ruckus at one of the tables at the bar. Derk pulled a face meant to look insulted but only made her laugh at him more, causing him sit up straighter on his stool.

"I don't see anything wrong with thinking highly of anyone-"

"Whose got a pair above instead of below?" Celeel laughed again. "Who knew fappers could be so genteel?" She looked at him over the edge of her mug as she drank, and he saw the smile in her eyes. Laughing at him. As well she should. Still, an accusation had been made and he had to address it.

"I'm no fapper, Gam, and what's wrong with keeping my boots clean and combing my hair? And offering a lady a compliment?" He didn't like being called self-centered, or made fun of for having manners. Derk didn't feel like he was more selfish than many of those he had come across in his few moons on the streets. He still ran the same games, slept in the same doorways they did, pulled in about the same amount of coin. He shared when he had made a few grips more than normal.

For the most part Derk had taken to this life quickly. It didn't give people time to adjust. It swallowed people up and they either came out on the other end intact or as shit. Some of the people seemed to wear their ignorance as a kind of badge, an excuse for why they did the things they did, and he thought it was rubbish. Celeel was like him. They stole not for survival, though they did take things to pay for food and other necessities. They felt themselves when sneaking about, sizing up a quarry and coming back with a little more than they had gone in with. It came naturally and they had embraced it. He peered over her shoulder, taking survey of the commotion at the table which would probably come to blows sooner than later. Derk fixed his eyes back on Old Gam when he had decided they were safe for now. "Besides, you've missed the point of my story entirely. I thought women were supposed to be sensitive to people's hurts."

"You ain't hurt, just sore that woman would have charged you for a throw."

"That's not it! I told you, I thought she was beautiful, one of the most beautiful women I've ever seen and I told her so-"

"Am I to sit here, having you basically insult me?"

"You'll sit there as long as I buy you drinks, Gam, and listen, for the love of tits." Derk huffed, taking a gulp of his drink. "I talked with this girl for almost half a watch, I said all manners of kind things to her, things I thought true. I'd seen her sing at Half Masts and thought she was a wonderful singer. And all she wants to do is sell her body for coin? With a voice like that? It ain't right!"

"Listen to you, saying 'ain't.' Ain't he clever?" Old Gam cackled

"Don't start with this, don't, or the drinks will stop." Derk threatened with a raise of his eyebrows, hoping to evoke a bit of concern from his friend. Instead she smirked and cocked her head, looking him over.

"I've never met one like you," she said, laughing again, nursing her beer. She wiped her mouth with the back of her hand, signaling to the tender she'd be needing another drink soon. "Saying brass ain't right. Maybe she likes having multiple callers and likes making money off of it. The demand's there."

"Multi-" The word stuck in his throat and he took a gulp of beer to clear it, raising the tankard up as he spoke for emphasis. "Maybe she does, but maybe she doesn't. Maybe she can't find no other work. And asides, people, men, women, should have one partner at a time. One to one is proper."

"Proper?" The barkeep set another mug of beer in front of Celeel, turning his attention back to other patrons, ignoring the fact she was choking on her last gulp of beer and her chuckles. "Proper? Where've you picked up this notion? It's so…even the Goddess takes on as she pleases. What an old-fashioned fellow you are!"

"I don't know," he said, tilting his glass to look down into it, noting the noise had grown louder and the banter more violent than jovial.

He supposed he had picked it up from his father. For all his faults, or maybe included among them, he was faithful to his partners. Darix Cartaskin could never be accused of sharing a bed with anyone other than his wives. Even after Derk's mother had died, he spurned female callers and only took Gela into his bed once the vows had been spoken. Other men, other Barons had their 'sometimes' women but his father never did. His father…Derk drained his tankard and set it on the bar, leaning toward Celeel with half-open eyes, smiling slightly. "I'm just a poor, old-fashioned man, aren't I? Endearing, isn't it?"

"Are you poor, now? How are you affording these drinks?" she asked, finishing hers quickly and asking the bartender for another with a hand signal. "Now you can find someone you love, you don't have to pay, your 'one to one' and do things…properly."

"Or improperly, as the case may be," he said, leaning in a bit closer to her. She was still pretty, he thought to himself. The time they spent in the bar together, no other woman had caught his eye but Old Gam, Celeel. The way her eyes sparkled when she laughed, her ready smile and how she spoke both plainly and jesting at the same time…was she drunk? He was surprised to see she leaned in as much as he was, a curl falling past her ear. Was she biting the inside of her lip? Was she in fact drunk? Derk leaned in closer, the blood pounding in his ears as her mouth came close to him. They'd kissed before, more than kissed. It didn't mean his heart didn't beat faster when she drew closer to him.

"Improperly, you say…?" Her breath was warm and she smelled the way women always did to him, warm and inviting. He breathed in Gam's distinct scent of honey which seemed very fitting. Derk placed a hand on her knee, giving it a gentle squeeze as he leaned in closer. He actually had something to say, quite good and clever. He brushed the curl off her face, tucking it behind her ear and let his hand linger on her cheek, which was soft and warm. He would have told her what he had in mind and kissed her, but instead he shoved her back forcefully.

Out of nowhere a large man came hurtling toward them. He slammed violently into the bar, gasping as wood and bone collided. Derk fell backwards off his stool, his head missing a table corner by a mere finger's width. The man who was pushed into the bar roared. He picked up the nearest object, their half-filled glasses. With a scream he charged his attacker, cracking both mugs over the man's skull. Derk winced as the ceramic shattered. Bright red blood bubbled up over the man's eye but he somehow shook off the blow. He unleashed a punch sending the other man spinning away like a drunken dancer.

"Hems!" Derk swore, ducking under a table as three more men joined in the fight. Apparently, it was to be four against one, with the fellow who was bleeding fighting by himself. He searched around for Gam, only able to see sets of legs and skirts rushing for the exit. A scream from the corner drew Derk's attention away from a possible escape. He dived under another table to shield himself from the action so he could see where the scream came from.

A young woman with gloves on her hands stood in the corner. The right sleeve of her dress was torn so her shoulder was exposed. She twisted her hands together, her mouth moving but no audible words slipping from her lips. Her strange green eyes sparkled with fear, and she looked around the bar as if to ask for help.

"You can cheat me out of my money! You can insult me," the young man with the bleeding scalp shouted. He broke off the leg of a chair with one yank, brandishing it skillfully. A well executed strike sent it across his attacker's face. The crack of bone and wood ran through the populated bar. "You can call me an idiot and boss me around!" He jabbed the stunned man in the stomach hard with the end of the chair leg. The man gasped and grunted before falling backwards, allowed to topple to the ground by the other two would-be attackers. "But if you ever, EVER lay a hand upon my sister again…I WILL RIP YOUR BLOODY TWIXT OFF!" The young man's face turned red as he shouted and the young woman with the gloved hands yelled in protest, her face ashen with fear.

Well, it wasn't right, Derk thought as he reached for his lucky dagger. Three now, against one, and all the one was doing was protecting his sister. The scrape of metal against metal was the sound of a shortsword being unsheathed. The young man traded the chair leg for a more dangerous weapon. He brandished this now, in an attempt to keep his attackers at bay. His face was a mess of rage and blood. Derk slashed his dagger across the back of one man's ankles. The blade sliced through meat and grated against bone. The man howled in pain, falling backward onto the floor. Curses bubbled from his lips as blood seeped through his fingers.

The screams redirected the attention of another attacker, a lanky man with a scar running under his nose like a mustache. Hard, dark eyes glared at the thief. The man dove down to pull him out from under the table. Derk crawled quickly backwards, hopping onto and over the table, sinking his dagger into the backside of the scarred man. The table jumped as the man shot up in pain, hitting his head on the underside. He still managed to get out from under it quicker than Derk had hoped, and Derk thought to make for the door. Most everyone else in the bar had apparently already done so. An arm reached up from under a table to grab their drink. At least there would be a witness.

The man with a scar for a mustache grabbed Derk by the shoulder, turning him toward him. A punch across the jaw spun Derk around as if in slow motion. He found it strange the only thought rattling in his head was the hope Old Gam was not watching. Another blow set Derk's head spinning in the opposite direction, quicker this time, the screams now not from the girl in the corner but the other patrons of the bar. The smells of hay and food and beer all faded as pain became the only thing registering.

His assailant swung and somehow Derk dodged the blow, being sure to sink the dagger deep into the man's gut, his hand pushing until it was up to its hilt in the man's insides. The man's face contorted with pain, his top lip curling up strangely because of his scar. Derk twisted the dagger before he pulled it out, the man sagging to the floor. The young man with the sword was fighting off two opponents at a time and had made good work of them. Derk thought to hasten the end of the fight by bringing a chair across the back of the closest one. A smack with the broad side of the young man's sword sent the last man to the floor. By then the only people standing in the bar were Derk, the young man whose head was bleeding, and the young woman with the torn sleeve.

"Many thanks," said the man, wiping off his short sword with a cloth on his belt but keeping the blade un-sheathed; his dark eyes scanned over the fallen foes, his knuckles white on the hilt of the blade. "It would've taken me much longer to get rid of those three without you." He reached out a large, muscular hand and Derk took it in his own, feeling weak for the first time in his life. "I'm Asa and the woman over yonder," he said, pointing to the girl in the corner who rushed over, picking over bodies and turned furniture, hugging the large man in front of him.

"This is Devra, my sister. We both thank you for helping us." His accent made Derk cock his head. This was apparently a country crow trying to pass as a city crow. Asa's dark hair and beard were trimmed to a more urban style, but his tunic and belt were dead giveaways. The sword and scabbard was nice enough though. The young woman was dressed eccentrically, colorful skirts and shawls draped over her frame. A little garish, but it suited her well, especially with her bright eyes. Her gloves were fingerless and embroidered.

"Yes, we do," she said, her voice shaking, her green eyes swimming with tears. She buried her face in her brother's chest. "I'm sorry," she said. "I'm sorry I didn't help. I just...I couldn't."

"I know," Asa replied, hugging his sister. Derk tried not to stare at the two. He took the opportunity to look around for Old Gam, wondering if she had ducked out of the bar when the fighting got bad or was still hiding somewhere.

"And your name?" After a few breaths, Derk realized the young man was speaking to him. The young man's bushy eyebrows were furrowed with the question, and Derk realized Asa was his age or a few years younger.

"Right, well...I'm Derk. At your service. Glad to be of help." He bowed politely as a joke, looking over the siblings. He narrowed his eyes at the girl, then looked up to her brother. "Will she be all right?"

"Yes, she will, long as I keep on watching over her." For a brief moment Derk thought the man was kidding, but the look on Asa's face told him he wasn't and he did his best to let his face match the man's. "Those men were gambling with us and carrying on and well, one of them disrespected my sister. I simply could not have it."

"Of course," Derk said, finding himself agreeing with the man. He never had a sister of his own, but courtesy dictated the proper treatment of all people regardless of sex, including not ripping their clothes unless they liked it.

"You were useful back there," Asa said, wiping the blood and sweat from his brow, his dark brown hair sticking to his damp skin. "My sister and I could use another sword where we're going. You could cut down on my workload by a third if you keep it up."

Derk failed to follow the man's math, but a look from his sister, still clinging to the large, formidable frame told him not to bother. "Right," he said, looking around the bar, trying to survey the scene for damages. A few bar patrons trickled in through the door and out from under tables, used to outbursts of this nature. They turned their chairs upright, sitting back down and checking on the status of their drinks, the din steadily rising in the room. The bartender returned from the back of the bar and sent a kitchen boy for the brown cloaks, making Derk's heart thump. A groan from one of the men made Derk look toward the door, eager to leave. "Perhaps we can talk about this outside?" he offered, looking around for Old Gam before he raised his brows at the pair hopefully.

"Not a bad idea," Asa said. Derk stepped outside while he waited for them to gather their things, taking the opportunity to look around in case Old Gam was hanging around outside the bar. The brother and sister popped out of the bar, Derk leading them to the street corner. "What exactly are you talking about? And where are you taking your sister that you'll be swinging a sword?"

"I've seen you at the Temple of the Full Moon at opening prayers, and this might be of interest to you," Asa said, pointing at Derk with the short sword, which worried the thief greatly. "It's a chance to do a service for our great Goddess. Would you want to come along?"

Derk looked around again, eyes scanning the streets, fairly certain Celeel had indeed left. He nodded, turning his attention back to the burly young man and his sister. "I might, I might…anything for the Goddess." Maybe it'd be good to get away from town for a bit. The thugs who stole and ran rackets were starting to wear on him and he hadn't swung a blade in quite a while. Plus, he doubted this oak of a man or his sister would be calling him disparaging names anytime soon. The Goddess had treated him well thus far; maybe it was time he pay Her back some of Her kindness. "When do we go?"

"Meet us in front of the temple at the beginning of first watch," Asa said, sheathing his sword, his sister finally managing a bit of a smile in Derk's direction. "Only bring anything you can't live without, as the good Church will be supplying us with most everything."

"Beginning of first watch…can't we meet up at the end of the second, perhaps? After mid-meal and a nap?" The life of stolen luxury seldom had him up for first meal or second. Asa laughed heartily as he and his sister walked down the street, a good, deep laugh, his bloodied face bright with amusement.

"Great, you're funny! That'll be good on the road." Asa had a big smile making him look younger despite his beard. "Remember, only bring what you need. If it happens to be raining, we'll be inside." And with that they both left, the girl with the green eyes and her burly brother crossing the street just as a pair of brown cloaks marched up to the building. Derk ducked his head and followed suit, leaving the street and walking off in the opposite direction of the young man and the girl once he was outside; he'd pay his tab when he got back into town.

He didn't have any trouble finding Celeel. He visited the room she kept a few times before, but this night he showed up at her door with a mission. The busted lip he suffered at the hand of the gamblers was almost scabbed by the time he reached the flight of stairs; he would have to bite it open to warrant the right effect. He knocked on her door, stumbling in, letting her lead him to her bed so she could dress his wounds and fuss over him. It wasn't the romantic display he had wanted but she was just as pretty and warm wiping the blood off his mouth as she had been sitting across from him in the bar.

Derk made sure she was asleep before he got out of bed, dressing as quietly as he could and checking how sound asleep she was yet again before he carefully and quietly opened the trunk sitting at the end of the bed. He cracked it open, keeping his eyes on Celeel to see if she stirred. The sun was threatening to be out soon and he wanted to be at the temple on time. Still watching the sleeping woman, he reached his hand into the trunk carefully, feeling around inside for what he knew was in the right hand corner, buried under two quilts and a piece of unfinished lacework. He had to open the trunk a little bit more than he had hoped. The hinges creaked quietly as the trunk pushed away slightly from the bed, the sound of wood rubbing against wood seeming to be amplified by the dark.

He crouched there, frozen, expecting her to at least stir in her bed if not wake up. Instead she snored quietly, brown curls masking her face, the blanket low enough to expose a bare shoulder. Derk stretched his fingers, wiggling them as he lowered his hand and closed it around what he was looking for. With as much care as he had taken to acquire the small, cloth pouch, he removed it, closing the trunk quietly and not bothering to push it back to its original position.

Old Gam's "meddling" tools, as she called them. He tucked them into the inside pocket of his coat, pulling up the collar as he headed down the stairs of the boarding house, the front door left open by someone who had risen even earlier than he. Cold morning air sunk into his lungs and made him breathe deep. It would be warm by the end of the watch, the sun giving away its location by painting the sky above it a faint orange. Derk knew where the temple was and he jogged in its general direction, the activity warming his blood. He was tired from lack of sleep and his face still ached from last night's fight, but if they were traveling there was a chance of a cart. He could always sleep in there.

As he turned the corner his eyes spied a small cart with a horse. Grey clad figures were still loading the cart, the large frame of Asa standing close by. The now familiar form of his sister stepped out from behind her brother and she saw Derk, waving heartily to the man who trotted toward them.

"Well, I'm up, I might as well come along." Derk stretched his arms above his head, looking toward Devra. She looked younger than Asa by a few years, her dark, plaited hair doing nothing to make him think otherwise. Her bright, unnaturally green eyes made him want to stare and look away at the same time. Her hands were still covered by fingerless gloves and Asa took her hand, helping her up into the cart. As soon as she was settled she promptly pulled a tablet out of one of the packs and started reading. Asa walked around to the other side of the cart, motioning Derk should follow, nodding to one of the robed figures who also nodded in greeting.

"We are lucky enough to be trusted by the Church to go to the Temple of the Ever Burning Sun and retrieve a holy relic. They're finally ready to give it back," Asa explained, the cadence of his words suggesting he was reciting something he had heard. "You know the history. Before the Great March, there was much fighting between the Four Factions. Before our ancestors left to follow the Goddess here, a holy relic was lost amid the violence and dealings, a glorious chalice said to have been given to Her people by Her own holy hand. Somehow it wound up with the brothers at the Sun Temple, who happened to come along with the first settlers of the Valley. They are now willing to give it back as an act of good will."

Derk was familiar with the first part of the story; the same tale told in most temples, churches, and squares on Founder's Day. Most tellings included a bit more bloodshed and bad talk about the land of origin, Holy Haran of the Sacred Family. Rarely had it ever included talk of goods to be got. "A holy chalice?" he murmured, stifling a yawn lest he offend the young man with the sword. "I see…and they're just giving it back?"

"As an act of good will," Asa said, tugging on one of the ropes running across the wagon load, testing its fastness. "They've been communicating with the Church for quite some time, almost the entire season. The Sun Temple wants the chalice returned to its proper place. They are hoping this act will encourage relations between the two churches."

"If they're just handing it over, why d'yah need me to tag along? You expecting them to change their minds at the last minute?" Though Derk was interested in doing something for his Goddess and the temple he had been attending for the last few phases, he still wanted to know if there was danger of his head being cracked open, albeit for a noble cause. Asa shook his head as he scratched the scar at his bushy eyebrow, finally walking into the temple itself.

"It ain't…it's not like that," he said, lowering his voice so it wouldn't boom in the quiet temple. "Getting the chalice isn't the problem, it's getting there. The Temple is in the Freewild Green, and while my sister could knock a few creatures onto their backsides, an extra set of eyes and a sword ain't…isn't a bad idea."

"What're you talking about, your sister?" Derk asked as quietly as he could, not able to keep confusion out of his voice. "I was about to say, the Freewild is a dangerous place. I've heard awful stories, mind you, and most of them from men who were only half drunk. Why d'yah think bringing your sister along is such a good idea? I mean, not to be rude or nothing but she seems a bit…bookish."

Asa actually smiled with pride, his handsome face beaming at the other man's observation. "She is, isn't she? My ma always said, one twin got the muscles, the other the brains." They approached the altar, the mural of the beautiful Goddess staring down at them from Her two dimensional throne, silver hair cascading over Her bare torso. Asa knelt, placing his hands over his heart as if to pray. Derk joined him, interrupting his would-be devotionals with more questions.

"That girl...she's your twin? And betwixt, it still fails to answer my question! Is she a good shot with an arrow?" Derk was less sure tagging along on this venture was a good idea. Maybe he could sneak back into Old Gam's and replace her tools before she noticed. If he didn't before she discovered them missing, he'd have to come up with something more than a split lip to get back in her bed. Asa turned and sat on the altar, rummaging around in his pouch for something, his hand emerging with what looked like some kind of root.

"Yes, she's my twin. My sister and my twin." He put one end of the root into his mouth and began to chew, a strangely sweet and spicy smell wafting through the air.. "She's not good with an arrow. She is better with finer things, more delicate...things unimagined." Again, Asa's words sounded like someone else's, though they came from his mouth. Derk was under the impression Asa put more stock in the words of others and tried to recite what they said in order to get things right. However, the thief was still unclear about a few things.

"That's well and good, but tits, what has the girl been studying? Poisons?"

Asa turned to him and Derk couldn't help but take a step away from him, the gravity on the young man's strong face taking him aback. Dark brown eyes hardened with all the seriousness Derk felt the man could muster and Asa licked his lips. "Swear to me you won't share this with anyone. I'm only telling you because you're coming and you seem like a man who understands serious things, and…you won't tell." It wasn't a question. It was as a fact Asa put forth, and Derk regarded the male twin with a narrowed eye as he considered what lengths Asa would go through to keep it true. Derk's eyes fell on the shortsword and then the man's arms. His curiosity was piqued for many reasons.

"Fine, I swear it. I mean, of course I swear it. I swear upon my soul, my restoration and my peace, I shall not speak on what you are about to tell me. May I suffer at Her Hems if I speak on it." The oath was said. For a moment Derk thought Asa wasn't going to tell him but then the young man turned his eyes up toward the mural of the Goddess.

"She's a…a user of power," Asa said quietly. The way he said it didn't suggest shame or fear. Derk felt the hairs on the back of his neck stand up and he took another step back, hands springing up as if someone was about to hit him.

"Hold on, she's a binder?"

"She ain't no binder," Asa growled, his face growing dark and hard again, the muscles in his arms twitching as if he held back a great deal of anger. "She's…a Wielder.." Asa watched Derk's face for a reaction and Derk tried not to look shocked. "Or apprenticed to one at least," Asa continued, trying to soften the blow. "She don't…doesn't do curses and nonsense like that. Devra's smart and good and patient and…she has self control. It's not a curse, it's a calling and it suits her." His eyebrows knit together, revealing his feelings before he voiced them. "Though I worry about her sometimes. Devra's been studying for a while, but she's not sure of herself. Her master wants her to go out in the world and start using what she has learned, experience…things. I mean, I've seen what she can do. But Devra second guesses herself and she's not good with a sword or a club in a tight bind." Asa took a deep breath and blew out through his nose, staring up at the mural of the Goddess. "She needs protection. I really appreciate having the extra set of eyes."

Derk sucked in his breath and stood up, turning around so he faced the large painting of the Goddess once more, Her deep eyes seeming strong yet gentle at the same time. The altar was empty of any religious tools. No bowl or arrow lay there for ceremony, only the Goddess and the two of them standing before Her. And a Wielder in the cart outside.

A Wielder was something Derk had never imagined he would come across. They were the subject of stories told at bedtime and in bars, tales of wonder and pain. Wielders wandered the land, able to harness the power imbued within the realm the Goddess had given them. No one knew how they were able to do it. Only the Wielders did. They were said to be dangerous, to be regarded with awe. Binders of spirits were feared and healers were sought out, but Wielders were outside of society.

The Church's position on Wielders was to leave them be. They were given something most people were not . Their numbers were small and as they seemed more than happy to keep to themselves, the Church chose to not intervene. Tolerance was important and since no one really knew how they worked, there was the fear a balance would be undone if they were disturbed. The girl with the strange green eyes hardly seemed like a threat. Except to Asa, if she couldn't protect herself. The chance to see a Wielder do anything was almost worth it. Almost.

A thought entered Derk's head and he held up a hand as he spoke, not wanting Asa to interrupt. "All right, fine…the Goddess, bless Her, has been good to me. I'll not be the first or last to say she's treated me well and kept me when I couldn't keep myself. She's guided me and it's time to pay Her back if it's what she wills. You're obviously good people, someone to trust or the priestesses wouldn't have asked you and your sister to fetch the relic. You must be capable if they believe you can get there and back. And like I said, I will not tell about your sister. You have my word."

Derk looked to Asa and he could see the thankfulness in the young man's eyes. For now. "However, one thing troubles me and perhaps you haven't thought of it. You say our Church and this temple have been communicating for some time and they're willing to give the chalice up to start some good will between the Church and this small faction. But I've been out and about and not everyone, including men and women in flowing robes, is always blue throughout. Maybe I'm being paranoid and such but how will we know for sure if what they give us is the right thing?"

"I would know if the chalice was not the one we were sent for." The voice came from behind him and Derk wheeled around to face the speaker. A figure in priestess robes approached them. Fingers adorned with silver rings pushed back the hood of the holy garment. The face stopped whatever words Derk had in his throat and his heart pounded as if to pump sound out of him but to no avail. She was an elven woman, a Forester. Her eyes were grey like those of the other priestesses of the temple, her black hair lustrous and flowing over her shoulders and down her back. She was the most beautiful woman Derk had ever laid eyes on. His eyes trailed from her eyes to her lips to her body, not caring she was a priestess of the Goddess he served.

She stepped soundlessly toward them, the light shining through the high windows seeming to gather at the hems of her garments. "Forgive me for being so forward," she said, bowing her head slightly to Derk, offering the faintest smile to Asa, who obviously knew her. "I am Sindra, the priestess who is blessed enough to accompany you...three?" She fixed her eyes on Derk, her calm gaze the inverse of what he felt inside. "I've been asked to go with you as a representative of our temple and to ensure the proper handling of the chalice, as well as its authenticity. I know Asa and his sister already, and though I have seen you in the temple before, I don't know your name."

Derk stood there for a moment before realizing she was asking for his name without asking a question. He managed to jump start his tongue and bowed courteously to the priestess, surprised at how formal his mannerisms had suddenly become. "I'm Derk, your holiness. Pleased to be of service to our Goddess and this temple. I really cannot stress how much it...well...really, there are no words for it. Happy, I suppose, might do. Something stronger, if I could think of it right now. Just. Excited." Why was he still talking? Though he said it, it sounded strange to him. He glanced over at Asa, who raised one bushy eyebrow. Sindra turned her head to the side slightly but her face gave away no trace of annoyance or disgust. Instead she graced them both with a smile. Derk smiled back, hoping he wasn't showing off too many teeth.

"Well, I hope we all share your enthusiasm, Derk, and please, call me Sindra. I am only a servant of this temple, much like yourself." She looked to them both and then to the exit. "I hope I have not delayed us too long. Forgive my tardiness; though it gladdens me to be of service to the Goddess and excites me to travel, I am loathe to leave my sisters. I was bidding them all farewell and I took too long, it seems."

"Oh, no, not at all!" Derk exclaimed, following her out of the temple and interrupting whatever Asa was about to say. "I'd be loathe to leave 'em too, your sisters. They're all beautiful people...on the inside. Aren't they, Asa?" Was his face red? Was Asa going to say something?

"And the outside," Asa said, apparently not ashamed to say so. "I've heard it said and I have to agree, those who commit their lives to our Goddess are the best looking."

"Tits, man, how could you say that?!" Derk smacked him in the arm, wincing at the impact of Asa's muscles against his hand, rubbing it gingerly. He jerked his head toward Sindra, only to have Asa look at him blankly. "Not that I don't think they're good looking, I just mean to say what should really matter is their attention to the other believers. Right?" Derk looked to Sindra hopefully.

"True, though I am sure the believers do not mind looking upon the fair clergy when they attend," she said with a wink, smiling coyly at the thief. She turned to them, offering her hand to Asa who helped her up into the wagon, the priestess sitting besides Devra who nodded in greeting and went back to her book. Sindra smiled at them both, Derk doing his best to not grin like an idiot as she set those grey eyes on him again.

"Well, we're off," Asa said, nodding to Derk before hopping up into the seat himself, settling in between the two women. "You'll take the gelding for now."

The gelding? Derk winced inwardly, looking over his shoulder. A horse was led toward him, another hooded figure leading the animal by its bridle. So much for a nap in the back of the cart. Derk mounted the horse in one fluid motion, surprised to find it easy after not having done so for quite some time. The horse snorted gently as it shifted itself under his weight. "Hope you ain't the sign of things to come," Derk muttered, patting the great beast on its neck.

"A prayer before we go, Sin?" Devra looked up from her tablet, gazing over her brother to the beautiful priestess. Sindra nodded and bowed her head, Derk and the others following suit as she spoke the holy invocation.

"Mother Moon, mistress of the night sky and the dark corners of our hearts, we humbly beseech thee; as your path is without hindrance, make ours so. Reveal what must be revealed and keep secret what must remain in secret. Keep the waters of the sky at bay and send your guardians to watch over those we love in our absence. Guard us always in your protective Bosom and may we reflect your pure, white light wherever we go. May your Black Hand guide us."

"May your Black Hand guide us." The words said, Asa looked around with a huge smile on his face, waving goodbye to the priests and priestesses gathered outside. "Farewell! We'll be back as soon as we can, and with the chalice! Keep us in your prayers!"

"And we'll take good care of Sin, don't you worry!" This was from Devra, turning around in the seat to wave farewell.

Derk followed behind just a few paces back, the lack of sleep starting to tug at his eyelids though he tried his best to size up the girl with the green eyes who could Wield. What kind of Wielding could she do? He'd heard a Wielder usually concentrated on one kind of power. Commanding animals, elements, bending the earth…more powerful than Binders, Spirit Callers, more dangerous than a forest fire. He jumped as he realized the Wielder in training was staring directly at him. Devra waved happily to him, her eyes bright with excitement. "Aren't you glad to be off? Isn't it exciting?"

"They didn't let you out much, did they?" He smiled sincerely, albeit wearily, wondering how long till he could catch a nap in the cart. Though his remark could have been misconstrued as unkind, the girl just smiled and turned back around in her seat, starting a conversation with her brother. The cart and the gelding and all their passengers trudged along on the city street, the smell of bread heavy in the air as the sky began to turn bright blue.

As they approached the gates of the city, Sindra turned around in her seat to gaze back at Derk, the thief sitting up as straight as he could in the saddle. After a breath, he shrugged and relaxed. He'd just be himself since it was easier than trying to be anything else. He leaned back in the saddle and waved to her, not bothering to hide his exhaustion. Her lips parted and she said something he didn't hear. "What?" he called.

"I said, I'm glad you are coming with us. It is always good to make new friends." She smiled primly at him before turning around, apparently joining in on the conversation with the twins. Derk shook his head side to side, feeling the cool morning breeze on his face, his hair disheveled and spilling in front of his eyes. He was tired. But he was leaving the thugs and other uncouth sorts of the city behind and heading forward into somewhat of an adventure. There was something energizing about that and he gripped the reins of the gelding more firmly, deciding he would take what came with open arms and with hope. And hopefully Sindra could be convinced in his arms was where she was meant to be.

Something metallic clinked inside of his jacket and he felt around with one hand as he followed behind the cart. Celeel's tools knocked against his lucky dagger again and his thoughts turned to the pretty woman he had left in her bed. He wondered if she had awoken yet and what she thought upon finding him gone. Would she miss him? Would she be in the city when he returned? For a moment he regretted having left without so much as a note and with her tools. But Sindra turned around in her seat again and just smiled and his thoughts were back on her and how beautiful she was.

"One to one, you said. Proper, as well. Which one is the one? You've just left, so wait it out." He had some time, he knew it. Time with his thoughts and some new people would do him good. Derk cleared his throat from behind the cart and began to sing to keep himself awake. It was an older song about starting a journey, one known by most anyone who went to bars often enough. Asa knew it and began singing in a surprisingly good voice and the women caught on. The party of four were soon singing as the sun rose higher in the sky, following them as they rode off toward its holy temple. Derk found himself thanking the Moon Goddess, hidden away in Her watery home for placing him on the path he knew would lead toward good things.

Chapter 6
Misguided Attempts

Derk fiddled with his dagger, watching as Asa chopped onions in the temple kitchen. The burly fighter was apparently good with a paring knife and a pot, humming quietly as the small white spheres separated in the wake of the fighter's blade. A priestess entered with a bucket of water, her blonde, curly hair pulled into a thick braid. Derk watched her as she peered over Asa's work, smiling at him and saying something which made Asa laugh. Asa volunteered himself to help fix the evening meal as soon as they were settled in.

Sindra and Devra apparently had a meeting with the High Priestess. So Derk found himself sitting on a stool, completely unaware as to how to chop onions or long onions or disjoint an old hen or knead bread. He

wrinkled his nose at the sound of a leg bone being popping out its socket and the hack of a cleaver coming
down. It sounded vaguely like some sounds he had caused
himself in his life and it made his stomach feel strange to
hear them.

"I've been cooking ever since I could hold a spoon,"
he heard Asa say, the young man's face beaming. "Devra
took to roaming about the woods with our pa so I stayed
by our mam and helped. She never got strong again, after
we came about. The least I could do was clean a bird to
thank her." Another whack of the cleaver made Derk
jump. He knew the sound from his childhood, from
scampers through the kitchen on the way to some other
adventure. He knew the basics of it, the cost for each item
and the technique. Derk wondered if he could cook a
meal worth eating, noticing a basket of berries. He looked
them over, smiling at the gentle bloom on their deep, blue
skins. Without a second thought he snatched a few from
the basket and popped them into his mouth, happy to
find they were not too ripe. A hint of sourness made his
mouth pucker but he chewed anyway. The berries were
perfect the way they were. They didn't need any dressing
up or cooking.

"That's very sweet of you," the priestess said, dunking
a handful of greens into the bucket of water. "And is it
true you're a twin?" Derk thought her name was Keala.
Her big eyes gazed at Asa as if he were a jug of wine and
she had been working in the fields all day.

"Aye, Devra is elder than me by three screams and
one threat to break my pa's arm," Asa chuckled, making
the priestess laugh as well. "It took the better part of a

watch for us to come out but we did, and both lived to hear the tale." Asa smiled at the priestess again and then over his shoulder at Derk. "Can you bring me those long onions?" He pointed with a finger covered in gore and vegetable matter.

Derk set the dagger on the table and slid off the chair and tried not to be nervous, knowing it was a simple request. He knew what long onions were, everyone did. He picked one up and raised his eyebrows at Asa. "One?"

"No, all of them. Well, maybe just five." Asa smiled broadly as Derk picked up the onions, piling them in his arms before he walked over. The priestess had a mound of greens on a square of cloth and Asa had taken apart the chicken quite expertly. "Tell me, do you like to cook, Derk?"

Derk slid back onto his stool and shrugged, picking his dagger up again. "Not really. Never really tried my hand at it. I think it's better when people cook for me." He smiled at Asa and Kaela, grinning, but the look on the priestess' face told him she was offended by his joke and Asa just nodded. He could feel his face grow hot with embarrassment as the priestess went back to washing things and Asa cut the onions, throwing them together in a pan.

"You should learn how to cook. It's fun," Asa said. "I can teach you, if you like. Unless you've no knack at all, like Devra. She can't even make a morning porridge without burning it. When she was little, mam would send her for a bucket of water and she'd come back when we were ready to start a search without the bucket and some fancy rock or a salamander she'd never seen before." Asa and the priestess laughed, still working on the meal.

Derk slid the dagger into his boot, hopping off his stool. "I can help. Just give me something to do. I can't be totally worthless." He smiled at the priestess in what he hoped was an endearing way, rolling his shirt sleeves up. "What can I do?"

"You can dry the greens for the salad," the priestess offered a bit to eagerly, raising her eyes toward him. She had a warm smile and dimples on her cheeks. Derk saw her eyes stray toward Asa and he managed not to laugh. He knew she wanted to get rid of him. The priestess handed him the sack full of greens and nudged him away toward the door. "Just take them outside and swing them around. It shouldn't take too long."

Derk smirked and took the sack from her, nodding to them both as he headed toward the door. "It won't. You'll see, I'll be the fastest drier of salad in the Valley."

"That's the spirit!" Asa said, raising his knife to him in encouragement. Derk just laughed and headed outside, instantly looking for somewhere to sit. It was quiet outside the kitchen, the summer sun starting its slow descent toward the horizon. Chickens clucked somewhere and a few people wandered the streets, finishing up their errands or work before going home for evening meal. He shook the bag of greens, not sure if this was the way to do it. He felt like a fool. Drying greens. Is this what he signed up for? It was a far cry from the brawl which had gotten him into this in the first place. Derk shook the bag, feeling the dampness start to seep through the fabric.

Two people came around the corner and Derk smiled at the priestess Sindra, and the Wielder, Devra, arm in arm as they approached the kitchen. He whistled in greeting and Devra waved at him, both of the women smiling as they walked toward him. "Meal's not done yet," he said, holding the bag of greens at his side. "Asa's fixing with some priestess in there. He's quite the cook, apparently."

"You're in for a treat if Asa's in the kitchen," Devra said. "Hes a better cook then our mam, though he'd never admit it."

"Do be sure to save me a plate," Sindra said, pulling her arm out of Devra's. "Maybe two?"

"Are you not going to share the meal with us?" Derk asked, genuinely curious. Apart from meal times Derk rarely had a chance to talk to the priestess. Last night she had turned in shortly after prayers and during the day she rode in the cart with Devra and Asa. There would be others at the meal but through careful planning he could maybe sit next to her or at least share an interesting story. He had to endear himself to the beautiful priestess somehow.

"I'm afraid not," Sindra said, shaking her head. She tucked her hands into her sleeves despite the warm weather. "I have to go into the town and meet our guide, the one who is going to take us into the Freewild."

"Well make it three plates to be saved because I'm coming with you," Derk said suddenly. Devra seemed a bit surprised but Sindra's smile dropped from her mouth, a bit of panic showing in her eyes. If Derk hadn't been so focused on her he might not have seen it, as she wiped all apprehension from her face before answering.

"It won't be necessary, Derk. I know where the tavern is and as a priestess, I don't need protection." She smiled warmly at him but Derk was curious as to why she wanted to go by herself, almost as much as he simply desired to go with her.

"It's not for your protection, not that I wouldn't lift a hand to keep you safe." Derk tried to think of a reason to tag along without seeming to obvious. "I'd just like to go with you. I'm...well, I'm bored here at the temple, to be honest and I could at least pick up a game of cards at the tavern. Plus, I hear the band playing at the Last Stop is very good." This was true. Kaela the priestess had mentioned it to him in an earlier effort to get him out of the kitchen. "I do like music. I'm a good singer, maybe I'll take up with them and leave you lot to find the chalice yourselves."

"I hope not! We like having your company," Devra said, taking the bag of greens from him. "Sin, you should take him. He's probably going crazy in the temple. Though promise me you won't run away with the band, Derk. I'd come but I have studying to do."

"It really isn't needed," Sindra said, insisting. "Besides, our guide might...he's a bit...to himself. I don't want him to feel surrounded."

"So you're meeting him in a tavern where a band is playing?" Derk chuckled. "Bad planning on your part already. What's one more person? And besides, he's going to have to meet the rest of us sooner or later. Half now, half later? Or one third, I suppose, since he already knows you, right?" The argument was sound enough. Sindra looked to Devra, defeated. Devra just smiled back, skipping into the kitchen with the bag of greens. Derk offered his arm to Sindra, hoping she wouldn't snub him. A quick narrowing of her eyes is what she gave him before she took his arm in his and together they walked down the street.

"Have you ever been to the Last Stop?" Derk asked, trying to keep the conversation light. "Or Bluemist?" It was Derk's first time in the town at the southeastern most point of the Tyeskin Barony. Last Stop was the name of many a tavern bordering the Freewild.

"I've been to both," Sindra answered, seeming a bit distracted. She managed to look up at Derk and he wondered if her dark skin was as soft as it looked. Her dark grey eyes were large, flecks of black dotting the irises. A smile tweaked the corners of her full mouth; if she noticed Derk staring she didn't say anything. "If you can manage to wake early, the Mist is a sight to see."

Derk surprised them with his ability to fall asleep in the saddle. Asa had asked for lessons but Derk thought better of it. He laughed out loud, glad the priestess was joking with him. "I think I can pull it off. I like things that are a sight to see." They walked for a few blocks without saying anything, Derk looking over the people in the town and glad to see a few were staring. He felt Sindra's hand grip his arm a little tighter. "Are you afraid of something?" he whispered.

"No, it's just...well, people are looking. You'd think they'd never seen a Forester before." She laughed, sighing quietly afterward. Her grip on his arm loosened slightly.

"You're the first I've met though my father told me my great-grandfather met one." The people from the Forest of Clouds showed up in the older, first stories of the Valley but now they were rarely seen. Derk had never thought he would meet one and now he was walking down the street with a Forester, a beautiful Forester woman.

"You'll be meeting your second in a bit," she said, nodding her head in greeting to someone who waved. The Last Stop appeared in the distance, a lone building standing apart from all the others. A girl fed some chickens in the yard and the aroma of dozens of suppers made Derk's stomach rumble. He grinned at Sindra's words.

"Another? You mean our guide-"

"Is a Forester, yes," she said. "Very knowledgeable about the Freewild. He...spends a lot of time there."

"Oh?" Not only was the guide a Forester, which was strange, but he spent time in the Freewild. Was he a criminal? From what Derk understood only miscreants and social rejects lived in the Freewild, though he never said this to Old Gam. The Freewild was strange with land often fertile one year and dead the next. Not to mention the threat of Freemen, the strange creatures living in the crevices and hollows, beaten back by the Barons. Derk remembered the depictions and stories from his youth, how the Freemen raided villages and stole food and weapons, having no language but shrieks and cries. Their numbers had dwindled to the point where they were almost just stories. Still, most people chose not to live in the Freewild. It was safer in the Baronies.

"Was your friend born there?" he asked, trying to steer the conversation back to the guide. It occurred to him maybe Sindra and the guide were more than just acquaintances. Perhaps this is why she didn't want anyone to come along.

"No, we were both born in the Forest." Derk and Sindra walked through the door of the Last Stop and Derk was glad to be within the walls of a bar again. It was noisy and warm, the way it was supposed to be with the aroma of sawdust, beer and food cooked all day wafting through the air. People played cards and dice at tables and in the corner a quartet of musicians were setting up. Sindra looked around and Derk did too, out of habit, though he had no idea who he was looking for. Instead of a guide he found a free table and pointed it out, the pair of them picking their way through the occupied tables and chairs.

"What'll you drink?" he asked. "Some food, maybe? A snack? A dance when the music starts?" That got a smile out of her. She seemed nervous, her arms crossed over her chest. "A drink?" Sindra nodded eventually and smiled without showing her teeth, keeping her eyes focused on the door. In the dim light of the bar her eyes seemed almost black but they were still pretty.

"One pitcher of your summer brown," Derk said. "Three cups. And a bit of whatever you have that's fried." The sinewy man behind the bar went into the back and came back with the pitcher and glasses, handing them over only when Derk laid down the money to pay for them. He raised the pitcher, showing it off to Sindra before sitting down with her and carefully pouring her a glass. Sindra took it all too quickly and gulped it down.

No sooner had she set her cup down when she stood up and waved, Derk looking to see who. Derk tilted his head to the side, slightly confused at the person who walked in. He was a Forester to be sure. His dark skin was a touch darker than Sindra's and when he pulled back his hood Derk saw they shared the same raven black hair. However his mouth was thinner and looked like it rarely smiled, his steely grey eyes hard as mirrorstone. On a face so young it was almost a shame.

What really made Derk stare was the armor he wore and the sword at his side. Who showed up to a tavern in armor? In this weather? The sword he could understand. Swords didn't fit in packs. But the guide looked like he was there for a fight, not to meet a friend for a job. Derk half expected to see dead animals hanging off of him but the sword was the only thing he saw.

Well, they aren't lovers, Derk mused, watching as the two Foresters regarded one another. They looked related. Sindra tried to display a happy face but the guide just sat down, letting his pack slip to the ground with a rather ominous thump. Maybe the dead animals were in there, Derk thought. As if sensing his thoughts the guide shot a glance at Derk, as if trying to stare him down. Derk smiled and waved two fingers in greeting. "Hi, I'm Derk."

The guide slid into his chair and raised his eyebrows at Sindra in a way which could only be described as annoyed. Then he started to talk. It must have been in Forester because Derk didn't understand anything he said. He could tell the Forester was not happy. He wasn't surprised when Sindra answered the guide back in the same foreign tongue, both of them seeming to whisper though no one could have possibly understood what they were saying. Derk wrapped his hand around his mug and took a pull off of it before he set it back down, pouring their guest a cup. Without missing a breath, the guide took the cup once it was full and took a drink.

Derk sat back in his chair and watched the two talk. It was obvious the guide was not pleased to see Derk there. He appeared to be trying to back out of whatever arrangement they had and Sindra was trying to convince him to help. Then Sindra said something and the guide corrected her, which made Sindra laugh, not in a kind way. She said something else to him and took a sip of her drink. Now the guide looked serious. He crossed his arms on the table and brought his tankard to his lips, setting his eyes on Derk. Derk just waved back.

"Why are you going?" the guide asked him. His words were accented, his Rs rolling too much as if he was still speaking Forester. Just then the tender brought a plate of food; vegetable fritters with sauce.

"Why, so you can steal my reason? Find your own!" Derk picked up one of the fritters and frowned, finding them to be too greasy. He took a bite and watched as the guide stared at him for a few breaths. Derk raised his brows at him and sat back in his chair, watching as the guide turned his attention back to Sindra and asked her something.

Finally Sindra laughed and the priestess stood. "I'm going to step outside for a bit. Don't let him leave." She pointed to the guide and addressed Derk.

"Maybe we'll leave together," Derk chided, taking a sip of his drink. Sindra narrowed her eyes at them both before she made her way out of the bar. The guide stared at Derk. It almost made Derk shiver.

"Come on, let us leave," The Forester said, grabbing his pack. Derk grasped him by the wrist and shook his head.

"Are you serious? I was only kidding, we can't leave!" Derk waited to let go of young guide's wrist, once he was sure he understood. "I mean, we could but Sindra'd be angry. They're counting on you."

"I do not want to take you into the Freewild," the guide said, shaking his head. "It is not a good idea."

"Why?" Derk said, lowering his head. "You afraid to take us? We can hold our own."

"No, it is not that," the guide said. "I simply do not like you."

"What?!" Derk wasn't sure if he had heard the Forester correctly. "You don't like us?" He couldn't believe it. But the guide nodded. "What are you, ten?" Derk sputtered.

"Ten what?"

"Ten years old! Is someone playing a trick on me?" Derk ran his fingers through his hair, trying to wrap his his mind around what the guide just said. "Look. What's your name?"

"Jezlen."

"Jezlen," Derk said. "I didn't give you a reason to come along with us because you have to have your own reason for doing things. Otherwise you'll just jump off the cart before you hit the gate. Sometimes you do things even if you don't like the people you're working with. Though to be fair, you haven't met all of us. I've been told I am very likeable. And Asa is fun. Devra's good to look at, sweet as well. And well, do you have anything better to do? Honestly?" Maybe Jezlen did. From the looks of his armor and his pack, he'd done a few things before this meeting. But obviously he had free time or he wouldn't have shown up at Last Stop. "Plus, what about Sindra? She looks like she needs you. Like...it would mean a lot to her. You're what, cousins?"

"She is the sister of the first wife of the brother of my father." Jezlen said it with a straight face so Derk tried not to laugh or make a big deal out of it. Instead he drained his beer cup and poured himself another glass, seeing Sindra enter through the door.

"So your...aunt. She needs you. I bet that means something." Derk tried to read Jezlen but when he wasn't talking he was hard to gauge. Sindra sat down and picked up one of the fritters, wrinkling her nose.

She talked to Jezlen in the strange language again, leaving Derk to try to figure out what they were saying. After a breath, he leaned forward. "You know, it would be nice if you would speak in Valleymen."

Jezlen stared at Derk and laughed, not with his mouth but with his eyes. "Do you speak Forester, Derk?" he asked, pouring himself another drink.

"No," Derk replied curtly, wondering what was his point.

"I speak Forester and Valleymen. How is it my problem if you do not know a language?" Jezlen rolled his eyes and reached into his pack, pulling out a pipe and some smoking herbs. "I am fine with switching. Your Forester is not very good anymore, Sindra."

"You're a terrible nephew," Derk said. He didn't care if Jezlen didn't like it.

"Everything I am, I am terrible," Jezlen said, pulling a match out and bringing it to his pipe, lighting the bowl with a few puffs.

"But you're an excellent guide," Sindra interjected. She was holding her cup in both hands and she leaned forward, drawing closer to the Forester. "Please, Jezlen. I...I already told the temple we had a guide-"

"Wait, you told the temple you had it arranged but you didn't?" Sindra's face looked as if it were blushing though Derk could hardly tell. Now he knew why she didn't want him to come along. One of the reasons, at least. "Did Asa know this?"

Sindra shook her head slowly, staring into her cup. "I was fairly certain I could get him to agree. Jezlen, you have to understand, I know you aren't a follower but it is important. And you do live in the Valley, where the Goddess reigns. Please?"

Jezlen dropped a fritter back onto the plate, making a sour face at them. "These are terrible. Their food is not good."

"Aren't you going to answer her?" Derk wanted to leap over the table and shake Jezlen but it probably wouldn't do any good. Plus, there was the issue of the elf wearing armor and having a weapon. Jezlen looked to Derk and sighed.

"I will do it. He is right. I have nothing else better to do." He looked to Sindra. "And even though you are family, you are still good to me." Sindra smiled at Jezlen as he puffed on his pipe again, exhaling a cloud of fragrant smoke. The band started to play louder, ready to start. "But I want to be paid in goods, not money."

"Of course," Sindra said, looking into the pitcher and seemed disappointed when she found there was no more beer. She looked to Derk and smiled, the same serene happiness taking over her features again. "Would you like to have another pitcher before we head back?"

"I was thinking we could dance," Derk offered, a little too hopefully for his taste. A few more notes eased over the patrons and Derk stood up, offering Sindra his hand.

"You should dance," Jezlen said, smoking his pipe and leaning back in his chair. "You never allow yourself to have fun." Sindra glared at Jezlen and looked at Derk, walking around her nephew and placing her hand in Derk's. Before she could ask him Jezlen groaned, waving them off with his hand. "Yes, I will be here when you are done dancing. Go. Leave me alone."

Derk led Sindra up to the dance floor and wrapped his arm around her waist, glad to hear the band was starting with a ballad. The song was She Left me, Cord in Hand. He much preferred the dances in taverns and barns and dance halls, two people touching one another and dancing as they liked to whatever was played. Sindra was almost as tall as he and felt light in his arms, allowing herself to be led around the dance floor.

"Your nephew's...." Derk let his voice trail off, not sure what to say and not sure why he brought it up.

"He's a stupid fapper is what he is," Sindra offered, breathing out. She laughed and she seemed to relax under his touch, her face brightening in the dimmed bar. Derk laughed along with her, glad to see her not looking sad. "You have to understand," she said, laying her head on his shoulder. "He had a rough start, Jezlen. He had to leave home when he was very young. Something happened to him, before he came to the Valley. "

"But you still trust him to get us into the Freewild and back?" He felt her nod against his shoulder. The music lolled and played and Derk inhaled the scent of moonflower on her hair and her skin, felt her pressed against him. As they turned to the music he saw Jezlen, smoking his pipe and watching them, his eyes glinting in the lantern light. Derk made a rude face at him but Jezlen remained impassive and Derk shook his head. "If you trust him, I'm fine," he decided to say. "Though I don't know how he'll get on with the others."

"They'll get on," Sindra said, lifting her head and looking up at him. Their eyes met and Derk felt his face grow warmer, wondering what Sindra was thinking. In a way he had helped her get her nephew to come along, hadn't he? It had to be worth something. Sindra pressed her lips together and Derk was surprised to see her look unsure of herself, almost ashamed. "Please, don't tell the others about this. That I didn't have the guide all set up."

"As long as he shows up in two days at the temple, there's no reason to tell them," Derk said. "Even if he doesn't show up, I wouldn't tell them. Make him look bad. Or rather, worse." The song ended and for a few breaths the dance floor bustled as people took their leave or came to dance as the band played the first few counts of the next song over and over. An uptempo song. Derk let his hold loosen on Sindra but didn't let go. "One more?"

"I'm not usually one for the fast ones," Sindra admitted, but she didn't pull away. Derk let his hand slide down to the small of her back and laced his fingers in hers. The last of those who wished to dance came to the floor and the band began their lively tune, sending the dancers spinning about the dance floor. Derk led and Sindra followed, laughing at a misstep but finding their place. The dance picked up in tempo and by the end the pair of them were laughing and falling over each other, Derk pulling Sindra away from the rest of the dancers to spare them their crashing about.

"It was a valiant effort," Derk laughed as they walked back to their table, pushing past those headed to dance. Sindra shook her head pushing her hair back to show her pointed ears.

"I told you I don't normally do the fast ones," she said, sliding into her seat. There was a full pitcher on the table but all the fritters were gone, Jezlen still smoking and eying the both of them.

"What, would you like to go for a dance?" Derk grinned at Jezlen, pouring himself a fresh drink. "You'll have to wait, I'm a bit tired from your aunt stomping me."

"I wasn't so bad, was I?" Sindra wrinkled her nose at Derk.

"Not the worst, but you definitely need practice. I can help with that." A gulp of beer was exactly what he needed and he drank from his cup, looking over the top at the priestess. If she didn't like the idea, she didn't show it on her face.

"As much as I love being in this bar surrounded by strangers, I think I am going to go," Jezlen said, standing. Derk wasn't sure how to feel about the Forester's departure but Sindra looked disappointed.

"Are you sure, Jezlen? You can stay in the temple with us." She sounded hopeful, sitting up straighter in her seat.

Jezlen just gave her a look, a look saying the idea was ridiculous and they both knew it. "I will be at your temple before first watch in two days. I give you my word." He cast his gaze at Derk and didn't smile. He looked slightly confused, Derk thought.

"I look forward to working with you," Derk said before Jezlen could say anything. Now the elf definitely seemed confused and he shook his head, picking up his pack and slinging it over his shoulder.

"If you say so," Jezlen said. He nodded at Sindra and then turned and left, slipping past the other patrons of the bar. They both watched his departure, pulling up his hood before he exited the bar.

Chapter 7
Early Rewards

Derk clapped his hands as the singer finished, a few other members of the audience applauding. He and Sindra had made their way up to the dance floor a few times though she pulled away at one point, the song too fast for her skill level. He heard her laugh and excuse herself. Without missing a beat Derk grabbed a skinny lad who looked like he wanted to dance, finding the young man flustered at first but they soon fell into the song, laughing and trying to figure out who was leading. Derk led and when the song was over Derk humored him and the laughing crowd with a bow, walking back over to where Sindra sat, her hands over her mouth as she laughed.

The music was winding down, the pitcher was empty and the greasy food cold. "I guess we should head back?" Sindra shrugged, looking at the grease covered plate. Another song started up, a slow song, and the singer sang in a clear, pretty voice. Derk finished his beer and nodded.

"Aye, I don't want to miss Asa's cooking," he said, standing up and offering her his arm. Sindra took it and they walked out of the Last Stop, the music from inside following them down the street. As they walked, Derk danced a bit, making Sindra laugh. "I like when you laugh," Derk confessed, smiling at her. The priestess smiled back, looking at him out of the corner of her eye.

"You've a talent for making people laugh, it seems," she said. "And Asa says you're good in a fight. And you can dance."

"I'm also a great singer," he insisted, making her laugh again. "I've got a good memory. I can recite 'The Graces and Deeds of Our Holy Goddess' from start to finish."

"Which version?" Sindra asked, her interest obviously piqued.

"The one by Sister Hila of the Temple of the First Quarter," Derk bragged. He had loved those stories since he was a child.

"Really?" Sindra seemed impressed. "Most people don't like it, because of the language. It's a bit archaic."

"It's more colorful, more fun," Derk remembered sitting on the bench at the front of the temple, Sister Kiyla standing over the scroll. "'In the days before our need, before the blood of the devout had been spilled by the belligerent, the Holy Goddess in Her wisdom and love stretched Her Black Hands over the land in order to make a dwelling place for all those who sought peace.' That's much more beautiful than, what is it? 'Before we came to this land, the Holy Goddess had already prepared it so those who sought peace would have a refuge.'" Derk shook his head. "I mean, it gets the facts across but where's the mystery? The wonder?"

"I'm surprised you've had such an intimate experience with Sister Hila's writings," Sindra mused. "Your priestess must have been exemplary."

Derk shrugged, trying to brush it off while trying to think of something which would satisfy the priestess' curiosity without revealing anything about his past. "She was a good priestess. Like...a mother, I suppose."

"Was your mother especially devout?" Sindra asked. She seemed genuinely interested and not prying but still, it made Derk a bit nervous. Perhaps he shouldn't have said the last bit. But it was true. Sister Kiyla had been more of a mother figure than his step-mother. What about Cira? He thought about their last kiss and what it meant, what it didn't mean. He wondered if she still thought about him. Even if she did, he was here now, with Sindra, and she had asked him a question.

"I don't remember, to be honest," he said. Derk kicked something in the street and sent it skittering across the dirt. "She died when I was young. I vaguely recall sitting in temple with her. My father wasn't especially devout." The Church was the only place Derk could find refuge from his father. His father had pulled away from the Church, hadn't he? Darix Cartaskin had abandoned the spiritual side of life to make something permanent in the material world. At least he had tried to. Derk saw the lights of the temple ahead and cocked his head at Sindra, thinking a change in subject was in order. "And Jezlen? He's not devout, is he?"

Sindra's face clouded. "My nephew...you have to understand, the people of the Forest have different gods. Different beliefs, and Jezlen...." She paused for a moment and this time he knew she was keeping something back. "Sometimes systems prey upon people."

"Is that why you left the Forest? Why you follow the Goddess?" Derk knew all too well what Sindra said was true, though he wondered what had happened to Jezlen. Sindra shook her head.

"I was called by the Goddess when I was younger. He was very little and so I hardly knew him when I left for the Valley to follow my path. Later on he left the Forest and Her hand guided him to me." Sindra tried to smile but her eyes looked full of worry. They reached the temple and instead of walking in she stopped, the pair facing each other on the dark street. "I am the only family he has here. I don't know if it means anything to him."

"Sometimes what we need isn't family, but a friend." Derk watched as Sindra looked at him, regarding him with her dark grey eyes. Eventually the corners of her mouth turned upward in a sad smile. Derk opened the door for her before following her into the temple kitchen, not surprised to find a plate of food waiting on the table. His stomach grumbled, suddenly feeling very hungry. He hopped up onto the table and Sindra pulled up a stool, both of them digging into the food Asa had prepared.

"I'm glad you helped Asa in the bar fight," Sindra said, licking her fingers. Derk reached behind himself and grabbed a spoon, digging into the barley and onion stew. He chewed and swallowed before he answered her.

"My jaw wasn't all too happy I did" he said finally, taking another spoonful. He smiled at her, looking up as he heard quiet footsteps approaching them. Devra walked into the kitchen, a pitcher in her gloved hands.

"How'd it go?" she asked. She set the pitcher on the table and grabbed a handful of berries. "Where's the guide?"

"He off preparing for the trip," Derk said before Sindra could. "You missed some good music. The singer could have been better."

"Think you could have done better?" Sindra quipped. Derk rolled his eyes and took another bite, trying not to smile with his mouth full of food. "You might not have known this, Dev, but our friend here is quite the singer."

"And dancer," Derk said, still chewing. "Also, I can do card tricks."

"Do you sing?" Devra asked, her green eyes bright with interest. "Would you sing for us?"

"I sang when we left Portsmouth," he offered, suddenly feeling self-conscious. But Sindra was laughing and Devra appeared to be waiting. "I don't know what to sing."

"Sing anything," Sindra insisted, her eyes sparkling. Both she and Devra focused on him. The best way to get someone to stop asking for something was to give it to them, Derk knew, so he cleared his throat and took a sip of water, the lyrics of the song coming easily to him.

I had a love fair as the night,
She was gone in the morn
Joined were we in the moonlight
But now my heart is torn

I loved the girl from far away,
I pined for her for years
All my hopes crushed in a day
And smiles have turned to tears

For now I know she sees in me
Naught but a bit of fun
In dreams, her I no longer see
And boyish love is done

I keep my love inside of me
For I am not the one.

Derk looked around, the kitchen seeming suddenly too quiet. Sindra and Devra were still staring at him and he thought they would laugh. But Devra and Sindra just looked at each other, not saying anything.

"The sad ones are the hardest to get right," Devra said, her arms crossed over her chest. "You have to make it sad but still keep them on the dance floor."

"Thank you for singing for us," Sindra nodded. "I hope you'll grace us with your singing at some other time."

"You'll have to sing for Asa, he does love a good song," Devra insisted, sitting next to Sindra at the table finally.

"Entertainment and protection, yeah?" Derk hopped off the table and winced. His legs had fallen asleep from sitting on the table top and he braced himself against the table, stamping his foot to get the blood flowing.

"Are you all right?" Sindra asked.

"I'm fine, just my leg. It fell asleep. I'll probably turn in myself." Derk bowed his head in farewell before walking carefully across the kitchen, not wanting to fall as the tingling sensation crawled through his legs and feet. "See you in the morning?" He heard them bid him goodnight as he walked out of the kitchen, recalling where the common hall lay. The corridor led to the temple and he couldn't help but gaze up at the statue of the Goddess behind the altar, Her serene face looking out over the pews.

Derk nodded at the priestess standing watch at the door separating the common area from the temple, not recognizing her from their brief stay in the town. She waited for him to show his pass before pulling the door open, the hushed tones emanating from within the chamber telling him most of the people slept. He saw a corner of the room was dimly lit and Asa sat on the edge of the light on his bedroll, sewing something. Derk stepped quietly to his bedroll and sat down, unbuckling his boots.

"Missed a good meal," Asa said, drawing the needle through the bit of fabric. Derk pulled one boot off, setting it next to his pack.

"It was still good when I got at it," Derk said, pulling off the other one. "Besides, I'm sure I'll get more of your hot meals in the next few phases." He set the other next to its twin before pulling off his socks, draping them over the boots. "How was cooking with the priestess?"

"Pretty good, though she cut herself," Asa said, finishing a few more stitches. "She wasn't being careful. I patched her up though." Asa finished the dart and then turned the garment inside out, revealing it to be a tunic. Derk could tell from Asa's tone nothing had happened between the young man and the priestess and Asa didn't seem to know what he missed. "Devra said you and Sindra went to meet the guide? How'd that ? You think he's a good man?"

Derk shrugged and pulled off his shirt, folding it neatly while he thought of what to say. "He's a Forester, so a bit mysterious. Looked the part. Cape and leather armor, a sword. Young. Willing to help." All true.

Asa smiled in response. "Sounds like a good match." He folded the tunic and put it in his pack, not bothering to secure it since they were in the safety of the temple. "Well, I'm going to turn in. Got a busy day before we head out to the Freewild. I've got to help Devra get a few things and pick up my sword from the smith. Don't stay up too late." Asa smacked him on the leg before he crawled into his bedroll, his mop of dark, straight hair the only bit of him showing.

Derk envied Asa, being able to fall asleep so quickly. Asa probably only had happy dreams, of his family or rescuing people from burning things. Derk still had dreams of a blackened skeleton reeking of smoke, the ring of his father's house on its charred finger. Or he dreamed of Old Gam, leaving him in a dark alley. One time he had a dream he was hiding somewhere in his father's house and Cira had found him, her beautiful face wild, eyes wide, her mouth twisted in a cruel smile. She shrieked and attacked him, all the other members of the household appearing behind him and doing the same.

The door opened and Derk looked up, seeing Devra and Sindra both enter, a few of the other travelers stirring as they both walked toward Derk and the sleeping Asa. He smiled at them before reaching into his pack, pulling out a deck of cards. He shuffled the cards as he listened to them slip out of their robes and skirts and dresses, noticing Devra's still gloved hands. Sindra's bedroll was beside his, and the priestess smiled at him before she slipped under her quilts. As Derk dealt himself a game he heard Devra whisper a goodnight before rolling over. He muttered in reply, not able to keep from turning his head toward Sindra as he heard her humming.

She hummed the song he sang earlier. After a few lines she rolled over onto her stomach and looked at him, her face darker in the lack of light. "It's a tune that sticks with you," she whispered.

"They're supposed to," he laughed, looking at the cards he had put down. He flipped over the third card in the deck and placed it where it belonged. "Like the emotions in the songs. They linger." Derk flipped over another card and then another, not sure why he said what he did. He pressed his lips together, thinking of the kiss he shared with Cira all those months ago. He thought of Old Gam and the way her skin felt against his, her long, thick hair brushing against his shoulders, tangled in his fingers.

He wondered what songs made her think of him. He remembered dancing earlier, how Sindra had felt in his arms, her cheek on his shoulder. The memory pushed the thoughts of Gam and Cira away. Derk looked up at her from his game, shuffling the deck again.

"What lingers in your mind, Derk?" Sindra asked. Derk narrowed his eyes at her. Was she asking him as a priestess or as herself? Were those things so different? He remembered how she spoke of her nephew, the look on her face and the words she said. How she had first spoken to him in the temple back in Portsmouth and how she gazed at him when he was singing. What part of him would answer her? Which part of her did he want asking the question? Priestly council wouldn't have been bad at this moment but his more romantic thoughts weighed in as well.

"You," he said. It wasn't a lie. Something on Sindra's face made him think she was pleased with his answer but trying to hide it. Part of him was surprised he'd been so bold, but it was an answer to her question and gave nothing else away.

"Goodnight, Derk," was the reply she gave him, though he knew she wanted to say something else. She rolled over in her bed, leaving Derk to watch her blankets rise and fall with her breathing, the rhythm changing once she had indeed fallen asleep. He went back to his card game, winning the first hand and dealing a second. Someone on the other side of the room coughed and a baby woke up and started crying. Derk heard the mother whisper quietly in the dark and bodies shifting before everything went back to being quiet, the only sounds that of gentle breathing and Asa's snoring. Derk looked over his hand and sighed.

Another sleepless night.

Derk leaned against the building, struggling to keep his eyes open. Even with the sun blaring down he was fairly certain he could fall asleep where he stood. But he had to stay awake. They would be leaving tomorrow morning and he had to wake with the rest of them since he would be riding the gelding. The iceleaf he had bought to chew wasn't helping to keep him awake like the woman said it would. It just made his mouth feel cold when he breathed in. Maybe some food would help him stay awake. With some effort he peeled himself off of the building he was leaning against and plodded down the street, trying to smell something besides iceleaf to tell him where he could find some food.

He wondered if Asa and Devra were finding everything they needed. He had gone with them to the herb shop after first meal. Sindra had a meeting with the head priestess of the temple, so keeping her company wasn't an option. The herb shop had been interesting, jars and baskets filled with peculiar smelling plants. Asa and Devra seemed equally interested in the wares, talking to each other and sniffing things. Derk walked up to the woman behind the counter, asking for something to help him stay awake and another to help him sleep. After a few questions she sold Derk the iceleaf and a blend of herbs he was supposed to eat before bed. He left Asa and Devra to their chores, thinking he would get bored following them around. Now he was too bored to stay awake.

Bluemist was a good sized town, bordering on a city. It was close enough to the Freewild to be the first stop in or out for many a cart or traveler, but not too far out it wouldn't make it into the territory on a Baron's Day. Derk yawned as he turned a corner, trying to recall if he needed anything. He had clothes and sewing supplies. The

Church was sending them with food and gear. His dagger was on him and Old Gam's meddling tools were tucked away in his belt. Maybe he'd pick up something for Gam, just to soften the blow of his departure. He planned on seeing her again, at least to return her tools. If Gam was true to her word, she wouldn't save a spot in her bed for him if he was gone. Still, he wanted to remain friends. Maybe a piece of pretty blue fabric for her work. Derk's stomach rumbled again, demanding it be tended to first so he sniffed the air again, finding a grill stand easily enough.

"One longfish, please," he asked, looking around while the woman behind the grill pulled a still living fish out of a bucket, hacking its head off with a cleaver. Derk surveyed the marketplace while the woman continued with her work, the smell of the the fish cooking over the grill making his mouth water. When the fish was done he paid her and took it, glad to see she had put a few slices of onion on the skewer as well.

Derk ate his food and looked around as he walked through the marketplace. Something glinted out in the corner of his eye at a nearby booth. He watched the person manning the booth call out his wares, a young man a few years younger than Derk crafting more jewelry behind the stall. A customer approached and Derk observed as he and the seller looked over the necklaces and bracelets. He watched as the customer touched the items and how the seller reacted. The seller kept a strong stance as the customer pulled out some money. Only then did the seller retrieve the bracelet which interested the gentleman. Derk watched and noticed how the items were secured on their displays.

His weariness clashed against his concentration but he noticed one necklace in particular, a white stone set in a small polished piece of wood. It would look pretty hanging around Gam's neck. Maybe he would wrap it in the blue fabric. To his relief the pendants seemed to be secured on a hook instead of being tied to the top of the booth as some more cautious vendors had them. His lack of sleep was making the world drone around him, like the buzzing of bees and he tried to push the sound away so he could take in everything around him.

Something brushed against Derk's leg and startled him. A cat rubbed back and forth against his leg butting his shin with its head. It was one of those cats the color of embers, black and orange all over with big orange eyes. Derk bent down to scratch the cat and at the same time a pair of city guards walked by, their plain but functional shortswords clanging at their sides. Derk gulped quietly, glad he hadn't performed the exercise in gift acquiring. Maybe when he was more awake.

He gave the cat an extra scratch behind its ears, which made it purr so loudly Derk laughed. There was still a bit of fish left so he pulled it off of the stick and held it out to the animal. The cat ate it enthusiastically but not ravenously. It probably received plenty of scraps as well as the mice skittering through the town. Derk wiped his hand on the cat's back when it was done, pretending he was petting it when he really meant to get the bits of fish off his hand.

"You should not be petting that animal." Derk recognized the voice. Jezlen stood in front of Derk, a dark eyebrow cocked in dismay. He wasn't wearing his sword or his armor but there was still something about him which looked guarded and dangerous. In the light of the summer sun he could see the true grey of Jezlen's eyes and Derk saw they were about the same height, though Derk was a finger or two taller. Derk stood up and wiped his hands on his trousers, giving the Forester a wry look.

"And why is that?" he asked, not sure he wanted to know the answer.

"They are evil animals," Jezlen replied. "They kill birds."

"And I ate a bird yesterday. What's your point?" Derk considered the fact he might be too tired to deal with Jezlen but was at a loss as to how to get rid of him. "They kill mice. Mice ruin crops."

"Cats kill for pleasure," Jezlen said. "Mice are only trying to survive."

"Are we really having this conversation?" Derk ran his hands through his hair, trying not to groan at Jezlen's words. "Cats are free spirited. They're cunning and agile and they don't just follow orders and wag their tails. Though this one is wagging its tail." Derk cocked his head to the side and stared at the cat, which was indeed wagging its fat tail back and forth. Derk shook his head and turned his attention back to Jezlen, irate he was still talking to him. "I'm too tired for this!" Derk waved Jezlen away, walking away from him.

"Cats hide their weapons!" Jezlen called after him, a bit too loudly. People were starting to notice them and when Derk looked back he saw Jezlen and the cat staring each other down. Derk couldn't help but laugh and wonder what that had been about. Jezlen was probably in the town to buy supplies like the rest of them. He wondered what kinds of items the elf would need. Probably something to shove in his pipe. Derk covered his mouth as he yawned, feeling slightly more alert after the weird conversation and the food. Maybe he'd make it to evening prayers.

Or maybe a nap was in order. A short one, out in the sun so he wouldn't sleep too long. Since he wasn't feeling completely exhausted he could probably wake himself up. If he fell asleep outside of someone's store he was guaranteed to be roused at some point by either the shopkeeper or a guard. The watch bells would wake him up if nothing else. Derk found a lamp oil store and sat down against the building, folding his arms over his chest and pulling his cap over his eyes. The sounds of the rest of the city going about its business were strangely soothing and soon they all seemed to melt into one sound. His muscles relaxed and his head dropped to his chest.

He startled as something thumped down next to him and he fell to the side, catching himself with his hand. His eyes widened to see Sindra sitting next to him, smiling broadly at his reaction. "Is the church too quiet for you to sleep, Derk?" she asked.

"I wasn't asleep," he lied. His heart still thumped from the shock and the presence of the priestess wasn't helping to slow it down. "And the church isn't too quiet. I'm just more of a night person." He shrugged. It wasn't entirely a lie.

"It's important to sleep," she said. "How will the Goddess sort our minds if we do not dream?"

Derk wasn't sure how to answer her question so he just nodded, looking at his hands. He thought about the things they had touched, the things they had held. Metal, blood, flesh, dirt, tears. He thought about how it felt to touch these things, how it made the rest of him feel. The pain, the exhilaration, the confusion, the pleasure and more. Emotions and ordeals revisited time and time again.

"It would be nice to be sorted out," was all he said in response, managing a weary smile. Sindra put a hand on the side of his face. It was soft and warm. She probably felt the stubble of his beard. Before he knew what he was doing he had turned his face to kiss the palm of her hand. He was too tired to care if he was being foolish. He looked into her eyes and then at her mouth. She didn't look shocked or repulsed. She looked like she was waiting and when he leaned in his head toward her she met him halfway.

They kissed, her hand stroking his cheek, and Derk wanted to sit in front of the store for the rest of the day, kissing the priestess. But she pulled away and looked to him, her dark eyes bright with excitement. He wondered what she thought she was doing by kissing him. For a breath Derk entertained the thought she kissed him because she had ulterior motives. Maybe she felt bad for him, tired and distressed as he was. He should care but at this exact moment, he didn't. Derk pushed the thought away and leaned in again, kissing her.

"What's this?" Derk heard Asa's voice, breaking away from the priestess and looking up. There he stood, mouth wide open. Devra grinned and looked at Sindra, a hint of mischief in her eyes. "I didn't know you liked men," Asa said to Sindra, shifting his packages in his hands.

"I told you she did, Asa," Devra said, slapping him on the arm.

"I must have forgotten," Asa sighed. "These kinds of things, I'm always missing them."

"I noticed," Derk said, slightly disappointed to be interrupted but glad to see no one was acting negatively to what just happened, least of all Sindra. "The priestess, Kaela, was shining brightly for you yesterday and you were too busy chopping onions to notice." Derk pushed himself up and took Sindra's hands, helping her up as well.

"It's one of Asa's more endearing qualities," Sindra said, putting her arm in Derk's.

"If you say so," Devra said, starting to walk down the street, the others following after her. "It has our mother sore. She'll never get a grandchild if Asa isn't noticing women."

"I've already explained it to her," Asa said, actually sounding slightly irritated. "I spent all those years in training, thank the Goddess, I want to give back for a year. Once I've made my gift of time I'll build a house and plant some barley. It was she who prayed for me to get an opportunity in the first place."

"What's he talking about?" Derk asked. "Where did you train?"

"He'll say nowhere but it isn't true," Devra interjected. "He trained at the armed combat school in Sedraholt, in the same class as the Baron's son. A merchant paid for Asa to attend." Devra's face beamed, though Derk noticed Asa rolled his eyes.

"How'd you manage that?" Derk asked.

"I beat up his son," Asa said simply, not seeing the reaction on Derk's face. Devra shook her head and slowed her pace so she was walking alongside Derk and Sindra.

"He's not telling it right," she said, green eyes shining with pride. "Asa had gone into town with our pa for Spring Market. Asa used to be shy in the city and he's always been big but never had the nastiness to use it on other people. He was getting picked on by some well-off brats. One of them said something insulting about our mam and he couldn't let it go. Gave him a bloody nose, in front of all the children.

"When the father found out," Devra continued. "He asked how old Asa was and knew my brother had held back. The merchant also knew his son was a fapper and so he had Asa become his study partner, in school and on the training field."

"We're friends now, before you ask" Asa said. "And his father helped fund this mission, since having the chalice back would be a boon."

"And we are grateful to him," Sindra said. She smiled at Derk and squeezed his arm. The excitement of kissing Sindra was still with him, making Derk feel lighter than he had before. Now that she had kissed him, the way she held onto his arm felt different, more intimate. He definitely enjoyed it. All the way back to the temple he couldn't help but glance over at the beautiful priestess, feeling genuinely lucky. He had been himself and it had won her over. Could he hold on to her after the retrieval of the chalice? He'd try. Tomorrow they would head into the Freewild. Derk could endear Sindra to him more, he was sure of it.

Chapter 8
Temple of the Ever Burning Sun

They saw the temple from the road. They couldn't not see it. The dying light of the sun glinted orange off the roof of the building. Two large fires burned outside indicating the entrance to the temple. The sound of a gong, low and reverberating through the hot air signaled someone in the temple had seen them as well, and the gelding snorted in response. Derk patted the beast on the neck. "I agree," he said, watching as yellow-clad figures came out from the temple. The building itself looked yellow, but as they drew closer they saw the the facade was made up of many smaller pieces of yellow, orange and red material, arranged to form pictures. It looked more like a place to be entertained by women than a temple, as far as Derk was concerned.

To the right of the temple were rows of trees, and people clad in normal garments came out from among the rows, a crowd of people starting to form. "Hello!" Asa called, waving his arm as the oxen plodded toward the temple, pulling the cart behind them. Devra looked back at Derk from within the cart, relief on her face, closing the book she had been reading. Jezlen sat up in the back of the cart, yawning after his nap. He had adamantly re-fused to ride any horse and so he rode in the cart most of the time, with Sindra riding the other horse the temple in Bluemist provided. The party rode into the temple court-yard, the end of what The Temple of the Ever Burning Sun considered their land marked by a several wooden posts, each one of them topped with a large, yellow glass orb.

The first thing Derk noticed about the people was they seemed nervous. It could have been because they were outsiders from the Valley proper and therefore strangers, but Derk thought it was different, something deeper. Something felt wrong. The laypeople just seemed cautious but the men and women robed in yellows, browns and reds appeared antsy. Their smiles seemed forced. It wasn't until one of the older of the clergy barked orders at them some came forward, offering to take the gelding and lead the cart to the stables for them. Something told Derk they should hold onto the horses and the cart. But he handed the reins of the gelding to the boy with the shaved head who approached him, his head bowed. Hardly prideful like the Sun, Derk thought.

A man emerged from within the temple, clad in sunny yellow robes and wearing a skullcap embroidered with gold thread. He must be the high priest, Derk thought. His beard was braided into two long braids and colored with an orange substance. He smiled warmly enough at Sindra and he held his hands out to the side and bowed to her in greeting. "Sister Sindra, we are glad you have made it to our humble community, and safely."

"I am glad to finally meet you after many correspondences. The journey was safe enough, with the Goddess' watch," she said, slipping the last bit in. It seemed to make the high priest bristle. "Of course, I also have my friends to thank as well," she added, looking back toward the three people of the Valley. "This is Asa and Devra, Jezlen," she said, pointing as her nephew jumped out of cart with a thump. He didn't look very impressed and didn't have the sense to hide it. "And this is Derk," she said, smiling at him. Derk stepped forward and bowed to the high priest, able to muster his courtesies while it seemed the others could not. Sindra looked at him thankfully as Asa and Devra followed suit, Jezlen hanging back with his arms crossed over his chest.

"This is a large party to come and retrieve one item." One of the other priests finally stepped forward. His hair was cut short and he too wore a yellow skullcap, but it lacked the gold ornamentation the high priest's bore. The stole he wore was white, the same color as the high priest. Derk thought he might be an important member of the clergy.

"The reports we received in your correspondences concerned the Church and we thought it better to err on the side of caution," Sindra answered, keeping her voice level. "And the Goddess has blessed Her people enough Her Church can send us all, with provisions for the trip here and back." Derk watched as Sindra's words made color rise in the high priest's cheeks, though he managed to take the comment graciously. Derk saw the hard look the other priest gave Sindra and he felt his hand ball into a fist instinctively.

"Yes, well," the high priest said, "We are most humbled to have you visit our holy temple and grateful you have come to receive the item as a token of goodwill, to foster camaraderie between our two holy establishments. I am sure you are weary from the road and hungry as well?" He smiled at the party, even at Jezlen who still insisted on hanging back. "We have been anticipating your arrival and we would consider it a blessing to have you share a meal with us. I will let Riyin take you to your quarters where you can wash and rest. Evening meal will be at two bells. And of course we hope you will join us at our sunset service."

"It would be an honor," Derk said before anyone else could say anything. "Taking part in one of your services would of course help to promote understanding between our two churches. We thank you for the privilege of being able to worship among you." Derk knew a few things about diplomacy. Sindra obviously knew but was too close to her own Church to not defend it at every turn. Asa and Devra could pull off polite, and Jezlen...he was still standing behind them. Derk gave the high priest a warm smile, which the older man returned, pleased with Derk's words.

"You are most welcome," the high priest answered, bowing his head in dismissal. "Brother Riyin, please show our guests where they will be staying. Dreya, please inform the cooks they will in fact be joining us for supper this evening." A woman with many braids and brown robes bowed and ran off. "I hope you will find your accommodations comfortable after such a long journey."

"I'm sure they'll be more than suitable," Sindra said, bowing.

"If you will excuse me, I must see to other matters," the high priest said, excusing himself. Derk watched as he bowed to Sindra, though not as deeply, and walked away, several other priests following him into the temple.

"If you would follow me," said the priest who had commented on the size of their party. He was Riyin, apparently. People scurried off as he walked, hands behind his back, to the left of the temple. Two large buildings made of stone stood the closest, each one with a large, yellow glass orb mounted at the top. Beyond the religious buildings Derk saw a stable and houses, several young children sneaking a peek at them from beyond the stables. All the girls had their hair done in multiple braids, tied at the end with ribbons while the boys had hair cut short, almost to the skin. One of the little girls obviously saw Sindra and Jezlen, her brown eyes growing as big as plates and she ran away, shouting something.

"This is where our unmarried priests stay," Brother Riyin said, pushing past a yellow and red tapestry serving as a door. "We've set aside one of the shared rooms for your group. I trust you will find them comfortable. If you're in need of anything, feel free to ask. We will eat in the communal kitchen, which is in the other building you saw," he said, pointing in the general direction at another building. "Again, it is our honor to have you visit out humble temple." He led them into a room rectangular in shape. Two beds were attached to opposite walls and Riyin turned and frowned at the group of them. "It seems as if we are short a bed. If you'll excuse me, I'll go see what we can do about this." The group shuffled out of the way to let the priest leave.

"I do not want to sleep here," Jezlen said. At least he had waited for the priest to leave before being so rude. Derk sat on one of the beds, testing its strength by bouncing lightly in his seat. Sindra eyed him strangely and then smirked at him.

"Why not?" Asa asked. "The beds look comfortable enough. Why, are you afraid they'll try to kill us in our sleep?"

"What?" Jezlen hissed, narrowing his eyes at the burly fighter. "Are you asking me if I am afraid of something?"

"No one is going to kill us in our sleep," Devra insisted, stepping between the two of them. "Asa is just making a bad joke. It's the only kind he can make," she said, glaring at her brother. Derk stood up and looked around the room. The four beds were covered with light, yellow-gold blankets and there was a lamp in the motif of the sun sitting on the only other piece of furniture, a set of drawers. The drawers were all empty when he opened them. Sparse. The rooms were obviously for sleeping only.

"Jezlen, you must stay in the room," Sindra insisted. "If you don't, they may take it as a slight. Don't you remember why we came? To befriend them?"

"That is not why I came," the Forester said. Derk looked above the doorway and noticed the two metal arrows placed over the door, one across the other.

"It might not be a bad idea to have someone keep watch," Derk said. He knew it wasn't what Jezlen meant but he didn't care. He would turn it into what he needed. Derk looked out of the window for some kind of training ground but saw nothing except the stables. Movement outside the window drew his attention and he stuck his tongue out at the two children who peeked in, the trio scurrying off across the dusty path. "Better too safe than not safe enough."

"Do you think we have a reason to not trust them?" Sindra asked. Derk shrugged.

"No," he lied. He knew something was happening, he just wasn't sure what. "Forget I said anything," he said with a wave of his hand. "It's just an old habit. Jezlen, you will sleep in here. We'll open a window if you can't sleep indoors." The look Jezlen gave him told him it was probably the issue. "Aren't you all tired and hungry? I could use a wash and a nap before evening meal."

The doors opened and a man and a woman brought in the belongings, their packs slung over their backs. The room was too crowded for a few moments as the packs were distributed but they all received their personal belongings and the man and woman left without saying anything. Devra opened her pack straightaway to check on the contents and Derk pulled out a clean tunic and trousers, wondering where his socks were.

"I think I'm going to make sure the gifts we brought for their temple are taken care of," Sindra said. She looked so cool in her light grey dress and robe, Derk felt less hot and sweaty just looking at her. Once he was clean he would see if she would go for a walk with him.

"I can use a clean up," Asa said, slinging his clothes over his shoulder. Devra rummaged through her pack and pulled out another colorful skirt and tunic. Jezlen snorted before he went to his own things, pulling out a set of garments to change into.

The four of them walked out of the building, asking a priest carrying two chickens by their feet where the bath-house was. He gestured past the stables with one of the chickens, the bird flapping its wings with displeasure and squawking. "Past the homes, make a right at the barn, you can't miss it," he said. They thanked him and continued on through the compound, waving occasionally at the people who stopped what they were doing to look at them.

It wasn't so different from other small villages back in the Valley proper, Derk thought, nodding his head in greeting to a young woman weaving outside of her home. All the women wore their hair braided and all the men wore their hair very short, their beards long and forked. Their clothes favored the warm colors of the sun but otherwise, it was a village with a large temple compound within it. Old women stooped over their herb gardens, old men smoked pipes and eyed them warily. Their fields grew green and tall out on the eastern side of the village. He saw boys and men practicing their archery on the north side of the barn, arrows thudding into the targets.

"Maybe you can have a go with them later, Jez," Derk said, pointing at at the archers with his chin. He knew

Jezlen had brought a bow and a quiver full arrows with him. The Forester had taken down a few rabbits in the Freewild.

"I could just run at the target with my sword and destroy it," Jezlen said.

"But where's the competition?" Derk asked, turning and walking backwards. "Skill against skill? What about that?"

"I could always run at one of the other targets," Asa offered. "I bet I could take it out with two hits."

"I bet I could do it in one," Jezlen said.

"Neither one of you is going to do any such thing," Devra said, laughing merrily at the both of them. "We're not here to destroy their targets."

"We should have a contest once we get back to Portsmouth," Asa offered.

"That also sounds like a bad idea," Devra said, cutting Jezlen off before he could say whatever contrary thing which had come to his mind.

"What could you do to the target, Devra?" Derk asked, facing forward. Ahead he saw a stream and three large, wooden tanks with covers standing on one bank. A small bridge led over the stream, a building on the other side of the river looking like a workshop of some sort. Men were fishing by the side of the stream and a priest stood by the tanks.

"Oh, I don't know. Maybe...set it on fire?" She sounded unsure, as if she was considering the possibilities. Derk, Asa and Jezlen all looked to each other with concern.

"I am not going to enter a contest with you," Jezlen said finally, walking slightly farther away from her. Derk and Asa laughed and Devra wiggled her gloved hands at him, grinning. Derk ran up ahead to the priest who stood by the tanks, looking around for the bathhouse.

"We were looking for the bathhouse?" Derk asked. He looked up at the tanks, noticing the lids overhung by a few fingers width, the material seemingly transparent. It was glass.

"Right there," the old priest said with a toothy grin, pointing. Derk turned and looked. The bathhouse was a platform. Derk blinked and then hunched over to see what was under it. The wooden platform had been reinforced but cut with holes so water used would drain into a basin below. With both the wash area and the basin being so close to the fields, it wasn't hard to imagine what the purpose of the wash area was for. The stream wasn't so deep to stand a very harsh summer and Derk could see where it had licked away from the bank.

Derk shrugged at his companions and then back to the old priest. "Do we just...?" The old man placed a bucket under the spigot and opened the faucet, the water filling the bucket quickly. He handed the bucket to Derk and got another one ready as Asa stepped forward. Derk walked up the steps to the top of the platform, the boards creaking under his feet. A railing was set up, probably to keep children from plummeting to their deaths, and in the center was a table with bottles of oil and scrubbing salts, as well as glasses for rinsing off. Baskets were stacked by the stairs, probably to store belongings and Derk started to undress, Asa trudging up the steps behind him. He had just placed his boots neatly by his basket when Devra came up the stairs, her lips pressed together so they almost disappeared on her face.

"Everything all right?" Derk asked. Devra looked to Asa, her green eyes wide. Asa just shrugged, pulling his shirt over his head. He had more scars than Derk would have thought.

"My gloves," Devra said quietly. Asa stopped getting undressed and looked worried. Jezlen came up the stairs next, not seeming to notice the tension between the twins and setting his bucket on the floor.

"I...I don't know," Asa said. "I thought the wash house would be indoors, like it is at home."

"What's the problem?" Derk asked. He wanted to get washing, naked as he was. "You can put your gloves in the basket with the rest of your clothes." He eyes Asa and then Devra, trying to figure out why they were so distraught. "Are you shy?"

"No, it's just..." Devra took a step closer to him, holding her bucket of water in her hands. "My hands. And my feet."

"Do you have a scar or something?" Derk said. He had wondered why Devra had insisted on wearing those gloves all the time, even in this heat. "I've seen worse, believe me."

"No," Asa said. "She has marks on her hands. For the things she does."

"Like brands?" Derk narrowed his eyes. Branding was for criminals and hadn't been practiced for some years by order of the Church. It didn't mean the people in the village knew the practice had stopped. Maybe Devra was worried they would think she was a criminal.

"More delicate than brands," Devra said. "Still, I'm worried. What if someone comes up while we're here?"

"Just blast them?" Derk offered. Devra tried not to laugh through her nervousness but she did, smacking him on the arm. Derk looked toward the stairs and then to the table. "Look, just get undressed. Asa, Jez and I will all stand around you and wash up, so no one sees you. It'll just look like you're shy." Derk raised his brows at her and then Asa, waiting for their response. "Besides, they moved here to escape persecution from the Holy Family. I don't think they'll stoke the fires if they find out you're a Wielder." Derk waited for Asa and Devra to get undressed. Devra pulled off her boots, socks and gloves last and Derk saw the marks there, thin, black lines on the front and backs of her hands, as if they had been burned through her skin. She folded her hands and Asa carried her bucket for her.

"Circle round Devra," Derk told Jezlen. The elf cocked an eyebrow at him.

"Excuse me?" he said, looking to Devra. Derk could tell he was trying not to look further but instead the Forester looked to the floor and then to Asa's arm.

"She doesn't want to be seen," Derk said, gesturing toward her. "Asa, you're the biggest, you get in front. We'll take the sides."

"This sounds really awkward, from where I'm standing," Devra said, laughing.

"Stop laughing and wash up. You can giggle while you scrub," Derk shot back. He looked over the bowls of scrubbing clay and grabbed one, mixing it with water in his hand and then rubbing it over his skin. The water in the bucket was surprisingly warm, almost hot, and he wondered how they heated the water without fire. They all scrubbed away the grime of summer travel, the water feeling good as it cooled on his skin. Derk couldn't help but look at Devra's feet, noticing how intricate the design was. Two circles, one within the other and letters and marks written as well. He noticed the marks on her feet were different from one another, different letters and symbols written in black ink on her skin.

No one else came up while they bathed, everyone too busy preparing for the evening meal to take time out for a wash at the moment. Derk dumped the remains of the water over himself and shook his head, spraying water everywhere. The scars on Jezlen's dark skin made Derk wonder what he had done to merit so many and he wondered if they were evidence of a lack of skill or recklessness. He guessed it was probably the latter.

Everyone seemed happier in fresh clothes, Devra wearing even brighter garments than before. "I'll see about getting these washed," Derk offered, sliding his boots on. Everyone dropped their laundry into one basket before leaving down the stairs, giving their thanks as Derk tried to arrange it so it wouldn't fall out. Derk walked carefully down the stairs and found his way back to the old priest manning the water tanks. "Excuse me," he said. "Where can I take these to get washed?"

"The clothes are washed downstream," the old man cackled. "Just give 'em to the women down there, they'll get 'em done for you." Derk thanked the man and walked by the side of the stream, listening to the sounds of the village. Sounds of metal carried over from the workshop on the other side of the stream. They had their own tank adjacent to the shop and he saw men in aprons, their faces covered with handkerchiefs. Large sunflowers grew on both sides of the stream, their yellow faces pointed toward the sun. Derk spotted a group of women down by the stream, laughing and washing garments while children played. A pair of boys were practicing with bows and arrows and a baby lay in a carved cradle hanging from a tree, its small hands grabbing at the air. Derk waved to the women as he approached.

"I was wondering if one of you could be troubled to wash these for us? If you're not too busy with your own items, that is," Derk said, smiling to them.

"I'll take on your wash," a younger woman said. Her hair was red and she looked like one of the youngest in the bunch. "I ain't got any babes to wash after, adding some more's no thing."

"Dayin needs to give you a reason to wash more," one of the women joked, her braids tucked within a pretty handkerchief. "Get him out of the range and in the bed, girl!" The other women laughed, scrubbing and smacking linens and garments against the rocks, rubbing soap onto them.

"There's more to life than slidin' out babes, am I right?" the young woman asked, her eyes glinting merrily at Derk. She took her basket from him, her arms strong and the hair on her arms bleached by the sun. "D'you have any babes?"

"No," Derk said with a shake of his head, feeling slightly out of place with the washer women. Deril didn't count, not really. He had treated Deril like his son in public and helped Jerila with the boy when he could but the baby wasn't his.

"You should try harder!" one of the women shouted, all of them laughing raucously. The young woman just laughed while Derk felt his face grow hot.

"I'll bring 'em by the dormitory later," the young woman said, smiling at him. She had a gap between her front teeth; it made her appear younger than she probably was. As Derk walked away from the women, he heard them laughing and joking. He stuffed his hands in his pockets and tried not to look back to see if they were pointing at him.

Movement on the other side of the riverbank caught his eye. A pair of horsemen rode in from the north, galloping toward the workshop. Quivers of arrows sprouted from the horse's tack and the men wore bows slung over their shoulders, leather bracers glinting in the fading light. A tree lent a handy spot to hide and Derk ducked behind it, making sure no one was watching.

The high priest came out of the workshop. He was still wearing his clerical garments so there was no mistaking him. Riyin was with him as well. The two horsemen slid from their mounts and said something to the high priest. The high priest looked down to the ground, obviously upset with their news. Riyin said something as well, moving his hands wildly, obviously agitated. One of the horsemen argued back and the two priests fell silent and looked to each other. The high priest looked toward the village as the horsemen grabbed the reins of their mounts, walking them toward the bridge.

Derk turned and strode back to the village before he could be spotted, trying to look nonchalant as he headed back toward the homes. When he looked over his shoulder the two archers were putting their horses into the barn, a woman running up to one of them and throwing her arms around his neck. Derk thought for a moment and headed to the temple.

The temple was not like the ones back home. Temples to the Goddess always had multiple entrances and exits. It meant they had to be guarded in order to keep out intruders, but it also meant people could escape if one of the entrances was attacked. It was a convention left over from the old days, when the people of the Valley were of Holy Haran and burned out of their temples by other factions. The Temple of the Ever Burning Sun had one entrance and it was the one he had seen with the two braziers outside the door. Derk walked through the front door, not sure what to expect.

It was sparser than he had imagined. It had pews within much like the temples for the Goddess, but whereas most temples had round windows opened to the air, this temple had colored glass in fiery colors. Candles burned, not lamps, and the altar was lit with many of them placed in glass holders. Derk wondered where they got the material to make all this glass and wondered if they couldn't sell some of it in the Valley for a good price.

What was really striking about the altar was it bore no depiction of their god. Instead, a large, golden ball hung in the air, suspended by thin chains from the ceiling. Carved depictions of the earth, clouds and the moon all had their place on the altar but the bright sun caught the light of the candles and gleamed like a thing alive. Derk marveled at the beautifully crafted arrows springing from the sun, its golden rays. Their shafts were coated in what appeared to be gold but their heads were made of glass. The altar table was made of glass as well, a huge thing remarkable to behold. Derk walked through the temple quietly, admiring the strange but beautiful craftsmanship the worshipers had used in reverence to their god.

A robed figure emerged from within the temple, jumping as he realized he wasn't alone. "Uh," he stammered, his eyes looking for an escape. "May I help you?"

"Yes, I'm one of the Valleymen here for the chalice. I was just wondering if I could see it?" Derk took his hands out of his pocket and rocked back and forth on his heels.

The priest's mouth fell open and then he shook his head. "I've been instructed to not show it to anyone. The High Priest wants to be the one to reveal it himself. I've been ordered-"

"I understand," Derk said, waving him away and turning to leave. "Orders." Derk turned and left. He couldn't help but listen as the priest's steps quickened till he was running away, the sound disappearing within the temple.

Chapter 9
Misplaced Trust

Derk found Sindra in the room, brushing her long hair loose after having it plaited for their travels. She smiled when he walked in, stopping mid-stroke. "Where've you been?" she asked. She set the brush down on the bed and stood up, looking toward the door before she put her arms around his neck and kissed him on the mouth. Derk kissed her back, glad to finally have some time alone with her. Still, Derk couldn't make use of the newly found time for what he really wanted. He had to find out something.

"When do we get to see the chalice?" he asked. Sindra pushed his hair out of his face and put her hand on his cheek.

"Tomorrow, Father Solin said," Sindra replied. "They're going to give it at first light, as the moon and sun will be there to witness it both." Her brows furrowed as she looked into his eyes. "Why?"

"I'm just curious," Derk said, shrugging under the weight of her arms. "We came all this way for it, I wanted to know when we'll be able to see it."

"I'm excited to see it as well," Sindra confessed, her eyes sparkling. "To have such an article of faith back in the Church's hands would be wonderful indeed. The legends behind it!"

"Right," Derk said. "The Healing of the Acolyte. And made by the Goddess herself! I'm sure many people will come to see it, to touch it. It'll inspire people throughout the Valley." Derk felt himself grow excited, thinking about the chalice. It was said to heal the Acolyte who drank water from it generations ago. She had been beaten and left to die on the side of the road. The Goddess had given it to the Acolyte and when she drank from it, she was healed of her wounds. Another version of the story said the Acolyte gave her attackers a drink from the chalice and it killed them, while yet another ending had the violent men beg her for forgiveness, giving up their lives of crime and devoting themselves to introspection. Regardless of the ending, it was supposed to have been made by the Goddess herself. The two horsemen and the exchange between the high priest and the man concerned Derk though.

"I think something is wrong," Derk huffed. He had to tell someone and Sindra seemed like the one to tell.

Sindra narrowed her eyes at him, her lips pressing together with confusion. "What do you mean?"

Derk shrugged, trying to think of a way of telling her what he saw and thought without having it seem like he was starting at shadows. "I saw some horsemen come galloping from the north, with weapons. They spoke with the High Priest and Brother Riyin. They all looked upset."

"If they came from the north, they came from the Freewild. It would be unwise of them to go unarmed," Sindra said. "Maybe they went looking for something mundane. A water source, a lost animal perhaps."

"That's not it," Derk admitted. "I went into the temple and...I saw one of the brothers there. I asked if I could see the chalice and he said the High Priest instructed him to not allow anyone to see it. Everyone looked nervous when we first arrived, Sindra."

"Because we're outsiders, Derk," Sindra laughed. It was a nervous laugh. She dropped her hands from him and stepped away, looking out the window. Her shoulders drooped. Derk felt terrible. He didn't want to be right.

"Well, you've seen it, right? When you went to get everything from the cart into the temple? The priest has shown it to you?" Sindra didn't turn around and Derk brought his hands to his head, blowing out his cheeks.

"Come with me. To the temple." She pushed past him and Derk couldn't do anything but comply, not sure what she was going to do. Sindra walked out of the dormitories, Derk chasing after her, her grey robes fluttering behind her as she made a line for the temple. Asa, Jezlen and Devra called to them and Derk just spun around and waved his hands frantically before he chased after Sindra again. Sindra entered the temple, doing nothing to dampen her footsteps.

"May I help you?" a different priest asked. He was older, wearing a white stole whereas the priest Derk had spoken with had worn an orange one.

"Yes, actually. I was hoping to speak with Father Solin," Sindra said.

"I'm afraid he is busy at the moment but perhaps I can help you. What do you need?" The old priest looked up as the sound of footsteps echoed in the temple. Asa and Devra entered and stood beside Derk.

"I have finally settled in and I was hoping I could perhaps view the chalice," Sindra said. Her voice was strong but low, and Derk watched the priest's face to see his reaction to her request.

"I'm afraid I'm unable to meet your request," the priest said, bowing his head. "The Father is the only one with the key to its case."

"Then I will wait for him," Sindra said, folding her hands.

"You will see the chalice tomorrow, at the ceremony," the priest said, his voice pitching slightly higher. Derk narrowed his eyes.

"I understand, but you have to understand, other relics have been thought to have been found in the past," Sindra said. "It would be an embarrassment to both of our churches if this ceremony was performed and the chalice was found to be inauthentic. If I could see it, I could be assured it was in fact the genuine article. I am learned in the history of my Church, both before and in the Valley and could easily save both parties much face in just a few breaths."

"Please wait here," the old priest said wearily, shuffling back through the door leading to the rest of the temple. Sindra turned to them, her eyes wide and lips pressed together. Derk thought she looked as if she were about to cry.

"What's going on?" Asa asked. Both he and Devra looked genuinely confused. Jezlen apparently hadn't followed them in.

"I came in to see the chalice and they're saying I can't see it," Sindra said, panic in her voice.

"They said the high priest has the key but he isn't here." Derk shrugged, hoping his words might calm the priestess down.

"He's in the stables," Devra said. "We just saw him. He sent out two men."

"Which direction did he send them?" Derk asked.

"North, northwest?" Devra said, shrugging. "He said if they didn't find anything by first light, to come back."

"The riders I saw came from the northeast," Derk said, wondering what reason the High Priest had for sending out the two men. Before he could ask, the sound of many footsteps made them all turn toward the doorway, where the High Priest and Riyin stood with several other priests.

"Sister Sindra, Brother Gilen informs me that you wish to see the chalice," the High Priest said. "I can guarantee you it is not a false replica. It is a thing of beauty we will happily return to your Church tomorrow, at the agreed upon time."

"I would like to see it," Sindra said. Derk had never seen Sindra angry but he sensed she was getting close. "A few hours difference will not challenge the importance of the ceremony tomorrow or infringe upon the relationship between our two churches. The wrong item being delivered into our hands will, however."

The High Priest held up his hand and the rest of the priests behind him looked to each other nervously. "Sister Sindra, we cannot show you the chalice because we do not have it." The priests behind him all started whispering and murmuring. Some of them eyed Asa with dread. Derk looked at Sindra, walking up so he could stand by her. Her eyes were full of disbelief.

"What?" she said, confusion in her voice. "We...we came all this way. You said you had it!"

"We did have it," Father Solin said. "And last night, some among us who were against returning the relic to you stole it and escaped into the Freewild with it. We have sent men out to find them and retrieve the item but have yet to find anything but tracks."

"What are they going to do with it?" Asa asked. Derk cringed. He didn't want to know the answer.

"I don't know, to be honest," the High Priest said. "They may destroy it. They may keep it as a piece to bargain with your Church. Their leader said as much, in his opposition to returning it to you. He said goodwill was not enough of a gain."

"So he's going to try and sell it?" Sindra asked. There was disgust in her voice. Derk found the notion sickening as well.

"Perhaps," Riyin said. His previous agitation was gone. Now he just looked tired. "They could try to get something from your Church. Land. Or medicine. Kirin was tired of living in the Freewild. He wanted our people to be integrated into the Valley proper, despite the misgivings of most of us."

"He might be riding for Whitfield," Derk said. "If I had something I thought the Church wanted, I'd go there first."

"You're probably right," Sindra said to Derk, turning to Father Solin. "Where are your people looking?"

"To the northwest, again," the High Priest said. "We will send some of our men to check the trail. It could be you are right." The priest came forward and took Sindra's hands in his, bowing his head sadly. "I am truly sorry for this. I hope that you understand why we kept it from you. We thought they would be found by now and had several days before your arrival. Please forgive us."

Sindra didn't say anything for a moment, but she nodded slowly. "I understand what you thought you were doing. Let us hope your men can find the chalice soon. It would be a terrible thing to have it used for personal gain or worse, lost once again." Sindra took her hands from him and put her hands together. "If you don't mind, I must retire with my travel companions. I will keep this endeavor in my prayers."

"As will we, as well as use our resources to find these men and your chalice." The High Priest nodded his head and turned, he and the priests going back into the hidden area of the temple.

Sindra didn't look up, her head bowed toward the ground. She walked toward the exit, the three of them following after her. The light had faded and as they left they heard the bells signaling dinner. Jezlen stared at them as they filed out. "Well?"

"They don't have the chalice," Sindra said wearily, walking back toward the dormitory. "They did, but several among them stole it, not wanting to return it to us. They have other men looking for the chalice and the people who stole it." Derk thought now the tears would fall but they didn't. He couldn't imagine how frustrated she was.

"What should we do?" Devra asked. She was rubbing the inside of her hand with her thumb. Asa stood by, his eyebrows furrowed across his face.

"We could go find them ourselves," Derk shrugged. "If they're not back by first watch. Since there won't be a chalice for a ceremony, there'd be no reason to stay." He watched as Sindra winced and kept his head down, thinking of something else to add. "And doesn't Jez here have extensive knowledge of the Freewild? And at finding people?"

"I would be able to find something," Jezlen said, too flatly for Derk's taste.

"Of course you could find 'something'," Derk said. He turned to Sindra "And Asa and I are here to defend if anything happens. They might respond better to you than the high priest. You're the representative of the Church. You could negotiate with them. If the High Priest finds them first, what do you think he'll offer them?"

"It's an opportunity to show the mercy of the Goddess," Asa said.

"You're not going to hit them?" Devra asked, obviously surprised.

"Maybe a little," Asa admitted. "I mean, they did steal from the Church."

"I'll give you my answer later," Sindra said, looking overwhelmed by what they were saying. She put her hands up and then dropped them to her sides. "I'm actually very tired. I don't have an appetite. Please, go on to evening meal without me." Sindra hugged herself and looked toward the dormitory, blinking.

"Are you sure?" Derk said. He looked to the twins and the Forester. "You go, I'll be there in a bit." Jezlen left first, Asa and Devra lingering, their concern for the priestess evident in their faces before they turned and followed the Forester. Derk nodded his head toward the dormitory and he and Sindra walked slowly in that direction.

Derk thought maybe now she would cry but she didn't. He slipped an arm around her waist and she let her arms drop from her chest. She sighed heavily, shaking her head and chuckling.

"I don't even know what to say," Sindra huffed, laying her head on Derk's shoulder. "I can't say 'I knew it.' Or blame myself for trying to do this. We haven't seen how it all ends yet. Only the Goddess knows."

"That's a good attitude to have," Derk said, resting his head on top of hers. "Try not to get caught up in blaming people. Better to make a plan to get out of it." He heard music starting in the schoolhouse, and the smell of food permeated the hot summer air. "You can't blame yourself for what happened. You didn't make those men steal the chalice."

"I know," Sindra said. They walked through the doorway of the dormitory, into the room. Someone had placed a low bed in the middle, making it more cramped than before. Derk and Sindra laughed as they tried to maneuver around it, sitting down together on one of the bunks. Derk rested his hands on his stomach, the both of them leaning their backs on the wall. "If they find the chalice tonight, I would be so relieved."

"It'll be found. The Valley is not a huge place," Derk said. He took her hand in his and brought it to his lips, kissing it. "Even if the worst happens, which it won't, trying to do good won't be punished by the Church. Though it won't end well for the people here."

Sindra nodded slowly, frowning slightly. What would the Church do if the chalice wasn't found? Derk didn't know. He wasn't sure if the temple in Portsmouth who had commissioned the party would react or if the situation called for the intervention of the main temple in Whitfield. "I just...I really wanted this to happen," Sindra said finally, disappointment heavy in her words. "I wanted to do something good for the Church. It seemed so simple." She laughed, rubbing the side of her face with her hand. "I should have known. The Goddess brought out the secrets, didn't she?"

"Looks that way," Derk shrugged. "Maybe the chalice being taken was a good thing? Now we know about the few of them here who want something, who wish to be integrated into the Valley proper. We wouldn't have known about it otherwise."

"I suppose," Sindra said. "I don't know what the Church will say but it should be brought to their attention." She smiled and then leaned over, kissing Derk on the cheek. "Thank you."

"For what?" he asked. He couldn't help but smile back, trying not to seem too happy about the kiss.

"For working this out with me," Sindra said. Her eyes lowered and she squeezed his hand. "I guess all we can do is wait and see. And maybe go try and find it ourselves." Sindra sighed again. "I would have packed more travel clothes had I known," she said.

"Me too," Derk said. They sat there for a while, listening to the sounds coming from outside. Derk leaned over and kissed Sindra, taking the opportunity since no one was around. She kissed him back, brushing her hand against the stubble on his chin. They sat there in the candlelight kissing till Derk wondered if the door had a lock on it. Just as he squeezed her leg a knock came at the door.

"Sister Sindra, are you okay?" the voice came through the door. It was one of the priests and it sounded like Riyin. "You are missed at evening meal. We were hoping to share a meal with you."

"I'm fine," Sindra called. She waited for a breath before she said, "I'll be there in a moment." She turned to Derk and bit her lip, an apology in her expression. Derk pulled away from her. Thwarted again. Sindra laughed and stood up from the bed, sidestepping past the cot placed in the middle of the room as she straightened out her robes. She opened the door a crack. Derk could see the priest on the other side of the door. "My apologies. After the news I felt like I should retire to my room and pray on the matter."

"Oh," Brother Riyin said. Sindra pushed past him and out of the room, Riyin looking into the room and seeing Derk there. Derk stood up and walked toward the doorway, Riyin staring at him.

"What?" Derk said. "I was helping her pray." He walked out of the dormitory, catching sight of Sindra as she headed toward the open-air dining hall. Inside people were playing music and sat on benches eating and drinking merrily.

Most of the people seemed to be members of the clergy, but a few of the townspeople were sprinkled among the robes. Asa stood up and waved at Sindra, then Derk, a place of honor set for Sindra beside the High Priest. Derk sat at the end of the bench, climbing into a space next to Jezlen.

"You missed it, there was a fire eater," Devra said, her green eyes sparkling. Derk poured himself a glass of whatever was in the pitcher, finding it very sweet. "There are going to be dancers later."

"The food is not terrible," Jezlen said. Round pieces of bread sat in piles down the length of the table and when Derk ripped one open he found it stuffed with herbs and bits of vegetable. It was still warm and shiny with butter.

"Are we leaving in the morning?" Asa asked Derk. He watched Sindra and the High Priest talking, seeming to be making polite conversation. Derk shrugged.

"If they don't get it, we'll get it," Derk said, stuffing food into his mouth. He wiped his hands free of flour on a napkin and watched as the other people ate.

It was a small gathering, about twenty people in all. They asked Sindra questions about the Church and how long she had been serving. A few even asked Derk, Asa and Devra about their involvement with the Church. Derk left out the part about being recruited in a bar fight but Asa rather joyfully filled it in. One priest asked Jezlen a question about the Church and the Forester answered by sipping from his cup and pretending he didn't understand him.

The fire dancers came and performed a stunning set, swinging torches, and a woman even wearing a belt of fire as she danced in time to the upbeat music, unscathed by the flames.

Asa was called to stand in the middle as several men juggled fiery torches around him, the young man's face screwed up in good-natured fear as balls of flame zipped past his head. The jugglers tried to get both Jezlen and Derk to stand in. Jezlen feigned ignorance of their words and Derk politely declined.

Derk laughed as Asa was roped into a dance with the woman who wore the belt of fire, his face turning red as she shimmied her hips in front of him. After the drama of the stolen chalice, it was a nice change. Derk looked down the table at Sindra and smiled, all of them clapping in time to the music. Eventually Sindra relieved Asa and danced, the stringed instruments playing happily in the hot summer air. Tomorrow would be fine, Derk told himself. They would find the men who stole the chalice and they would return to Portsmouth triumphantly. And if they wound up having to go after the chalice themselves, they would find it and still bring back the holy item. If Derk had anything to do with it, he would turn a bad situation into a good one. It's what he did.

"They are definitely dead," Jezlen said coolly, releasing the hand of the body he was standing over. Its arm flopped to the ground, lifeless.

"This is bad," Devra murmured, turning to Asa, her green eyes wide with fear. "Who could have done this?"

"Only one thing," Derk said, grimacing. The camp hadn't just been attacked. It had been destroyed. The fire had died down and the morning mist dampened the entire camp. Bodies lay scattered, broken arrows littering the ground. The only sword they found was broken and black with blood and gore, all the bows gone. Whoever had attacked had taken the weapons as well as the chalice. There was no doubting the victims were the zealots the High Priest had spoken of. The male victims wore their beards forked and had shaved heads, moisture making their beards sag. A gash from a claw across the face of the only woman in the group made Derk's stomach turn. "Freemen."

"Here?" Devra asked. "Why?" She wrung her hands together, a habit Derk noticed she did when worried, and Asa took off his hat.

"They probably have a base close by," Jezlen said. He walked around the camp, crouching down and scratching at the dirt with his fingers. "The Freemen mostly raid in lean times. If the zealots had not stolen the chalice, this would not have happened to them."

"These men and woman have families, you know." The young priest who had accompanied them on their search shot Jezlen an amazed look, looking surprised by his seemingly heartless comment. The priest gestured toward the bodies, his face stricken with grief. "They didn't ask for this."

"They should have kept a better watch." Jezlen said. He stood up and walked over to the edge of the camp, ignoring the angry looks of the priest and the other men.

"What am I supposed to do?" the priest said. The priest hugged his arms to his chest and began to weep, seeing the bodies of the villagers. "I can't believe this" he sobbed. "Our community hasn't known a violent death in two generations. What do I tell their families?"

"You comfort them," Sindra said. "You use it to bring the community together. Honor their memories by speaking on the good they did in their lives, not the terrible nature of their deaths. But do not make them out to be martyrs." The young priest looked up to Sindra and then nodded slowly.

"Sometimes death is senseless," Derk said, looking over a body face down in the mud. "When Freemen are involved, especially."

"We'll put them in the cart and take them back to the village for last rites," one of the villagers said. "Will you come back with us?"

Sindra shook her head. "The chalice is still missing. We will try to track the Freemen and see if we can't get it back."

"But how will you face them?" the priest asked. His eyes were red-rimmed and his brown hair plastered to his head. The sound of the cart made one of the villagers run to meet it, no doubt to deliver the news of what they had found. The cart had been brought to carry back any sick or wounded, and Derk frowned as he thought of the shock of the villagers.

"It does not look like many attacked the camp. They most likely caught them by surprise," Jezlen said. "Probably in the dark. Whoever kept watch most likely sat too close to the fire and was blinded."

"We have to at least try," Asa said, looking grim. "We can't go back to the Church and say, 'Well, it looks like some Freemen got a hold of the chalice so we let them have it.' It would look stupid."

"Maybe they dropped it along the way?" Devra said. "What use would they have for it? They can't eat it and it isn't a weapon. Maybe they opened the box and abandoned it?"

It was very hopeful of Devra to think so but Derk nodded, watching as the men began to load bodies into the cart. The priest closed their eyes, his hand over his mouth as he looked on the deceased, tears falling once more.

"If we are going to go, we need to leave now," Jezlen said. "This weather may get worse and the tracks will disappear in the rain." Sindra nodded slowly, walking to the cart to tell them they would need their belongings after all. Derk just stood there and watched as the bodies were moved, Jezlen gesturing with his head for Derk to follow him. Derk looked around to make sure no one was watching and he followed Jezlen out of the camp and over a small rise, past some tall grass.

In the grass lay a Freeman, dead. Its face was small and its head virtually hairless. The eyes were black orbs with no pupils and its lips were pulled back in a snarl of death, showing pointed, razor sharp teeth. Grey skin was barely covered by scraps of fabric and an arrow protruding from its abdomen revealed the cause of death. Blood stained its ragged nails dark. It was hardly a man. Derk had seen drawings of Freemen in his youth and heard the stories, but seeing one filled him with dread. Jezlen just gripped the hilt of his sword.

They walked back to the camp and Asa handed him his pack and the shortsword he had asked for back in Portsmouth. He couldn't help but wonder if it would be enough. Derk gulped as he slung his pack over his shoulder and fastened his weapon around his waist, remembering the dagger sitting in its sheath. Devra had a walking stick, Asa a sword and a club and Sindra...a dagger. It looked ornamental.

They said their goodbyes after the last of the bodies were put into the cart. Derk shook hands with the villagers and the priest, avoiding the man's tear streaked eyes. When the villagers and the priest trundled down the path, the group was left in a strangely abandoned clearing, the remains of the campfire a black stain on the ground. Jezlen led them wordlessly to the body of the Freemen. Devra gasped and put her hand over her mouth. Asa narrowed his eyes at the body and Sindra's face grew hard. She looked determined.

They mounted the horses they had been given except Jezlen, the Forester scouting ahead and tracking. Derk held the reins of the gelding in his hand and stared up at the cloudy sky. If the sky was clear he would have been able to take comfort in the fact the Goddess was watching them, Her pale face looking down from a blue sky. Instead grey clouds surged and rolled, the threat of a summer rain making him hunch his shoulders and wish to be indoors. The foul weather matched the situation. Derk sighed and prayed both the weather and the undertaking would turn to their favor.

Chapter 10
Trespassing

"Are you sure?" Derk asked, furrowing his brow. The cave a stone's throw away looked unobtrusive. A few scraggly trees grew around it, the soil too poor to grow anything more impressive, and the ground littered with shards of stone. No sign of life could be seen or heard.

"The tracks lead here," Jezlen said quietly. "It is the type of place a group of Freemen might dwell. As you may recall from stories your mother told you." Jezlen's mouth twitched as if he might smile and Derk rolled his eyes. Quietly they walked back to the others.

"There will be at the most twenty of them within," Jezlen said, his voice low and steady. "Larger groups of Freemen have not been encountered for two of your generations. They will have a central area where they convene and keep the fire and maybe a separate area where they keep their belongings. Food. Weapons. They can see in very low light, and the only lights they keep are glowing mushrooms. If you hear a sound like a puff of air, do not worry. It is only sporing. But try not to walk into a cloud. It will make your face glow."

"Twenty?" Devra gulped. Her green eyes were wide with apprehension. "Will they all be together? Will we have to face twenty at a time?"

"I have not had to kill more than five at a time, at the most," Jezlen said nonchalantly, pulling out his sword. It looked well-used but well-kept. "It is possible you will make it out alive." It would have helped if Jezlen smiled at her but he only stared. Derk snickered nervously, looking to Asa, who stepped in front of Devra slightly, dark eyes shining with fear.

"No one is going to die," Sindra said, stepping forward and facing them. "We are going to get the chalice back from these beasts and return it to the Church, where it belongs. They don't have the training or the determination we do. The chalice means nothing to them."

"What should we do?" Asa asked. Derk looked in the direction of the cave.

"One of us should scout ahead. When the way is clear, the others can come up." Derk looked at Jezlen. "Which one of us will stick our neck out first?"

"Not Asa. He's too loud," Devra said, drawing a look from her brother. She widened her eyes at him and folded her arms. "What, you are!"

"Well, you aren't going. Someone can use a weapon." Asa looked past Sindra to Derk and Jezlen. Derk considered Jezlen with narrowed eyes, wondering if he should allow the more experienced Forester to take the lead or if he should volunteer. Derk knew he could be quiet, probably quieter than Jezlen. But Jezlen knew Freemen patterns and tactics. However, Sindra was there.

"I'll do it," Derk said, hoping to sound as brave as possible. Jezlen actually looked surprised for once, his dark eyebrows raising on his face. "I know how to be quiet and not be seen." He also knew how to use the shortsword and the dagger tucked into his belt.

"They like to attack from behind," Jezlen offered as a parting comment, moving out of his way. Asa and Devra both nodded at him at the same time which might have been funny if Derk's heart wasn't pounding in his chest. Sindra leaned over and kissed him before he left, which made the blood swish in his ears as he walked away up the hill, keeping to the edge of the excuse for a path leading to the mouth of the cave, a hot summer wind rippling through the tall grass.

He didn't want to get down too low or an escape would be difficult. Derk was painfully aware his friends were watching him, possibly judging him on how he approached the cave. Carefully he placed one foot in front of the other, aware of the ground and its consistency, feeling for what was around him. Was anything close by? Did something wait for him just on the other side of the stone entrance? His gut told him no and he stepped forward, turning to look to the side just as a bird flew out of the grass, startled by his approach. He felt the weight of the sword in its sheath and the pressure of the dagger tucked into his belt. After he made sure he was breathing slow and steady, he peeked past the edge of the stone.

The entrance looked bigger than it actually was. The ground sloped down rather steeply and the entrance to the cave was probably only wide enough to allow two people side by side, though six or seven people could stand comfortably on the outermost rim. He looked back at his four companions, Sindra's dark eyes disappearing as he slipped past the lip of the cave, toward the actual entrance.

The Valley was dotted with caves and caverns, low hills sitting atop naturally formed rooms and tunnels carved from the earth. The Freewild itself was more rock than dirt in many places, making it hard for those who preferred absolute freedom from the seat and the sword to scratch out a living. Derk set his hand on the cool stone, craning his neck forward. His feet moved quietly over the ground and the sound of his sword scraping against the inside of its hilt as he drew it made him shiver.

Derk stepped into the cave, the lack of noise almost reassuring. He kept his blade down, careful not to let it catch light from the outside and give him away. Derk wondered if the Freemen could smell him. Maybe they could hear his heartbeat. He wondered why they were called 'Freemen' and not something else. They were hardly men. Two arms, two legs, and a head were all they shared with the typical inhabitant of the Valley. The drawings from his childhood stories hadn't prepared him for the reality. There used to be more of them in the first days of the Valley. His grandfather's generation had campaigned against them and now Derk was creeping toward a remnant.

The cooler air within the cave would have been refreshing if he hadn't been so nervous. His eyes adjusted to the light and he saw a stone chamber, piles of unremarkable rocks stacked around. Two tunnels led down into the earth, and he could see the glow of the mushrooms Jezlen had referenced. A blue green light emanated from within, telling Derk each tunnel lead to a hallway. But which one should they choose? A brown, wet spot on the floor drew his attention and he knelt down, glancing about quickly to make sure it was safe. Derk reached out and scratched his finger against the spot, bringing it to his nose to sniff.

Blood.

Derk looked in the direction of the passageways. Another brown spot lay in front of the entrance that led to the right. The glow at the end of it was brighter. Derk noticed a distinct heel print pressed into the dirt and sand. Derk picked his head up, listening before he stood and turned, walking out of the cave.

The party looked relieved to see him though anxiety still wracked all their faces. "Well, what did you find?" Devra asked, her eyes wide.

Derk almost made a joke but thought better of it, glancing over his shoulder toward the cave before he answered. "There's an atrium of sorts, a big room with two tunnels leading deeper underground. One of them has blood leading up to it. I'm fairly certain they went down that way." He still had his sword in his hand and he didn't feel inclined to put it away just yet.

"Derk, you take up the front with Devra," Jezlen said. He avoided the panicked look the twins both gave him. "She will be able to create a light if needed. At the very least." He looked to Asa, pulling his bow out and looping the bowstring over one end. "Then Asa, Sindra and myself in the rear."

"Are we trying to sneak in, get the chalice and sneak out, or are we trying to launch a surprise attack?" Asa asked.

"Whatever results in us not getting killed, I'd say," Derk offered. He turned to Devra, wondering if they should give her a weapon, just in case. She had a walking stick. "Can you make a light?" he asked, trying not to sound incredulous. "Or, I don't know...just find where the chalice is and...." He waved his hands, not sure what he was doing or what he was asking her. "What can you do?"

"I can make a light," Devra offered. "Most of the time. Unless I'm nervous."

"Good thing we're not about to do something nerve-wracking," Derk huffed.

"You obviously do not understand how Wielding works," Jezlen said to Derk. "She has never seen the chalice or the caves. She is not a seer."

"You have to give her a chance," Asa said. "I've seen her blow up lots of things. I'm sure she'll be able to do something once we're in there." Asa looked to Devra hopefully. His sister didn't have the same confident look as her brother.

Derk looked to Sindra. Devra had mentioned being able to set things on fire in the village. It occurred to Derk he was flammable and wondered if leading the party with the Wielder was the best idea. But Sindra couldn't fight. Sindra took Devra's gloved hands and smiled at her. "I know you'll do your best. I've seen what you can do. And we all trust you." Sindra looked to Derk, giving him a look which told him he should at least pretend he trusted her. Derk sighed.

"I just wish I would have brought my helmet," Asa said, pulling out his sword. The scrape of metal against the scabbard was so loud it made everyone cringe.

"You'll have to be quiet," Sindra said to Asa. "You can be quiet, right?"

"Can we just go already?" Jezlen asked, pulling an arrow out of its quiver. "All this talking is boring to me. Asa, be quiet, Devra, set something on fire, Sindra, do not do anything. Derk, lead us through. There."

The members of the group all looked at one another before Derk sighed, turning to go. He heard Devra walking behind him, trying to catch up. "I imagine you can be quiet?" he asked, slowing his pace as they approached the cave.

"Yes," Devra said, whispering. "I learned in my training. The forest is a quiet place and my master taught me in the ways of listening. Though when one begins to listen, it's actually quite loud." She smiled, holding her walking stick in her hand. It was carved with symbols, Derk saw. He just nodded.

"Well, let's both be quiet." They walked into the cave, the others following behind. Derk waited outside the entrance of the cave to make sure nothing had moved into the atrium in the meantime and then pointed to the entrance with a jerk of his head, indicating Devra should follow. They entered the coolness of the cave. Derk glanced over his shoulder, seeing Sindra slink in next and then Asa, moving behind them. Jezlen brought up the rear. Derk walked ahead, waiting till his eyes adjusted to the light before advancing toward the hallway. He wondered if they could be cut off. If they went down the one tunnel, there was no saying Freemen couldn't come down the other tunnel and come up the rear, trapping them. Jezlen and Asa were back there at least.

The natural hallway turned and Derk drew in his breath as he saw the source of the light. The mushrooms. They walked further down the hallway, mushrooms occurring more and more frequently until the ceiling and walls were covered with a proliferation of glowing fungus. The caps were bigger than a chicken's egg and a sweet, earthy scent permeated the air. A breeze made the fragrance stronger in Derk's nostrils and he realized he was holding his breath. The only sound he heard were the footsteps of those behind him. Out of the corner of his eye, a hand reached out and his eyes went wide as Devra's tattooed hand reached out and plucked one of the mushrooms off of the wall. He wanted to ask her what she was doing but he didn't dare speak, watching as she placed it into her belt pouch.

"What're you doing?!" Asa asked for him, too loudly for Derk's liking. Derk cringed and looked down the tunnel, expecting a horde of Freemen to come charging toward them. Instead he just heard Jezlen sigh.

"Be quiet," Jezlen growled. Devra wiped her glowing hands on the inside of her garments.

"I've never seen this kinds of mushroom before, I had to take one," Devra said quietly. "We might not come back this way. I wanted to be sure I got one."

"Business and pleasure," Derk said. "Now can we all shut up?" A scratching sound up ahead made the entire party wheel their heads around. Derk felt his face twist, his heart kicking against his ribs. They all stood there for a long anxious breath. Derk let out a sigh of relief as a rat skittered toward them. Its mouth was glowing, iridescent whiskers twitching as it regarded them in the low light. Derk turned to the rest of them and put two fingers across his lips, signaling they should remain quiet before he walked ahead.

The path turned again and Derk held his hand up, signaling them to stop. The glow of the mushrooms looked strange on his sword and he held it behind him, peering around the corner. The ground sloped downward and opened up into a chamber. A different kind of light came from this room, yellow in hue. He sniffed the air and smelled something burning. A torch, most likely. Derk pointed at himself and then at the end of the tunnel, signaling the rest of them should remain while he scouted ahead.

Quietly he stalked toward the room, listening for anything which might be another life form. Maybe they would be lucky. Maybe the box holding the chalice would be right there and they could grab it and get out without any hassle. Derk licked his lips, listening to the sounds in the room before he walked forward, knowing if anyone was in there, they would see his feet first. He gripped his sword in his hand and took a deep breath before he stepped forward.

The room was roughly square with a tunnel directly across from where he stood. A crude table sat in the middle. No one was in the room but there was a torch set in the wall emitting a feeble but adequate light. A quick glance around and Derk stepped out into the chamber, out of the line of sight from the opposite tunnel. What was on the table?

It looked like several packs of the dead men had been taken, their contents strewn about. Clothes, a broken necklace, a pipe. No food. He wondered why no one was there to guard anything. Derk almost laughed as he thought how the Freeman probably weren't expecting company, but he remembered the sword in his hand and kept a sober face. Did the Freemen know the people they killed belonged to a bigger community? Did they not fear retaliation? What did they think about the chalice? A tunnel went off of the left hand wall. If he remembered correctly, it ran parallel to the original tunnel they entered. The one across from it went perpendicular, deeper into the earth.

Derk walked up to the first entrance and peered around the corner. The ground also sloped downward, the same mushrooms lining the walls. A musty smell wafted up from whatever was down there. If he walked down this way there was a chance someone at the very end would see him before he could see them. He would hopefully be able to hear them first. Derk looked at the ground, his feet quiet against the stone as he slunk to the corner. Looking behind him he could barely make out Devra in the dark. He lowered his head to give himself a better vantage point of what lay down the hall.

It seemed like it opened up into another room, lit by another torch. A faint noise made Derk stop in his tracks but after a few breaths with nothing happening he thought it was probably just another rat, scuffling in the dark. He took a few steps down the hall, keeping his back as close to the wall as he could. Mushroom caps brushed against him like soft, fat fingers.

Derk stopped. The noise again. Another step closer made the sound slightly more audible. It sounded like a mix between chittering and growling. It wasn't loud and he thought he could hear two distinct voices, if they could be called such. He heard a faint scratching as well. Derk glanced back down the way he had come, making sure Devra was still there before he took another step forward.

The talking stopped. Derk gripped the hilt of his sword. He looked back and waved his hand. The way Devra moved told him he had her attention. Quickly he placed one foot in front of the other, walking back to the start of the hall, pointing at Devra and beckoning her over. When she pointed behind her to indicate the others, he shook his head and pointed at her, the Wielder slinking to his side.

Derk pointed to the room and then held up two fingers. "Are you ready?" he mouthed, hoping she would see what he was trying to say. Devra's mouth was a thin line cutting across her face but she nodded. He was certain the knuckles on the hand clutching her walking stick were white.

Derk stepped forward as quietly as he could but quickly, his sword feeling too light in his hands. Steps behind him told him Devra was following, and he tried not to scream as he entered the room,

Two Freemen were bent over weapons, sharpening them. Despite their alien faces, they still managed to look surprised to see them, scrambling up from the whetstone, weapons at the ready. Derk gulped as he saw a third Freemen in the room, a croak rasping from beyond its ragged teeth. It was making for the passageway leading deeper underground. "Stop him!" Derk said, managing not to shout.

Devra reached out an ungloved hand and pulled back, the tattoo on her hand seeming to animate. The Freeman who was running stopped suddenly, its head snapping back unnaturally with a crack before it fell to the ground. Derk rushed the other two, parrying a swing with his shortsword before he pulled his dagger out and drove it into the belly of the one of the Freemen. A backhanded slice sent the other to the floor with a clatter that seemed too loud. Derk panted as he looked to Devra, her eyes wide. "We need to move."

The pair of them rushed back to the others. The questions on their faces would have to be answered later. "We must be quick," Derk said. "They might know we are here." The five passed through the room, taking the tunnel the other Freemen had tried to escape through. Derk couldn't help but look at the one Devra had dispatched. The dead Freeman's neck was split open. In the faint torchlight he saw the splintered bone gleaming red with blood. It was grisly. He shivered as he thought of Devra. So that's why she hadn't done anything in the bar that evening.

Derk slid down the hall, the adrenaline from his previous kill making his skin hot. He listened, emboldened, dashing silently ahead. The mushroom glow was stronger here. Derk stopped before he reached the end, trying to make out the bit of the room he could see. No one was in this cavern and the only other exit went to the east. He wondered if it would spill into another chamber and how long the system went. Derk held up his hand and listened, hearing nothing in this chamber and stepping out cautiously.

Derk wondered what had carved the system. The ceiling of this section was also covered in glowing mushrooms and he was astounded at the amount of light they gave off. He tried to recall what Jezlen had said about the Freemen and knew eventually they would come across the center of their home. They didn't dig out the caverns. The Freemen weren't known for ingenuity or building. Why were those three Freemen in that part of the cave and how soon would they come across the rest of the assembly? What did they live on, deep in the earth? Grimly, Derk thought they would never find out the answer. He doubted the Freemen would be willing to provide the information.

Another stretch of stone, void of life save the mushrooms. As the five companions walked through the caverns they would occasionally hear something, a scrambling, chittering. When Derk looked behind him he could see Jezlen walking backwards, watching their rear. Asa's face looked as dark as it could possibly look, determined to protect them all. But nothing showed its face. Derk tried to keep a map of the caves in his head, trying to recall their path. One section was much like another. Some rooms has spots on the wall obviously meant to hold torches but they passed through no other torch lit rooms.

After several chambers with no one in them, Derk was starting to feel nervous. Where was everyone? Could Jezlen have been wrong? Perhaps the three they had killed were all the Freemen there were? Still, there was the chittering they occasionally heard. What did it mean? Perhaps their own nervousness was making their venture more serious than it had to be. Derk came to the end of a tunnel and peeked ahead.

Derk felt his heart leap into his throat. There it was. In an enclave cluttered with various objects, a wooden box marked with holy symbols and script lay off to one side. It had to be it. What else could it be? Derk wanted to thank the Goddess out loud but stuffed his joy inside of him. After the trouble with the Temple of the Ever Burning Sun and the dead dissenters, the Chalice was within their grasp. Would it be so easy? Derk hoped it would be, for their sake.

Chapter 11
Malfunctions and Mysteries

Derk looked over the scene once more, counting the steps to the chalice, the objects in the way, the layout of the room before he turned back to Devra.

"It's here," he whispered. He said it so quietly even he could barely hear it. Devra's eyes went wide and then a hopeful smile tugged at the corners of her mouth. She turned around and relayed Derk's message back. Derk listened carefully, over the beating of his heart, making sure he wasn't ignoring some key sign of life in his excitement. Everything was quiet. And the chalice was there.

"I'm going to sneak up and get it," he whispered. "Is there anything you can do...to help? Just in case?" Derk looked to Devra hopefully. She just pressed her lips together and shook her head. He tried not to sigh as he nodded as well. He ran his fingers through his hair, push-ing it out of his face before he took a deep breath and took a step forward.

Derk felt as if he were naked in the room. It was big-ger than the others and had more tunnels leading off of it. Derk held his breath as he crept quickly past the first en-trance. He stepped quietly, with the tiptoes of his feet past the second one, keeping his head away from the entrance. Derk was glad to be unencumbered by bulky armor or metal chains that could clink or rattle.

He exhaled and took a breath in. Quiet. Wait. Listen. Step. Step. Look back. See Devra's green eyes, still green in the dim light. Everything appeared the same in the dark. Step. Step. He reached out with his hands and placed them on the box. He felt the grain of the wood and the rough edges beneath his fingertips, the smoothness of the paint where someone had written on it. It was in his hands.

A sound made him turn his head to look over his shoulder. It was so quiet, he almost thought he didn't hear it. But after the sound he heard Asa swear. Derk picked up the box and put his back to a wall, looking to Devra. She was backing away from the rest of the party, obviously staring at something down the hallway. Derk felt his heart thump in his chest and somehow over the thumping he was able to make out the sound of something coming down the hall closest to him. They were coming.

Derk set the box down and pulled out his sword as quietly as he could, so as not to give away his position. Now Sindra was in the room and Asa yelled. Derk heard Jezlen cursing at Asa. And then a head came around the corner.

In the low light he couldn't make out the color of the Freeman's skin or the true color of its eyes. But the faint blue-green glow of the mushrooms made the terrible form even eerier. Derk inhaled and as he exhaled, struck at the head, jerking his sword free and readying his blade again. Devra stared down the hallway and her eyes went wide, taking on the same glow of the mushrooms. She put a hand up as if to gesture to someone to stop but then she jerked her hand back, fingers bent in a strange fashion. He heard meat tearing. It made Derk cringe. Then the chittering started.

Sindra careened around the corner, running. Derk picked up the box and saw Asa and then Jezlen back out of the hallway, Jezlen placidly firing off a shot while Asa stepped back. His hand was on his bicep, blood trickling down his fingers. Derk noticed the strange color the fungal light gave Asa's blood. Derk picked up the box and locked eyes with Sindra, deciding now wasn't the time for whispers. "SINDRA!" he shouted, tossing the box in her direction.

He didn't bother waiting to see if she caught it. Derk didn't hear the sound of wood breaking on a stone ground so he assumed she did. What he did hear was the strange chittering and keening of the Freemen. He ran to the other tunnel and looked to Devra. "A light?"

Devra picked up something from the ground, a rusted sword. As she held it, light from the mushrooms started to drift to it, collecting on the surface till it shone brightly, enough to cast light a few throws ahead. She ran to Derk's side, Sindra behind her.

"More are coming," Jezlen said, cocking an arrow.

"Can we go back the way we came?" Derk asked. He heard his own panic in his voice and the torch Devra had made glowed brighter.

"They are probably coming around to trap us," Jezlen said. He looked behind him and shot into the dark, a screech sending a shiver down Derk's spine.

"Tits, this way!" No sounds came from down the hall so Derk charged, sword drawn. He slowed as he reached each adjoining corridor, trying to keep track of where they were in relation to the exit. The chittering continued, louder behind them and to the sides. As they came to one entrance glowing eyes stared at them. Devra pointed the torch at the Freemen and said something Derk couldn't quite make out. Blue-green lights shot off of the torch. More screams. It smelled like cooking meat.

"I really wish at least one of them Zealots had survived their attack," Derk shouted as he ran down the corridor, the magical light illuminating the stone walls before him. "I'd really like to throttle one of them right now for getting us into this damned mess." There was no point in being quiet anymore. He wondered if Gam would wonder what had happened to him, if they would ever find their remains. And Sindra...he had just gotten involved with her.

Was it to end here? Murdered by beasts underground? Derk wanted to live. He wanted to drink beer and make love and take things and see the light of the moon. He wanted to pray and beat a man and feel the warmth of a fire. These Freemen might take it all away from him. From all of them.

The sound of four other sets of feet running as quickly as they could still didn't manage to drown out the high pitched war cries of their pursuers. Their shrill, manic sound made the hairs on the back of Derk's neck stand on end. The distinct voice of Devra yelped in fear and the light on the walls glowed brighter as the Wielder ran faster. There was a whizzing sound and then a screech as an arrow cut through the air and into the bodies of one of their assailants. Derk felt relief, and then panic washed over him as the corridor ended, letting them into a large, rectangular chamber. A large, stone door blocked their way.

They were trapped.

The other four party members spilled into the room, Jezlen crouching down notching off another arrow into the black. Another shriek signaling the projectile had hit its mark. "Quickly!" Derk shouted. He pointed to them. "Barricade the corridor the best you can." Sindra and Asa started to drag a stone bench to the entrance, Sindra running off to push a table. Jezlen let another arrow loose. It bought Asa and Sindra time to move another bench into place. Derk stared at the wall before him. "Asa? You went to school for this, right?"

"Jez and I'll take the front and whoever hops over. Sindra, stay off to the side and guard the chalice. Devra, get as much room as you need and stay by Derk while he gets us out of here." Asa unsheathed his longsword, finally having the room to pull the long blade out of its scabbard. "You will be getting us out of here, right?"

"As long as there is a way to get us out of here." Derk looked at the large stone door, twitching visibly as a strange, reptilian howl rippled through the air. "I'm hoping there's a way to get us out of here."

"Things are going to die," came the overly calm words of Jezlen. His eyes showed no mirth and not a single, black hair was out of place on that cool head of his. He could be singing a dirge for all Derk presently cared, as long as he kept the arrows flying toward whatever bizarre creatures were attacking them. The thief turned his attention to the door, hoping to get a good idea of how it worked before the din and energy of battle made it harder to concentrate.

Derk placed his hands on the door. It was a single, carved stone, without any sort of decoration and without any handles. There was no sign of hinges, and the edges of the door were flush with the walls, meaning it wouldn't swing. He looked up, noting a small gap in the ceiling above the door. It went up. That meant there should be a switch somewhere.

"Devra, check the wall over there, see if you can find something, a nook or an opening of some sort. Unless you think you can just blast a hole in the door?" Devra just grimaced. "Well, please, just find something." It couldn't be harder than casting a spell, could it?

Asa didn't want her at the front of the fray. And Derk didn't want to consider what would happen to one of them if they got caught in the path of one of her wieldings. He told himself he would be able to jump out of the way in time. He was quick.

Derk tapped on the wall quickly with the hilt of his shortsword, listening for the sound indicating a hollow space behind the stone. The bizarre reptilian howl sounded again, closer this time. The tapping of clawed toenails on stone grew louder and more rapid. Jezlen let one arrow and then another fly and the hiss of his quiet words told Derk something bad was about to happen. A quick yelp from Devra grabbed his attention. He raced along the wall to where she was standing, her quarter staff leaning against the wall perpendicular to it.

"Paps, I ain't never seen nothing like it!" shouted Asa, his eyes finally seeing what the elf saw, his voice sounding slightly less sure than it usually did. Devra looked over her shoulder, eyes wide, so distracted Derk had to shake her to get her to focus.

"Which stone is it?" he asked, finally getting the girl's attention. She pointed to the rock and then picked up her quarterstaff, pulling off one glove and then the other before she held the wooden implement over her head.

Derk took a deep breath, trying to push the fact out of his head there were horrible creatures the likes of which he had only heard about from half-crazed drunks heading down the corridor. The stone was before him and it must be moved. He had to help his friends. And Jezlen. They were protecting him. He pulled out his lucky dagger and kissed its hilt before jamming it between a small space between the rocks, using the tips of his valuable fingers to pry the stone out.

He was annoyed to see there wasn't a switch behind the stone. He heard the sound of a creature scrambling over the makeshift barricade. Luckily it was quieted by a few curses and the melody of a skilled hand slicing into enemy flesh. The twang of a long bow punctuated the story of a dead monster. Derk snapped his fingers at Devra, trying to keep her attention. The girl managing to rip her wide gaze away from the scene and looked to Derk. "The light!" he shouted, pointing into the open space.

Devra's tattooed hands fumbled in a pouch at her waist. With a few words a small stone began to emit a cold, white light suitable for inspecting the hole. "Take care," he said, nodding to her. He looked to Asa and Jezlen, attacking whatever was trying to rush over the barricade. Derk looked to Sindra. She stood in front of the box holding the chalice, a long, thin knife in her hand. Even when nervous she was beautiful, he thought, taking another deep breath before inspecting the hole.

It wasn't a hole but a short tunnel leading to the other side of the wall. He shone the light in, inspecting to see its dimensions. It was obviously meant for one, normal sized person, and even then it would be tight. A thick, burly person like Asa would be able to make it but not very quickly. Lengthwise, it would have fit between two to three people of average height end to end. Carefully he removed another stone to expose the full entrance to the shaft and put the rock serving as a light in his mouth. Behind him Asa emitted a short, sharp cry. Derk had to focus on getting the good warrior out of there so they could see to his wounds.

Derk took a deep breath and crawled in. Once his whole body was inside, he noticed two small holes on the right wall about where the giant stone door stood. He leaned both his elbows on the floor of the tunnel so he could get a better look inside the hole. Derk's elbows pushed down on a hidden switch, meant to look like one of the many stones lining the floor. He strained his ear to hear what it could have possibly affected, trying to find the source of any mechanical workings within the wall. All he heard was the wild screech of a beast as it forced its way over their barricade. It was followed by the steady, powerful prayer of the elven priestess. Derk looked over his shoulder, hoping Devra heard him when he shouted. "I don't suppose anything happened to the door just then?"

"No!" she cried. He could see her putting her back to the hole, apparently readying herself to face anything coming her way. Derk took a deep breath, sweat starting to bead on his brow. Had the tunnel just grown narrower? He licked his lips, easing off the switch and listening again for any possible sounds which might hint at what the hidden switch had triggered. Instead Derk heard grunting, sword slashes and shouts in a strange reptilian language. There was a popping sound and then a sizzle and a scream. Devra shrieked something unintelligible, and the hole became obstructed as she placed her back right against it.

I've got to get them out of there, Derk thought. He looked at the two holes set into the tunnel wall. Maybe there was something in here. Maybe another trap he had just set off. But he had to check. If this was the mechanism he needed, it would mean the difference between life and death for his friends. He took a deep breath and tossed the glowing rock into the hole. Nothing happened. He nudged it further into the small hole on the right, his hand lacing its way through and to the left...the two holes were connected and there was nothing there.

"Hems," he cursed. Derk picked the rock and placed it between his teeth, crawling further through the tunnel.

He had just set off a switch which didn't do anything and wasted valuable time throwing a rock down a hole. The sound of battle muffled by the stone walls rang behind him, urging him on. Hands and knees took him through as quickly as he could, the light in his mouth revealing the stone wall that lay at the end. Probably a fake, he thought, approaching the end. Derk shifted in the exit so he could push it out with his elbow.

And then he pressed down on another switch with his other hand. Farther away from the din of battle, he could definitely hear chains and gears scraping against each other, the ticking sound of a primitive timer clinking behind the stone. "Betwixt," Derk managed to whisper. His heart thumped in time with the metal workings readying themselves. He half whimpered, half screamed as he threw his weight against the stone, knocking it clear out of its niche and threw himself out onto the floor, landing on his side. Pain shot through his wrist and shoulder but he got himself on his feet, coughing as he looked back at the end of the tunnel.

Nothing happened. There was a strange, grating sound coming from somewhere but more importantly there was a lever on the other side of the wall. He turned to run for the lever when the sudden sound of metal slamming forcefully into stone pierced his ears. Derk jumped and screamed, wheeling around to see what had made the sound.

Right at the exit of the tunnel where his neck had formerly been was a large, metal plate, rust hiding its true color. Small clouds of dust billowed around the metal plate and Derk had no doubt it was still very sharp. He gulped, pulled away from the thoughts of his own mortality by the shouts of his comrades from the other side.

"Don't worry!" he shouted, his throat dry from stress and running, hoping they heard him. He jumped up to grab a hold of the lever, missing the first time, screaming the second time as he grabbed it with both hands, his injured wrist burning with pain. He gritted his teeth as he crouched down and leaped up growling, grabbing hold of the lever and using the weight of his body to pull the switch down and hopefully the door up.

He heard the sound of chains moving and gears moving yet again but a series of metal bangs and a few booms from somewhere below made Derk's heart sink. He thought of the blade which would have killed him and how it had deployed late. If it had rusted, there was a good chance the chains working the door had rusted as well and snapped from the counter weights deployed after all these years. Tears of frustration sprang to his eyes. He wouldn't be able to open the door. They were trapped. He would have to go back through the tunnel....

The tunnel. Derk ran back over to the tunnel, the way blocked by the metal plate. He rapped his knuckles on it to judge its thickness, ignoring the blood stains now painting the orange colored metal. As most metal things meant to slice through flesh and bone, it was heavy but thin, flakes of rust scouring his skin. Maybe he could get the blade moved. Maybe someone else could.

"DEVRA!" He screamed the girl's name, his voice hoarse but desperation propelling his plea forward. "DEVRA! I NEED YOU TO SHOOT SOMETHING DOWN THE TUNNEL! I NEED-"

He didn't finish his sentence as something did indeed come down the tunnel. There was a high pitched whizzing sound as cracks he hadn't noticed in the walls went from black to white as something made of light shot toward the metal plate. Derk was unable to take cover as the metal plate flew out and hit him in the head, knocking him sideways. For a moment everything before him was blurry and then black. Something told him he had to keep his wits about him.

Derk stumbled in the direction of the tunnel, the sounds from the other side telling him where to go. "Devra! I can't get the door open, we'll all have to come through the tunnel! Tell the others and then come on!"

Light and dark played at the other side of the tunnel before it remained dark, wood scraping against stone telling him she sent her staff first. Derk placed the light stone on his end of the tunnel, beckoning the young woman to come quickly. Devra stopped suddenly, her eyes wide with alarm. "I think I pushed something!"

"It's okay, it's been disarmed!" he called, urging her to come forward. Above his head he heard the rusted workings of the trap resetting itself, never to kill again. Devra crawled through, another shadow falling across the opposite end of the tunnel. This time a box was placed in the tunnel, a set of grey eyes peering from behind it as Derk helped the Wielder. First came the intricately carved box and then the priestess, pulling her robes along with her, her face wan and drained though she smiled at Derk as she exited. "We have pushed them back," she said quietly, kissing him on the lips briefly, taking his hand in hers.

"Asa and Jezlen gave them such a fight, they grew disheartened and retreated."

"Asa and Jezlen need to get in," came a quiet voice from within the tunnel. The pair moved away from the tunnel exit, first the elf and then the human emerging. Asa was the worse off of the two but he was smiling in his usual fashion, bushy eyebrows almost hiding the relief in his eyes. He went over to his sister and gave her as much of a hug as he could muster before looking to Derk. "Couldn't get the door open?"

Derk shook his head grimly and looked at the tunnel everyone had just crawled through. "That door won't open ever again. We should place the stone over the mouth of the tunnel and wedge it in so we can be sure not to have any followers," he said, holding his injured wrist in his other hand. "This door only opens from this side and the switch is broken so we should be safe. Best we get to sealing up the tunnel," Derk said, not wanting to be surprised by more creatures anytime soon. "Asa?" Asa nodded and walked over, the two of them managing to put the stone back in its place, the others handing them spare cloth and rock chips to wedge it into place. Sore as he was, it was difficult work and Derk wondered how he had managed to move the stone himself. He eventually had to chalk it up to fear. Once they were satisfied the stone wouldn't be moved by anything weaker than Asa, Derk slumped against one of the walls and waited for his turn to be patched up.

"I am glad we got the chalice before they moved it," said Sindra, turning her interest to the ornate box on the floor, kneeling before it. She placed her hands on its lid for a moment before removing the key from around her neck and unlocking the receptacle for the holy object. The party gathered around, forgetting their aches and troubles for a moment as they all tried to see the object.

It was a two handed cup. The body was carved of white stone and engraved and inlaid with silver holy symbols. The phases of the moon danced around the rim of it, waxing and waning in antiqued silver. In the bottom of the cup was set a pearl of great size, milky white and round like the celestial body it was meant to emulate.

Devra gasped in awe and Derk and Asa bowed their heads in reverence. Derk hadn't thought seeing it would have drawn any emotion out of him but it did. It was beautiful and it shone with its own light, a soft glow seeming to radiate and bathe its rescuers in its glory. Sindra closed the lid and locked it, placing the key back around her neck before looking up to the others, eyes shining with tears of happiness. "That's been tended to," Sindra said, a proud smile tugging at her lips. "Let's see about getting us all patched up."

Jezlen came to his aid, but a look from Derk and the elf just smirked faintly, going over to a corner to see to his own wounds. Eventually Sindra came and sat by Derk looking over his wrist and shoulder, judging them both bad sprains. She took several bandages from her pack, wrapping them tightly. She finished by applying balm to his hands. Derk could have done it himself but he wasn't going to turn her away.

"All right, everyone's patched up. We need to figure a way out of here," said Asa when the gashes on his neck and shoulder were treated.

"I don't think we'll have to search hard," Derk said, sitting up a bit straighter. He pointed at the lever and door with his chin, rubbing his rough face with his hand. "That door only opens from this side. There must be a way to get to this side up ahead."

"I agree with Derk," said Jezlen. He looked up from his weapons, all laid out in front of him in size order for inspection, his face looking as if he had just been roused from sleep and not facing bloody battle. "When we first entered the cave, it was clear the caverns were natural. The chamber we are in now was made. The cave we entered must have been the rear entrance while what lies ahead would most likely be the main entrance to this underground structure."

"Well, those creatures didn't build this," chimed in Devra, her hands gloved once more and replaiting her thick hair. "If what you say is true, they obviously hadn't found the tunnel yet and are kept back by the door. If not them, who?"

Derk lifted his head slightly, blinking as they all finally looked over the sides of the chamber they were occupying. He stood up and taking the still glowing sword Devra had made in his hand, thrust it before him. "The answer to that," he said, turning to his comrades, "I believe is in the writing on the wall."

The party puzzled over the carvings on the walls around them for a while, trying to make sense of the figures and the activities they seemed to be carrying out. They couldn't agree on what or who the figures could have been and became more and more unsettled as they agreed upon their actions. The stone room seemed to become darker as the discussion trailed off, no one willing to end it properly, unwilling to say what was on everyone's minds.

The empty eyes of the stone figures seemed to be watching them. At one point Devra suggested they make camp elsewhere, but by then everyone was too tired to move. Their wounds had been tended but most of the company had sore muscles and all needed a good night's sleep.

Jezlen offered to take the first watch. Sindra said she would take the second, and Derk was glad to hear it. But as tired as he was Derk couldn't manage to fall asleep. Every time he drifted off, he would think he heard something and wake up. The noise always seemed to come from one of the engravings on the wall. He rolled over on his bed and looked around, noticing one of the others sitting up or tossing and turning as well. Sindra sighed beside him and he drew closer to her, smiling as she opened her eyes and gazed into his. He kissed her on the forehead and rolled over again, hoping to drift off soon. After tossing and turning a half dozen more times, he sat up, looking over to Jezlen and raising an eyebrow. A wry smile played on the elf's face, his eyes turned toward the weapons he was cleaning.

Derk contented himself with carving into one of the stones on the floor, carefully etching a waxing crescent moon, sure to close the shape with a heart before carving, "Derk loves Sindra," his tongue stuck out of the side of his mouth. Thirsty, he reached over his sleeping love to feel around for the water skin. He took the opportunity to squeeze her backside, trying to feign innocence as she rolled over to smack his hand and laugh quietly.

"Since you are awake, perhaps you should take your watch, dear Sindra," Jezlen said. Derk looked up at Jezlen, the elf finally putting his weapons away. "Not an issue, correct?"

"No issue whatsoever, Jezlen," Sindra said. She kissed Derk on the cheek before she sat up on her bedroll, pulling out a book to read before she moved to where he couldn't reach her. He huffed and glared to Jezlen.

"You should try to sleep as well, Derk," Jezlen said. It sounded as if the elf were chiding him. Derk considered throwing something at him but couldn't find anything to throw, so he scowled instead before he rolled over on his bedroll.

Derk tried to get some sleep once more. He was finally able to nod off, but he didn't dream and he felt as if he was being watched the entire time. He was glad to be woken up by a kiss on the cheek, turning his face to return the kiss only to find his lips on a face in need of a shave and he pulled back, shocked to find a grinning Asa. Chuckles rose up from the other party members as he sat up in bed.

Derk wished this had been the first time they played this trick on him, but it wasn't, and for some reason they never tired of it. He jabbed the burly Asa in the shoulder, still not able to hold back his laugh at the old joke, though his chuckle was dampened as he looked up at the walls of the room. He couldn't help feeling uncomfortable at the carved figures looming above the laughing group.

First meal was quick and uneventful. They ate their dried biscuits and fruit in silence, except when Jezlen told

Asa to chew more quietly. The five of them packed up, the stone wedged in the tunnel still intact and untouched. Devra made a few lights and anxiously they set off.

"Is it just me or is there something off about these figures?" Derk asked, casting a light up onto one of the reliefs. They didn't bother to stop but gazed over the walls as they hurried on, eager to leave. The group walked through the silent halls, the figures lining the walls and some even flowing onto the floor or ceiling with their height. All of the figures were carved in great detail, the weave in the fabric of their clothing or the flow of curls in their hair obviously etched by a careful, observant hand.

"None of them have eyes," Sindra said. Her words seemed loud and Derk swore he felt a cool wind blow through the intricately carved passageways. No irises or pupils were carved into their stone faces. The figures depicted carried out their deeds without seeing what they were doing. Yet at the same time the people carved in relief onto the walls seemed to be watching the intruders while their hands worked, bent over bodies, sacrifices, bowls.

"We should leave this place," Jezlen said.

"We're trying, Jezlen, really we are," Derk grumbled, pulling ahead of the group and setting a quicker pace, eager to put all of this place behind them.

More than once Derk found himself reaching for his shortsword. Occasionally he heard the cocking of a crossbow or the stretch of a bowstring from Jezlen or Asa. Yet nothing gave him a reason to draw the entire time they stalked the quiet halls, ascended the silent staircases, passed through the noiseless rooms. They were the only things alive in the entire structure, menaced by the images of speculated horror that adorned the ancient walls. Still, his hand moved to the hilt of his blade.

There seemed to be no end to the temple, and they had to make camp within its stone walls once again. Derk dreamed of being sacrificed by those beings, smooth cold hands of stone gripping him by his limbs. They carried him to a gate leading to an inky darkness which made his stomach cramp with fear and his brain scream in terror. He was glad to take his watch and the next day found all of them hurrying through the vast temple, eager to put it all behind them.

After what seemed like two watches of walking a beam of light popped ahead of them. Derk stood up straight as the welcome natural illumination reached his eyes. He could hear Devra gasp with delight behind him and Asa thanked the Goddess for bringing them to the end safely. The group ran toward the exit, almost knocking each other over to get out of the breathless oubliette.

They squinted in the bright light and grinned at each other as they spilled out of the temple, relieved. White, bright sunlight bathed them all and Derk knelt down on the ground, laying his face on the sparse grass sprouting from the dirt. They were high up though not at an extreme elevation, rolling hills spreading below them. Huddles of farms and the white roof of a church welcomed them from below. Derk blinked a few times and looked out over the land, his lips pressed together as he cocked his head to the side.

"How fortunate for us," said Jezlen, looking over the green that lay before them, finally resting his longbow across his back. "We find ourselves above the Moorlands, a good place to be after such an ordeal. We shall find...."

Moorlands. Derk went pale and he felt panic rising. Jezlen stopped talking and Devra was asking him questions, clapping her gloved hands excitedly. He felt the sensation of Sindra squeezing his arm but couldn't react accordingly, only managing to utter a single sentence.

"You sure you all don't want to maybe go back through the way we just...came? No?" He hadn't even managed to say it loud enough for anyone to hear, and his companions were all too excited to be out of the cavern to notice his state. Though his knees were knocking together, he managed to follow the group down, taking the tail end instead of the lead like he usually did. Moorland. Through a lack of luck or by trickery, he was back where he had started.

Chapter 12
Laid Bare

Derk drew the razor one last time over his scalp, wincing slightly as it nicked his skin. It wasn't the first time he had done so, and he imagined his pink scalp was dotted with spots of red blood, noting there was the definite feeling of a trickle on the right side. He ran his free hand over his head, not surprised to find it stained crimson, rinsing his razor and then his hand in the cold water of the stream. Derk dipped his head in the stream, the icy water stinging the cuts but the pain was minor and bearable. Lifting his scalp out from the waterway, water dripping down his face and around his nose, he looked to the priestess who watched him with crossed arms, her lips hidden with dismay. Derk held his arms out to the side, presenting himself to her. "Well? What d'yah think?"

"I still don't understand why you have done this," Sindra said, turning away and walking back the short distance to the rest of the camp. "You have beautiful hair, or did. You look like a peasant or a prisoner."

"Well, for your information, I am a peasant," he shot, surprised how quickly the words escaped his lips, like a projectile and not a fact. "And high summer is upon us. I'll be cooler this way." He closed the razor with a snap, almost cutting his finger on its edge.

"I agree with the priestess," said Jezlen, sitting up straight as he spoke. Derk shot Jezlen a look, not remembering asking his opinion. The elf stood up, cocking his head to the side as he inspected the now bald thief, eyes half open. "I believe she is being too kind with her comparisons. You look more like one who is…wrong in the head." Jezlen pointed to his own head as he said it, nodding as he agreed with himself.

"Well, if I could think about something mean to say about you right now I'd say it. Except I can't think of anything at the moment," Derk snapped, going to his pack and fumbling through it, looking more for something to do than anything in particular. He found himself irritated by the elf's inspection, looking to Asa and Devra, the girl counting coins and the warrior redressing one of his wounds. "Well, how do I look to a Valleyman's eye?"

"Keen. Intense. Skilled." Asa said. The warrior scratched at the bandage on his shoulder, looking over Derk. "Like…like a hired killer!!"

"What?" Derk shot. He wasn't sure if he should be amused or angry.

"I mean a soldier," Asa said. "One of the guardsmen. Alert!"

"What my brother means to say," said Devra, gathering up the coins and placing them in a small leather pouch, "Is it is a very bold look. Now that your hair isn't hanging in your face, you can see how blue your eyes are."

"Do I look like myself, though?" Derk asked. This was the heart of the matter and he needed an honest opinion. They were back in Cartaskin territory and Derk would not take the chance of being recognized. The chance was slim, given the fact no one was looking for him, but Derk would rather be over cautious than over confident. He avoided Sindra's gaze.

"In a way, but not really." Devra offered. She gestured at him with a finger as she went over his appearance, smiling broadly at him. "Your beard's more scruffy than before and well, you're shinier up top."

"I think it looks good," Asa blurted. Derk figured he was trying to make up for his ignorant comment from before. "Maybe I'll do the same," Asa continued. "So we can match. That'll draw the attention off of you. It is getting to be hot, it's not a bad idea."

"I'm not...I'm not looking for us to be triplets now, Asa. Thank you but two knob heads bobbing around might actually call more attention." Derk took a breath, placing his hands on his head and remembering something he wanted from his pack. "Are you two going into the town proper or not?"

"Yeah, who's got things to be taken in, who needs what?" Devra tucked the pouch into her belt, exchanging it for her gloves and pulling them on. "We might be long.

Asa's shoulder isn't healing the way I'd like. We're going to try and find some medicine for it, if not a healer. No offense, Sindra."

"None taken," Sindra replied, sipping from her waterskin. "My training in the healing arts is basic, as required by my order. Us priestesses rarely have to mend these types of wounds. I'm sorry I can't help you more, Asa."

"No need to apologize," Asa mumbled. Asa wasn't facing them as he spoke, but Derk knew his face would be red with embarrassment. Derk spared Asa from further humiliation by keeping his worry for the burly fighter to himself. Asa had fought valiantly and taken most of the blows, protecting them. "I know you did your best." he said to Sindra, so gracious even as he scratched at his wound.

"But something to take into town, right?" Derk asked Devra. He did have something to send off, though, so he dug around in his bag for the letter he had written a few days ago. Plus, he was sure Asa would be glad to have the attention off of him. He pulled the letter out and handed it to Devra.

"Back to Portsmouth, eh?" Devra said, looking over the address. "I thought you said you didn't have any family?" She smiled, her eyes sparkling in the summer sun,

"What, I can't have friends besides you all?" Derk asked. "Is it hard to believe?"

"Yes," said Jezlen, not looking up from whatever he was doing.

"That's not what I meant," Devra laughed, sticking her tongue out at the Forester. "Just, two letters in under a moon. You must be nervous, or have someone nervous about you." Before Derk could think of what to say Devra turned her attention to Sindra and Jezlen. "And you two?"

Jezlen handed Devra a small pouch. "Some tobacco," was all he said as Devra brought it to her nose, sniffing it.

"What is this?" she asked. "This isn't money."

"Heartberry seed," Jezlen said. "Enough for tobacco."

"Jezlen, you have to give her money for tobacco, not trade. She's doing you a favor, not asking for work." Sindra sighed and waited as Jezlen muttered something and handed Devra a few coins.

"Sindra?" Asa asked. "You need anything?"

"I'm fine," Sindra said. "Good luck in town."

Derk watched the siblings as they disappeared down hill. They were three days into the Cartaskin Barony and as he started to recognize different land features and bends in roads, Derk had grown more nervous, talking less and keeping to the center of the party. All the towns with walls were collecting gate taxes and some of the roads even had guards, demanding fees to use the roads, so the group started traveling through the woods to avoid being pecked to death by fees. Sindra's standing with the Church did nothing to lessen the cost. Derk's convenient rumors of the area further convinced the group traveling off the road was a better idea and when pressed to answer how he knew so much, he simply credited stories he had from other bar patrons.

Derk settled down on the ground, deciding to clean his nails and maybe take a nap. As soon as he sat down, Sindra sat beside him, laying her head in his lap, her long, dark hair spilling over his legs and onto the grass. He played with her hair absentmindedly, finally able to relax for the first time in what seemed like far too long. The cavern from which they had emerged took the primary toll on his nerves. The constant worrying about what could possibly happen in the lands he grew up in kept him awake at night and nervous during the day. Plus they would have to cross the Freewild again to get to Portsmouth, though above ground travel would be far less dangerous. He thought Sindra had fallen asleep and was about to close his eyes and do the same when she spoke.

"Sending letters to that woman again?" she asked. Derk blinked, trying to ascertain her mood by the tone of her voice, not sure why she was asking. He paused, confusion making the skin on his forehead pucker, blinking again as he laid a hand on her side.

"Again? You mean for the second time?" Why had she asked? He traced his finger around her pointed ear, tucking her hair around it so he could see her beautiful face. The sun turned her skin even darker and her cheek was smooth under his caress, as always. "This is only the second letter. Letting her know where we are and I'm safe. Can't have her worrying, you know?"

"Of course not." She sat up so she faced him and he was surprised to see her face was very serious, her grey eyes dark and heavy lidded. "You are good friends, aren't you?"

"Old Gam's my best friend, after you all. First person I met worth talking to in Portsmouth. Smart. Helped me get my bearings when I got into town. Y'know?" The expression on her face never changed but Derk felt sweat starting to pop on his forehead for some reason. "Put me up when I had no place to go. A drinking buddy." He felt as if she was searching for something else and he wracked his brain for what it could possibly be but came up blank. "What? I'd write you a letter if we were apart, if that's what's bothering you." Maybe that was it. Perhaps she wanted reassurance she was worth the parchment and ink. "I love you, Sindra, you know that."

The elven woman sat up and then stood, shaking her robes free of dirt and grass as she walked away. Derk stood up, alarmed, tripping over his pack as he chased after her. "What, where're you going? You can't go into town by yourself! The entry tax!"

"I have money to get into town," she said, her words curt and low, her eyes not fixing on him but looking past him as she addressed him. "I'll be back before evening."

"Sin, I mean…come on, don't go. What did I say?" Her hood was already up despite the heat and she walked through the brush toward the road, a grey splash swaying among the sun burned greens and browns of the plants. He couldn't help but watch her move as she walked away and once she was out of his sight, he spun around, looking to the other Forester who had been watching. "How can someone so beautiful be so…."

"Annoying?" Jezlen finished braiding his long black hair, tying the end with a leather cord and wrapped his arms around his knees. "Sindra and I are both of the Forest. It does not mean I understand her."

"Yeah, women, eh?" Derk shrugged and walked back over to the camp, sprawling on the ground across from Jezlen, the sun peeking out from behind some clouds overhead. He ran his hand over his scalp as he got comfortable on the grass, not able to keep himself from looking in the direction Sindra had gone. "I mean, I treat her well, don't I? I practically worship the woman, as if she was the Goddess herself and she never protests, does she? I tell her she's beautiful and smart. What more does she want from me?" Derk pulled out a handful of grass and tossed it aside, wiping the blades stuck on his hands on his leg.

"What women want, which is whatever we cannot figure out at the moment," offered Jezlen, his face still morose as if he did not understand the hilarity of his statement. Derk laughed out loud, though not as long as he would have liked; the elf's serious face dampened his enjoyment of what he thought of as a jest. Jezlen often said things that seemed like they were jokes but he rarely laughed or smiled. Derk cleared his throat, unable to keep his eyes from wandering to the trail again, considering how to ask the Forester a peculiar question heavy on his mind.

"So, Jez, I've a query for you," he said. Jezlen gave no indication he was listening nor that he wouldn't answer so Derk dove in. The worst that could happen would be Jezlen tuning him out. "I don't mean to be rude or such but…what's going on? I mean, you're related to Sindra and granted she's got her own little oddities, but you? I don't get you." Derk shook his head and looked over Jezlen, his sharp features unfazed by what Derk said. Maybe he had tuned him out, Derk thought, waving his hand in front of the elf's face. Jezlen set his eyes on Derk with a snap, and they shone as they fastened on him. For a moment, Derk wasn't sure if Jezlen was about to laugh or strike him but he waited to see the outcome before placing a bet on either emotion.

"You do not...get me?" Jezlen asked. He seemed amused by the question. "And you compare me to Sindra. Sindra and I are not...alike." The elf looked down to the ground, playing with the edge of his bedroll, his face thoughtful as he spoke "I was born and raised more...secluded than she. She was born in a village and moved to the city. In her temple she is often with other worshipers, able to enjoy the communion of the other followers of the Goddess. I....." The young man just shook his head.

"So, spend a lot of time alone, eh?"

"One could see it that way, I suppose," Jezlen said, curiosity starting to streak across the lines on his forehead. "It is interesting you say you do not understand me, when in truth, I could say the same about you. You are a difficult man to follow, Derk."

"I can't say I follow your meaning," said Derk, breaking eye contact with the elf whose gaze had become too intense for his liking. He set his own eyes on his shoe and started to undo the laces, busying himself with the banal task of tightening them. "I'm just the meddler, good for a jab every now and again. Asa's brains, Devra's brawn and Sindra's, well...I keep her warm enough at night, I suppose. Sorry I can't be of much help to you. If you're ever cold at night, be sure to give me a tug, I'll see what I can do."

"You are trying to distract me with your jokes," said Jezlen, chuckles changing the cadence of his words. "I think you may indeed 'follow my meaning,' as you say. You are a strange mix of the high born men drinking wine at their long tables and the common streetsman begging for blueies for a mug of beer. You punch like a bastard and wield your dagger like it's the finest blade ever forged," Jezlen smirked, his expression sly as he locked eyes with Derk again, the thief not pulling away this time but staring back. Jezlen slapped at a bug that landed on his neck, muttering something foreign under his breath before looking at Derk once more. "Where does this come from?"

"If I tell you, it takes all the fun out of guessing, don't it?" Derk wasn't going to back down and he wasn't going to give Jezlen what he wanted, as simple a request as it was. He thought he would have been more unnerved by the confrontation but he realized he had been expecting it for a long time. Derk was only surprised that it was Jezlen, who knew him least, who brought it up. Something told him Jezlen asked not out of concern, as might be the case with the others but out of curiosity. His words seemed to intrigue the elf more and his ears actually perked up, his eyes wide with amusement.

"Your past life is a puzzle for me to figure out?" Jezlen asked, laughter finally lilting in his voice. The Forester chuckled, the serious expressions he had pulled the last two weeks seeming miles away from the person who sat before Derk. Jezlen reached into his pack, pulling out a pipe and filling it with tobacco from his tin before bringing it to his lips. "Well, most people are so obvious to read, a challenge is a nice change."

"You're the one making the challenge for yourself. I'm an open book!"

"And the story seems to change every time you turn a page," Jezlen said, pulling a twig out of the campfire to light his pipe. He puffed on it a few times, his mouth twisting, taking a few drags before he wrapped his arms around his legs and stared at Derk, locking his gaze on him again.

"It is obvious you were born to a higher station in life, since raising oneself up in the Valley is difficult, especially in your lifespan. In addition, no one who has started off low and manages to raise himself goes back to the lesser ways of living, if he can help it. You do not strike me as a man who lets things happen to him, but rather as one who makes his way. So you must have thrust yourself upon this lifestyle zealously, probably burning a few bridges in his wake, as they say." Jezlen puffed again on the pipe as he collected his thoughts like the smoke in his lungs. Derk saw his eyes watering as the herbs worked their way into his brain. Still, Jezlen cocked his head at Derk, something like a smirk showing on his mouth. "You never think what you are doing is wrong. Ever."

"Oh, everyone thinks that," Derk said, looking away again, the same previously nervous feeling prickling at his stomach again. He tugged at another handful of grass, trying to toss it into the fire, most of it blowing back on him. "Most people are stubbornly against taking blame, faulting someone or something else."

"But you actually believe it," said Jezlen, leaning back on the rock. "In your eyes, you are without blame. If it works for you, fine, and you are conveniently optimistic about the consequences which might befall others. You are definitely the hero of your own story."

Derk sat there, still pulling up grass with his hands. Was he really all those things? He shook his head, sneering sightly as he looked the elf dead in the eye. "Well, if you're so smart, what about you? You're finished gutting me out here on the grass, how about you make me feel not so sheepish and show a little bone?"

Jezlen grinned, a peculiar smile which seemed more wolfish than anything else. "Ah, you will take the safe bet and not try to analyze me yourself, fearing you may be wrong. I am not a complicated person." He held up his hand, counting off as he spoke, starting off with his thumb. "I am driven by the base things. Hunger, thirst, lust, things of that nature. I want peace of mind. Sometimes while looking for peace, I am led to danger." Jezlen took one last drag off of the pipe before offering it Derk with both hands. "I have found both with you, I think."

"My bedroll offer was a joke, Jezlen!" Derk laughed, taking the pipe from him and bringing the tip of it to his lips. He had never smoked before and it showed as he puffed on it, immediately exhaling, choking on the first real pull he took. The smart comment he had meant to say stuck in his throat as he coughed. He felt his eyes watering.

"You do not smoke?" asked Jezlen, laughing loudly. It was an awkward sound, almost rusty as if he wasn't used to being amused "What kind of ruffian are you? At least tell me you play cards!"

"Now that, I do," Derk said after a good while, tears streaming from his eyes, his throat feeling raw. "I'll go get my cards."

"Oh no, we will be using mine," insisted Jezlen, reaching into his pack and pulling out a deck, untying the ribbon keeping the cards together. "You may not smoke like a dog but I imagine your card skills include tricks. I do not wish to be thrashed outright."

"Do elven dogs smoke? And I can play for pleasure," Derk said, chuckling slightly as the elf began to deal, watching the cards he lay in front of him. Jezlen didn't trust him. Derk had to laugh, sighing as he picked up the cards and looked over them. "It'll be nice to play for fun and not for supper. Though I warn you," he added, eyes glinting merrily at someone he now considered a friend. "The thrashing will come whether we use your cards or not."

Chapter 13
Past, Present, and Future

"Thanks, mam," Derk laughed, taking the food from Asa. Asa blushed and Devra looked up from her journal, glaring at Derk. "Tits, it was just a joke," he shot, panic rising in his voice. "Lay off me."

"I know it was," Asa said, handing a plate to Jezlen. The Forester wrinkled his nose at the food. "Didn't your pa ever cook for you?"

"My pa never cooked a day in his life," Derk said. That was the truth. If his mother cooked, he didn't remember, and his step-mother never had. "You just...you're a mother hen, Asa."

"He's always been that way," Devra shot. "Asa's a caring person. It's just the way he is. You should be glad someone can cook, and cook well at that."

Jezlen screamed and Derk jumped in his seat, wondering what had caused the elf to startle so. Hot grease dripped down his chin. Derk smirked and cut into his food, shaking his head. "Too simple to know how to eat a sausage?"

"We do not have exploding meat where I am from," Jezlen said, wiping his chin with the back of his hand. He had a red mark under his mouth.

"You should put something on that," Asa said, putting the spoon back in the pot and turning to Jezlen. "It's going to leave a scar if you don't."

"Maybe you should kiss it and make it all better," Derk offered. Jezlen batted his eyelashes at the brawny Asa and soon the three men were laughing. Devra didn't seem to be amused by Derk's joke.

"Don't fret, Devra. You know Derk was only kidding." Asa said, retrieving the medicine bag.

"Maybe a kiss from you would be work better," Jezlen said to Devra. He tilted his head to her with something like hope. The corners of Devra's mouth curled upward slightly.

"I'll break your neck, Jez, and no amount of kisses would heal it," Asa said. Derk laughed loudly, and Asa and Devra joined in though the Forester seemed less amused. He rubbed the salve on his chin.

"When is the priestess coming back?" Jezlen asked.

"Eh, she said she wanted to fellowship with the other priestesses but she wouldn't be too long." Asa served himself food finally and sat down next to his sister, bringing her plate as well. "The service was very good. The priestess spoke on the Goddess and the Sympathy of the Willow Tree. "

"I'm familiar with the sermon," Derk said, finishing his meal and pulling out his handkerchief to clean his hands. He knew the story by heart. It was one of favorites, actually. He huffed, actually disappointed he had missed it. "Did they sing 'In Thine Arms'?" Derk found the small bag he kept his dice in and pulled them out.

"Yeah, actually." Asa's brows furrowed on his face. "I'd never heard it before."

"It's a shame. It's a beautiful song," Derk said quickly. He rattled his dice in his hand. "Written by the Sister Kerida of the Silver Heart."

"Did Sindra tell you this?" Devra asked, smirking.

"No, I know about it because I pay attention and read," he shot. "I'm probably the most devout out of all of you, I'll have you know. And not just because of Sindra." It seemed like a lifetime ago, but afternoons spent with the priestess and evenings with his brother had embedded the information in his brain. His own loneliness fueled his devotion. The more he attended temple, the angrier his father had seemed. And ever since taking up his new life he didn't see the reason to stop attending service. It was quiet and peaceful. Under The Goddess' cool gaze he could sort out his thoughts, packing the ones he didn't want to deal with away and giving them over to her, keeping gladness in his heart. He had to be devout. In his own way, but he did love the Goddess.

"Definitely more devout than I am," Jezlen muttered. The elf rubbed at his chin and looked at his hand, grimacing.

"That's not saying much," Devra said.

"Anyone up for a game of dice?" Derk offered. Only one was loaded. "Crow Catcher? Blossom Fall? Chaw?"

"I like Chaw," Asa said, eyes brightening. "We used to play it in training school. I won a pair of britches once." He smiled proudly.

"Are you a lucky fellow then, Asa?" Derk asked, throwing the dice into his other hand. He'd won more than a pair of pants in his time but he wasn't about to go into the details and dissuade his friends from play. Besides, he wanted to play to pass the time, not for supper.

"My mam says I am," Asa said without a trace of irony or sarcasm. Derk managed to not laugh, but he caught Devra giving her brother a pained look.

"I am playing," Jezlen said quickly. Derk squatted down, the rest of them circling around for the game. A rustle in the grass drew Derk's eyes and he smiled as he saw Sindra come up over the hill, the sun setting behind her. She smiled primly at Derk and the rest of them.

"I'll play in a bit, I'll get you some supper fixed, Sin," Asa said, starting to rise from his seat.

"No need to worry, Asa. I had evening meal at the temple." Sindra bowed her head. Derk narrowed his eyes at her. She seemed a bit less jovial than normal. What had happened in town?

"Are we going to play or not?" Jezlen said impatiently. He put a clean bowl on the grass to throw the dice into. "Play, play, play, now."

"Calm down!" Derk chided, the Forester pulling his attention away from the priestess. They all circled round and played, the dice rattling merrily in the bowl as the sun set over the hills. Asa's mom was right. He was lucky. They played for points and the simple warrior quickly accumulated twice as many points as all of them combined.

Jezlen and Devra didn't seem to mind. The elf rather seemed to enjoy the thrashing but it was too much for Derk. He left the circle in the second round of Crow Catcher, deciding a walk in the surrounding forest would do him some good.

It was hot but with the evening came a cool breeze and wispy dark blue clouds stretched across the sky beyond the tops of the trees. Derk wiped his nose with the back of his hand and stared up at the sky, a few stars bright enough to shine through the dying sunlight. He knew the stars and the view. Derk hadn't been here before specifically but the roll of the land, the types of trees and the splay of branches were all familiar. It might have called up nostalgia in another man, but in Derk it conjured something like panic in his belly so he pulled his eyes away, bringing his hands to his face.

"I know why you have been uneasy since the cave and I have something to tell you." He jumped, surprised to hear Sindra's low, sweet voice floating over the night air. Something about how she left and the expression on her face when she returned from temple told him something happened. While her approach had surprised him, the fact what was bothering her was about him did not, though he dreaded it. Derk bent down to pick up a few twigs, tossing them end over end at a tree up ahead, not bothering to turn around and face her.

"Do you, now? Well, it's a day for analysis, and such. I'll let you have your turn." Derk felt hostility rise up over him, like armor. He threw his last stick before turning around, Sindra's shape blending into the trees and ferns around her. He saw her face, her eyes shining in the dark. "Out with it. I don't want to be up all night."

"Dershik...." Whatever she said after that was lost. It was as if all the air and sound had been sucked out of the forest suddenly. The name washed over him like an enchantment, a low buzz humming in his ears and spreading up to his brain till his senses were awash with confusion, blending so that he felt sound and heard colors. Then something broke through: anger and fear. It bubbled in his belly, red hot yet icy, slimy black breaking through the fog, snapping his brain back into the forest with the priestess, who was still speaking. Derk turned away sharply, his face twisted with disgust, trying to push what threatened to emerge down into himself.

"Don't say that name! How dare you speak it to me!" he hissed, fixing his eyes on the ground. His fists were balled and the knuckles white circles surrounded with red. "I don't know where you heard it or what made you think should address me as such but...don't."

"But it is your name, isn't it?" Derk heard her words as she approached him. It was just a few steps closer but it made him more anxious. She stood beyond his reach as a priestess, not the woman he kissed and loved. "It is your given name, though, isn't it?" Sindra asked. "The name your father gave you?"

It struck him like a blow to the chest. For a moment Derk thought he might actually strike her. Anger burned in his heart, in his brain and hands. But wrath melted to fear and then betrayal as he took a step back from her. "Who told you these things? Who told you this?"

"The priestess at the temple of Moorland told me," Sindra said, her voice slightly above a whisper. There was a moment of silence, the forest seeming dead around them. Derk considered what she said and what should be his next statement or question. He looked at the priestess out of the corner of his eye, glancing at her briefly before shamefully looking back to the ground.

"There...there is no temple in Moorland," he muttered. "Not here. There is only a shrine."

"A temple was built. And a priestess assigned to it." Sindra spoke the words as if they were to offer hope and not condemnation. She took a step toward him as Derk tried to think of what could have led to this. "I spoke with her, intending only to vent my own personal issues and you came up. I spoke on you and the priestess...well, she said she...might know you. You sounded familiar to her. I spoke more and she said she did know you. Then she told me about you." Derk found himself pacing angrily across the small clearing, running his hand over his bald head, agitated with what Sindra just said. "Don't be alarmed," she responded, her voice calmer than how he felt "Your secrets are safe with me."

"I would rather have it safe with the person I left it with," he spat, stopping short on his path and gesturing violently toward the town. Derk paced a few more times, breathing heavily as he considered what Sindra might have told Cira and what Cira had revealed. "I don't understand how she could have done this! She is a priestess of the Goddess! Who keeps secrets! How could she speak a word of anything I said to anyone?!"

"As ladies of the White Calling, we make each other available to one another in order to help share the burdens of what we know," she said. Something in her words sounded like annoyance. "The secrets are safe within the

Circle, but their weight must be spread evenly, lest one part bear too much and break. And…I am not just anyone. I am your lover and she thought it was important I know something so I could tell you. Derk-"

"What, do I have a child running around somewhere from her? Is that it?"

Sindra turned her face away from him and her face grew dark. She looked as if she had just been slapped. The priestess stood there for a moment, looking at the ground. Sindra pressed her lips together, breathing out forcefully before she spoke, her words quiet and robbed of any sentiment.

"No, Derk, your father…he's dead."

Derk managed to find the ground under him, sitting cross legged as he stared forward, dazed by what he had just been told. His father, the great Baron who aspired to unite entire Valley under his Crown, with his Coin. His beard was hardly streaked with grey when Derk left home, his eyes a steely, fiery blue. The sword and strike of Baron Cartaskin had been feared by many a man within a day's ride. In truth, Dershik had feared him; but Derk was shocked. He couldn't understand how this could be true. Derk turned his eyes to the priestess, unaware there were tears threatening at the corners of his eyes. "Was it…how did he die?"

"It was an accident," Sindra said, her voice steady. There was a hint of pity in her voice and it drew Derk's eyes to her. "He was out riding a horse given to him as a gift for Baron's Day. It threw him off and he was gravely injured. He suffered for a half a watch before passing on."

Derk wished he hadn't shaved his head so he could run his fingers through his hair and pull at it. His father, the great Baron, killed by a feisty horse? It didn't seem right. His father had been a great horseman as well; the fact one dared to even toss its head in his presence...a thought shot through his mind and he looked up suddenly, hoping Sindra had the answer. "And my brother...how is he doing as the Baron?"

"Not well, actually," she said as she drew in her breath. Her face was tweaked with discomfort. "Your father didn't declare him his rightful heir after you di...left, nor did he any of the times he told his men he would. He only passed on the seat to your brother on his death bed and now some of the nobles and magistrates are saying there were not enough witnesses there to attest to the fact he ever did. A faction of them are saying your son is the rightful Baron now and his maternal grandfather should be his regent."

"Deril is not my son. He's my brother's son."

"I don't understand how that works exactly since he is your former wife's son-"

"I didn't father that child. And she's not my wife. I'm dead; by law, Ceric can marry Jerila and adopt Deril." Derk knew that. But something on Sindra's face pricked his confidence.

"You forget who your father was, don't you?" Sindra said. There was a cold anger in her words. Now Derk saw it on her face. He saw the resemblance between her and Jezlen. But her anger was worse, keen and quiet. For a moment he thought Sindra knew everything, about how Darix Cartaskin had thought to make himself King of the Valley but he waited, wincing under her gaze.

"Your father was a stubborn man. Hard against the Church. And cruel to those he should have protected," Sindra said, sounding angry. "Jerila was forbidden to remarry. He turned her into a rather pathetic figure. The widowed young woman, her husband torn away from her by miscreant peasants. He had all the common folk afraid of him and the nobles on his side. Now he is dead." She paused for a moment. Sindra didn't sound pleased or saddened by the Baron's death. "Your brother, who by some grace of the Goddess, was allowed to become a priest is left at the helm, not sure who to endear himself to or how to go about doing so. There are rumors of some of the northern holds pulling away. The other Barons have kept it under their beds to keep people from growing nervous but it may get worse, Derk. Because you wouldn't bear a title."

"Because I COULDN'T!" he shouted, springing up from his seat, finally grabbing a hold of Sindra by the shoulders, pulling her forward so violently her forehead knocked into his nose. He felt the force but the pain would not register as he shook her, her hair falling across her face. "I couldn't! I'm not a Baron, I'm not a lord to be over people! I never believed I was better than the crowds who tilled the land or the hordes in their finery storming our home with fancy words and lavish gifts! You know me! Could you see me doing any of it? The bowing, the ordering, the...if I had taken the seat, it would be worse, I assure you, because I'd be doing another man's job and not my own. Miserable men do not make good rulers." Sindra looked up at him as if he were mad and he probably did seem that way. He loosened his grip on her shoulders and drew her close to him, burying his head in her hair as he spoke, the tears threatening all this while finally falling. "I just...Sindra, you know me best. Am I a lord?"

"You're not a lord of any land," she said quietly, gently pulling away from him, a sad smile playing on her lips as she gazed up at him. "You're not. I'm...I'm going to bed." She sighed and bowed her head before she turned and made her way back to the camp, leaving him there in there in the midst of the trees.

He stood there for a while. Clouds had rolled in and kept the starlight and moonlight from penetrating the canopy. Derk found himself in the dark rubbing his arms, feeling chilly and alone and turned heel to get back to the camp, walking more quickly than he realized. He popped out from the ring of trees, Jezlen looking up from the fire. The Forester's face actually colored a bit with surprise. Derk blew on his hands, sitting in front of the fire and staring into it, hoping the elf would start the conversation. He wasn't sure if he could come up with anything to talk about.

"Good time or bad time with Sindra?" Jezlen finally asked, raising a dark eyebrow at the man. He sipped something out of a flask. His hair was slightly less neat than before, a few stray wisps falling into his face. They do look alike, Sindra and him, Derk thought to himself. He probably stared at the elf too long because Jezlen took another drink from his flask and turned his gaze into the fire.

"Y'know, it's rude to talk about your...aunt like that," Derk retorted, still rubbing his arms. His chest was warm enough now, but his back feeling the chill of the night air. Jezlen laughed, short and harsh, still looking into the flames

"Do not make me laugh, Valleyman. Like I care." Derk laughed out loud, almost giggling as the words registered. He looked over Jezlen again, trying to ascertain if he actually was younger than the woman who usually laid her bedroll next to his. Jezlen took another gulp from his flask before he abruptly offered it to Derk. "You look like you need this. Your eyes look as if you were just crying."

"I…." Derk held the flask in his hands, the thing too warm to have just been opened. He sighed, his breath whistling in the neck of the flask as he brought it to his lips. "I just found out my father died." He took the sip, the liquor hot in his mouth and rough on his throat, warming as it made its way into his gut.

"Ah," Jezlen said, taking the flask back from him, draining it in one gulp, turning it upside down to speed the task. The elf wiped his mouth with the back of his hand, tightening the lid and tossing it at his pack, missing completely and almost hitting Asa in the head. He turned woozily back to Derk. "Was he a great man or a man not worth mentioning?"

"He was a great man, to be sure," Derk offered, momentarily worrying Jezlen would pitch into the fire. He waited till the elf leaned away before continuing. "Great. An idealist, like me, as you suppose. Only his ideals…he wanted to press on other people. He thought things should be a…a certain way. But he's dead now." He nodded, wishing Jezlen hadn't finished off whatever was in the flask. The fact of his father's death was sinking further into his brain. He could use a drink.

"And do you feel the bite of your own mortality, Valleyman?" Jezlen stood up somehow, teetering forward. He had to lean on Derk to stand up, his shadow long and quavering as Jezlen swayed by the fire. Derk stared up at him, hugging his knees to his chest. He considered what the Forester said.

"No, actually. I don't," Derk said, turning his head back into the fire. He wondered why this was when Jezlen leaned down again, resting his hand a bit too heavily on his shoulder, almost knocking him down.

"Well, you should. At least your father had children to keep himself going. You have no one to leave your legacy so if you die, you are done." Jezlen leaned over and kissed Derk sloppily on the forehead, patting him on his bald head before stumbling over to his pack.

"Jezlen, you're drunk! You said you'd take the watch!" he hissed at the elf, the young man already sprawled out on his bed roll. The drunk elf lifted an arm in the air, not bothering to roll over as he replied.

"I am too drunk to watch and you will not sleep…you watch." Derk hissed a few more words of protest but as far as he could tell, the elf was out cold. Derk cursed under his breath, grabbing a blanket to draw over his shoulders as he sat watch. A slow chuckle bubbled up as he looked over the drunk elf snoring a few paces away.

It was a bit too much. The chuckle changed to a laugh and then a low sob as he pulled the blanket closer around him, the edges of the fabric growing damp with his tears. The elf was right. He wouldn't be able to sleep. Derk thought of the father he feared and respected, the brother he thrust in harm's way, and the nephew who might be treated more like a tool than an actual person. And what legacy was Derk leaving on the earth? All the ideals he had for himself...what was the point if he never passed them on? If they didn't change anything? If all that remained after him were the results of his mistakes?

He cried as he looked into the fire, sobbing until he felt he was actually tired enough to sleep and sleep well. But the elf snored and Derk's eyes still burned from salt water and too much rubbing. He would take time to get himself together and in the morning would present himself as a brand new man to his mates. The truth was he wouldn't be able to help his brother or nephew with his presence. It would probably cause more problems. He would continue to lay low as they passed through the territory. All he would offer them were his prayers and good wishes. It would have to be sufficient.

Something moved behind him and Derk looked, catching sight of Sindra rolling over, her beautiful face showing faintly in the firelight. She was an aunt. Maybe he could make something more of her. He wished he could crawl up beside her but he knew if he did, he would most likely fall asleep, leaving the camp vulnerable.

Derk rose from his seat to stretch his legs, still looking at Sindra, a smile playing on his face. She made him happy and loved him, didn't she? More than he infuriated her and vice-versa, they loved each other. After they returned the chalice he would see how they played out and do what he could to keep her. After all, he was an honorable man and loved her with his heart. That was more than enough, wasn't it?

The elf snored again, jarring Derk from his thoughts of a thief and a priestess building a home together. He sat down by the fire again, sitting to the side of it so he wouldn't be blinded by its brightness. There were a few more hours to go and more than enough tree seeds around to throw at Jezlen to keep him occupied. Derk gathered up a handful before he tossed one overhand, the seed almost landing in the sleeping man's mouth.

The fire popped suddenly, jolting him and Asa stirred, looking at Derk for a moment before smiling and going back to sleep. Legacy. Derk sighed. He still felt cold and wished he could get his thoughts on death far from his mind, its black imprint sullying the more cheerful thoughts he had been entertaining before. A life of being a husband and thief…he could manage it, right? He could have his Sindra life, as well as his Old Gam, surely?

But violence would still come, stars would still fall. People would try to come up against him and try to tell him he couldn't have either. A cinder falling into his hand and the low, sad cry of a bird were all it took to start the tears in his eyes again, not for his father, but for himself.

Chapter 14
Acceptance and Rejection

Derk wore his second best shirt and his best pair of britches, with boots cleaned and buckles shined. His short, sandy hair was combed and slicked back with sweet oil, his face clean shaven, the bit of pink dancing at the surface of his skin suggesting he hadn't sharpened his razor as keenly as he should have.

In his hands, the fingernails void of dirt, was a small wooden box, the decoration without hinting at the value of the contents within. Yet for all this, Sindra walked away from him, her back turned, hands engulfed by her dark, lustrous hair as she ran her slender fingers over her head in frustration. Derk stood there, his hands still poised to open the box, the words he was about to speak stuck in his throat. He managed to push them back and find the appropriate words for the situation, taking a step toward the priestess. "What, Sindra?" he asked quietly, his boots sounding noisy in the small room as he approached her.

"What's the matter?"

"Don't," was all she said, but the urgency in her voice was clear, her hands trembling as she brought them out of her hair and to the sides of her face. Cold, white sunlight streamed through the one window in her chamber, the square of illumination falling on the table and the wooden floor. Derk crossed into the square of light, his excitement temporarily quenched rising up in him again as he undid the clasp on the box.

"Sindra, please…will you marry me?" He opened the box and a necklace gleamed in the corner of sunlight, tossing up a chunk of reflected light into a corner of the room. What he expected was for the priestess to wheel around and throw her arms around his neck, kissing him passionately on the lips before saying yes. He would pick her up in his arms and walk her over to her bed where they would enjoy each other till vespers.

Instead she bowed her head and brought her hands to her face, her shoulders moving up and down ever so slightly. She pulled her shoulder length hair behind her ears before turning around, her expression saying she pitied the man rather than she wanted to spend the rest of her life with him. Her eyes settled on the contents of the box and they widened, her lips parting slightly as if to speak but she took a breath instead, slowly shaking her head.

"No," she said, closing her eyes as she continued to shake her head. "I will not."

The small room seemed to fall apart around him, the cold from outside suddenly making its way into the room, into his bones. Surely, she hadn't just said what he heard. What had he heard? She stood before him and she looked the same as she had this morning. He last saw her in the temple during morning prayers. He had been there to ask for the blessing of mystery in his next mission as well as traveling mercies. She had been the priestess officiating over the liturgy and rituals and her hand lingered on his jawline as she prayed over him. Now she stood before him and the tenderness was gone. There was an expression on her face he had never seen before and a cold sweat broke out on his forehead as he looked upon her.

"No? Why not?" The box was still open, the gift he had acquired for the occasion still exposed to the open air. He trembled slightly, placing the box on the table, not able to keep the edge off his voice. "Why? I don't understand."

"Because, Derk." She walked up to him, laying a cold, soft hand on the side of his face, her eyes glinting as tears formed in their corners. She still shook her head, laying her forehead on his. Sindra didn't look him in the eye when she spoke. "I don't want to."

"D...don't want to? Why?" Derk felt confusion creeping around his brain, a sensation he rarely felt and did not enjoy. The words were said and he thought he heard them but he didn't understand how they could have come out of Sindra's mouth. She was still the beautiful woman he fell in love with, the same woman he vowed to start a family with all those seasons ago. By the time they had returned with the chalice, he had been under the impression she was going to turn him off. Instead, she embraced him, letting him call upon her when he was able, even going so far as to let him kiss her in public, never refusing him. Now she was saying no. How could she say no?

"How could you say no?" he asked, his voice piqued more with annoyance than grief. Her dark eyebrows raised, a hint of confusion furrowing her brow.

"How? Derk, you can't believe the relationship we have should end in marriage…can you?" She asked him the question as if she was unaware of the answer, curiosity playing on her words.

"Well, I did, obviously. Till now." That part was painfully obvious. "But I was thinking maybe you and I could have a family. A child. And I thought you'd be more likely if we took vows." It was one of the reasons why he asked her to marry him. The first was he loved her but Sindra already knew this. What she wanted was information and he offered it up, hoping by exposing his good intentions and reasons, she might change her mind.

Sindra laughed, a dry, amused chuckle echoing in the chamber. She let her hands drop from her face and she pulled away from him, nodding slowly. "I see now. That is something you would think, isn't it?" She stood behind one of the chairs, resting her hands on its back. Her eyes wandered over to the contents of the jewelry box but she closed them and turned her attention to Derk again.

"What?! I figured with you being a priestess and all, and a recently promoted one I might add, congratulations yet again." He bowed to her in a way which wasn't supposed to be mocking but she looked at him as if it were. Derk straightened up and threw his hands in the air, sighing, exasperated with her disdain. "I know they like priestesses to be bonded if they are to start families."

"Now you consider my calling," she said, glancing to the side. Her hands gripped the back of the chair, the smile on her face wry and her eyes gleaming. "Now. Do you know why our relationship has worked thus far, and don't say love, whatever you do. Actually, don't answer. I am going to tell you why.

"Our relationship worked because my duties as a priestess and your profession as whatever it is you call yourself made us readily available to each other when the other called. I busied myself with my studies and devotions. You busied yourself going on your missions and learning your little tricks in the bars and inns and taverns and alleys of every town you passed through. When I was made the High Priestess of the Temple, you conveniently started going on longer…excursions. It was of little consequence. I had less leisure time as you seem to have plenty of projects to take up yours. However, shortly after my ordination, it was brought to my attention the types of places you frequented and the company you keep."

Sindra paused for a moment, loosening her grip on the chair and bringing the tips of her fingers together, her robes undulating like an ocean in the winter as she crossed the small room. She stood in front of the small screen and wardrobe taking up much of one of the corners of the room, turning to face Derk, who now sat on the other chair. "I know some of the things you have done, I know some of the people you have been working with, and I do not like it. As a priestess, I can grant you secrecy but as a friend, as more than a friend, I cannot and will not approve. You are endangering me as a person and therefore, you are endangering my position and the people I have been charged to care for. I will not marry into trouble."

Derk leaned forward in the chair, rubbing his eye with his hand, his once well groomed hair falling into his face. "I'm not asking you to marry into trouble, Sindra, I'm asking you to marry me. I'll stop doing such shady things once we've settled down and such. I promise."

"No, you won't," she shot. "You won't, I know you won't." Her eyes went over to the open jewelry box, turning her head to the side as she looked at it again. "You keep secrets from me even now, even when you come to temple to give up your cares you still hold things in, I know it. You don't do anything just to get by, you do them because...I don't know, because you feel you must." Sindra's eyes grew cold, her face as hard as one of the moonstone statues adorning the temple just below. "Where have you been the last week?"

"I told you. I was out with some of the fellows, getting some goods back for one of the merchants. Harik. Asa was there."

"I saw Asa three days ago and he said he had been back in town three days before that."

"Once we got the goods back, I sent them ahead and had to stay behind and do something."

"And what was this something you had to do?"

"I had to get you this present!" Derk didn't flinch as he spoke, closing the jewelry box with a loud snap. He stood from his chair, holding the wooden box out to her, eyes narrowed with ire. "I knew I was going to propose to you and I wanted to have a proper gift to give you. It was supposed to be a surprise, so naturally, I didn't tell you where I'd been."

"So you stole it?"

"I got it for you!"

"But you stole it?"

"Chew Her Hems, yes, I stole it!" he shouted, slamming the case down, the wood of the box buckling under the force of his hand and bits of the inlay flying off, skittering across the table and floor. "I saw it and I wanted to get it for you. I also stole the sheets on your bed, most of the jewelry I've given you, if not the whole thing then the components. If it wasn't stolen it was bought with money I took or won gambling." He shook his head, looking down at the crushed box, picking up the scraps of scented wood. The necklace lay haphazardly on the small piece of fabric in which it had been wrapped. Derk stared at Sindra, her eyes on the necklace, her lips pressed together so they disappeared on her face and he sighed, throwing his hands in the air. "But you had to have known this. I don't understand what the trouble is, all of a sudden. I don't know why you can't be with me."

"I can cover your sins, Derk. I cannot stand by them. But that is just it. I don't think you see your deeds as sins."

Derk stiffened, the room suddenly quiet as they stood there, the sounds of the busy street outside muffled by the stones surrounding them. He walked over and kissed her on the cheek, taking her hand and putting the fractured box in it, closing her fingers over it. "I don't." He kissed her on the lips, the priestess pulling away. Sindra pushed the box back into his hands. She shook her head slowly, pulling herself away from him completely before walking to the door of her chamber and opening it.

Derk walked over to the chair, grabbing his coat from the back of it, yanking it on as he gazed at Sindra, trying to drink her in before he left her private chambers forever. Her face was calm, her mouth smiling slightly, her grey eyes sparkling, hinting at a few tears. Derk couldn't understand why she was crying. She wasn't the one who had just been rejected. He buttoned his coat, taking his time with the buttons so he could linger longer, stuffing the box into his pocket before he walked over to the door.

"What will you do with the necklace?" she asked as he stepped over the threshold, her words stopping him short of the stairs. Her eyes looked away from him, her body leaning against the open door. The post of her bed was still in view from where he stood, and he briefly considered ripping off his coat and pulling her after him onto the mattress they had lain so many times. But she asked a question he never considered and he shrugged, feeling the weight of the box in his coat pocket. He reached in, wiggling his fingers through the splintered wood and lifted out the delicate item. Derk held it up, letting the links of metal cascade over the contours of his hand, the weight of the carved stones pulling here and there.

"Will you give it Old Gam?" Sindra asked. Her voice sounded strange. Derk blinked, startled by the question, wondering what she was implying.

"No. She was there when I got it, naturally, and knew why I was after it. It wouldn't be right, y'know?"

"Ah. No. It wouldn't be." Sindra slammed the door with such force, the wind nearly knocked Derk off his feet and down the stairs. He caught himself on the banister, a jagged splinter of wood jamming into his skin. Derk cursed out loud before he brought the injured digit to his mouth. He glared at the door, his now disheveled hair and old coat making him look more like himself than how he appeared on her doorstep just a little while ago.

Maybe it was better off this way, he thought, sucking on his finger as he descended the stairs, his boots clomping loudly. She was beautiful and he loved her but if she couldn't live with what he did, it was probably for the best they didn't get married. The trouble he had gone through to get the necklace had been worth it, though. She had seen it and thought it beautiful. Maybe in a few seasons she would change her mind and decide she could live with him. He would hold onto it until then.

Derk screamed out loud, the jolt of being hit in the back of the head with a snowball unexpected and unwelcome. The snow was already melting against his skin, dripping down his neck despite his efforts to scoop it away. He tried not to glare at the elf who laughed obnoxiously in the doorway where he'd been hiding. Derk wiped his nose with the back of his hand, stuffing his hands back into his pocket as Jezlen ran out onto the street, sliding past him on a patch of ice.

"See you didn't leave town, like you'd said." Derk muttered at the Forester not bothering to grace him with his gaze. Jezlen came to the end of the icy path, misjudging where to put his feet and tumbling head over heels into a pile of snow. Derk just chuckled as he continued down the street, blowing out his cheeks so his breath came out as a plume of smoke. He had made it about five doors down when the elf rejoined him, still brushing snow and ice out of his scarf and clothing.

"Well, I had to find out the result of your attempt to become my uncle," the Forester said, spitting to the side. Derk heard his teeth chattering and the Forester started rubbing his arms. Jezlen was almost able to pass for human as his scarf hid his pointed ears and long hair. "However, I am cold. Take me to your house, I want to get out of this horrible weather."

Derk laughed out loud, tossing his head back. "Cold? I thought elves could stand winter and rough weather?"

"Well, it does not mean we like to be out in it! Where is your home? I need to warm up."

Derk drew in his breath, the cold air warming in his lungs and he continued down the street at a quicker pace, hoping the elf would hurry along. He turned a corner and pointed at something with his chin, his eyes set in the direction they should go. "I ain't got nothing at home to eat. Let's get a quick bite, it'll warm you up."

The elf made a terrible sound in his throat as he trotted behind Derk, laughing out loud as Derk almost slipped on a piece of ice, grunting with dismay as the human kept right side up. Derk sniffed the air, following the welcome aroma of food permeating the cold. He indicated which stall he thought they should go to with another nod of his head.

"What should I ask for?" Jezlen asked, scanning the small board nailed to the side of the booth, a dozen hearty scents heavy in the air. "I cannot read human script."

"Well, with meat pies, you can't go wrong, really. And those are pictures, not words" Derk brought his hands out of his pockets, narrowing his eyes as he read over the list. "They've got a mutton pie and…a few pork ones. What'll it be?"

"By the mists, not another one of your minced-meat-stuffed-in-something inventions!" Jezlen growled. The old man frying the meat pies looking up suspiciously as he flipped one over in the boiling oil. Jezlen continued to rub his arms and hopped in place as he tried to keep warm, staring down into the snow. "Why are you people always grinding meat and putting it into things? It is unnatural! No wonder your cities are so ugly and your people are uncivilized. You spend all your free time mincing meat!"

"Uncivilized? Jez, I've been to your 'house' and it's a platform in a tree. It's a tree house, and without walls. Don't come telling me 'bout lack of civilization and things of that nature." Derk shook his head and looked to the fryer, holding out a few coins. "'Scuse my friend here, he's a Forester and a stupid one at that. Two rabbit pies, please." The old man gave Jezlen a weird look, pulling one of the frying pies out of the oil and wrapping it in a square of fabric before handing it over and taking the coins. Derk handed it over to Jezlen, who at least seemed happy to have something warm in his hands. The second pie was handed over and the two walked away, eating them too quickly and burning their mouths on their way down the street.

"So, I take it she said no," Jezlen said finally, grabbing a handful of snow and bringing it to his mouth. Derk just nodded. There wasn't much more to it, though he would spare the details to save himself face. Jezlen spit something out, cringing as he looked into the handful of snow before tossing it away, spitting again. The elf cursed out loud, something Derk had heard often but never knowing exactly what he said, understanding the meaning of the word by the intonation alone.

"Look, I don't know if you've gathered it yet, but I don't got a home here. I used to stay with Sindra and that's gone to pot. I spent my last blueies on those pasties we just tore our mouths on so…." Derk shrugged, kicking a clump of snow that looked like it needed it. He couldn't lead Jezlen around town forever and it was better they start thinking of something now before his friend froze to death. He laughed as he thought of Jezlen, the elf from the Forest of Clouds, dying from exposure to cold. It just seemed silly. "Why didn't you dress more warmly? Didn't your mother teach you not to catch cold?"

"I was under the impression you had a room somewhere or a shack or a…." Jezlen shook his head, chuckling to himself as he shivered, yawning as he looked down the street, turning his eyes back to Derk. "I have no idea why I thought any of those things. I am going to freeze to death because I thought you were a normal person."

Derk looked around the empty street, his eyes lingering on the entrance to an alley. He heard something coming from within and thought he recognized the voice of one of the approaching people. With a few fluid motions, he undid the buttons of his coat, placing it around the freezing elf's shoulders, sniffling slightly as he did. "Look, there's two blues and a fullie sewed into the lining of the coat. I was saving them for an emergency, but it looks like an emergency has shown itself to us. I've something to see to, get to the Ale's Well. It's down three blocks, take a right. You can't miss it." Jezlen eyed him suspiciously and for a moment Derk thought he was going to protest. But the warmth of the coat and the promise of four walls was all the persuasion Jezlen needed to take Derk's belongings and money before the elf left, almost falling into another snowdrift on his way down the street.

Derk watched his friend leave, the cold seeming to trickle through his pores as he stood there. A few snowflakes began to fall. It was the part of the winter day when it started to grow dark though one felt it was too early to be doing so. His second best shirt was meant for autumn. Derk stamped his feet and wrapped his arms around himself, wondering if he should avoid the confrontation altogether or get it over with so he could spend the next few days in peace.

Before he could decide, a body came flying out of the alley, sliding on a piece of ice and tumbling over a barrel left out of doors. A few peals of laughter came from the alley, the owners of the voices walking slowly out onto the main road.

The person who had been evicted from the alley scrambled to his feet, breathing loudly as he tried to run away. Derk could see he was young, his dark eyes wild with pain and worry as he ran off, making little headway in the deep snow. The largest of the three men who came out of the alley pointed in the direction of the boy, urging his lackeys on with curses to follow after the lad, his left hand wound tight with a chain. The two cronies gave chase, having trouble in the snow themselves, their feet sliding out from under them so they laughed as they chased after their quarry. The man who had given the orders watched them go for a while, his breath forming a halo of steam around his dark head.

"So, you ready to give me that shirt of yours or not?" the man said, not bothering to turn around to address Derk. He still held the chain, the metal no doubt warm in his hand but freezing cold in the air. Derk rubbed his arms briskly, thoughts of the chain and the young fellow pricking him with anxiety. He couldn't show fear in front of Sersena the Bastard. He felt fear but he told himself he was shivering from the cold and nothing more.

"How 'bout my third best shirt and an extra set of boot buckles?" Derk didn't blink as the large man turned around and approached, his shadow growing ominously as he walked toward him. Was the snow melting around him? Derk managed to put a smile on his face as the muscled brute drew closer, the swagger in his step causing the chain to dance in the frigid air. He stopped when he got within a pace of Derk, the chain finally shimmying to a halt, its shadow long and hard against the pale, white snow.

Sersena the Bastard was two handwidths taller than Derk. Steam rose off of his shaved head, his dark eyes sizing up the shivering man. A smile cracked his lips as the words finally seemed to register in his head and he laughed out loud, a booming laugh that would have been louder had the snow not been there to muffle it. He reached out a large gloved hand, setting it on Derk's shoulder and giving it a squeeze. It made the thief want to wince. The sound of a faint commotion made its way over the snow drifts, the distinct crack of wood against skull obvious to Derk and his eyes darted down the street, hoping the boy was okay. The Bastard finally stopped laughing, letting his hand fall from Derk's shoulder, much to his relief.

"How 'bout you come wif us on a job instead. I'd make more than what your shirt is worth. Call us even."

Derk stopped rubbing his arms for a moment, a cold wind making snowflakes twirl in the space around him. He knew what job The Bastard was talking about. Hock had been bragging about it in the Unders a few days ago, his claims almost lost in the chaos of the gambling den. It had reached Derk's ears and caught his interest and he listened to Hock's plan. The potential gain was formidable but the plan had obvious holes and he had told Hock so, pointing out no less than two issues which hadn't been considered in the plan.

Hock raised an eyebrow and offered to buy him a drink if he stuck around and discussed the plan over with him, unless of course Derk didn't have anything else to add, his jealousy and input unloaded. This had pricked Derk's pride and he sat down and listed five more things wrong with the plan, mentioning the states of the streets and the roads out of town, the relocation of several watches recently on account of a take which had backfired a few weeks ago, and the fact the lock on the shed would take know-how to undo, something The Bastard and his gang lacked. He had taken his ale thankfully, thirsty after his tirade and out of money after having gambled it away.

Derk shook his head, managing to laugh despite his nervousness. "No thanks, Sers. I've just had a bad shot to the head and it'll take a few days to sort it all out. Wouldn't want to put you out on account of having a muddy brain." He hoped this would be a good enough excuse for Sersena to leave him alone, at least as far as the take was concerned. "Look, it's cold out and I'm looking to be indoors soon as I can."

"Right, so I'll be taking my payment now." The Bastard grinned, a menacing leer chilling Derk more than the weather. Derk sighed and began undoing the buttons on his shirt, pulling it over his head and handing it over to the thug. The Bastard took it and brought it to his face, sniffing the fabric and laughing out loud. "So, fappers do sweat, eh?"

Bare chested, Derk couldn't stop shivering, the thin layer of fabric having done more than he had given it credit. He was about to turn and run off when The Bastard held up a hand, signaling for him to stay. The tall thug turned to look in the direction his two toadies had gone and he laughed out loud, the chain jingling merrily at his side.

Where three man had gone, one emerged. The young fellow, limping and breathing heavily, stumbled toward the pair, groaning quietly as he held the side of his head in his hands. The Bastard just laughed, snow falling off windowsills as his guffaw echoed through the streets. He motioned for the youth to approach him. "Don't you worry, this is just what a 'bootin' in' looks like," speaking to Derk as he put an arm around the boy's shoulders. "He wanted in, and he had to fight for it. Now, it's rightfully his. Though I was expecting at least one of those asses to come back. He must've given 'em quite a whoopin' eh?

"Now, since this man here didn't give me what was mine when I asked for it, there's interest to collect, ain't there, Scald?" The Bastard addressed the youth, who nodded, his eyes seeming unable to focus as he stood there in the snow. "Now, you're new here, Scald and I've a mind to teach you how to go about doing business so stupid bastards like this know better than to cross you."

Stupid? If he wasn't shivering so hard Derk was sure he would have turned red with rage, having someone like The Bastard call him such petty names. Even if he had his shirt, though, Sersena was cruel and feared. He ran the Unders of this town and was not to be crossed; Derk was lucky enough to only owe him a bit of money and would be mostly free of his influence once he left town, which would be sooner than he had originally anticipated. Even still, if anyone was stupid in the trio, it was Sersena. Derk spoke through chattering teeth, his eyes wide with annoyance. "Well, if-f you're g-g-gonna t-t-take it, be qu-quick...I've a d-d-date with either a f-f-ire or a c-c-c-offin in the m-meanwhile." His urging didn't seem to affect the two as The Bastard looked him over from head to toe, his dark eyes resting on the shiny buckles on Derk's boots.

"Those look like they'd fit you, Scald." They didn't. Scald's feet were definitely smaller than Derk's but it didn't keep the boy from nodding, obviously not wanting to disagree with The Bastard. "You could use something nice for the job anyways...off wif 'em."

Derk managed to bend down and undo the buckles, loosening them both before stepping out of them. His feet felt as if they were being jabbed by a million needles as he set them on the ground, the snow melting as he stepped into it. He grabbed the pair in one hand, keeping his other arm wrapped around his torso for all the good it would do, handing the boots over to The Bastard who handed them to the boy.

"Pleasure, always a pleasure doing business. Best you win a few hands next time you play wif me. Now, off wif you." Derk managed to bow courteously to the pair, more mocking them than anything else, before he turned around and started off down the street. He waited till he was out of eyesight before he attempted a full on run, each step tortuously cold, each pace of air his body moved through threatening to crush his lungs. Stupid Bastard, Derk thought, his instincts hurling him away from the man he so desperately wished to kill. A string of curses bubbled in his brain, keeping it alert enough to find his way to the Ale's Well. His dark thoughts began to thaw out as soon as he stepped through the door, all his vicious plans and vile words streaming from his mouth as the snowflakes melted on his pale shoulders.

A loud laugh directed at him gave away Jezlen's position and Derk stumbled toward him, his feet not working properly. He was out of breath and the cold was still very real under his skin. Derk starting to shake more violently as he settled next to Jezlen in front of the roaring fire. The elf was still wearing his coat and didn't offer it to him. Derk's teeth were chattering too hard to ask for it so he pointed to the coat and then to himself. The elf wrinkled his nose in dismay and reluctantly handed the coat to the freezing man.

"Whatever just happened, I wish I had been there to see it," was all Jezlen said, turning to the side to lift his mug of something warm off of the table. Derk tried to think some murderous thoughts about the elf but he was still shivering and his desire for revenge against Sersena the Bastard seared at the forefront of his mind. All this over a simple game of cards.

If Derk didn't think so highly of himself, he would have counted himself lucky for escaping with a few less belongings. People who angered the thug usually had his gang after them, and those who did worse than anger him learned why he kept his chain in hand. Many a debt had been taken out in broken bones and torn open flesh in the Unders and sometimes for debts smaller than two shirts. Apparently Sersena the Bastard thought Derk might be useful. Derk could have gone along on the job and maybe made some money, as well as endeared himself to one of the more dangerous folk in the city.

But Derk wasn't one to get on other people's "ledgers." Though not as well known as The Bastard, Derk knew he was a better thief and a better person in general than the dirty cur. The best way to make was one's own. That was his general thought, and he figured he'd rather make a few blue pieces and answer to himself than be given a bag of fullies by someone he had to call "boss."

Jezlen, in his saintlike generosity, offered Derk his pipe, the man finally noticing his hands stopped shaking as he took it. He would do something to hurt Sersena the Bastard. A long pull set his nerves aright, his bare feet finally registering the hard floor below and he stared into the fire. Sersena would pay.

Derk never got the chance to pay back Sersena the Bastard. The job went horribly and Sersena and all the men who were there as accomplices were rounded up and tossed into jail. They were sentenced to hang. Apparently, Hock hadn't been at the job, nor had he been fingered as the mastermind behind it all; Derk saw him enjoying a mug at the Northside the day the group was convicted. When Derk cornered him later and asked him how he could let them go through with his original plan, Hock narrowed his eyes, hopping off his bar stool and leaning in close, his mouth by Derk's ear. All he said was: "It's trash off the streets." Derk stood there, stunned, realizing what he was implying.

The plan was supposed to have gone wrong. Sersena the Bastard really was an idiot.

Derk, wearing a pair of boots and a shirt bought with Jezlen's tobacco money, attended the hanging. Each of the criminals was bound and chained to the other. Two guards drove the wagon, two guarded the prisoners. All five of the convicted were led up the stairs to the platform where they were made to stand on stools. Sersena the Bastard fought back, cursing wildly. One of the guards pulled out their sword and plunged it into him. The large man doubled over and then went limp, his body unceremoniously loaded into the cart which had brought him there.

Among the four remaining, the boy was one of them. Derk felt a cold sweat break out on his forehead as they forced the boy up on the stool, tightened the noose around his neck and placed a sack over his head. Their crimes were recited in front of the jeering crowd: attempted robbery of ten barrels of lamp oil, destruction of private property, destruction of public property, assault of city officials, public inebriation and performing crimes within one hundred paces of a holy temple.

Their faces were covered but Derk imagined the dread wracking their faces, the tears in their eyes, the last minute prayers or curses springing to their lips. He imagined himself in their place, imagined where the boy might be instead if he hadn't decided to join Sersena the Bastard's gang. Derk held his breath as the crowd seethed around him, throwing things, shouting things, hungry for entertainment in the form of death.

The Bastard had gotten what he deserved; or had he? He was a cruel man, but even he didn't strike a man when bound or in the back. Derk looked over to the cart, the booted feet of the dead man sticking out past the end. The crowd boiled around him but he didn't notice, didn't see what they did, didn't hear what they said. The hangman went behind each prisoner, kicking the stool out from under each, their bodies bobbing up and down as they kicked desperately, the false hope for ground underfoot causing the bodies to dance, suspended as they were. One stopped, than another, followed by the other two, the crowd shrieking and hooting all the while. Derk stood there, frozen, numbed not by cold but an overload of emotion. He stood there in the square as the crowd dispersed, trembling slightly as he watched the four men cut down, loaded into the cart and led out by a simple peasant.

He stood there in the square for a while in a daze, the snow starting to fall yet again. People began to pass before him and behind him, some of them staring at the man who was staring at the small raised platform where five men had just died. Derk didn't care about the cold beginning to bite at his face and legs. Trash. He wasn't trash, was he? He didn't deserve to have a stool kicked out from under his feet, did he? As if able to read his thoughts, someone came up and stood beside him. The voice of Hock was crisp and clear in the cold winter air.

"You are better than them. And you know it. Jezlen is getting your boots. Now come with me."

Chapter 15
Questionable Beginnings

Derk drank from his glass, trying to keep a smile on his face. The bar was loud, the lively exclamations of card players and revelers filling the air. Normally Derk would have joined in but not tonight. Across from him sat Hock, Drink and Paint, all three of them regarding him with different emotions. Hock looked hopeful, a smile plastered under his bushy mustache. Paint looked disinterested. And Drink...the woman with red hair and a face full of freckles did not look pleased.

When Hock had first taken Derk on last winter the big man made it seem like he was the head of the Cup of Cream. As Derk has asked more questions it became more and more clear Hock wasn't. Nobody was in charge. Everybody was. But there were senior members who were regarded as the most knowledgeable, the best at what they did. Everyone could recognize each other and most knew of one another but finding each other got easier only the longer you'd been in. Hock said it was like 'magic,' the way they were able to come together when needed. Derk thought it was more about habit and a bit of luck. Hock could always be counted on to be in Bluemist eventually. Paint worked at a singing house called the Piper's Dream. A man named Shot spent a lot of time in the 'Wicks and the Holy Bowl. And Drink rode between Reedwood and Redtree at least once a season.

But now three members of the Cup of Cream were sitting before him. Under the table Hock's dog wagged its tail, whacking everyone. Derk could felt its wet nose pressing against his leg, sniffing him over and over. Hock slipped the animal scraps of barley bread from time to time. Drink raised a brow at Derk but turned to Hock. "I still don't understand where you found this boy," Drink said. "He has a big mouth and a big claim. Horse riding, letter writing, mapping, prowling. Tell me, boy, what can't you do?"

"I can't break a man's nose with a flick of my finger," Derk started looking at Hock. "I can't sing the high parts of 'Cross the Sky Came My Darling'." That was meant for Paint. "I can't shoot an arrow into a man's neck from a hundred paces." He looked to Drink. "But I can do lots of things you all can't. And we all share abilities."

"Who cares where he picked it all up?" Hock said. "No one's looking for him, he don't owe anyone anything. You know better than anyone, living is learning, Drink. Some manage to live a bit more than others. Faulting someone for making better use of their time?" Hock laughed and dropped another crust of bread under the table for the dog. "Too useful, sorry Derk. We'll find a bigger fapper to work with."

"He's very pious to boot. He goes to temple to honor the First Thief more than anyone I've ever met before, more than Shot even. He knows his scriptures too." Paint played with the handkerchief tied around her neck but Derk knew what hid behind it. Born a man but living as a woman, Paint wasn't the first of her kind Derk had met. Apparently Hock and she had something together. They had been kissing when Derk had arrived at the bar. Drink had been sure to sit between them.

The three of them didn't need to know Derk went to temple to think about Sindra and to beat back thoughts of Gam. He missed both women, not able to see them as much as he would have liked while taking on with Hock. He had seen Sindra after Baron's Day. The visit had ended with him sneaking out the window with his shirt in his mouth, Sindra feigning being ill as the priestess who had come to check on her asked various questions. Derk had damn near broken his neck jumping off the roof. "The Black Handed One is the Mother of us all and she stole the light so we wouldn't be afraid in the dark times," Derk said. Everyone knew it, sang about it in temple. Derk had said it to Sindra and she never had a response for him.

"We don't need sermons, we don't need priests. The Church means well and the Goddess might have made the first Take, but she risked burned hands, not a life in jail. Have you ever been to jail, boy?"

Derk shook his head. He had been to jails. He remembered the jail at Cartaskin Keep, dark and wet and underground. Rarely did prisoners occupy its cells. He'd seen people who had been released from prison. It was a deterrent to many.

"You don't want to wind up in the Jugs," Drink said. "We're lucky they don't brand criminals no more."

"Didn't I just say he's good enough to stay out of the Jugs?" Hock exclaimed, exasperated. "Drink, I don't just talk to hear my own voice."

"That's one good thing the Church did," Paint offered, pouring herself another glass of wine. "Getting rid of branding. You know it was the Church which forbid it, right?"

"I do," Derk said. "One of the few times the Church crossed the Barons."

"Enough about the Church," Drink snapped, glaring at Paint and Hock. She was obviously tired of them. She looked to Derk. "Hock here says you're good at hiding. Strong. Smart. Paint says you're loyal. Devout." Drink looked again to Hock and Paint, the expression on her face telling them what she wanted before she said it. "Clear out, you two. I want to talk to this pretty boy myself." For a breath neither of them went anywhere, but then Hock rose whistling for the dog and Paint went round the table, putting her arm in his before they walked away, the dog scurrying behind them. Derk watched them go, feeling nervous as they disappeared through the crowd. He hoped he didn't seem nervous.

Drink took a bite of the food from the bowl, chewing it quietly while she stared at Derk. Her eyes were green like new leaves in spring and sharp. Derk squirmed in his seat.

"Hock'll vouch for you. Paint'll vouch for you. Why should I?" Drink said.

"What about Jezlen, he'll vouch for me," Derk offered.

"Nice try, trying to find a work around," Drink said. It almost sounded like a compliment but Derk knew better. "But he can't vouch for anyone."

"Why not?" Derk said, trying not to sound disappointed.

"Well firstly, no one will vouch for him. He's not right," Drink said, taking another bite of the food. "The fact you two seem to get on is a puzzle to me."

"We've a bit of history," Derk said. More than a bit, but he wasn't going to dominate the conversation or get into how they knew each other. Talking too much would only make Drink angry, he was fairly certain. And that history involved Sindra and the Church, two things he wasn't sure he wanted to bring up.

"He's not right. Be careful around him," Drink said.

"Is that advice? Look, you've taken me under your wing already," Derk laughed, flashing a smile at the woman. He thought she would smile back at him. Her eyes did but her mouth just frowned.

"You think you're so cute, boy. You've got Hock and Paint in your bed, don't you?" she said, drinking her beer.

"Not literally," Derk said. Derk scooped up some of the barley salad with his spoon and looked at it. The bit about Jezlen still bothered him. Jezlen wasn't a bad person. He just wasn't very good and was sometimes a pain to get in on something. The reasons why the Forester did things were mysterious to decipher but apparently something about Derk got Jezlen on board with him. As far as Derk could tell Jezlen did things for Hock because Hock hated cats. "So you're just using Jezlen?" he asked.

"It's what he's good for," Drink said. "He's fine not being vouched for. He's also not a Valleyman."

"He...." Derk squinted. "What?"

"He doesn't follow the Goddess."

"He's not the only person in the Valley who doesn't hold the Goddess high," Derk said. Most of the people in the Valley did, but there were people like the ones at the Temple of the Ever Burning Sun, spirit workers. Most of them lived in the Freewild but they came into towns and villages to trade and for festivals occasionally. It wasn't a reason to not deal with someone. The Church encouraged tolerance.

"The Cup of Cream is based on the idea the Goddess was the first Taker. She made something that wasn't hers, hers."

"I thought we were keeping the Church out of this," Derk said, narrowing his eyes. "Which is it? Is the Church good or bad?"

"The Church is one thing. The belief in the Goddess is another." Drink gulped her beer. "If you can't see the difference, you're not as clever as Hock says."

"But Hock says I'm clever," Derk said, taking the opportunity to turn the conversation back to him and the Cup taking him in. "More then clever. Good at making things wind up in my pocket." Derk leaned forward in his chair, using the knife the kitchen had provided to sever one of the legs off of the roasted rabbit. "You need more smart people. More planners. And you need new people who are eager to please, eager to impress."

"Oh, and you think you can impress me?" Drink said.

"Maybe you have to impress me," Derk said, taking a bite out of the roasted rabbit. It was a bit dry but still tasty. "I mean, I know what I've done, which is more than you might think. I've tracked down and killed Freemen. I've recovered lost property. I've retrieved jewelry for pretty ladies, I've run street games and slept in feather beds and in doorways. I've snuck in and out of bedrooms, kitchens and great halls. I've killed. I've drawn blood and made men disappear. What have you done?" he asked.

Now Drink smiled and Derk wished she hadn't. It wasn't a cruel smile or even an ugly smile. It was a smile that would lead to something terrible, Derk knew it.

"And what is the most impressive thing you've ever done?" Drink asked. Derk watched as she picked up her mug and took a gulp. He wondered if she was getting drunk yet. With a name like that, probably not.

Derk narrowed his eyes and smirked swallowing his bite of food. "I haven't done it yet," he said.

"Ah, looking to the future, I see." Drink poured another mug, nodding to herself. "And why do you even want to be in the Cup?"

"You can get more done with a few people," Derk said. It was the simplest way he could say it.

"Get some friends," Drink retorted.

"I have friends," Derk shot. "More than a few. Some of which you might want to meet."

"Well, just give me their names and where I can find them and I'll be on my way." Drink held her drink out to the side, seeming a bit exasperated.

"Do you not like me for some reason?" Derk asked. He heard seats scrape behind him as people got up and left, people yelling farewells, the sound of the temple bells ringing in the distance. His food was cold now and he didn't want it. Before she could answer he put his arms on the table and leaned forward, looking over the table and into his drink. "I don't need for you to like me, or for Hock to like me, or Paint. Hock came to me. He told me about the Cup. About how you work together when you have to, to get what you want. How you part ways. How you don't always do things for yourselves, out of selfishness, how together you can all see the bigger picture. More than just yourselves."

"What is the bigger picture, Derk?" Drink asked. Her voice was quiet but keen and Derk was trying to make sense of all they had said to each other in the last few moments. He looked up at her, his eyes meeting hers.

"The bigger picture is...everybody wants things." His voice trailed off. The Valley, his childhood, the life he was living now. His old friends, Sindra, Gam. Jezlen. He thought about the hands which had tried to hold him down, the ones he had pushed away. The ones he had held and kissed and the ones which had slapped him. "I want things. The Barons and the magistrates and others want to take from me, from other people. I can take too. But I also want to give. In my own way, on my own terms."

"You seem to think very highly of yourself," Drink said.

"Someone has to," Derk said. "It has to start somewhere. And I've reason enough."

"I think you're just lonely," Drink said.

"Don't mean I'm not good." Derk was tired of talking in circles with Drink. "Look, just tell me what to do to get your approval or, I don't know, slit my throat or whatever it is you do to people who know about the Cup but aren't in. Well, try to slit my throat, I won't go down quietly." He took another sip of his beer and then set it on the table, hard. "Hems, I'll fight you to get in. I don't care you're a woman."

"Don't you have anything better to do than get yourself killed and try to roost with us? We don't need no simps, us big crows are doing just fine."

"Well, it's clear you don't feel the Cup is important. Just let it all die off. Nothing to leave to anyone, is it?" Derk finished his drink and thought about leaving but the look Drink gave him made him stay, made him lean back in his seat. "Who brought you in? Isn't there an old saying, 'A family without children is a grave waiting to be filled?' Is that it?"

"I always heard it was a 'A mam without a babe is a dead woman.'" Drink said. She stopped drinking for a moment . "Do you have any children?" she asked

For the first time since he had walked in Drink didn't look angry. Something about her face looked sad or wistful but she set her eyes on him, waiting for an answer. Derk shook his head. "No," he replied. "I don't."

"The truth is, of course, everyone makes their mark, their difference. And everybody dies. Only the marks remain. It only follows a few can make a bigger mark together. Deeper." She poured the remains of the pitcher into her glass and drained it, the two of them sitting there, not saying anything. The barkeep called out the last call for warm bread and the sound of people leaving and paying and talking grew for a few breaths.

Derk looked at the plates. She agreed with him. He didn't know what to say, concerned any remark would set her against him again so he just sat there, waiting and wondering where Hock and Paint were. Drink finished one of the other cups and stood up, wiping her hands on a napkin.

"Can you take orders?" she asked. Drink was shorter than Derk had expected, wearing light colored britches tucked into her dark brown, leather boots. She still wore a woman's belt, laced in the front. At her neckline he saw the glint of a rosary, the pendant tucked away under her tunic.

"I can," he said, sitting up straighter. "I can give them too."

"You looking to be in charge?" she asked. There was a hint of a smile on her lips, the same smirk bordering on cruel.

Derk laughed and shook his head. "No, I don't want to be in charge of no one or nothing, not for long anyway."

"You laugh too much, Derk," Drink said. "I can't figure out if it's a good thing or a bad thing." The woman pulled a stick out of the pouch she wore at her hip and brought it to her mouth, clenching it between her teeth. A faintly herbal smell wafted through the air and Derk was reminded of the sticks Asa used to chew, all those seasons back. Drink motioned for Derk to follow her and Derk got up and grabbed his bag, slinging it over his shoulder as he followed her to the bar.

"I've a job for you," she said, the stick threatening to fall out of her mouth as she spoke. Even her hands had freckles on them, Derk noticed, as she handed a few coins to the barkeep to pay for the food and drink. They walked past a card game and a few people throwing darts before the slipped through the doorway and into the late spring evening.

The breeze was chilly but the night was warm, and the few people milling around the singing halls and bars mostly walked without cloaks or jackets. Derk pulled his hat out of his pocket and pulled it over his head just to make sure it wouldn't fall out as they walked. Drink inhaled deeply, still chewing on her stick, the scent more sweet than medicinal now.

"I hear you've got a woman, grey in eye and garment," Drink said. Derk stiffened slightly, putting his hands on his pockets. They walked, back to where Paint kept a place from what he could tell. "What's she do in the Church, eh? Light candles? Lead prayers? Count allotments?"

"Look, I ain't going to involve her in any schemes, I won't," he said, holding a hand up in protest. He didn't like the way she asked. Hock had brought up how having someone in the Church could be useful, but Derk said no and quickly. He knew better. He was careful not to mention anything about Sindra beyond the fact she existed since even that seemed to perk up ears and raise eyebrows. "She knows a bit about what I've done," Derk said, his tone meant to tell Drink Sindra knew general ideas and not specifics. "But she doesn't want any part of it."

"So, she's not the one you spoke of before," Drink said, pulling the stick from her mouth and smirking. She spat to the side before the stick found its way back between her thin lips and white teeth. "Don't be so touchy," she murmured. "I will say this, speaking as a person who's been in relationships before, if she don't like it, she don't really like you, Derk." She smiled at him in a way which wasn't meant to be comforting. Derk frowned, thinking about what she said. "In any case," she continued, turning onto the other main street. More respectable and mundane stores fell behind them as they walked. "She's a priestess. They don't sit on the Seat or fear the Sword. But they still make sure the Seat is in place and the Sword is sharp.

"I want you to go into the temple and steal the offering from the collection plate," Drink said.

Chapter 16
Personal Gain

Derk stood there, not sure he heard correctly. Drink was still strolling down the street, leaving Derk a few paces behind her. Finally he ran to catch up, falling in beside her and continuing down the busy street.

"What?" he hissed, trying to keep his voice down. Just the idea of stealing from the plate made him feel guilty, made his heart thump in his chest. "What?" he asked again. "Are you missing a bit in the brain box? Why?"

"Just do it," she said. "It's easy. I doubt they'll even have anyone watching the plate." She was so nonchalant about the whole thing as if she was asking him to buy a pitcher of beer at the bar and not steal from the Church.

"But they need the money!" Derk said, quietly. He was afraid someone would hear them and turn them in. "Why?"

"Do they really?" Drink said. "They grow food and get donations from farmers. They brew beer and sell grey ale to bars for coin. The Church has their own flocks in Tyeskin Barony. Food, drink, coin, clothing. They have everything they need and more, Derk. And we still give."

"The clergy still has to pay gate taxes," Derk pointed out. "Entry taxes. And they help the people. They offer help, charity. Peace, comfort. The food they get, they share."

"Is that what your bed mate tells you from the pulpit of her bed?" Drink laughed.

"It's what I've seen," Derk said. He left Sindra out of it. Sindra was a good person. She wasn't involved in the charities her temple performed but he knew Churches gave food during lean times. A quiet refuge from the day, the peace of a priestess' blessing. These were good things they gave.

"Every temple isn't the same," Drink said. She stopped and faced him. The stick was still danging from her mouth, making her shadow look strange on the ground. "Who do you care about more? The Church or yourself?"

Derk drew in his breath, sharp and quick, sticking his jaw out. This was the task Drink was setting before him. He thought about the times he had visited Sindra, the jobs he had done for the Church. They had always paid well. Sindra never seemed to want for anything. He knew not every Church was able to thrive under the Barons. The temple at Cartaskin Keep had been subject to the whims and patronage of the Baron and that had waned. If it happened to one temple, it could happen to others. But in all his travels in the Valley he had never seen a temple in serious need, its priestesses wanting for food or clothing. People loved the Goddess and they loved Her servants who were kind and gentle. They still charged for people to sleep in their basements and the incense they burned...how much money had Derk spent over the years for scented prayers and a bit of roof to sleep under.

How much would even be in the collection plate? Not a lot, he supposed. It was late, after supper and vesper bells had already rung. Would it be missed? Did he want to be involved with people who stole from the Church? But what of what Drink said? She wasn't lying about the things the Church was able to do and entitled to in the Valley. All these years, he had never questioned it. What were the chances of Derk working for the Church ever again?

Drink was shoving the question in his face. He didn't want to falter, have her think he had the heart of a mouse. "Where should I go once I've got it?" Derk said, trying to keep his voice steady and mostly succeeding.

"Bring it to Paint's," Drink said. "All of it. And don't take forever. I'll come looking for you." She smirked at him and turned, her eyes lingering on him before she continued down the street, toward Paint's home.

"Chew Her Hems," Derk cursed, looking down the street in the direction of the temple. He knew where it was. The temple had been the first place he went to on his own. A temple was a bit of familiarity, a place of comfort no matter where he was in the Valley. He knew where the collection plate was. It would be easy, almost too easy. It was set on a table against the wall in the foyer, before entering the temple proper. He had walked in, dipped his fingers in the holy water and dropped a coin into the collection plate. His coin had probably been collected by now.

The walk to the temple seemed to take both an eternity and pass too quickly, his heart beating faster the closer he drew. Sweat popped on his brow despite the cool evening. The weight of his dagger felt heavy hidden away under his shirt and he prayed he wouldn't have to use the weapon. Why would he? If a priestess caught him, would she fight back? What if there were people in the temple? They might attack him. And if Sindra heard? The chances of getting back in her bed and her good graces would be destroyed. Still his feet moved, drawing him closer to the temple.

Derk shoved all these thoughts to the side, focusing his mind on prayer instead. He prayed to the Goddess for forgiveness. He prayed no one would be in the temple, for the Black Hand of the Goddess to guide him.

The steps leading up to the Temple of the Blessed Hope were bare. No one stood on the steps selling wares, no priestesses discussed the merits of one translation over the other or sang hymns over the marketplace. Lamps hung on either side of the door and the sign of the temple, the waxing moon, almost full, carved out of stone so light shone from the almost perfect circle. Almost.

The soles of his boots skipped against the stone steps as he ascended, the sound of music from the streets growing fainter in his ears. For a breath he considered just walking through the temple and out the back door. All temples had back entrances available for the public to use. He could leave the temple and then the town, go somewhere else. Back to Sindra. Maybe try to watch the Cup from afar, see if they were taking advantage of the Church and then do something about it.

Hock hadn't made it seem like it was the case during their talks. All of the stories before had been small robberies, foiling block lords, intercepting weapons. Derk had mentioned his lover being involved with the Church and Hock had seemed interested but never protested. The Church...Derk remembered the solace he had found within its walls so many times. Had it been the building? The Bosom of the Goddess? Or the bosom of Sindra? And what would the Cup give him? He remembered Sersena and his cruel chain, killed by the guards. Hock had made that happen, in a way. The brown cloak had shoved the sword into him but Hock had allowed Sersena and has gang to take on the bad job.

Was it kind of the Goddess to let people like Sersena lord over streets and back rooms? But things changed, didn't they? Her Black Hand could set things in motion. A powerful man, killed. A Baron's son, now a thief, about to steal the ten coins from the collection plate. Ten coins, all of them blue.

Three were Goddess side up, Her eyes lowered to look into the bowl of the Valley. Ten coins and no one watching. The temple was empty save the quiet burn of the oil lamps in the vestibule. Perhaps a few people sat inside but they would be looking at the altar or their heads bowed, hands over their hearts in prayer. He had walked into the temple quietly enough. No priestess came out to greet him, no one stood at the altar singing or reciting.

Sindra. The painting of the Goddess behind the altar looked like her. It was the hair, mostly. Dark hair spilled over Her shoulders in thick waves and stars gleamed among Her tresses. One hand lay on Her belly, swollen yet perfect in its roundness. Her other hand was outstretched, the palm black. Evidence of Her previous deeds, forever marked on Her divine body. Derk's hand tingled.

He approached not the altar but the collection plate, his hat already in his hand. He had pulled it off when he had entered the temple. A quick gaze around the temple, listening for footsteps, heavy breathing. Square fingers reached forward, brushing the lip of the plate and finding the first coin.

The coin wasn't cold or warm. It was round and hard. The tips of his fingers felt the familiar patterns hammered into the dark blue metal. He picked up the first coin and dropped it into his hat.

The second went in. It jingled against the other and Derk felt his heart stop. He listened to hear if anyone had noticed, waiting. The scent of incense wafted past him, mixing with the night air. People could enter at any moment. Derk held his breath and quickly, unceremoniously picked up the rest of the coins, gathering them in his fist. The coins rubbed against each other as he settled them into a stack within his grip, metal against metal, cold and grating. Eyes darted from the collection plate to the temple to the painting, expecting someone to stir.

The remaining eight coins were in his hand. He turned and put his hand into his hat, walking toward the main exit. As he exited, he turned back, casting his gaze upon the painting of the Goddess. Even from here, he swore he could see a faint smirk on Her face, a smile in Her eyes.

Derk turned his head, careening into a priestess before he could stop and cursed. The priestess exclaimed as well, both their voices echoing in the temple. The sound of several of the coins clinking against the floor made his skin hot, the coins he had managed to hold on to starting to make his hand hurt. The priestess was sitting on the floor, rubbing her elbow, a book lying a toss away from them answering the question as to why she hadn't avoided the collision. Derk dumped the coins in his hat and stood up, offering a hand to the priestess. She gave her elbow one more rub, a wince twisting her face as Derk helped her up.

"I'm so sorry," he said. He was only apologizing for knocking her down, he told himself. He bent down to pick up her book, catching the title before she snatched it up in an effort to keep the book from him. He knew the title and tried not to smirk, knowing it would only make the priestess angry. "I...I didn't see you there," he added, bending down to pick up his hat. He balled the end of it so it looked like a purse, looking the priestess over. "You're bleeding," he said, pointing to her elbow.

"Hems," the priestess said, bending her arm to see. Sure enough a patch of bright red showed the pattern of the weave, criss-crossed against her elbow. "I'm sorry, I was...I was busy reading," she said. The priestess looked young. Her face was round and she clutched the book to her chest, hiding it with her arms. She was probably still an acolyte, a student. More than likely she was supposed to be in quarters. The younger priestesses usually had the chores done earlier in the day.

"Gotta get it in when you can," Derk said, smiling. The priestess managed a smile back, averting her eyes from him. "Best get it looked at, you don't want it to get infected," he said, pointing to her elbow. The coins were heavy in his hands but the young priestess' attention was on herself. "I knew a man, bumped his elbow one day, two phases later had to get his arm chopped off at the shoulder. If you're right handed, it might make dealing with your book more difficult." Derk tried not to grin but the priestess blushed and straightened her back to counter her embarrassment.

"It's still a holy text," she said quietly. "One of the blessings of the Goddess, is it not?"

"Well, it is. Still, get it mended or blessing yourself will be uncomfortable at best." Derk turned and left, pressing his lips together so as to keep from laughing. As soon as he was at the bottom of the steps he laughed out loud, recalling the priestess' face. She looked both shocked and amused when he had warned her. Maybe because the piece of work she held, 'The Illustrated Workings and Enticement of the Holy Mother Over the Powers of The Valley' wasn't a religious work every Valleyman was familiar with. He only knew about it because Cira had mentioned it once. Later in his love life when he had asked Sindra about it...he remembered how her eyes glinted, the smile on her full mouth. The pictures in the book had made Derk's eyes go wide. Derk laughed again as he walked down the street, the weight of the coins lighter in his hand.

Paint's home was found easily enough. A knock on the door evoked barking from within, followed by cursing and the sound of things being knocked over. He heard Hock shout something and Paint say something back, followed by a laugh by Drink. Metal raked against wood as the lock was pulled back and the door opened. A wet, black nose snuffed at the door, the large dog from earlier in the bar joined by two others, all of them pushing past Hock to see who was at the door. "Get back! Lock! Stock! Paint, call them!"

Derk walked through the door, the smell of beer and bread frying making his stomach rumble. The three dogs all circled him, making it difficult to walk. A tail knocked someone's mug over, one of the dogs lapping up whatever spilled as the other two still crowded Derk. "Paint, call your dogs!" Hock insisted, locking the door once more.

"They're your dogs too," Paint said, ducking into the kitchen. "Stock's the only one I brought home, Lock and Barrel are your pups."

"Pups? They're full grown, dumb as children. They sprawl out on the bed as if it's theirs," Hock grumbled, sitting down. In response Lock sat in front of Hock and leaned over, licking him on the face. The large man's expression softened and he reached out and pet the dog, evoking a grin from the beast. "At least they don't talk back."

Derk sat down at the small table, setting his hat before Drink. The weight of the coins made it slide open, the coins glinting in the lamplight. Before he could say anything, Barrel crawled up onto the couch after him, laying its large body across his lap. Derk felt its feet and claws dig into his lap and he stifled a groan, looking to Paint with thanks as she whacked the dog's backside with a dishrag, shooing him away. "Let's not forget, they can rip out a man's throat," Paint said, kneeling over to wipe the floor. "Not many children can do that."

"Not many," Drink said. She didn't bother moving as Paint knelt down to clean, instead keeping her attention on her cards. "Hock, we still playing?"

"Give me a minute," Hock said, stepping around the dogs. "Paint, you need any help with the cleaning?"

"No, just check your bread, don't want it to burn," Paint said, wiping the table. "Derk, dear, are you hungry?"

"I don't want to put you out," Derk insisted, wondering when Drink was going to look up from her cards.

"Nonsense," Paint said. "You're our guest, though we're not very good hosts. You might have to use a dog for a pillow. At least they're warm."

"No sleeping at the temple commons for you, eh, Derk?" Drink said, finally turning an eye his way.

Derk sat back on the couch, scratching at a patch of bare wood on the arm of the seat with his finger. "No, not tonight," he said.

"We've got cold ham and whitberry jam. Hock can share his bread with you."

"Hock won't!" Hock called from the kitchen, one of the dogs trampling over to the kitchen. "Get out of here! Paint!"

Paint laughed and put a large hand on Derk's knee. "You let me know if you need anything. Let me go make sure he don't burn the house down." Derk watched as she took one last swipe at the ground and left, her skirts swishing behind her.

"So, was it hard?" Drink asked, rearranging her cards in her hand.

Derk looked at the pile of cards on the table and then to his hat, filled with coins. "At first," he admitted. "I didn't want to do it. But then, my heart started to race. And I wanted to do it. So I did." He leaned over and picked up one of the coins, wondering who had left it in the plate.

Drink leaned over and pulled three coins out of the hat, putting them in her coin purse. "Buy yourself something nice," she said, tucking the pouch away into her belt. Derk must have been looking at her strangely because she stared at him. "What? I saw something for three blueies in the market this morning. Thanks for it."

Derk scooped up the rest of the coins and put them in his pouch before any more could be claimed, wondering what had just happened. He put his hat back on his head, only to have Hock knock it off as he walked back into the room. "No hats in the house, it's rude," Hock said, sitting down at the table. He held the plate of food in his hands, high enough the dogs couldn't grab a nibble off of it. "I don't even remember what we were playing, Drink. Can we deal again, let Derk in?"

"You don't remember you was losing?" Drink said, throwing her cards onto the table anyway. "Sure, we can let Derk in." Slender fingers picked up the cards and she shuffled them, the stiff paper rattling . "Paint, you in?"

"I'll play a hand," Paint said. "Wish I had a bigger table. It's usually just me or me and Hock."

"The dogs don't play cards?" Derk asked, sitting up closer to the table.

"These dogs don't do much else besides make messes," Hock said, talking through a mouthful of food. The dog called Lock put her nose on the arm of the chair and looked up at Hock with big eyes. "And beg," he said, offering the dog a tidbit with his fingers. The dog managed to wait, drool starting to dribble from her mouth before she lifted her muzzle up, taking the morsel gingerly between her teeth. "Ah, that's a good girl," Hock said.

"We're playing Crow Catcher," Drink said, dealing out the cards.

"Haven't played Crow Catcher with two pairs in years," Paint said, smiling at Derk. "You and me, eh?"

"I've played a bit, I'm sure we'll get it sorted," Derk smiled. He picked up his cards and looked them over before he took a quick glance around the table. Sitting with Hock, Paint and Drink around the table, one of the dogs chewing on his boot. Drink caught his eye and winked at him. It was different from the comfort of a hard pew and the Goddess' gaze. He hadn't had this kind of comfort for a while. Was it worth ten blueies? Derk grinned as he set his first card down, Hock cursing and Drink punching him in the arm in protest.

Yes, he thought. Yes it was.

Chapter 17
New Alliances

Derk rubbed at his eyes as he clipped up the temple steps. Midday meal was over and done with for most of the town, but Derk had woken up just earlier that watch. Dogs had crowded around him in his sleep and as he smacked at them to scatter he had knocked over beer bottles and other things. Hock and Paint were still sleeping in the one bedroom, he guessed. Drink was nowhere to be found. He would go to temple and then to the baths for a scrub.

He didn't have to go into the temple this time, just to the top of the steps where a small table was set up. Behind it sat a priestess, the same priestess from last night, funnily enough. Derk squinted at her and smiled, wiggling his fingers in hello. She stuck her chin out at him, fiddling with the wares on the table. Derk clasped his hands behind his back and looked them over.

Prayer beads and icons of the Goddess were arranged on the grey square of fabric laying on the tabletop. The icons would be painted by hand. Some were done on carefully shaped pieces of wood, some were carved into stone or clay and one was even etched into metal, bright enamels in silver, black, white and blue depicting the Goddess. Too expensive for him. Some of the necklaces and bracelets were series of knots with the beads at the cusps. He had enough for one of those. "Did you make any of these?" he asked, pointing at jewelry with a wave of a finger.

"I painted some of the icons, yes," she said, sitting up straighter in her chair. "I learned from the High Priestess Kerla of Whitehill. She's the leading expert in depictions of the Goddess in art."

"But you painted as a girl, right?" Derk asked, cocking his head to the side. She nodded. He could tell she was pleased with herself. More than likely she showed promise at an early age, ability which was noticed and cultivated. He wondered how old she had been when she left her family to learn. "Is your mam or pa the artistic one?" he asked.

"My pa was, truth be told," she said. Her light eyes brightened, as if she was hungry to tell the story. "He makes pots, you see, with clay from the lake bed. And he used to paint them and I used to help him." In the young priestess' face, he could see the memory, the happiness with it all. Digging out clay. Watching her pa mold it.

"Which did you do?" he asked, leaning over the table.

The priestess pointed to a clay piece. "I did that one." She pointed to another. "This one too." Derk leaned over as close as he could, not touching the icons with his hands. They were good, actually. Carefully painted lines, the black spiral representing the palm of the Goddess artfully stylized on her work.

"Well, I've got four blueies to spend. I need the rest for a bath. I'm going to see my lady in a bit, so what've you got?"

The priestess' face fell, looking over pieces. She picked up one of the knotted bracelets. "This is five pieces."

"I've got four, I told you. Five and four ain't the same in the Valley yet, are they?" He looked it over. The knots were careful and tightly woven and the beads were a beautiful mix of black and white. "I mean, will it even fit?" he asked, holding out his wrist. "I'll give you the four for the red one."

"What moon were you born in?" she asked, exchanging the black and grey bracelet for the red one. "What's your line of work? Because-"

"I know what red is for, Sister. Four for the red one," he said, still holding out his hand. Pale brows furrowed on her face and she picked it up, tying it around his wrist. Her fingers felt smooth and tickled his skin. He thought about the book he had caught her reading last night but thought better than to bring it up. Derk reached into his purse and pulled out the four blue coins and put them on the table.

"And what's your name, in case I have more than a few coins and want to purchase an icon by yourself? Your work is lovely." He leaned over and looked at it again, wondering how much they were. "I'll say, this piece is by Sister So-And-So, isn't it? I recognize the art. I'll take it."

He wanted to smile but the look on her face made it hard to grin. Her disappointment was evident.

"It's...Arika," she said. "Sister Arika of Three Pines of Ayilkin. I mark all my pieces like this," she said, picking up one of the pieces. On the back the letter 'A' was written three times, the points of a triangle. "I'm...I'm glad you like them," she said.

"Or maybe you can do a new version of the Illustrated Workings?" he suggested, raising his brows. The priestess laughed. "I'd pay for that. Have a blessed day."

"May the Goddess hold you in Her Bosom," the priestess replied. Derk walked backwards a few steps and almost fell down the first one, catching himself just in time before he turned around and went down the stairs.

He didn't bother to stop, just slowed his pace as Drink fell in beside him. "Giving it back?" she asked. Derk held up his wrist to show his new bracelet.

"No, just thought I could use it," he answered. "Spending the rest on a bath. You could use one yourself."

Drink laughed. "I guess you'd be the expert on being wet."

"About that," Derk asked, lowering his voice. "I was wondering about last night-"

"You're not in yet. Though I don't hate you," Drink said, locking her eyes with him. "Just stick with Hock or whoever he passes you on to. Do what he says. Do your thing. Meet a few other people." She nodded, slipping her hand under the strap of her pack. "Come this time next year, you'll be feathered and not fluffed, and floating to boot."

Derk laughed. "You like crows, don't you? You're from Ayilkin, aren't you?"

"Most commoners like crows. They're smart, loyal to their families, adaptable. Black as the night, they can hide in the Goddess' hair. And," she added, gritting her teeth but still smiling, "being from Ayilkin Barony, I'm more than partial to their sayings." Red brows furrowed on her face as she tilted her head slightly with her question. "You the son of a priestess?"

"No," Derk laughed, amused she was guessing. He supposed knowing a bit more about his background was important to her, knowing what the Cup was taking on by taking him on. Perhaps if she knew more about him, she would just let him in. "Just in love with one." It was all he would offer her right now.

Drink didn't seem satisfied with his answer but she drew back, stopping in the street so Derk had to stop as well. "I'm heading to the Holy Bowl. I'm sure I'll see you again."

"I'll make sure you do," Derk said, with a bow, a bow too proper for the occasion but he didn't care. The confusion on her freckled face was worth it. He tipped his cap to her and she turned and left, not bothering to look back as she cut across the street. Derk just shook his head and turned. The bathhouse was waiting. He'd have a bath and try to plan out the best way to impress Drink and the rest before the year was through.

Chapter 18
Finished Business

"From your bed I've been turned, from your life I've been spurned, yet in my heart you remain. Though gone from my eyes, in my thoughts you arise, my love for you, Sindra, the same." Derk looked over the verse, holding the lamp black pencil in his mouth. It was good. Not the best poetry. But sometimes the most heartfelt emotions were best relayed in small phrases. A grip of birch paper couldn't hold all his thoughts and feelings about Sindra, easily filled with his requests for her to reconsider his offer. But hearts weren't won with logic.

He signed the letter, "All my love, Der-" He cursed. After all these years he still wasn't used to signing his name and he had started to write an 's.' Looking it over and considering the letter, Derk managed to turn it into a rather convincing 'k.' He added the vowel marks, careful not to smudge what was already there. "All poetry should have the vowels put in," he said, waiting for the pigment to set before he carefully folded it thirds and then folded the sides, carefully fashioning the letter into the shape of flower. The customary shape for a love note.

Derk took a sip of his beer and set both the letter and the drink aside before he looked at the second sheet of paper. "Cel," he started. "I'm doing well but not good. Always busy and swimming as you say. I've something for yeh when I come see you next, shud be afore our first dance. Stay good." He stared at the words, wondering how to close the letter to Old Gam. Derk missed her. He had left it out of the letter but he did.

Derk glanced over at the letter intended for Sindra and wondered, if he could have either one of them sitting across from him, which one it would be? Intelligent, gorgeous and good Sindra? Or cunning, crass and boisterous Celeel? He loved Sindra, loved who she was. A woman of importance and conviction, who he could talk to about things he couldn't talk to others about. She talked about Church policy, history and scripture with authority. She was kind. He loved to look at her to the point it was almost blasphemous. Celeel on the other hand...he could be himself in a different way with Old Gam. The Derk he always knew he was. She made him laugh and told him plainly when he was being stupid. Except when it came to Sindra. Then her advice was 'Do what you want, you dumb fapper.' What he wanted now was one of them on his lap. He couldn't even decide which one he enjoyed sleeping with more. Each had their charms. Derk shifted in his seat and blew out his cheeks, trying not to think of either of them. He drew two crescents back to back and overlapping, the symbol for 'friendship' and just wrote 'Myself' at the close of Gam's letter, draining his glass before he folded the paper in thirds. He scrawled their final destinations on the backs and then got up from his table, not bothering to push his chair in behind him.

Derk shoved his letters and his pencil in his bag as he headed toward the lightening sky. All the carts heading out would be leaving through the East Gate and one was bound to be heading to Portsmouth, another to South-of-Downs. A bit of cold night air still hung over the city but the approach of summer put a hint of heat in the breeze. Derk yawned, eager to get to bed but still having a few things to do before he turned in.

The bustle of carts getting ready to depart beckoned to him and he listened out for the locations and spaces called out by drivers willing to take letters or people to other locations. Derk helped a pregnant woman and her little boy up into a cart, handing them their bags before he bowed his head to them, listening, straining his ears.

"Portsmouth!" a woman called, waving her whip in the air. Derk pushed his way past a guard and approached the woman, waving his hat above his head to get her attention

"I've a letter for Portsmouth," he said, pulling out the letter for Gam. He handed her the letter and two blue coins, one to get it to Portsmouth, one to get it to Gam's door. He'd only know if Gam got it when he went to go see her. As his plans stood now a month would be the earliest he could get to Portsmouth. A letter would have to do.

"You wrote the address on the back?" the woman asked. Despite the chill she wore a sleeveless shirt. Her arms looked like they were made from ropes, strips of muscles stretching under skin and over bone. Her straw-yellow hair was tied in two long braids hanging down her back.

"As much as I could recall," Derk said hopefully. He had written 'Portsmouth of Tyeskin, The Apartments above the Bone Carvers store on Blue street, second level, Celeel.'

"Better for you, not me," the woman laughed, putting the letter in a bag. "If weather holds fair, should be in Portsmouth in a phase and three," she said.

"Sooner than I'll be there," Derk smirked, tipping his hat to the woman, letting her go back to her shouting and trying to sort out the rest of the calls. A woman in grey robes caught his eye and he rushed over. "Where are you headed, Sister?" he asked.

"Taking priestesses where they need to go, new assignments and all." Derk looked behind her to the cart. A half-dozen girls, wrapped in grey and white shawls sat in the back, holding packs and bundles on their laps.

"Will you be stopping at the temple in South-of-Downs?" Derk asked. "I have a letter."

The old priestess pointed over her shoulder. "You can give it to Darika back there, she's assigned there." Derk walked to the back of the cart, reaching into his bag. He was regretting having folded the letter the way he had. It was obvious what it was. All the girls were looking at him.

"Which of you is Darika?" he asked. A girl with a round face and a slightly upturned nose raised her hand, her short brown curls spilling beyond the edges of her headscarf. "I've a letter for...the High Priestess." He pulled it out and handed it to her. The girl's eyes went wide and he heard the other girls giggle, one of them snorting with laughter. "I would appreciate it," he said. Feeling bad for putting the girl out, he handed her two coins, hoping the extra would save her a bit of face.

"Are you plowing the High Priestess?" one of the girl's asked, a little too loudly for Derk's taste. He avoided their stares and looked around, as if the answer was to be found in the air. He couldn't think of anything so he just bowed to them and turned on his heels and left.

Another errand before he turned in for the night. He would need his rest. Derk had planned a sizable heist for tonight and Hock was in town to help. But before he could do that he had to lay down a bet for tonight's fight. A young man just kicked out of the Martial Academy of Gorskin was to go up against one of Block Lord Sunny's better boys. Hock thought Sunny's boy was going to win. While the fight was going on, Derk planned to pop into Ferix's dye shop and steal a few packets of dye.

Autumn was making its way through the Valley and Lover's Moon would have people wanting to wear their finest clothes for the festivals before they went indoors for the cold months. He would save a bit for Gam. Gam would make something beautiful with the colors and her fibers. She had a talent. Sindra wouldn't be taking him on for the winter, he knew that. It didn't mean he couldn't spend the night with her and get her something. Maybe a scarf this year, to keep her warm. Last winter she had gotten sick to the point she couldn't speak except in a hilarious rasp. It seemed like a long time ago. He had kissed her anyway, not caring. Even after she reminded him she wouldn't take vows with him. Derk yawned, a smile pulling at his mouth as he remembered her heavy lidded eyes, flushed, dark skin and slender fingers in his hair.

The bar where the fight would be taking place was serving customers already, the front doors propped open with barrels. Someone was slumped in their seat at the bar, head on the bar top. Derk knew the situation well. He cast a glance about the bar, managing to not look surprised at the table of three browncloaks at the corner table, eating their morning meal after getting off watch. Last night's beer barely wafted through the scents of toasted barley cereal, pork belly and ember cooked eggs. Derk hopped up onto the bar stool, feeling very tired. The bartender looked like he was about to get off shift as well. He laid his eyes on Derk, eyed the guards and then looked back to Derk, business written on his scruffy face. "What'll it be?" the man asked.

"I wanted to ask, what'll you have for midday meal?" Derk asked, hands in his lap. "Just curious as to what I should have when I come back."

"We've got custard and greens but if you want something heavier, barley bread and rabbit shred made with dried fruit and beer."

"Those both sound good," Derk mused, tapping his fingers on the counter top. The noise did nothing to wake the sleeping man, just quieted the snore emitting from him. "How about for now, an ember cooked egg and creamed beans if you have any leftover."

"Bread?" the man asked, pulling out a mug from under the counter and setting it in front of Derk.

"Yeah, on the bottom. And just boiled water to drink," Derk added. As soon as the barkeep went back to get his meal, Derk leaned his head against his hand, barely able to keep his eyes open. He pulled out paper and pouch, rolling a cigarette while he waited. Running his tongue over the edge, he raised his brows at the barkeep as the food was set in front of him. It was simple fare, the egg cut into slices so rounds of nutty white nestled the rich, orange yolks, atop white, creamy beans and brown bread. Tired as he was, Derk's stomach gurgled in response.

"Did you decide on midday?" the barkeep asked. Derk tried hard not to look at the browncloaks. The food definitely gave him something to pay attention to so he looked at his plate.

"Yeah, I'll probably go for the custard. Been in the mood for eggs lately." Derk picked up the bread and took a bite out of it, tearing into the food. He put a hand over his mouth, talking through the mouthful. "What do I owe for the food?"

"Four blueies altogether," the barkeep said. Derk didn't bother to comment on the price. It was one blueie more than he liked to pay for breakfast, but he wasn't about to haggle when he had food in his mouth. With his free hand he reached into his pocket and pulled out the four blue metal coins, careful to sandwich the white lunar in there for Hock's bet. "You're new here, aren't you?" the keep asked, tucking the coins away. Derk could hear them clink, the blueies in one purse, the white coin in another. "What's your name?"

"Eh, my friends call me Lurk," Derk said, taking another bite. He'd have to come back and pick up the bet after all was said and done. If he was lucky he'd get to see part of the fight. Hock wouldn't come around. The man who had taken Derk under his wing owed a bit of money but didn't want to pay it back just yet. Hence why Derk was in the bar. The barkeep nodded and went into the kitchen leaving Derk to finish his meal in peace. By the time he had wiped the last smear of beans off his mouth his water was cool enough to drink and he gulped it down before he hopped down off his bar stool. He lit his cigarette on the oil lamp sitting on the edge of the bar top, saluted the browncloaks and stepped outside.

It was too bright. Derk squinted as he closed his purse, his cigarette dangling between his lips. It was going to be a warm autumn. People were starting to get to work, booths popped open like mushrooms since he walked down the street just before his meal. He turned down an alley, noting the group of younger men laughing and jumping over some crates. Derk walked past, keeping an eye on them. One of the boys' heads popped up, and called out, "Lurk! Hold up!" Derk slowed and then turned, sure to keep his attention on the small throng. These were streetsmen in training, self-training as it may be. They weren't to be trusted but they were good to have at one's disposal at times. He flicked a bit of ash into the gutter and took another drag off his cigarette, waiting to see what would happen.

The boy named Shamsee stumbled over, pulling something out of his pocket. Derk watched as the boy with the curly hair and big brown eyes pulled a stack of cards out of his pocket. When the boy looked up and smiled at him, Derk noted the black eye. The boy had a knack for getting into trouble but always managed to avoid serious injury or legal consequence. He claimed his whole family was lucky, that his mam had birthed five children, of which he was the last. It was the biggest family Derk had ever heard of but he suspected the mom didn't have any brains left to give the boy by the time he was made. But the Goddess gives out luck at least.

"I've a stack of cards here and I can guess yours. If I guess, you owe me a blueie," Shamsee said. He shuffled the cards on his knee, several of them spilling to the ground.

"Quick, Sham. I'm on my way to temple for a sleep. Gotta be up in time for the fight tonight," Derk muttered, pulling at his cigarette one more time before he looked to the other boys behind Sham. "Any of you want the rest?" The smoke and the flavor began to wind its way around his brain, making his head swim a bit but not so much he wouldn't be able to avoid getting taken by a pack of young trouble-makers. The boys shook their head and kept their distance. Sham lifted his head, rearranging the cards in his hands.

"Oh, you're going to be there?" Shamsee said. His hands were dirty and his shirt sleeves too long for the weather. "I might go, if I can sneak in. I got kicked out of the Two Fisted a phase ago. Not my fault, mind you, he just got mad when I said the Skinner got sick on his food. Helping people not get sick on his food, you know, I didn't say anything about his beer. The beer is good." Shamsee splayed the cards out carefully, his tongue sticking out of his mouth as he did. "Okay now, pick one!"

Derk reached out with the hand holding the smoke and pulled out a card, looking it over. His face fell and he threw the card into Shamsee's face. "Sham, you chicken-brain, these are fortune telling cards! Get these away from me!" Shamsee tried to catch the card Derk threw and dropped the others in the process. Derk turned to leave, hearing the boys all laughing, most of them directing their ridicule at Sham.

"No wonder I couldn't play Four Are The Seasons with these!" Shamsee cackled. "Hey, you owe me for telling your fortune then! One blueie!"

"Grab betwixt, Shamsee," Derk called back, gesturing rudely behind his back and flicking the butt to the side. A peal of laughter followed him onto the main street. Derk patted his shirt and pockets to make sure nothing had been taken from him during the failed bit of showmanship. He still had his pouch and dagger. Ignoring the increasing hustle and bustle of the street, he turned down the side street and entered the temple through the backdoor, nodding to the priestess there, noting the cudgel across her lap. As always it was quiet within the temple, the soft notes of a hymn being played in the sanctuary. Derk made his way to the basement stairs, pulling out the wooden token given to him that morning in exchange for the one they had given him the day before. The older priestess looked it over and then let him pass.

The room downstairs was almost empty, most of last night's previous inhabitants already up and probably wandering the streets or on their way to the next town. A trio of people who had shown up right when Derk had left for the evening were still asleep, probably weary from hard travels. It had been obvious from their appearance they had ridden hard. Derk went to the wicker boxes the Church provided to hold belongings and pulled out his pack and bedroll before he looked at the trio once more, finding a corner to set up his sleeping space. He unfolded a mat provided by the church and put his pack where he could lay his head. His boots found their way to the foot, his pants folded and placed atop them. Sitting on the makeshift bed, he pulled his shirt off, knowing in the basement of the church he could sleep soundly

As soon as he laid his head down the thoughts came flooding in. The heist. The door. The store. His tools. The store owner. He was supposed to be at the fight that night, another reason Derk wanted to have it done within a certain amount of time so he could make an appearance toward the end. Getting in at the end would be hard but doable. He'd have to pay to get in. The trapdoor where the special dyes were kept. Derk knew where it was because he had sent Jezlen in to trade. One look at Jezlen and the shop owner suspected nothing when the Forester entered, claiming he had something rare to trade. It wasn't entirely a lie. Jezlen did know how to prepare and transport plenty of things in such a way their effects would be maximized. It had more to do with the fact his mother was a healer than it did with Jezlen being an elf. His mother being a healer meant the Forester knew the best things to put in his pipe or soak in alcohol.

The effects of the herbs Jezlen had given him to smoke earlier were kicking in a bit more, slowing down the once racing thoughts. The trap door. He would climb in through a window since the back door was locked from the inside with a padlock and the front door was on the main street. A lamp was lit on the street corner, and putting it out would draw more attention than breaking in through the front door. There was a lock on the trapdoor leading to where the special dyes were kept. Just powders. He would pick up a bottle of fixing powder as well. And then he'd go to the fight. And then he would pick up Hock's money. Head South to Bluemist to meet Hock and wait for Jezlen.

Derk anticipated succeeding. Hock had hinted if he did this, there could be others in Bluemist waiting to congratulate him. If this was the step Derk had to take to get into the Cup, he would ride to Sindra and ask her to marry him again. But first, the window, the lock, the trapdoor.

In his thoughts when he opened the trapdoor there wasn't anything there but the card he had pulled from Shamsee. The New Moon Card. The empty card. He hated fortune telling. Something about the card made him not want to touch it but it was where he needed to go. Without bending over it was in his hand, the thick paper between his fingertips. The gaping emptiness of the black moon in a black sky, offering nothing. Something beyond the card moved. When he looked, Sindra was there, smiling. There were tears in her eyes, making her normally dark grey eyes look like metal, sharp and cold. Before he could say anything, he was in her arms and her mouth was on his, kissing him hungrily. He couldn't speak or say anything, just succumbed to her hot skin and warm body, the walls of the shop falling away so they were left in darkness, naked.

Derk woke with a start, finding himself in the temple and feeling disoriented. His dream had felt so real but the time spent so short. His heart still rattled in his chest and his skin was damp and hot. Derk cursed Jezlen under his breath, turning over on his bedroll. Waking up dressed, in the church, alone...Derk took a breath, breathing in and out slowly, feeling air fill his lungs, his belly, pouring into his arms and legs. The sound of people talking quietly registered at the edge of his mind and he slowly sat up on the bedroll, letting the blankets pile in his lap.

Two priestesses were quietly cleaning the room. The trio was gone and in their place a mother and a child sat against a wall. The child played quietly with dolls made of scraps of fabric. The mother didn't seem to notice. The woman stared off into space, mouth slightly open. Derk noticed her arm was in a sling, the hand bandaged. A reddish spot on the off-white the dressing hinted it would need to be changed soon. Derk took one last deep breath, fully in the room, in the Valley, his dream pushed away.

Reaching over, he grabbed his shirt, pulling it on over his head before he stood up, dressing quickly. There wasn't a mirror in the room so he looked to the little girl, noticing she was staring at him. He held his hands out to the side and smiled warmly at her. "How do I look?" he asked. The little girl's eyes went wide and she buried her face in her mother's side. But he saw one blue eye peek out and the corner of the girl's mouth curl in a smile. Derk stowed his pack in the wicker box and tapped one of the Sisters on the shoulder. "Sister, I think you should see to that woman," he said, indicating the mother with a nod of his head. "Her hand needs to be tended to, I think."

"Thank you," the priestesses said. Derk gave one last look to the little girl and the woman before he went upstairs. He was sure to get the new token for the night from the priestess at the top of the stairs, turning to enter the temple for a blessing before he headed out.

The temple was full of people who came for prayer before evening meal, sitting in the pews. Derk slid into an empty row and pulled his bracelet off, finding the white bead through feel more than sight. He put his hands over his chest and bowed his head. A priest was at the altar, playing a small harp and singing "Light of Revelation." Not really what Derk wanted.

He rolled the knots between his fingers, reciting the Titles, the Attributes, the Loves and the Mercies. At the beginning of each list he felt each stone bead, felt their polish, the unseen nicks in their surfaces. And when he came to the end, he felt the Goddess Bead. He had replaced it with a bigger one, a finer one. Derk held it in his hand, holding the image of the Goddess in his mind as he made his prayer.

"Blessed Goddess, Holy Mother, put your light in my eyes. Guide my hand with your own. Hide me in my work and grant me success in my endeavor. Show me the way through the dark. May your Black Hand guide me and those I love." He kissed the Goddess Bead and slipped the bracelet back on before he slid out of the seat, dipping his fingers into the bowl of holy water set up in the vestibule, anointing his head and heart before he stepped out onto the street.

Chapter 19
Stealing Away

Derk wasn't hungry but he would grab something to eat and drink while the sun went down. He'd go by the Two Fisted and get seen around there before ducking to the dyer's store and make his score. Then back to the Two Fisted to get Hock's money if there was any to be had, and then maybe a game of cards. The Happy Owl was supposed to have good singers. He should celebrate a bit by himself before the congratulations from Hock and Drink came rolling in. A smile curled up his mouth as the thought solidified in his brain.

He stopped at a food stall and sat at the small table set up beside it, trying not to get grease on his face or clothes. Bread fried in bacon grease with onions. It was a bit too rich for his taste so he left the last few bites for whatever man or beast cared for the rest, deciding he would get a beer at the Two Fisted before he went to the dyers.

The streets were full of people heading home for their suppers but Derk felt alone. Alone in his purpose. He missed his friends, the few he had. He missed Sindra. He even missed Jezlen. Maybe he'd take Jezlen to meet Gam sooner rather than later. Jezlen never seemed interested when he mentioned it, and Old Gam always seemed apprehensive about meeting him after Derk relayed stories. Jezlen was a...reliable person. Derk could rely on him. The Forester had a peculiar sense of humor and strange tastes but Derk appreciated the change in pace from the average Valleyman.

The Two Fisted was busier than Derk thought it would be and he quickly ordered a beer, the barkeep narrowing his eyes, and then nodding as he recognized him. Derk raised his glass and smiled, feeling his tools pinch and press against the skin of his arm. "I never did come by for lunch," Derk said.

"Maybe some other time, Lurk," the keep said. "They've got some in the back if you wanted to try it."

"I'll probably do that," Derk said, taking another sip of his drink. Someone else called the tender over and Derk took the opportunity to finish his beer and walk out the door, presumably to the fight. He guessed there was a staircase in the kitchen leading to the basement. For now, he would go down the street for three blocks, a left, then another left to the store. After it was done he would come back. Usually there would be a few matches so he wouldn't miss the main event if he was quick.

Derk felt his heart race as he walked casually through the streets, ignoring the other people, ignoring the lamps being lit on the corners. He could smell the oil burning but kept his eyes on the dark corners of the street, trying to make out what was in the shadows. The nasal invitation of a woman with bells at her bosom drew a shake of his head so as not to seem out of place, but he pushed her and the rest of those on the streets away from him, ignoring them as he walked. Solitude pushed against him and he recalled the tools under his shirt sleeve and the dagger laying against his skin, warm.

The dyer's lay ahead, the lamplight illuminating the street but still he kept his eyes averted from the bright lights. It was called 'Red Rabbit,' a red rabbit fur hanging down from the name board. Beside it was a fiber store specializing in thread for embroidery. He knew more about embroidery than he cared to, thanks to Gam. Gam would like a bit of dye. Derk wasn't doing this just for himself, or even just for the recognition from the Cup. He would get something for Gam, and once he sold everything, something for Sindra. For all her dislike of his stealing, the priestess did like beautiful things.

These stores closed earlier than the others since most people did their daily shopping before evening meal, so the streets were emptier. The residences in this part of the town numbered less and were nice, with some shop owners living above their establishments. The embroidery shop owner lived above her shop, but the dyer didn't. The space above the store was used to dry and prepare some of the rawer materials they received. The money was probably kept there as well.

Derk walked behind the building, looking around and listening for voices or animals. It was quiet and empty and dark, the lamplight having no effect back here. Derk stared up at the side of the building, looking around once more before he walked over, putting his weight on a crate to test it before climbing up onto it. He pulled his knife out, feeling his shirt pull out of his pants. He listened for a breath and then wedged his knife in the space between where the windows were latched closed. The hook lifted after a quick flick of his wrist, freeing the two sides from each other. The windows swung outward so he pulled them toward him, stowing his dagger in the back of his pants before he placed both arms in the window, trying to swing himself in without waving his legs around too much or losing his bearings. Below the window the floor seemed low and there was a table littered with plenty of things which could fall and break if he wasn't careful.

He fell back onto the crate, careful not to make too much noise and listening again for another soul. A cat mewed off in the distance but Derk heard nothing else. Leaping up, he caught the ledge above the window where it had been set into the wall, getting a foot on the bottom of the sill and quickly maneuvering hand and weight so that he was perched in the window, like a dark bird with a yellow crown. He peered down at the table and slid down onto it from the window, testing its sturdiness before he put his entire weight on it, turning and closing the windows behind him.

The lamplight from outside poured through small windows close to the ceiling but the backroom was dark. He saw the staircase leading up to the airing room. Derk hopped down onto the stone floor, looking around at what was in the backroom out of habit more than out of interest. Packages of herbs and substances were stacked on another table, unlabeled, herbal and animalistic scents faint in the air.

He slid the lock picks from where they were strapped around his bicep, crouching down. A lock had been built into the floor and he saw the outline of the door, the metal ring used to pull it up. The floor creaked. Derk wondered why they just didn't keep the pricier dyes upstairs. He yawned as he eased two picks into the keyhole. He felt almost disappointed as it clicked open easily, yielding to his gentle prodding. A grin crossed his face as he replaced the tools and opened the safe in the floor.

A few off-white packets were stacked in the hole in the ground. If everything was pulled out, the edge would have gone a bit past his ankles, if that. Derk picked them up and noticed words written on the packets, wondering what they said. Pulling a few out, he ventured into the front room, knowing the shuttered street level windows kept him from detection.

"Dried bog snake venom. Rockcrawl blossom, dried under the 3rd full moon. Marrowroot seed, grated." No need to be picky. Derk tucked all of them away. He then looked behind the counter for a glass of fixer. It would make the colors brighter, though it itself didn't lend any color to garments. He could cut the first three with more common and easily acquired items to make a good product at a good cost. It was stolen, so it was all profit but he could make more if he 'had' more. Gam would get the unadulterated stuff though, he would be sure of it.

A glint of metal caught Derk's eye. He crept over and investigated, almost groaning out loud when he saw what it was. A key, probably for the trapdoor. Derk sighed. If he ever had a store it would be the least easy thing to break into, he told himself, pulling the key off the nail and going to close it. Before he could do it, he thought of the envelopes in the backroom, going back to retrieve several to carry out the newest part of his plan.

Derk set the key on the table and lifted their folds, bringing the envelopes to his nose. He opened the ones he had taken, already labeled. If it was brighter back here he could be clever and just take unlabeled stock. But the pen was right there...carefully he wrote the labels from the three stolen envelopes onto three of the ones from the backroom. After blowing on them to dry the ink he set them in the safe and closed it. His handwriting was nicer than whoever labeled the envelopes. He locked the safe before returning the key to the nail, pulling the bag he had tucked into his belt and stowing the fixer and three packets in there, securing it to himself. Now the number of envelopes in the safe matched what was there before. The man who ran the store might be more likely to think it was a mix up between his workers than a theft if things were mislabeled. Why not confuse them a bit?

Now to get out. The table under the window was not very stable. It moved when he put his weight to one side or the other, risking knocking things off. Even if he could steady it, he might kick something off which wasn't his goal. And when he got up into the window there would be getting down. He would have to get out quickly and quietly.

The front room had a side window with a heavier latch, but the alley it opened into was dark. And he wouldn't have to jump down from anything. Derk walked into the front room, opening the shutters and peering out into the street, listening. He then quickly opened the window and stepped over the sill, careful not to catch his pants on the apron. He then quickly reached in and pulled the shutters closed, his fingers wedged into the slats to fix them in place. The window panels were next, and he took the extra step of wiggling his fingers in and latching the hook so it would look as if no one had opened them.

Derk inhaled through his nose and blew out through his mouth, the Goddess Bead warm against his wrist. He brought the bracelet up and kissed the image, exiting the alley quickly but cautiously. If anyone saw him sneaking out it could raise suspicion but he wanted to get away as quickly as he could. A few street cleaners were out picking up debris, putting it into barrels. They didn't seem to notice him so he walked down the street, back the way he came, his heart racing not with anticipation but excitement. He imagined the praise from Hock. Drink's smirk of approval. Old Gam's underhanded admiration. Jezlen's indifference. And Sindra. How did she fit in? He wanted her. What was she to him? Next time he saw her he would get it sorted. Once he was in the Cup.

The streets grew busier the closer he got to the Two Fisted, the music he heard in the distance growing closer. Derk didn't bother going into the front door but swung around to the back, making sure the dyes and fixer were secured. The back window was open, a bald man with a huge cleaver hacking at a bird carcass. "I heard you had some of midday meal still? Custard and greens?"

"You're a bit late," the big man said. The man's arms suggested he did a bit more than hack at dead animals and he was missing a few teeth on the bottom. Derk fought the urge to take a step back and leaned over the back door.

"I've got money to pay," he said. The cook smiled and walked over, opening the door and letting him in. Behind the pantry was a staircase, the sound of shouts and cheers coming through the hole. The big man looked Derk over, wiping his hands on his apron.

"I think someone is down there looking for you," the big man said. "Forester type. You know a Forester?"

Derk's brows furrowed. Jezlen? He wasn't supposed to meet Jezlen till the next town. "I know of one," Derk lied, just in case. "What's he look like?"

"Like a hem chawing Forester, you know," the big man guffawed. "Keep your eyes open. You going in or what?" He looked into the pantry and gestured. "I've got food to cook."

Derk nodded and walked past the potatoes, beans and barley, stepping down the ladder into the lower room. The room was packed, barrels and ropes keeping the audience back from the fighting ring, a circle drawn on the floor in white powder. It was hot and it smelled like sweat and alcohol, a hint of blood tinging the stuffy air. The sound of every smack and punch and grunt was followed by the shouted commentary of the audience, pushing and jostling to get a better look. Derk tied his belt tighter and waved to the man behind the table.

"Lurk, I put a bet this morning on Sunny's boy, one lunar." The man looked over a ledger, a small knife used as a pointer.

"Just in time," the old man said. "This fight's almost over if you can't tell." A shout rang up, louder than before and Derk wondered how no one upstairs heard them, even with the band playing. Derk nodded and looked over the crowd, trying to figure out the best way to get to the front. In one corner of the room he could see Sunny's boy, hair cut close to the scalp and skin shining with oil. Sunny stood to the side, towheaded and melancholy.

Derk pushed through the crowd, wondering where Jezlen was, if he was still around. At the same time he scanned the crowd for the other fighter and a good spot to watch the fight. A chorus of screams, curses and laughs went up as one of the fighters stumbled and fell.. Hands flew into the air and a man pushed into the middle to see if the man could keep going. People stomped the floor so loud Derk thought it'd make the ceiling fall in. In another corner he saw the boy kicked out of the military academy. His hair was a bit too long for a fight but his nose looked like it had been broken a few times. He looked angry. Very angry.

Across the ring Derk saw the dark face of Jezlen. They saw each other at the same time, the Forester's eyes growing wide and his face dropping as their eyes met. Derk waved. He expected Jezlen to make a face and wave him over but to his surprise his friend just ducked his head and started pushing through the crowd. Derk started to make his way in his direction, finally walking around the push of people, waving as he saw the elf pop out of the crowd.

A shout dampened the words Jezlen called and Derk walked up to him, patting his own belt to make sure his belongings were all still there. If he hadn't been so intent on finding Jezlen, a few more items might have made their way into his possession. But the look on Jezlen's face drew Derk close "What's going on? Everything alright?"

"Sindra-" Jezlen started but a scream from the crowd said the fight was over, the clang of a bell and a shout announcing the winner. Derk didn't care. Jezlen put his arm on Derk's back, turning them both away from the crowd.

"What about her?" Derk said.

"I went by her temple on my way up from the South," Jezlen shouted. "To see her. She is dead."

Derk pulled away from Jezlen. What? He felt as if all the air had been sucked out of the room along with the sound. "What?" he said, too quietly. "What?" Maybe he had misheard. The room was noisy. People were starting to push past him, bumping him. "Jez-"

"She is dead," Jezlen said putting his mouth close to Derk's ear. "I had to tell you."

"What? HOW?" Derk grabbed Jezlen by the collar of his shirt. He felt like he had been punched in the stomach but he was still standing somehow. He needed to know. "HOW?"

"Let go of me!" Jezlen shouted, putting his hands on his chest. Someone saw the two of them and shouted in approval, a crowd starting to form around them. "Stop, people are staring!"

"If this is a joke-" Derk started.

"Why would I joke about this?!" Jezlen screamed.

"Punch him in the face!" someone suggested, drawing laughs and more shouts from the crowd. It knocked Derk out of his stupor and he let go of Jezlen, drawing boos and jeers from the crowd. He loosened his grip on his friend and Jezlen dropped his hands from him.

"Just a misunderstanding!" Derk said, draping an arm around Jezlen's shoulders. "Just a matter of money!" he said, laughing it off. He could feel Jezlen tighten under his hold, the Forester not a fan of being touched. To appease the crowd and anger Jezlen more he reached over and ruffled his hair, waving till the crowd turned their attention back to the ring, leaving the pair of men to themselves.

"I am going to send you to the Tits of your Goddess if you do not stop touching me right now," Jezlen hissed in his ear. Derk might have found this funny under other circumstances. But he needed answers.

"Is that the only thing you could think to say right now?" Derk asked. He wanted to slap Jezlen across the face. He could feel his hand twitch, wanting to hit him. But he didn't. His breath came quickly as he waited to think of what to ask, letting his hand slide off the Forester. "What are you talking about?" The referee was announcing the other two fighters, the crowd commencing with their ruckus, but still Derk kept his eyes on Jezlen. He found himself leaning against one of the walls. "Jezlen?"

"We should leave," Jezlen said, loudly, so Derk would hear him. "It is too loud here."

"I...I have to stay. I have to collect Hock's bet. He made a bet. On Sunny's boy." Derk pointed at the crowd.

"The boy is going to lose," Jezlen said. "I hope Hock gave you the money to pay."

"I've two extra lunars. But..." Derk didn't care how Jezlen knew. He pushed himself off the wall and nodded toward the exit, Jezlen falling in behind him. He waved two fingers at the old man at the betting table before he climbed up the ladder into the dark pantry. When Jezlen had climbed up Derk knocked on the door, waiting for the cook to let them out. The bald cook looked them over and grinned.

"Ah, see you found each other," he laughed.

"Yes," Jezlen said. The annoyance in his voice was obvious to Derk. The cook just continued to smile

"Is there reentry?" Derk asked, walking toward the door. It was cooler in the kitchen than downstairs and a cool breeze still managed to make its way through the half-door.

"If the fight is still going, yeah, but if it's over you can settle with Ferix. Open all night if you get hungry."

"Right," Derk said, wanting to leave already. He pushed the bottom door open and walked out into the late spring evening.

Sindra. Dead. "How could this be?" Derk asked. "Jezlen, tell me?"

"I went by her temple on my way up from the south," Jezlen began. He didn't look at Derk but across the alley as if he was ashamed to tell him, avoiding his eyes. "When I went and asked for her, the priestess looked concerned and asked if I was related to her. I told her I was her..her nephew." All these years and Jezlen still had trouble with certain words. "She took me aside and told me Sindra was dead."

"But how?" Derk asked. Jezlen's lack of telling was starting to make him anxious and he wanted to shake him but he stopped himself. "An accident?"

"It looks like...someone killed her?" Jezlen said it like a question, as if he himself didn't believe it. "Or as if she killed herself."

"She wouldn't kill herself," Derk insisted. "She had no reason to. Sindra was never in despair."

"They found her in her tent. Her knife was in her hand. Her throat." Jezlen didn't bother to say anything else. His hands were shaking. Derk leaned up against the building, his head swimming with Jezlen's words.

"It had to have been someone else," Derk said. "Someone. Who? Who could have done this? Who? She never...she never mentioned anyone to me besides the priestesses, never said she was in trouble. She would have told me, right?" His last few words were muffled by the lump forming in his throat. "Who could it have been?"

"It...Derk, no matter who it was...she is still dead." The Forester's words were quiet but clear. Derk was grateful for the sadness in Jezlen's words. He dropped his head to his chest and now the tears fell, burning his eyes and making his face feel tight. Sindra...gone. Pulled from life, from his life. He balled his hands into fist and set them on his legs, not caring Jezlen could see him cry. He loved her. He still did. His heart ached for her, ached for her in a different way now. Knowing the hole would never be filled. He would never hold her hand, kiss her cheek, lay beside her. He would never hear her say she loved him. He would never hear her refusal. Smell the sweet scent of her neck or hair, taste the salt of her skin, feel the press of her lips.

Derk slumped to the ground, sobbing. He cried for the loss of the woman he loved, for the future they wouldn't have. His plans for the both of them, destroyed. Her own plans, the history she wanted to write, the ways she wanted to help the Church and the Valley. They had been robbed. He had felt alone before hitting the Red Rabbit but he felt even more alone now. Though he wasn't. Derk wiped his nose with the back of his hand, pressing his palms into his eyes. He still had the Cup. And Gam. And Jezlen. He turned his reddened eyes to the Forester, not surprised to have Jezlen's metal flask offered to him. The lid was already undone. Derk brought it to his mouth and sipped from it while Jezlen pulled out his pipe. Derk didn't say anything when Jezlen went to the kitchen door for a light. He just waited for Jezlen to hand him the pipe.

"The smoke you gave me last time wasn't good. It gave me strange dreams." Derk thought about the dream he had and how Sindra had been in it. "I...Sindra was in the dream." Derk took a pull off the pipe. His lungs burned along with his eyes. Something about it made him feel more calm.

"Oh?" Jezlen said. He took the pipe from Derk. Derk nodded, taking another sip from the flask. It was strong, whatever it was, but Jezlen's stuff always was.

"Yeah." Derk looked over at Jezlen, trying to keep too much hope from his voice. "You don't think...maybe. Maybe it was Sindra?"

Jezlen exhaled a chestful of smoke, staring off in the distance for so long, Derk thought perhaps he hadn't heard him. Derk was about to ask him again when Jezlen shook his head, turning to give him the pipe again. "No, I do not think it was."

"Oh." Derk frowned. He held the pipe in his hand, looking at it and the flask. He wondered what Sindra would say if she saw him. "Out of curiosity, how d'you figure?"

He saw Jezlen stiffen slightly, crossing his arms over his chest. "Because," came Jezlen's reply. "The people from the Forest of Clouds do not dream." Dark eyebrows on his face raised at Derk, annoyance in his voice. Derk knew he hadn't wanted to give up the piece of information but he had given it to him. It surprised Derk. But it answered his question.

"What happens to Foresters?" Derk asked, knowing what he was about to ask was strange. "When they die?" The contents of the flask were starting to make him woozy, his stomach growing warm.

"They rot. Like Valleymen." Jezlen's eyes smiled but he managed to keep his face calm, one of his more annoying traits. Derk managed to laugh, shaking his head.

"No, to their souls," he said. "What happens?" Again, Jezlen didn't answer. This time he stared at the ground, his lips a thin line on his dark face.

"To tell the truth, I think Sindra will go to be with your Goddess. Her body was made in the Forest but her soul was made here, I think. Why else would she have come here?" Jezlen took the flask from Derk and held it for a breath before he took a large swig from it. Derk thought he looked like he needed it.

"And what about you?" Derk asked. He stood up slowly, his back sliding against the rough wall of the bar. "What'll happen when you die?"

"Hopefully I will just be dead," Jezlen said. This time Jezlen did smile, one of the rare times he did. It was such a terrible reason to smile but it made Derk laugh. They both laughed for a while, the dark mood lifting slightly. Derk handed the pipe back to Jezlen and started to walk down the street.

"I could steal a horse today but getting out of the gate would be the issue. Unless we left and hit one of the farms outside the wall but there's no guarantee any of the horses will be good for riding, and not in the dark. Plus, the noise." Derk looked up at the sky. "When is New Moon?"

"Two evenings from now."

"I'll never get to Southpoint by then."

"For what?" Jezlen asked, sounding genuinely confused.

"The Goddess comes on the New Moon to collect the souls of the living. I thought-" Derk put his hands on the back of his neck, realizing what he was going to say. "I could say goodbye. Talk to her one more time." Doctrine said the souls remained in the bodies until the Goddess came to collect them. People kept vigil over the dead to keep them company, singing songs or speaking so the souls wouldn't grow lonely or crazed while still trapped in their bodies.

Jezlen handed him the flask once more, his face stripped of the mirth which had just been there. "Derk. She is dead. There is nothing left to say. She knew you loved her."

Derk let Jezlen's words wrap around his heart once more, remembering the last time he had kissed her. Before he escaped out her window. "And a good amount of help that afforded me." He brought the flask to his lips and drained it, feeling the hot liquid snake down his throat, burning away his pity and regret for now. Sindra.

"Come on. I have to pay Hock's stupid bet. We can go from there to Bluemist. Give him his money. Then...." The thought of being inducted into the Cup floated through his brain. For some reason he wasn't as excited for it anymore. He needed it, now more than ever. Now Sindra was gone. He remembered Drink's words, about more people together making a bigger mark. He wouldn't do anything with Sindra. This was his chance. The fact this was the way he would leave his big mark, this way alone, filled him with something. It wasn't hope. It was something else, something darker and more desperate. Derk didn't like the feeling.

"Let's just pay the bet," he said finally, walking ahead and Jezlen falling behind once more. "I'll decide what to do next after I deal with Hock and the Cup." Derk pushed open the doors, not surprised to see some of the faces from the fight in the bar now, singing along with the girl on stage. The ex-student from the military academy was sitting at a table, his nose obviously broken again but he was obviously too drunk at the point to care. As for Sunny and his boy, they were nowhere to be seen.

Carefully they wove their way through the crowd, Derk carefully relieving anyone who bumped into them of their purse, passing them back to Jezlen as he made his way to the bar. He pounded his fist onto the bar top, wanting to deal with the bet and leave. The barkeep from earlier came to him, looking dreadfully tired. "Can I help you?" he asked. He look like he was about to fall asleep on his feet.

"I placed a bet," Derk said, not bothering to keep his voice down. It was so loud no one would have heard, and anyone who would have heard was probably at the fight himself. "Lurk," he reminded the keep. The keep nodded and ducked into the kitchen. Jezlen squirmed on his seat beside him, obviously uncomfortable with the volume of people.

"Here you go," the barkeep said, sliding him a piece of bread. Under the bread were three white coins. Derk frowned, tucking them away before the barkeep could take them back, looking around the room. The man beside him looked like someone from the fight so he tapped him.

"Eh, who won the fight?" Derk asked. The man swayed in his seat, drunk as well and seemingly happy to be so.

"Oh, Sunny's boy!" the man exclaimed. "It was a great fight!" Derk held up his hand and thanked him before the man could get any further and he hopped off the stool and wove his way back through the crowds, the effects of the liquor and the heat pushing toward the cool night air. As soon as they got outdoors, Derk looked to Jezlen.

"I thought you said the other one would win," he accused.

"I just wanted to get you out of there," Jezlen admitted with a comical shrug.

Derk snorted. "Ass," he said. A quick glance around the road and Derk realized they had nowhere to go and they wouldn't be able to get out of the town until first watch. He didn't want to sleep in the Church. Not tonight. Even though he had been awake for only a few hours he felt tired.

"You have any money?" he asked Jezlen. Jezlen raised a brow. "Come on," Derk insisted. "I know you've got a pack stashed somewhere. You don't just wander the Valley with your knife and you don't stay in temples." He put his hands on his waist and waited for Jezlen to answer.

"You just received a good bit of money in that bar," Jezlen reminded him, raising his brows. Derk hit himself in the head and laughed.

"Right you are!" he said. "Let's go get a pitcher of beer and a room. Something with a few beds not on the floor. Something...nice."

"If you crawl into my bed, I will kill you," Jezlen said.

"Don't flatter yourself," Derk laughed, walking in the direction of an inn he knew, one which didn't have a band and a fight on the same night. "I know a place that makes a nice ground apple brandy. I could use...I could use a drink. And a good sleep." Derk took a deep breath and he and Jezlen walked down the street in silence. Derk couldn't help but hold the Goddess Bead from his bracelet in his hand, casting a glance at the almost New Moon in the sky. It was too late, he told himself. For some things. Not for all things. If he couldn't make a future with Sindra, he would find another way. He was already well on his path. The thought of anyone wanting to kill the gentle priestess...the moon looked cold and sharp despite the warm air and Derk shivered. It was a cruel end to a good woman. Derk crossed his arms across his chest, wishing he could hold Sindra one last time.

Chapter 20
Personal Business

Derk dipped his spoon in his cup, watching the hot tea dissolve the honey at the bottom. He still smelled the incense from the temple in the chamber, but the High Priestess' office was scented more like parchments, oil lamps and sunshine on stone, the windows opened wide to the streets outside. Derk rubbed at his chin, scratching his beard with recently cleaned fingernails. The High Priestess was dressed in robes of simple but sharp grey and white. Derk knew her hair was dark and very curly but the woman somehow kept it wrapped in a dark grey shawl. Her stole embroidered with silver thread was the only thing giving away her position within the Church.

He was glad to have the audience with the Priestess. After over a year of traveling through the Valley on business and some of Sindra's old assignments he was back where they had started. Portsmouth. Her first assignment out of Whitfield, where he had met her. He had avoided coming here, always making some excuse when Hock mentioned some gain to be had or Drink asked if anyone knew the town. Walking the streets from the gate to the temple after all this time felt strange. He found himself walking toward Gam's place but stopped short in the middle of the street, reminding himself he was there for her, but not yet. Personal matters first, then business.

"I am glad to see you doing well," the High Priestess said, sitting down. "After Sindra was taken from us I thought I would never hear of you again. The others of you who aided us check in from time to time."

Derk nodded, putting his tea down without sipping from it. Asa and Devra were of course living and getting on. Both married. Devra had two children. Asa apparently caught on to a woman who liked him and married her, a woman who didn't follow the Goddess. "I move around a lot, and my business affords me strange hours, Sister," Derk reasoned. "I barely have time to get letters off. And I know you are busy with matters of Church. I didn't think you would remember me."

"Sindra spoke of you so much, I had no choice," the High Priestess said with a warm laugh. "Especially when she came back from the first mission, for the Cup."

"Pardon?" Derk asked. He realized what she was speaking of as soon as she turned her eyes on him and he looked into his teacup, hoping he didn't seem as flustered as he felt.

"The Goddess Cup, when you went into the Freewild." The Priestess sat down at the table finally, making Derk feel less nervous. "I remember her making sure any letters you sent would make it to her assignment in Tyestown."

Sindra had always seemed to be happy when she saw him. Initially. It was just the rest of the visit which wore on them both, ended in a disagreement or a fiasco. Never done. Derk took a sip of his tea and wondered if he could pour a bit of his flask into the cup without the priestess noticing. He was feeling strangely nervous. "Right, I remember when she took up the position at Tyestown. She did a good job there." Derk set the cup down, frowning at the delicate silver dishes.

"She was exemplary," the High Priestess said. "When she arrived here from Whitfield, she was very eager to please. She had a lot to prove, she felt."

Derk fiddled with his bracelet. "Why?" he asked.

"Well, not being from the Valley there were some who didn't know what to do with an elven woman who felt called by the Goddess. Some didn't trust her intentions. Some made it very clear they didn't. Did she ever tell you about the time her fellow students cut her hair in her sleep?" The High Priestess raised what were her eyebrows; Derk noticed they were painted on. "To a Forester, to have your hair cut is...." The High Priestess paused, taking a sip of her tea. The skin on her hands gave away her age, silver rings adorning her wrinkled fingers. "From all accounts, she could sit on her hair when she arrived in Whitfield."

"Why were they cruel? Had she done something to them?" Derk asked. He had gone to Whitfield to see what he could find but even the lower ranking priestesses were busy. He had gone during the Blooming of the Field, when all the moonflowers surrounding the city bloomed, which had been a sight to behold but made doing anything with the clergy close to impossible.

"Sindra was different and it was reason enough for them." The High Priestess smiled but it was a sad smile digging into the creases of her face. "Among the clergy, she was known as a devout student, a good leader, good with council. Wherever she was assigned she dealt with the Tower of the Moon in the Trees, till they dissolved."

"They dissolved while she was here in Portsmouth, right?" Derk asked. He remembered Sindra seeming upset about something during one of his visits.

"Yes, there was a small group of Foresters who had their own temple but they disappeared. A temple to the Goddess." The High Priestess poured herself more tea, steam rising off and out of the cup as the aroma wafted to Derk's nose. "They probably just wanted to go home. Life in the Valley for Foresters isn't always easy."

Derk sat up straighter in his chair, remembering the first time he had walked with Sindra and the stares they received. In Tyestown she was called 'the Forester Priestess' more than by her title. People weren't mean but they noticed she was different and pointed it out. "Do you think perhaps her being different had something to do with the manner of her death?" Derk asked the question plainly. There wasn't any polite way to ask it. The nature of the question itself wasn't polite. It was disturbing.

"I doubt it" the High Priestess said, lines of worry creasing her forehead. He thought she looked more upset he could assume such a thing more than the idea itself. "The people of the Valley are not a hateful people, you know this. We left Holy Haran because of hatred toward us, and know what it can do." The High Priestess shook her head. "They were more...curious. The Foresters have all gone back to their forest, whereas the stories of the beginning of our people here, they are often present. When I was a little girl, my grandmother said the Foresters were around on holidays and roamed the festivals when she little. By the time she bore my mother, they were gone. I would find it hard to believe that anyone could hate a Forester for being a Forester. Or even hate Sindra. As a priestess, as a student, as a woman?" The High Priestess shrugged. "She would have risen to serve many, if she was still living. She would be in Whitfield now. Probably scouring the library." The High Priestess smiled.

Derk remembered the parchments and books of Sindra's quarters, the table always littered with books so the food he brought always wound up on the floor. The smell of her ink stained hands. Her calligraphy. Her belongings were probably scattered throughout the Valley now, taken by those who lived and loved her. She had given him a few trinkets over the years but most of them had been lost. He always thought there would be more. He took a deep breath and forced a smile. "Probably," he agreed. "I just...her death, Sister...I've been trying to sort it out and move on but...I'm having trouble. I've been all over the Valley, picking up pieces here and there but all I have is someone killed her and no one knows who or why. I know the Church launched an investigation and found nothing within or without but...." He thought about

Jezlen's answer when he had asked him plainly if the Forester had any idea. The elf had looked just as bewildered as Derk felt. "Do you think a Forester could have done it?"

It was the High Priestess' turn to look confused. "I don't know why they would. Sindra only cared about the Valley. She wrote about the history of the Valley and was working on a complete history. Why a Forester would kill her for that escapes me."

Derk didn't know enough about the Foresters to fill in the large gaps the possibility presented. Derk only asked Sindra about her childhood briefly, lest she ask about his childhood. Jezlen always grew agitated when questioned about their upbringing and going to the Forest to ask was out of the question. He had hit a dead end. Another one.

"Darik," the High Priestess said, using the name he had given her. She reached over and put her hand on his. Her skin was soft and he thought maybe she washed her hands in rosewater, as her skin smelled faintly of it. "I know it is hard to let someone as good as Sindra go, even harder when they are suddenly taken. I know she meant a great deal to you. She was loved by many. But she is in the Bosom of the Goddess. Finding her killer won't make her love you any more. It can't."

Derk felt her squeeze his hand. He nodded slowly, considering her words and his presence there. He shook his head and exhaled sharply through his nose, running his free hand through his long hair, combed back to look more presentable for the High Priestess. It was probably messy now. He looked to her and pulled his hand back. "You're right. It was just...." He shook his head again, trying to sort out his thoughts. "I prayed for the Goddess to shine a light on this, so I would understand. But she doesn't want to give me understanding."

"The Goddess has gone through Her phases, Darik. And you?" Derk sat there for a moment. A lot had changed over the last year. He had been inducted into the Cup. He didn't answer to Hock all the time but roamed the Valley as he pleased just like he had before he joined. But now he knew the signs to look for, for a face which appeared more than friendly. But as much as he liked the security he still felt like something was missing. Like his life was on a path but he couldn't see where the road was going. Aimless. He had tried to focus on Sindra, still. And it was wrong.

"Thank you for your time, Sister," Derk said, bowing his head to her. He drank his tea, now cool. The honey had pooled at the bottom and was too sweet at the end but he drank it anyway. "I appreciate you sharing with me and your...advice. You're right."

"I didn't pay someone to become the High Priestess," she said with a broad smile, standing first so Derk could stand. She took his hands in hers, her rings cold on his skin, her skin warm on his. "May the Goddess watch over you."

"May Her Black Hand guide us all," Derk said, smiling. He turned and left her quarters, bowing his head to the priestess who stood outside her door. The honey sat thick on his tongue and made his mouth water. He would probably grab a pitcher of beer to take with him.

Derk stopped in the temple, paying the priestess for a stick of incense, putting it in the censor and letting it burn. It seemed only fitting to light a prayer for a new beginning. He watched the scented smoke curl and spin up into the air, hopefully taking his hold on Sindra with him. She was dead. It was unfair to think on her. One sermon said the obsessive memories of the living clawed at the souls of the dead. He didn't want his thoughts of Sindra to be a source of pain to her. Or himself. He sat on a pew and watched the incense burn, grey smoke emitting from bright orange, the smell of moonflowers and red tree gum and sage wafting through the temple. Maybe he would come back for vespers. But first, he had some business to attend to.

Derk's pack was light, lighter than it had been last time he left Portsmouth. It was autumn, almost time for Lover's Moon. It seemed like a good time to come back, to see Gam again. He walked the familiar streets to the bar selling the beer Gam liked best, not bothering to complain about the deposit for the pitcher. He'd just be sure to not break this one. Derk rolled a cigarette while the barkeep went to get his pitcher and happily smoked as he walked the streets to her home, noting what had changed since last he'd been in town and what was the same. The door to the building she lived in was different. It looked stronger, newer. Not a bad thing, he thought as he pushed it open, clipping up the stairs. His boots scuffed merrily up the wooden boards, creaking under his weight.

Hers was the one on the left. He knocked three times and then waited. After a few breaths he put his ear to the door, listening within for a sound. He knocked a few more times to be sure, straining his ear to make out anything. When no one opened the door he set the pitcher on the floor, dropping to his knees and pulling a pick out of his belt, his cigarette dangling from his lips.

The door swung open. Derk froze in midair, the pick still in his hand, hands reaching for the lock. He looked up. Relief washed over him as he saw Gam, wrapped in one of her quilts, bare shoulders and legs sticking out of the top and bottom. Her curly hair was messy. It was obvious she had been sleeping. It was also obvious she was confused to see Derk there.

"Hello," Derk managed, standing up awkwardly on the landing. He bent down and smiled stupidly, holding up the pitcher. "I brought us some beer. Your favorite."

Gam didn't even ask him in. She just walked back into the apartment and left the door open so he could follow her. Derk walked in and closed the door behind him, locking it before he set the pitcher of beer on the table. Gam walked over to the fire, still wrapped in her blanket and poked at it, trying to coax the embers into flames. She shuffled over to Derk and plucked the cigarette from his mouth, bringing it to her own lips with a smile and a slow drag making the tobacco crackle and the ember glow. She exhaled, looking at him sleepily as her hazel eyes darted over his face "You've a beard now."

"Aye," he said, not sure how to respond.

"I've a headache," she muttered, turning around. She took his cigarette with her. "I went out last night and stayed out too late and drank too much. The band was playing all the songs I loved." Gam watched the stove, taking another pull off the cigarette. "Stoke this while I get dressed," she said, smiling. Derk blinked, taking the cigarette from her when she offered it to him and brought it back to his mouth as he watched the woman disappear into the backroom. He heard her moving things, throwing clothes. She came out wearing just a long shirt, the ribbons tying the sides of the garment loose and dangling. The garment was loose around her bust and shoulders. He could see the scar on her leg and imagined the mole on her stomach.

"Sounds like I missed a good time," he said, pulling his eyes away from her. He picked up the poker by the fire and jabbed at it.

"Yeah, you missed a lot," she said. Her words were sharp and Derk knew she wasn't speaking about only last night. He could feel her eyes, wide opened and awake staring at him.

"Did you get my letters? And the gifts I sent you?" Derk asked. He watched the sparks shoot up and grow as he stabbed at it. The heat from the fire threw itself at his legs.

"Yeah, who was that fellow you sent? The dark fellow who holds conversation like broken glass?" she asked, her anger momentarily gone. "He was strange. Don't like the look of him."

"That's Jezlen, remember?" Derk opened the cupboard and found it was bare, the breadboard sporting a few crumbs and nothing else. "I...wrote you about him. Though I'm not surprised he never introduced himself."

"Sending strangers to my door. Many thanks," she said. Old Gam sat down at the table and put her feet up on it. Her ankles and feet were dirty. Around one ankle was tied a blue anklet, frayed from being there too long.

Derk could see the light line it had made where the rest of her skin had darkened in the sun.

"Do you want to go out for some food?" he asked quickly. "You've got nothing here to eat here."

"Are you sure you don't want to go out of doors for some other reason?" Gam asked. She smiled crookedly, untangling a snarl in her hair with her fingers. "You think I won't yell at you out of doors? You're mistaken if you think so."

"Celeel-"

"You're gone for more than a year chasing after a dead woman," she said. It sounded like an accusation. Gam started working her fingers through another snarl, shaking her head. "You're the stupidest man I know."

"Really, I'm the stupidest?" Derk asked, anger rising in his voice. "Me? Out of all the idiots who walk about Portsmouth?"

"And the most selfish," Gam added, smiling while narrowing her eyes. "I bet you're back to ask for something."

"I-" Derk stopped cold, his cigarette falling out of his mouth. He dropped the poker in his hand, cursing as he fumbled to catch it and burned his hand when the cigarette fell onto it. Old Gam laughed at him, like she always did. It made him angry he still loved her laugh, even when it was directed at him.

"Derk, why're you here?" she asked. Her words were quiet and she sounded tired. Derk brought his hand to his mouth and snuffed out the cigarette with his foot, taking his time to grind the black ash into the floor. Then he picked up the poker, setting it back against the wall carefully so it wouldn't slide. He went to where she kept the cups and pulled out two of them. One of them was new.

"Why're you always making me feel like an ass, Gam?" he asked, walking across the room and sitting down. He set the glasses on the table.

"You make it so easy," she quipped, taking her feet off the table and leaning forward, resting her elbows on the surface. Derk poured them each a glass of beer, noticing the tablecloth as he set hers in front of her. She had changed the cloth from the old one. It looked newer. He poured himself a glass of beer and rubbed at the embroidery with a finger, feeling the raise of the stitches. A sip of his beer told him the recipe Gam liked hadn't changed after all this time. Gam sat with her own beer, her hands wrapped about the cup but she didn't drink. She just waited.

"I don't have something to ask for. I've something for you," he said, looking up.

"Oh well then, you should give it to me," she said. Old Gam said it quietly, in a voice he remembered well. He lifted his eyes to her and bit the inside of his lip, a grin tugging at his mouth. His eyes wandered to her bare legs, bruises on her shins dark on her skin.

"Don't you get tired of doing things by yourself?" he asked. Gam's mouth fell open, a bark of laughter skipping from her lips. If it had been a younger Derk, he would have blushed but he only chuckled and rolled his eyes. "Not like that, Gam, come on, stop it!"

"What, is that why you're back?" she asked. Gam ran a finger around the rim of her glass before she picked it up, eying him over the top. "Tired of doing it by yourself?"

"I'm not talking about matters betwixt," he laughed. "Please, I'm trying to be serious!"

"You always take the wrong things too seriously." The smile faded from her face and she crossed her legs under the table, her foot bumping against his leg as she did. "What is it then? What do you have for me?"

"Well, I actually brought you something," he said, leaning back and reaching into his belt pouch. He pulled out a pendent made of wood, carved with the image of a starry sky. Chips of shining stones made the stars twinkle in the dark wood. "I hope you like it. Just for you."

Genuine surprise crossed Gam's face as she reached over and took it, her fingers brushing against his as she picked it up. She looked it over, her eyes darting over the tiny individual stars. "It's...thank you." It was a genuine bit of thanks with a hint of surprise in her voice. Gam looked to him, her smile warmer than usual. "I...I think I have the perfect ribbon to hang it on."

"If you still have the dark brown one, I think it'd be good," he said, taking a drink. "It makes your eyes sort of...." He shrugged. If he said 'shine like the stars,' it would sound like a line. But Gam's eyes twinkled more often than not. With mischief. With secrets. With wrongdoings wrapped in a raucous laugh. "It'd be best."

"Out of all the men I've ever met, you've the keenest eye for color and sparkle," she said. It sounded like a compliment. Derk took the chance and leaned in, tilting his head to the side.

"I'm here, aren't I?" They considered each other for a few breaths, Derk trying to figure out how Celeel took what he said. Celeel held the pendant in her hand.

"What d'you mean by that?" she asked. He was surprised by how plainly she asked. Was it an opportunity? He missed playing with Gam, quipping back and forth till they were exacerbated with each other, laid bare with sarcasm. Today, Derk thought, the skin would be removed more plainly.

"Celeel," he said. "I know you're a good taker. I know it. You know it. You could do more with other people. The right people." She gave him a sidelong glance but recognition showed in her narrowed eyes. Her mouth pulled to the side, as if many answers lay in her mind and she was sorting through which one to let out.

"And how do you know I'm not already working for someone else?" she asked. Her tone didn't match the serious face she had just shown him. Someone else? Who? For a breath Derk entertained the thought that he didn't know everything about Gam, her sewing and love for taking and her laugh. How she stayed in Portsmouth because she moved so much as a child she wanted to stay put and have a home. How it felt to be smacked by her, kissed by her. There was the Church, the Barons, the Block Lords and the Cup. She sometimes sewed for the Church. She wasn't lawful enough to work for the Barons. She disliked the Gangs. So why not the Cup?

"Are you sewing things into your quilts for someone else now? For more than just deals here and there for extra eggs, a barrel of beer?" He knew it was one of Gam's tricks, though she never said it plainly. It hadn't been difficult to figure out. Derk had stayed with her too often not to. Quilts she worked on at night with an inconsistent bit of batting in the morning. Money, packets of items sewn into the quilting. He watched as she tried to wash her guilt down with a sip of beer. "Your quilts are beautiful, Celeel, they shouldn't be pulled apart for a take."

"And how do I know all the people in this...Cup of yours? That they care about what happens to me?" she asked. "Why should I throw my lot in for the big take, when I can happily pick away for the things I want?"

"Since when do you need anyone to care about you, Gam? I thought you were happy caring for yourself?"

"There's no point in being with people if they're dumb fappers who don't care about you," Old Gam said. She took another drink and poured herself another glass. "I don't need another set of people who don't care about me. It's a kick in the twixt to deal with." She topped off Derk's glass without asking him if he wanted her to.

"But they won't just...Gam, I know these people, I've told them about you. I've vouched for you."

"Oh, you've vouched for me, you sweet thing," she laughed. "Let me light a stick of incense on my altar in thanks." Gam squinted at him. The look on her face was probably the closest to a pout she could do. It still managed to look sly somehow. "You know," she said, wagging her finger at him. "It was I who took you in all those years ago!"

"And now I want to take you in, Gam! Please! I know you do a bit yourself but you can do more with others. You're smart, you're cunning." Derk left out the other compliments he had for her. They didn't matter at this point and she would just think he was trying to grease her up. "And when I get something good in my lap, I want to be able to let you in, with more than just a packet of dye. I want you to get recognition. Respect."

"Not everyone wants those things, Derk," was all she said. She sighed and leaned forward and Derk couldn't help but ease in to meet her. Old Gam put her hand on the side of his face. Her fingertips brushed against his forehead and his hair, running along and lingering along his jawline. She scratched at his beard and smirked. "What's with the beard?"

"Last time I was here, I didn't have one, so I grew one," he said, shrugging. He pulled away from her and sat back in in his chair, putting his hands behind his head. Derk could still feel the touch of her hands on his face, the warmth of her skin.

"Takes a while to grow a beard," Old Gam mused. She laid her hands on the tabletop, her nails pink ovals. The pendant lay under one of her hands, star side up. Even from this angle, Derk saw the glint of the stars.

"Well," he said, looking to the side. "I had it in my mind to come here for a while." He said it and he let it hang in the air. Derk stared at the table, wondering what she would say in response. "I've thought about you," he said. He ran his fingers over the tablecloth, trying to re-member what the sheets on her bed felt like. "More than you probably think. More than you tell yourself I do." He looked up at her. As soon as her eyes met his she stood up from her seat, leaving the pendant on the tabletop. Her back was toward him, her long, curly hair spilling down her back. He could see the curve of her backside under her garments, the backs of her legs and the hint of the scar on her calf that crept over her skin.

"You think what you want is more important than what other people want. Like you know better. You're so stupid." He could see her fingers, her arms wrapped around herself.

"You know, Gam, it is possible for two people to want the same thing," he said, leaning forward. She spun her head around looking over her shoulder.

"Oh yeah? Like what?"

"Happiness. Being themselves. Alongside one another," he said. "Even if they don't want the same thing, it can be sorted." He believed that. "You want to be happy, don't you? And if you join the Cup, no one will ask you to be anything but yourself. And I'd be closer to you."

"We're close now, Derk." She turned around and faced him, her arms still wrapped around her middle.

"Closer?" He said it and couldn't keep a bit of hope out of his voice. "You could always find me." He walked over and stood in front of her, sliding his hands around her hips, not bothering to start at her waist and slide down. "I could always find you. Or others."

"Or each other," she said, gazing up at him. He saw the laugh there before it jerked in her stomach, played on her lips. "Ain't your new friends good enough? You still need Gam?"

He wanted to say he wanted her. It would be the sweet thing to say. More than he needed her, he wanted her, more than the other women he had dallied with over the last year. Dark haired women with sweet smiles. Not Gam. Gam, whose mouth was more likely to grin, with her curly hair as raucous as her laugh. The scar hiding under her skirts. He could probably trace the outline of it with his eyes closed. The thought made his fingertips press into her skin harder but Derk forced himself to loosen his hold on her.

"Gam, everyone needs you in their life," he said. Her eyes narrowed at him but a pleased smile curled her mouth and she put her hands on his chest. As she put her head back to up at him, he could feel her hair brush against his hands.

"Is that a fact?" she asked. "I think you're a liar." She wrapped her arms around his neck and drew him closer so his forehead rested on hers. Her nose brushed against his, and he felt her breath against his mouth.

"Have I at least gotten a bit better at it?" he whispered. He wondered how they had once again started with sharp words and yelling and wound up whispering in her front room. Derk had come there set on business but the two of them together had turned the meeting into something else altogether. Or at least it was heading that way.

"You can fool other people, but you can never fool me," she said, quietly, so closely her lips brushed against his. He thought she would kiss him but before he could blink she slipped out of his arms and away from him, walking to the stove.

Derk cursed himself. Working with Gam was never just business or pleasure. Business, he reminded himself. He brushed his hair back, trying to think of how he could bring it back to the Cup, get her to say yes. He wanted her in because it would be more like a family if she was in. And he wanted to bring something to the Cup besides himself. Gam would be the best thing he could bring, for now. And as much as he hated to admit it, he wanted to give her something in return for all the nights he had shared her bed and covered for her, for all she had taught him. Gam had taught him how to mend his own socks. She had taught him how most garments were made and the best way to put your hand into a pocket without getting noticed. With Sindra gone, Celeel was the one who knew him best. Celeel knew him the longest out of anyone. As long as he had been Derk, this had been the case.

"Look, I only asked because I thought you'd be interested," he said. "There's no question as to whether you can do it or not. You'd probably be running it in a few months time," he said. Her eyes darted toward him as she put a pot on the stove.

"Why don't you run it yourself?" she asked. She ladled water into the pot to boil, turning to look over the cupboards herself.

"What?" Derk laughed. He laughed so hard Gam actually looked surprised. "Me? I don't want to run anything," he said with a shake of his head. He picked his beer up and chuckled, thinking about how funny it was. "I just want to have some fun, get my heart going, a grip of coins in a day. A laugh, a drink with a friend and every once in a while, sleep in bed. Maybe with company." He drank from his glass, watching Gam's reaction to his words, wondering if she would take the last bit as an invitation. "And have some people to talk about the triumphs of the day."

"And the failures," Gam said.

"Of course, in the most comical way possible," he said. "Give 'em a show." He sat on the edge of the table, looking at the spot on his hand he had burned. It was red and still throbbed but nothing too serious. Derk watched as Gam found some herbs in a tin to make tea. "Oi, d'you have anything to put on my burn? It's starting to hurt."

Gam dropped her chin to her chest and glared at him. "Really?" she asked. "That little thing?" She sighed, though to Derk it didn't sound like she was too upset, walking toward her room. "You're such a baby."

"Ah, yes, such a baby. I'm Gam's little baby," he said, trying to sound whiny through his laughs.

"Oh stop it," she said, slapping at him as she walked into the bedroom, Derk following behind her. Derk looked around the room as she looked through the boxes she had under her nightstand. She blinked and looked at him, frowning slightly as her eyes traveled up and down his frame. "You're dressed mighty fancy," she said. "What's that about?"

"Can't a man put on his best shirt and best pants and walk around?" he asked, incredulous. "If you like, I can take them off." He laid down on her bed, trying not to react when she wrinkled her nose at him, hands on her hips.

"Get off my bed!" she demanded. "I don't know where you've been."

"I've been here the last bit! And the bar!" he half-shouted, not able to keep from laughing. Gam huffed through her own laughter and sat on the bed, putting the box with her medicines next to her.

"When did you get into town?" Her fingers pried open a a stone box of salve and she ran her fingertip over it before she took his hand in hers. She had callouses from hew sewing, her hands rough and smooth in different spots.

"I got in last night, slept at the Church, as I'm like to do." Old Gam dabbed her finger a little too hard against his skin, making him wince.

"As you're like to do," she said, looking at him out of the corner of her eye.

Derk sat up in the bed, pulling his hand away. "I wasn't going to show up here late at night. I wanted to get a good night's sleep and wash up."

"Trim your beard," she said, sticking out her tongue.

"What is it with you and the beard?" he demanded. "It's just hair. Things change, Gam!" He looked over his burn, moving his fingers to see what his hand felt like. Not too bad. "I can't believe you're all mad over a beard." He grabbed her hand and put it on his face again, looking into her eyes. "I'm still Derk. Your Derk." He didn't think Gam could blush but she was. She seemed to know she was because she looked away, as if trying to hide it. He kissed the palm of her hand, rubbing her hand against his face. He could hear the scratching of her skin against his facial hair. Gam reached up and tousled his hair, smiling.

"That's more like Derk," she said. "My Derk. Just you and me."

"It's just you and me right now," he said. She looked over his clothes again. He wondered if she guessed he had been at the temple, asking after Sindra. It was all behind him. Behind them.

"And the Cup," she mused, sitting up straighter on the bed, the mattress settling under her.

"Not in bed," he said.

"You need a good plowing, don't you?" Old Gam asked. She grinned at him.

"I'm trying really hard to not just come out and ask," Derk laughed. "Not that I think it's all you're good for,

Gam. I-" He stopped short, looking around the room as he tried to think of what to say.

"Don't stop, say something nice to me," Old Gam said. "You know how to get me in bed."

"That was before the beard," he said, as seriously as he could. Gam laughed, loudly, her face scrunching up like it always did when she laughed. They both laughed for a few breaths before Gam sighed and laid down beside him, forcing him to scoot over in the bed.

"You know, you missed me and I missed you," she said, laying her hand on his chest. He could feel his own heart beat under it, his heart beat slightly faster as she wrapped one leg on top of his. "And you treated me bad, Derk. You left me in bed all those years ago and took up with that woman. You spent all your time with her and even when she didn't want you, you kept after. She didn't even know you. Not like me. And you would come to me and sit at my table and mope over her. You always looked so stupid when you did."

"Gam, you never told me you wanted me to stick around." He rolled over onto his side so that he faced her, close. He brought his fingers to her hair and laid his thumb on her cheek, his legs brushing against hers.

"I knew even if you did stick around, you wouldn't be happy. Why ask you to do something you're not supposed to do?" Old Gam moved closer to him, her hips inching toward his, her shirt creeping up her legs. "It wouldn't have been fair or kind."

"You've always been too kind to me," he chuckled.

"I'm glad you recognize when I'm being kind," she said. Celeel leaned over and kissed him, Derk's mouth meeting hers. Her mouth still tasted the same, the beer she always drank on her tongue and lips. He put his hand on the small of her back and pushed her hips gently toward his, feeling the curve of her backside and slipping his hand under her shirt to feel her skin. They kissed on her bed, Gam's hands running over his thighs and tugging at his shirt. She pulled her lips away from his and laid her cheek on his, rubbing her fair skin against his beard, making Derk laugh.

Derk rolled over on top of her, moving her legs and lifting up her shirt, past her legs, thighs, hips till he could see her stomach. He knelt down and started to kiss the inside of her thigh when she grabbed him by the hair, too hard for it to be playful.

"I left the pot of water on the stove," she laughed. Derk looked up from between her legs. Whatever his face looked like it made her laugh even more.

"Are you kidding me?" he asked, his arm still wrapped around her leg. "Just let the hem chawing pot go!"

"I could set the whole building on fire!" she laughed. "There's a woman with a baby living above me! I need to take it off." She patted him on the head before she awkwardly unlaced her legs from his grasp. Derk groaned after her as she skipped into the front room. Between grumbles he pulled off his boots and socks, setting them at the foot of the bed neatly. He started to pull his tunic up over his head, raising his eyebrows when he had it off. Gam stood in the doorway, naked. She posed quickly like the way women did in pictures before she walked back to the bed, one hands reaching to undo his pants as she pushed him back onto the bed. Derk was happy to help her with the belt. Both their bodies were patchworks of lighter and darker shades of beige, showing where they had allowed the summer sun to color their skin. Derk kissed her shoulders, raking his teeth against her skin as she straddled him, more and more of themselves touching, her heat and taste familiar to Derk's tongue and body.

Afterward they lay in her bed, not bothering to get under the sheets. It was too hot for it. Derk lay on his belly, watching Celeel's stomach rise and fall with every breath. They had both dozed off but Derk was awake now. Her hair was in her face but she didn't seem to notice as always. He heard her stomach grumble and realized he himself was hungry. Leaning over he kissed her on the mouth, sweetly, glad to find her kissing him back, her hand in his hair. He pulled away and she smiled at him, yawning lazily before she sat up.

Gam sat in the bed, leaning forward slightly, her back curved in an arc. She looked to Derk sleepily and yawned again. "You know," she said. "I think I will join your Cup," she said. "I could use with knowing where you are."

"It would be nice," Derk said, rolling over and propping his head on his hand. "I'd like that."

"And," Gam said, sitting up a bit more straight on the bed. Her hair fell down across her shoulders but he could still see the curve of her breasts. "Well, if you're not going to eventually take charge of it, someone will have to." Gam smiled at him, her mischievous grin. It made his heart skip a beat.

"Right," he said, sitting up in bed. Relief swept over him, glad to finally have her say yes. He wouldn't be with

Gam all the time. He couldn't be. But a bit more would be nice. He sat up and kissed her shoulder. "Let's go get some food. We can talk more about it later."

They both got up from the bed, searching the room for their clothes. Derk thought about pulling Gam back to the bed before they went out but he found all his clothes too quickly to make it happen. Gam dressed in a dress he hadn't seen before, the embroidery around the neckline and shoulders intricate and beautiful. He offered her his arm and they walked out onto the streets of Portsmouth together looking for a meal.

"Where's the pendant I got you?" Derk asked. They were several blocks from her home and he noticed she hadn't bothered to wear it. "You didn't wear it?"

"Oh," Gam said, rolling her eyes at herself. "I must have forgot to put it on. Got caught up in being hungry and all." Gam leaned over and kissed him on the cheek in consolation. Derk tried not to look too disappointed. After all, she had agreed to join in the Cup, hadn't she? He had brought his past to the present. As they walked to the bar Derk couldn't help but feel like even with Gam closer to him, the road before him was still unknown.

Chapter 21
Little Girl Found

Derk took a moment to have a seat in the back alley, shaking out his coat so the tails fluttered behind him as he sat down, groaning. His head ached horribly and his eyes were still having a hard time focusing. The blows he had just taken were still with him, apparently. He had gone to the End Side to wallow a bit, intending on blowing off some steam by picking a fight with one of the other patrons. Instead, someone started throwing chairs right when he finished his first bottle. What was meant to be a therapeutic trip to the bar ended in a brawl involving most of the people there. The inside of his mouth tasted like salt and iron and he spit to the side, cursing at the blood shining bright red on the dark cobblestones.

Fenwick was one of the worst places Derk had ever been, and yet he had stayed here the longest. It was a town full of people with bad tempers, horrific manners and dark secrets. Its reputation as a den of thieves had been what attracted Derk in the first place. After much carousing with others from the Cup, as well as going on a few more diplomatic exploits, he realized his skills had reached a plateau. He would have to be pressed to grow and when he asked Hock how he should go about doing so, the man had said, "Fenwick." The suggestion had both intrigued and frightened him. Before he could decide otherwise he set out, telling Jezlen to meet him in a year's time. The Forester had said something to the effect of, "If you make that long." This of course convinced the thief Fenwick must be done and so he left, determined to last a year.

It had been a fruitful year. Among the lowest of the low, he had learned a few new tricks, most of them meaner or sneakier than those he was accustomed to. He learned a few names and matched a few faces. He now had the ability and nature required to strike a man down with one blow. Even more so, he fell back upon his old habits of disappearing and reappearing when it was most convenient to him. "Derk the Lurk" came into Fenwick from quite a few cities down, and in the streets, alleys and halls of the city, he lived up to his new name.

Of course, not everything had been educational. Shortly after arriving in Fenwick, Derk fell in love with one of the brass, a thin, dark haired girl named Benna. Shortly after she took him on, she informed him she was pregnant. The attention he paid her was apparently unwelcome because she threw him out, informing him she wouldn't give up her profession or be told what to do by any man. During the following months, he checked up on her, sending her money and offering to move them all out of the city, to some place safer. When the child was born, it was very obviously not his and Benna evicted him from her life. It was the reason why he had gone to the bar.

"Stupid hem chawers" he muttered to no one in particular. His mouth still tasted like blood and his head still pounded. He crossed his legs and placed his right ankle on his left knee, opening the compartment in the boot heel only after making sure no one was looking. Inside was a fullie and a silver colored charm, meant to bring him good luck wherever he stepped. Derk contemplated tossing it into the gutter and spitting on the old soothsayer who had sold it to him. But the old woman told him only in the death throes would peace come and then, life. Riddles. The fortune teller was almost as bad as the priestesses in this city, with their meandering liturgies and cold prayers.

A few more phases sounded like an eternity at the moment. He secured the charm and the white coin in his heel before he stood up, surprised at the pain shooting through his leg as he put his weight on it. Had someone kicked him there? His knee felt slightly loose and he grimaced as he walked through the alley, limping as he made his way onto the busy street.

Derk's eyes scanned the teeming streets, only slightly sure of what he was looking for. When Derk was hurt, he generally wanted one thing: to be pampered by a beautiful woman. Beautiful women weren't hard to come by in

Fenwick, but the chance of finding one who would care for him would most likely prove fruitless. His stomach growled despite his other bodily pains, commanding food before doctoring. The aroma of something pleasant seemed to be mixed in with the other ranker scents and so he followed his nose toward what he hoped would be food for sale.

The first thing he noticed about her was he almost didn't see her. The small body bumped into him and a tiny voice said, "Sorry," before the speaker scurried away, trying to get lost in the sea of people. Derk stopped dead in his tracks, letting the people stream around him like water around a river rock. He knew the feeling.

There was the sensation of someone being clumsy and bumping into you. And then there was this; a sizing up upon impact, deliberate, meant to tell the "bumper" something about the person they bumped into. He turned his head and strained his eyes, trying to see if he could make out who had done it. The pressure had been too low for a full grown adult and the voice too high for a man or a woman. He turned around altogether, shoving someone who was giving him dirty looks for holding up the flow of traffic in the street. His eyes scanned the crowd and fell upon a small group standing in front of the temple.

The little girl was like a tattered butterfly fluttering to and fro among the people on the street, eventually lighting upon the white-washed steps of the temple. In the short time it had taken her to run between five people she had acquired something to eat and was now chewing it quickly, hiding behind the skirts of one of the women in the group. They were obviously all brass and the one who the girl was hiding behind obviously the ring leader of the three. The woman, buxom and blonde, looked down at the little girl, tossing her head back as she laughed and patted her on the head, playing with one of the girl's long, black braids. The little girl smiled slightly, still gnawing at whatever she had taken. The blonde woman said something and the little girl's large mouth frowned slightly as she turned her dark eyes up toward the woman. The woman knelt down and tucked a braid behind the girl's ear, revealing its slight point. As soon as the woman turned away the little girl made a face and let her hair fall back over her ear.

Derk held his breath as he looked not upon the woman but the girl, finding his heart pounding in his chest. He would never admit the little girl reminded him of someone, but she did. Instead, Derk saw the look in the girl's eyes as she scanned the crowd, remaining inconspicuous as she took everything in around her before she walked up a few more steps and sat down, setting her face in her hands. He almost laughed out loud, thinking the look on her face comical. He reached into his coat pocket for his hat and pulled it onto his head before he headed straight for the temple steps, not able to keep from limping more as he neared the women.

The three hawked their wares on the steps of the New Moon Temple, bells on their corsets jingling enticingly to passers-by. When it came down to it, he would have preferred the thin one with the long hair to the blond one, but he wasn't there for pleasure, though he would take it if it came to that. He tipped his hat to the three women, focusing his attention on the buxom one who had been laughing earlier, even managing to get his legs to aid him in a courtly bow The women laughed, the one he was looking at placing a hand on her chest.

"Well, ain't it nice to see a body with manners?" she said, pushing a few curls behind her ears. The woman adjusted her skirts and walked down the steps toward him, stopping short at the bottom. She lifted her chin slightly, a smirk playing on her coral lips before she spoke again. "You look like you've been worked over and need a bit of doctorin."

"Right you are, good woman," he said, placing his hat over his heart, hoping he looked as pathetic as he felt. He knew he didn't have to go through all this; he could have just pulled out some money, pointed and they would have been on their way. But he was more here for information than for the exchange of purses and so he appealed to the prostitute's apparent boredom, giving her a chance for a bit of conversation before business. He let his head hang slightly, his dirty hair falling into his face. "Some loving care would be nice right about now. Have I come to the right place?"

"Right you are," she said, walking toward him coquettishly, her skirts dragging on the temple steps. Derk couldn't help but look over her shoulder, eying the little girl sitting on the temple steps. The little girl stared at him, frowning at his face before her dark eyes scanned down and set on his shoes. She tilted her head the side, a quizzical expression scrunching her features. The prostitute opened her mouth to speak, stopping herself as she turned to see what he was looking at. A wry look managed to creep its way past her make up as she put her arm in his, leading him away. "She's green yet, so keep yer blues off of her."

"Pardon me," he said, managing to tear himself away from the girl and turn his attention to the woman. "Just I ain't used to seeing little ones around your type. If they have 'em, they don't generally let them hang around. It's bad for business, I hear."

The woman laughed, the same melodic cackle as before, the bells at her bosom jingling. Derk knew she wanted him to look at her chest so he did, playing into her little game. The woman took in a breath after she was done having her chuckle, leading him around a corner.

"Ah well, I have to keep an eye on her and she ain't no fuss. She knows when to make herself scarce," she said, looking over her shoulder as if to make sure the girl wasn't there. The alley was quiet and bare, save for the two; off from the distance came the sound of the nearby streets. The woman cast quick glances in either direction before lifting her skirts up past her ankles.

"Hold on!" cried Derk, holding one hand out toward her feet, urging her to stop. "Not here!" He managed to keep disgust from his voice, forcing a smile and tapping his left leg. "I've a bum knee at the moment and money. Don't you have a place hereabouts?" Derk really did want a bed to lie on; his knee was starting to ache and possibly swell and the sooner he got off of it, the better. However, Derk also was of the opinion anything more serious than kissing should be done away from other people and preferably on something soft. He was also curious to see where the little girl lived. A part of his brain told him to have nothing to do with the brass; they were foolish and wayward and his last involvement with one had put him in the physical and emotional state he was currently enjoying. But Derk told himself he wasn't getting involved. He was casing a scene. He was going to make a grab and sleeping with the prostitute was just one step in the plan.

The woman laughed out loud, dropping her skirts and looping her arm in his, leading him down the alley as the bells jingled at her bosom. "I see, you're one of them old fashion, romantical types, ain't you? I had a feeling, just from looking at you. It's a nice change of pace for me, I tell yah…." She talked some more and Derk tried to listen, the throbbing in his head and knee becoming more acute with every step he took. Mostly he nodded and tried to seem charming, hoping to endear himself to the bubbly woman leading him to where the little girl lived. When his pants were off, they revealed a swollen, purple knee which would need to be dressed sooner than later. He paid her before she asked for payment, reminded her to be gentle before he started his plan to investigate and possibly obtain the little girl.

The little girl's name was Tavera, though the women called her Tavi. She was probably somewhere around nine or ten years of age, though it was hard to tell on account of her Forester blood; it was said they grew differently from both Valleymen and Foresters and no two half-breeds grew alike. In all his wanderings, Derk had never come across another like the girl. Prisca, Gia and Sera found her on the street just last winter. Prisca had taken the girl under her wing, having lost a daughter just a few seasons back to an epidemic. She was raising the girl as her own and training her to live the lifestyle of a woman who sold pleasure in Fenwick.

Derk watched the girl every day he could, which was almost every day as he had few obligations and answered to no one. He found himself caught up in her every public activity. He cheered for her when she managed to pocket something of worth, cringed when she was lambasted or struck down by an annoyed street vendor, laughed when she danced in the street for a half a blueie. The day after he met her, he was shocked to see someone, most likely Prisca, had cut off all her hair. The long, black tresses were gone, the bonnet on her head and the expression on her face doing nothing to hide the fact. Obviously upset by the cosmetic loss, she still managed to be of service to her benefactors, returning from a particularly long stint with a string of sausages, though she herself did not partake. The hair gone, he could see the top point of one of her ears was missing, cut clean off with a knife, most likely. He wondered what had happened to the little girl to warrant such a wound, admiring the tiny thing for having such tenacity and perseverance.

It became obvious after a few visits to Prisca the little girl stole from the woman's clients. He had figured the girl's rudimentary prowess at pilfering would be exploited somehow by the woman and he decided to test the girl. He hid things in various parts of his clothing before he visiting the woman, noting where he put them and checking to see which ones he lost to the girl's invisible hand. The little girl never did figure out the the heel of one of his boots was hollow and if she did, she never searched them. Derk was careful to keep anything of real value out of his coat and pants when he visited the peculiar house which was the home of the three women.

She wasn't a pretty little girl or a courteous one. She was more likely to frown than to smile. But her hands were quick and when she narrowed her eyes and took in a scene Derk knew she saw everything. She was an ass. She kicked stones at people and then hid, causing more than a few fights in the marketplace and more than a few distractions. Her small, skinny fingers were adept at picking up bits here and there and one day after she had nicked a pretty button he followed her. He watched from the shadows and he saw it. The smile on her dark face, the grin, the light in her eyes. He knew how she felt. He could imagine her heart thumping in her chest jubilantly, the pride coursing through her.

Derk wanted her to feel that again, to see the smile on her face. The girl was a thief, a natural. Prisca didn't know it, but Derk did. And he could help this little girl along better than the brass. As he thought about his legacy the girl looked up, her dusky face frowning as she peered into the dark. Derk ducked away and ran, hearing her walking to investigate. But by then he was gone and he had already decided.

Eventually Prisca figured out how Derk kept himself fed, though it didn't deter her from keeping him as a client or make her think he was there for something more than what she had for sale. He was sure to bring her plenty of trinkets and gifts to endear himself to her and never pressed her for anything more than he paid her for. As far as Prisca was concerned, he was there for Prisca. As far as Derk was concerned, he was putting up with Prisca to get the girl. He was convinced despite all the experience he had acquired in Fenwick, the girl was to be the better gain.

On the final day of the year, Derk stood in Prisca's room, naked, his dagger out and pointed at the women in the bed. The little girl was knocked out and still hanging halfway out of the crawlspace. He knew the door was locked, having done so himself. He listened for a moment to be sure no one was coming; shouts and screams weren't uncommon in this house, and so Derk grinned triumphantly at the vulnerable Prisca, turning his dagger so the light glinted off of the blade.

"Now shut up," he said before she could speak, her mouth popping open and closed, fear glittering in her eyes. He stood between the girl and the bed, keeping his eyes on the woman for the moment, making sure she wouldn't fight back. Prisca's eyes weren't on the dagger but the slumped over girl. Tears started to stream down her face. Derk huffed, bending down and feeling around in his bag for the sack he had brought.

"I'm taking the girl and you ain't going to stop me," he said, shaking the sack open. "You won't say nothing to no one and you're not coming after us either. If you do, I will warrant you another nickname you shall not like, if you catch my meaning." He kept his eyes cold and his face hard as he spoke, not hope but power propelling his words toward the shaking woman. He placed the dagger on the small table, being sure to set it down so it pointed at Prisca as a warning. Derk gave her one more icy glare before he bent down and carefully folded the girl up and put her in the sack, tying it up and leaving it on the floor as he got dressed.

"But...but why are you taking her?" Prisca's voice was quiet but still full of alarm, a tiny, keen sound which seemed to cut his ears with its controlled grief. For a split second Derk almost felt pity for the woman, her hair loose and spilling about her pained face, her make-up smearing. But all his pity was reserved for the girl in the sack, and so he offered Prisca none of it.

"It's none of your business why I'm taking her. Because I want her." He buttoned his pants and pulled on his shirt, tucking it in before he fussed with his belt, finding his own hands shaking a bit. "You're here, fixing to waste her away on blue piece takes and men, and you've a set on you big enough to ask me what I'm doing with her? It's shameful, really." Derk pulled on his coat and hat, grabbing his bag and the sack, swinging it over his shoulder before he took the dagger up, pointing it at her again. "You think your men will like coming here, knowing their pie monies ain't safe? Don't worry about this girl's well-being. I'll see to it she grows up proper. Gold don't belong with brass." He sneered at her as he tightened his grip on the neck of the sack, turning around and unlocking the door.

"Please...please, Derk, don't take her." Prisca's voice was muffled by her sobs. Derk sighed, looking over his shoulder at her.

He just stared at her. He didn't say anything. He didn't wait for her to explain why she wanted or needed the girl. Instead, he walked out and shut the door behind him, letting it slam. The dagger was still in his hand as he walked down the hallway, down the stairs and out the front door, into the fetid night air. People strolled around after vespers, hawkers shouting their wares, the aromas of beer and evening meals making their way through the scent of dirty people. Other denizens of Fenwick pressed upon him, pushing against him and giving him dirty looks as he paid them no mind.

Derk had the girl. The girl was in the bag. His hand gripped it at the top, slung rather awkwardly over his shoulder as he made his way down the street. Singing to himself, Derk cut across the main street to the bar where he was to meet Jezlen. He passed by Gia and Sera in the street as he went on his way and Derk was sure to tip his hat to them as he went by.

ABOUT THE AUTHOR

Tristan J. Tarwater is a writer of fantasy novels, comics, and RPG bits. Her titles include Hen & Chick, The Valley of Ten Crescents series, Shamsee: A Fistful of Lunars, and Reality Makes the Best Fantasy. She has also worked for both Pelgrane Press and Onyx Path.

Born and raised in NYC, she now considers Portland, OR her home. When she's not making stuff up, she is usually reading a comic book, cooking delicious meals for her Spouse and Small Boss or petting one of her two cats. Her next RPG character will most definitely be an elf.

www.backthatelfup.com
@backthatelfup